LOST LANDS: The Game
ATLANTIS
Book 1 of the Lost Gamers Series

A. E. McCullough

Copyright Information

Copyright © 2014 by Andrew McCullough

This book is a work of fiction. Names, character, places and incidents are the products of the author's imagination or are used fictitiously. Any resemblance to actual events, locales, or persons, living or dead, is coincidental.

All rights reserved under International and Pan-American Copyright Conventions. No part of this book may be reproduced in any form or by any electronic or mechanical means, including information storage and retrieval systems, without permission in writing from the author, except by reviewer, who may quote brief passages in a review.

Cover Art by A.E. McCullough
    Background image for the cover art: *Autumn Moor Cold* by Lvxion @ DeviantArt

First Edition: February 2014

www.aemccullough.com

www.facebook.com/brotherlobo2

www.twitter.com/brotherlobo

www.brotherlobo.deviantart.com

DEDICATION

This novel is dedicated to Irl and Sollie Stambaugh.

I have had the pleasure and privilege to meet and chat with people from all over the world and yet, rarely do I ever get to know their real names. As an avid gamer, I have developed friendships with people that I only see during my trips into cyberspace. However, there are a few that become more than their avatars or faceless voices over chat channels. They become true friends. Irl and Sollie were in this last category.

Sollie was an early supporter of my writings and always encouraged me to keep plugging away at the keyboard. She even got to read some of the earliest drafts of this novel. Unfortunately, she passed from this life and into the next before I had the chance to complete Lost Lands.

I have lost touch with Irl over the years but their friendship and kind words of encouragement still warm my heart. Nonetheless, this novel is for you two.

ACKNOWLEDGMENTS

It would be a great injustice not to acknowledge and thank my test readers. DJ, Alex and Venus have been reading my work and giving me insights ever since my 2nd novel.

Although, with this novel came a new test reader – Jeff – who fell in love with the concept of this novel even as I was writing it. Jeff would hound me to get another chapter written just so he could proofread it.

Thanks guys. Your support, insights, edits and friendship mean the world to me.

Cast of Characters

Guild: Keepers of the Flame
Taote 'Tao' Ching – Human Samurai – Patrick 'Mac' MacIntyre
Gamble Giantbane – Dwarven Skald – Marvin
Bjørn Bluebear – Norse Berserker – Earl Stamper
Moira Ravenclaw – Wood Elf Druid – Kaslene Stamper
Mathias Strongbow – Half Elf Archer – Matthew
Pixi Firewings – Faerie Wizard – Whitney
Roland Darkslayer – Human Paladin – Steve

Guild: Society of Night
Arieal De'Morte – Dark Elf Necromancer – Annie
Cozad – Human Dreadknight – Edward
Tariq al'Nasir al'Rafiq – Human Hashashin -- Brandon

Other Known Outlanders
Callistra – Vampyre Witch – Cassandra MacIntyre
Kastle Rook – Human Warrior-Priest – Richard
Jagoda Wartooth – Human Gladiator – Leon
Aaliyah – Human Sha'ir – Ashley
Marrok – Human Knight – John
Andraste – Elf Warden – Amanda
Sartael – Human Wizard – Alex
Sanguine Bolt – Human Wizard – Wayne
Wynn – Half-Elf Nightshade – DECEASED
Argos – Human Centurion – DECEASED
Albiona – Wood Elf Druid – DECEASED
Geirolf – Norse Berserker – DECEASED
Bertram – Dark Elf Warlock – DECEASED
Kano – Human Ninja – MISSING IN ACTION
Amerisky – High Elf Wizard – MISSING IN ACTION

Prologue

A lone figure slowly paced back and forth in the dark, featureless room.

Actually, that was incorrect. There were two unusual features about the room. The most obvious was the huge silver mirror which dominated one wall and the fact that there was no visible entrance or exit from the room. No doors or windows, just the mirror.

Unconsciously, the lone occupant stretched his white feathered wings and gave them a small flap. He longed to fly through the open skies once more. He momentarily wondered how long it had been since he had been incarcerated. While his back was to the mirror, it shimmered and an image appeared on its silvery surface.

"Hello brother."

Without turning, the prisoner asked, "Is it time again?"

"Yes. Another group is about to attempt the trial."

Grigoris turned to the mirror and waved his hand. The image shifted to depict sixteen people sitting in front of their computer monitors all across the globe. He even noted that the group contained a husband and wife team, a teenager and one that radiated sorrow and loss. It was on this last one that the trapped seraph focused his limited powers on. There was something familiar about him. Something...

The images shifted once more to show the red-skinned face of his brother. "You do realize that if you just admitted defeat, I would free you. None of your so-called champions have even come close to accomplishing their quest."

Grigoris grinned. "I like my chances with this group. Even so, my other champions are still in play. They are just waiting for the right leader to come along."

"Ah brother, how can we be siblings? You still believe in the goodness of man while I believe in their weaknesses, especially greed. They will always fail."

Grigoris shook his head. "Nay brother, I have faith in mankind. Every fire needs a spark and every rebellion needs a leader. Just wait, you will choose one soon that will upset this little game of yours and make a complete mockery of it."

"We shall see brother, we shall see."

Once more the image of his sibling faded to be replaced by a faraway land where his future champions were doing nothing more than playing a harmless game. Completely unaware of what their future held. Grigoris could do nothing to aid them, except watch and pray.

Chapter 1

Patrick MacIntyre, known as Mac to his friends, stared at his twenty-seven inch monitor and took a sip of his lukewarm coffee and grimaced. Pressing the button on his keyboard which activated the microphone on his computer he said, "One of the things I hate most about these raids is not having time for a kitchen run."

Mac heard a few of his online friends laugh over their guild's voice-chat channel. Onscreen, Mac watched as Earl's avatar Bjørn turned to face his avatar. The towering Norseman was bare-chested and wore a blue tartan kilt with his upper right arm covered in ornate plate armor while his left was heavily tattooed with blue glyphs.

Bjørn rested his huge claymore over one shoulder when he spoke. "Mac, you need to plan ahead. You know these things take time."

Mac had always thought that Earl's deep baritone voice matched his onscreen image perfectly. Personally, he had chosen to play a samurai named Taote Ching and had outfitted him in the traditional Japanese-style armor that was crimson red with highlights of black. This was his main avatar since he began playing *Lost Lands*. Even after three years of gaming, Mac was still impressed with the game's graphics. From the flickering shadows cast by their torchlight on the rough stone walls to the echoing sounds of dripping water in the darkness, *Lost Lands* did it's best to fully immerse the player into the game. It had been the premier MMORPG (Massive Multiplayer Online Role-Playing Game) for the last three years running and deserved every award it had won. The interface was easy to learn but challenging to master.

Since Mac was acting as the rear guard, he panned the view of his avatar around the passageway to make certain that no enemies were sneaking up behind them as he keyed his microphone. "I know, I know, next time I'll pack a thermos."

Whitney's laughter echoed over the chat channel as her faerie wizard mimicked the laugh out loud emote, a pre-designated action for the game avatars. In this case, her faerie bent over laughing and slapped her knees. However when Whitney spoke, her British accent was readily apparent. "You say that every week but me mum would suggest tea instead of that coffee you Yanks drink."

Mac was about to respond with a snide remark on their ongoing argument over the virtues of coffee versus tea when Arieal's voice came over the raid voice-chat. "Keepers…estimate thirty seconds till entry."

Turning serious, Mac keyed up the raid channel. "Roger that Society...breach in thirty seconds...mark," and started a countdown timer which would be visible to all sixteen members of the raid and watched as the rest of his group moved into position.

Onscreen, Bjørn moved to stand behind one of guild's members and Earl slipped back into the role-playing aspect of the game as he said, "Alright dwarf, the Society of Night is about to make entry. Time for you to earn your keep."

"Shh...this isn't as easy as you might think," responded Marvin. The dwarf was a skald, a hybrid class of thief and mage from Norse mythology. Marvin was hard at work trying to pick the lock of the door. He worked through the controls on his keyboard which allowed his avatar to pick locks. It was a fine balance of timing, reactions and guesswork but after three years of gaming, Marvin nearly had the lockpicking skill down to a science.

Mac glanced once more at the passageway behind them, it was still empty. Manipulating the keyboard controls on his computer, he turned his avatar back to the door and prepared to enter the final room of the Tomb of Immortality.

As a guild, they had been trying to raid this particular dungeon for over six months. The problem was that the entry took a combined effort of two full groups of eight; one group for the followers of Law and one for the minions of Chaos. Since this was a role-playing server, many times getting the two factions to work together was more difficult than the actual quest. Mac's late wife Cassandra had purposefully created a witch four months earlier to give their guild, the Keepers of the Flame, a chance at completing this particular dungeon. She had been grinding out experience in an effort to advance her newest avatar to a high enough level to allow the when a fire gutted their home and claimed her life. Mac had been at work that night and had come home to fire trucks and broken dreams.

Glancing up from his monitor, he stared at the only picture of his wife to survive the fire. It was of their wedding day. They were standing in front of the Cape Hatteras Lighthouse, full of smiles. It was a wondrous day and a great memory. Feeling the clutches of despair and sadness on his heart, Mac turned his attention back to the game.

The game.

Lost Lands had been his lifeline since the fire. Work seemed tedious. Food was tasteless. Only when he immersed himself in the game did he truly feel alive. After digging out whatever was salvageable from the fire, he'd rented a cheap apartment, bought some old furniture and a brand new high powered computer. Now he lived for the game and played almost every waking minute that he wasn't at work.

It was during the last month when Mac had ran into Arieal while working on another quest. Even though she was a dark elf necromancer, an evil wizard who summoned undead minions to serve her bidding, they had paired up and hunted together. Over the preceding weeks, they had adventured together a few times and a friendship had formed. At some point in their hunting, the subject of uncompleted dungeons had come up and they discovered that neither of their guilds had been able to complete this particular quest. It had taken some juggling of schedules but they had finally been able to arrange this raid between their two guilds.

Mac watched the countdown timer in the upper right-hand corner of his monitor. Both groups were supposed to breach the door on the count of zero. With seven seconds to go, he glanced at his team once more and noted with pride that everyone was ready and knew their roles.

Gamble would push open the door and step out of the way of the tanks before slipping into the shadows to move behind enemy lines. He would backstab tough opponents or alert the group about wandering enemies – commonly referred to as 'adds' or 'mobs.' The tanks, heavily armored warriors, would rush inside the room and engage whatever mobs confronted them. Bjørn would lead the charge flanked by Roland the paladin and Marrok the knight. Mathias the archer and Pixi the wizard would engage targets from a distance, raining death and destruction on all foes. Since Moira was a druid, she would pull up the rear casting her healing spells on injured group members or using her command of nature to entangle rushing mobs. Which left Mac's avatar Tao to act as a free safety, going wherever he was needed the most, adding the weight of his bow or swords to whatever needed to be done. Mac's guild, the Keepers of the Flame, had other members but these eight were the core members and had gamed together for the better part of two years. Their entry plan had been developed through trial and error and it worked well for them.

Mac had often wondered how other guilds breached rooms. The few times he had attempted a serious dungeon in a PUG or 'pick-up group' – a group consisting of random gamers working together toward the completion of a certain dungeon, they had all been a joke. Mac soon realized it wasn't so much a lack of knowledge of the game but a lack of teamwork since most ended in a party-wipe, when everyone dies. Of course, Mac knew going into them that PUGs typically had a low success rate but sometimes that was the only way a gamer could complete a certain dungeon.

Mac looked up from his computer monitor for a moment and glanced at the clock on his desk. It was just past midnight. Wiping the sweat from his palms, he stretched his back. It was amazing that a game could elicit such a response, but between the thrills of the unknown and the intense graphics, *Lost Lands* sucked you into the game.

Mac placed his hands back on the keyboard just as the timer flashed three…two…one….zero.

As his guild breeched the door, Mac scanned the room.

It was a large circular chamber, divided into two halves; one black and one white. Kind of like a large yin-yang symbol with a dark hole in the direct center. They were standing on the white half, while the members of the Society could be seen on the opposite side. A number of black cloaked monsters were clustered around a glowing black orb centered on the white area.

The Keepers' tanks had already engaged the leading edge of the monsters. Bjørn's huge claymore cleaved the monsters in two with every strike. Roland and Marrok's swords weren't as deadly but they efficiently hacked the monsters apart. Mathias's arrows and Pixi's firebolts never missed a monster but as quick as one fell, two spawned to take their place. Mac instinctively knew that in a battle of attrition, the monsters would win. They were only seconds into the battle and all three tanks were injured and threatening to be overwhelmed by the increasing numbers of the monsters. A quick glance at their counterparts told a similar fate on the opposite side of the room.

Arieal's voice came over the raid channel. "This isn't working. Two of my team are already down."

Matthew keyed into the conversation. "They're spawning faster than we can kill them."

Mac yelled. "That's it! Don't kill them."

"What!" echoed several voices across the raid chat-channel.

"Two spawn for every one that you kill, so stop killing them. Go for crippling attacks."

"You're the boss," replied Matthew as he shifted his avatar's aim lower on the rushing monster and fired again. The barbed arrow flew true and punched through the leg of the monster, dropping it. Instead of disappearing and two spawning to replace it, the injured monster crawled about the floor slowing the progression of those around it.

Earl grunted. "I'll be damned…I'm on it."

All throughout the room, both groups changed their tactics and the increasing number of monsters slowed. They were still outnumbered five to one but they weren't about to be overwhelmed any longer. Since the wounding action bought them a few minutes of breathing room, Pixi dropped back to stand with Moira and the two began to conserve their power. Spellcasters have a limited amount of power for their magic and constant casting drained it quickly.

Marvin broke into the conversation. "Tao, I'm near the orb and there is something odd about it."

Mac switched the conversation over to the raid channel so the Society of Night members could hear it as he replied. "What 'ya got skald?"

"The orb isn't an orb."

"What do you mean?"

"It is more like a half of an orb."

"Arieal, do you have anyone near your orb?"

"Let me check," she responded. After a brief pause she added, "Tariq...one of my assassins is close by and moving to check. Why?"

Mac had a glimmer of an idea. "If it looks like half an orb as I suspect, I bet the only way to control the spawning of these mobs is to rejoin the two parts."

"Yes, it looks to be the white half of a yin-yang symbol," came a new voice with a slight northern accent on the raid channel. Mac guessed it to be the assassin.

Since Mac was the raid-leader, the Player Interface on his computer screen showed the statistics of all raid members. The warriors on both sides were down to less than half their starting health and a few were below a quarter. Two members from the Society were knocking at death's door but the healers were doing their best to keep them alive. Unfortunately, every caster was near critical levels on power but thankfully no deaths…yet. They would have to do something and fast.

Keying up the raid channel Mac ordered, "Gamble and Tariq…grab the orbs and move toward the center of the room as fast as you can. All warriors break off from your current target to cover your carrier. Casters be ready to throw your spells where needed."

Putting actions to words, Mac moved his avatar forward while using his samurai skills to dodge or parry oncoming attacks but not fully engaging the monsters until he was beside the dwarven rogue. "Let's roll, mate."

Marvin had his avatar Gamble grab the orb and grimaced as he took damage with each pulse of the orb. "On your six, old man!"

Everyone heard Mac's laughter over guild chat. The inside joke was that Marvin was actually two years his senior but since Mac always seemed to slide into the leadership role, the guildies had taken to calling him 'the old man.' Seeing the monsters beginning to swarm after them, Mac used one of his avatar's special abilities called whirlwind, a magical enhancement which would temporarily increase his weapon speed and began slicing and dicing the monsters' arms as they attacked.

Mac glanced at the raid display on his interface.

Both Gamble and Tariq were taking constant damage and it seemed that the closer they got to the center of the room, the more damage they took. Glancing back at the distance left to travel, Mac knew the dwarf didn't have enough health left to carry it to the end and keyed the raid chat. "Arieal, they aren't going to make it without help."

"I agree. Any suggestions?"

"Only one...are you a basketball fan?"

Arieal's laughter echoed over the raid chat. "Nope, I prefer football but I can guess your plan."

Mac turned back to the dwarf and said over the guild chat. "Give it to me."

Guessing what he had in mind, Gamble passed off the pulsing orb. "Here you go." Free from the orb and the attention of the chasing mobs, the dwarf used his rogue skills to slip into the shadows and fade from sight.

"Arieal, on the count of three; One...two..."

"Three..." came her response as she pitched the white orb toward the gaping hole in the center of the room.

Mac threw the black orb.

Everyone watched in fascination as the two halves collided and exploded into a brilliant flash of light, destroying the cloaked monsters. Mac's screen flashed white, rocking him backwards in his chair. Judging from the gasps and curses over the raid chat, he guessed everyone's monitor had done something similar. As the screen refocused on to the room they saw the fuzzy image of a very large beast glowing with an inner light in the direct center where the orbs had collided.

Mac glanced at the health meters of the raid members on his interface. No one was dead but everyone was injured and their power levels were critically low. If it came to another fight, it was going to be a slaughter, short, brutal and very lopsided against the gamers.

Once the image cleared up, they were confronted with a huge beast with the face of a man, the body of a lion and the wings of an eagle. Mac recognized the monster as a Sphinx, a creature from Greek and Egyptian mythology which typically parlayed wanderers with riddles. When it spoke, its words echoed across both voice channels and scrolled up the chat windows also.

"Greetings mortals. Only the cooperation of the twin forces of Law and Chaos would allow such as you to reach this point. You are not the first but only the latest. Now, you must pass my tests to gain your reward. The challenge shall be three; one for the Light, one of the Darkness and one for all. Answer the first or second and gain a great reward. Answer the third for a chance at immortality; fail all and your lives shall be forfeit." Without waiting for a reply, the Sphinx turned his body to face Mac's avatar and spoke. "Taote Ching, you are the leader of the Keepers of the Flame. It shall be you who gives the final answer for the followers of the Law."

The Sphinx shifted his body to face his counterpart. "Arieal De'Morte as the designated leader of the Society of Night, you shall give the final answer for the minions of Chaos."

Once more turning his gaze back to Mac. "Taote Ching as raid leader it is your responsibility for the final answer. You shall have one minute to answer per riddle."

Unsure if the Sphinx would respond to a voice chat answer, Mac typed his answer as he spoke. "I understand."

Arieal did the same.

The Sphinx looked at Tao and said, "I am four letters and can be seen in the sky, yet I cannot fly. I am found in the ocean, yet I cannot swim. When you are down I am around. What am I?"

The Sphinx switched his focus to Arieal and continued, "I'm as smooth as any rhyme, I always fall but never climb, what am I?"

The two guilds began to talk amongst themselves over the guild chat channel. As raid leader, Mac could actually listen in to the Society's chat if he wanted to but didn't. He needed to focus on his guild's riddle. Bjørn suggested 'fish' but wasn't truly convinced that was the answer. Mac had panned his camera controls to stare at the image of the Norseman. There was something in his image that tugged at Mac's subconscious. Suddenly, it hit him. Bjørn's kilt was a blue tartan and his surname was 'Bluebear.' He had named his avatar after a character in one of his favorite books and the answer came to him. Mac typed his answer. "Blue. The answer is blue."

"Correct," replied the Sphinx.

It was about that time when Arieal's answer was seen on the local chat channel, "A waterfall."

"Correct," answered the Sphinx.

Turning his attention back to Tao, the mythical beast spoke again. "This last riddle is for everyone and for a chance at immortality. Fail and spend your days in mediocrity." The Sphinx paused for a moment before asking, "I walk on four legs in the morning, two in the afternoon and three at night. What am I?"

The raid voice-chat channel went wild with answers, ranging from a cat to a bird. Mac just sat back in his chair and let them guess. Finally he leaned forward and asked, "Hasn't anyone ever read Greek Mythology?"

There was a chorus of nays and only a few ayes but only Matthew elaborated. "I did back in High School but that was many years ago and only because it was required reading."

"I did too but mythology was always one of my favorite subjects in school. As a matter of fact, it got so bad that I was forbidden to do another book report on mythology while in High School." Mac grinned at the memory.

Kaslene asked, "Interesting but what does that have to do with this situation?"

"This is the original riddle of the Sphinx from Greek Mythology. I can't remember which hero it was who confronted the Sphinx, I want to say Oedipus but I could be wrong. However, I do remember the answer...Man."

"What?" came several responses over the raid chat channel.

Mac typed his answer. "Man. The answer is man. He crawls on four in the morning of his life; walks on two during middle-age or the afternoon of his life and three, with a cane, during old age or at the evening of his existence."

"Correct," replied the great beast and with the completion of the riddle game, the Sphinx bowed his head once before fading into nothingness.

The sound of clapping echoed through the empty chamber as a red robed figure appeared in the center of the room next to a large iron bound chest. One feature of the game that was consistent with every character or monster was a nametag floating above their heads and this one read: Al Shaytan <Game Operations Designer>

"Outstanding....absolutely outstanding."

Since he wasn't in their raid or guild voice chat, it was odd that they heard his words on both voice channels while his words scrolled up the chat box. Al Shaytan was thin of frame with pale skin, black hair, red robes and had the unmistakable look of a wizard. However, after his opening remark the wizard fell silent and waited.

Unsure of what to do, Mac fell back on his default action and decided to be polite. Many situations in real life and in the game could be diffused by a simple conversation. "Well met Al Shaytan. I am Taote Ching, a humble Ronin and speaker for the Keepers of the Flame."

Al Shaytan pivoted to face him. "I know much about you Taote Ching. Actually, I know much about all of you. I am here because you managed to defeat this dungeon." Gesturing to everyone gathered. "You are the first, both server wide and game wide, to do so. Your names shall become legend."

"Anyone ever heard of this guy before?" asked Arieal over the raid chat.

There were a great many nays but Whitney spoke up. "I think I've seen his name on some of the game forums."

Matthew agreed. "Now that you mention it, I think I've seen it also. He must be legit, look at his nametag. I've never seen that before...ever."

Al Shaytan continued speaking as if he hadn't heard their exchange. "This particular dungeon has been my pet project for several years. Many have made it to this room but only one other group has ever made it past the orbs but they didn't make it past all three riddles. You are a special group and I have need of your skills."

Mac moved his avatar forward slightly. "Pardon my directness but who are you and what are you talking about?"

Al Shaytan pointed at the nametag floating above his avatar. "I thought this would explain who I am but you are a straight speaker, so I too will be blunt. I'm one of the designers of *Lost Lands* and I have an offer for you." He gestured at the chest before him. "Here is your reward for completion of the Tomb of Immortality; one legendary item of your choice. You may take it and depart." With a wave of his hand, the chest opened to reveal sixteen glowing items. "Or you can choose not take it and bet on a chance at an even greater prize but you must make your decision before we go further."

John, the gamer who played Marrok the Knight, moved forward and pulled forth a new sword which glowed with a yellow light. Sparks of electricity could be seen as they raced up and down the blade. "Sorry guys, I have to go. The wife is calling. Good luck if you take his offer." He turned to face Whitney and the two avatars hugged. "Princess, tell your mother hello for me and make sure you do all of your homework."

Whitney stepped back. "Dad! Tomorrow's Saturday, I don't have any homework."

"Okay. Love you girl."

"Love you too Dad."

Stepping away from the rest of the group, John used his recall stone and disappeared. Recall Stones were a magical device which all guild members carried that would teleport them back to their respected guild halls. Several members of the Society of Night followed suit, grabbed their prize and departed to their own guild hall. In the end, there were only ten left. Seven of the Keepers and three from the Society: Arieal the Necromancer, Tariq the Assassin and Cozad the Dreadknight.

Al Shaytan smiled. "I've been developing a new expansion for *Lost Lands* and I would like you to Alpha test it for me. If you agree, each of you will receive the new expansion disk tomorrow morning."

Whitney typed quickly. "Will it cost us anything?"

Al Shaytan shook his head. "Negative. It is my gift to you for your accomplishment."

Marvin asked, "What's the expansion called?"

Al Shaytan grinned. "Atlantis."

"What is it you want from us?" asked Arieal.

"Simple. Install the disk and enter the game normally. Tomorrow shortly before noon, Eastern Time, a portal will open in your respective Guild Halls which will bring each of you to the gateway. I will reveal the rest of the quest at that time." Al Shaytan gestured to the chest and added, "Go ahead and keep these. They may aid you in your quest and I will see each of you at noon tomorrow." With that, the wizard faded from view.

Mac moved over to the chest and pulled out his reward. It was a katana of immeasurable beauty. Drawing the blade, it flared to life with a pale-white light and radiated an area of frost. "Wow! A Frostbrand and look at the stats on this thing."

As each of the remaining raid members pulled forth their weapons and chatted about the possibility of exploring a new expansion. Mac only vaguely listened. Now that the raid was over, he once again felt the loneliness of the real world pressing in at the edges of his consciousness. Realizing that someone had asked him a question, he turned his attention back to the group. "What was that? I'm sorry, my mind was wandering."

Earl asked again. "Do you think Al's offer is on the up and up? I mean, we're supposed to have the expansion disk tomorrow morning? Come on, get real. Kaslene and I are in Alaska. Snail mail isn't the quickest reaching us."

"I don't know. Only time will tell but either we will have the disks tomorrow and the chance to explore Atlantis or we won't. It seems pretty simple to me."

Tariq said, "Now I see how you chose your name. You sound like some sort of Chinese fortune cookie."

Mac had his avatar shrug his shoulders. "Could be one reason but it is true. Either we will or we won't. There is no use worrying about it. But it's late here and I need sleep, so I'll see everyone tomorrow."

Arieal said, "Good idea. Goodnight Tao. Thanks for the fun."

Everyone else said their farewells and teleported back to their guild halls and logged out.

As the screen went dark, Mac looked around his empty apartment and felt the loneliness of his existence once more. Glancing over at the framed photo of his late wife, Mac fiddled with the gold band that he still wore on his left hand. With everything that had happened to him over the past four months only the game kept him going...only in the game did he truly feel alive.

Chapter 2

It wasn't his alarm clock which awakened Mac but the ringing phone.

He stared bleary eyed at the annoying device and wondered if he should answer it. Looking up from the phone to the clock on the nearby mantle, he saw that it was a quarter past eleven. He knew that it was sometime around sunrise when he had finally fallen asleep. Of course, the empty bottle of bourbon laying on the floor had helped him chase down that elusive prey.

The insistent ringing finally stopped.

Mac laid his pounding head back on the pillow and was about to close his eyes when the phone began again. He realized that whoever was calling wasn't going to leave him alone until they talked to him, so he picked it up it.

"Hey mate!" came the voice of his best friend. Leave it to Marvin to be cheerful in the early hours.

"Morning."

"Did you check your mail yet?"

"No dammit, you woke me up. Why?"

"It's here."

Mac bolted up fully awake. "The game? It's here? Then it's true?"

"Yep. I already have it loaded up and so does everyone else. We are just waiting for noon to roll around before using the portal." After a brief pause Marvin added, "And our fearless leader of course."

Mac glanced at the clock. "I'll be there in thirty minutes. Gotta go!"

Slamming down the phone, Mac rushed over to his apartment door and found a small brown shipping box sitting on his doorstep. Ripping open the package, he was greeted with a DVD jewel case with the artwork of an island dominated by a shining crystal city and with dragons flying around its many spires.

The title read: **Lost Lands: Atlantis** by Infernal Online Entertainment.

Mac sprinted to his computer and inserted the disk. He clicked the agree buttons without taking the time to read any of the agreements which popped up until he got to the prompt to begin the install and glanced at the clock.

Eleven twenty-seven.

Stripping off his clothes, he tossed them on the floor to join the other discarded garments and hopped in the shower. Five minutes later, he was in the kitchenette slapping together a few peanut butter sandwiches, starting up a pot of coffee and grabbing a bottle of water before returning to his desk. By eleven fifty-two, he was logging into the game.

Mac felt the pressures of reality fade from his mind as the graphics of the game filled his senses. He felt his pulse quicken at the excitement of the unknown.

Everyone was in the Keepers of the Flame guild hall when he arrived including the three members from the Society of the Night who had chosen to join them on this quest. One of the first things Mac noticed was that they were able to form everyone into one group of ten, not the normal limit of eight. This would make things easier for everyone, especially him as leader. Trying to juggle two groups in raid-mode was frustrating and tended to pull away from the enjoyment of the actual game.

A few minutes later the chatter of small talk died when a shining white portal opened in the center of the guild hall. Without hesitation, Mac maneuvered his avatar to the portal and stepped through.

The rest followed.

Al Shaytan <Game Operations Designer> was waiting for them. Dressed in his now familiar red robes and leaning on an onyx staff capped with a glowing red orb, he was standing in front of a huge ebony archway which was filled with swirling smoke. Ivory letters marked the face of the arch which read: *'Abandon All Hope Ye Who Enter Here.'*

Seeing the group pause to stare at the archway, Al Shaytan gestured to it and asked, "Too much?"

The game automatically executed the emote of Tao shaking his head as Mac typed. "No...very mythical and dramatic."

Arieal said, "I kind of recognize the saying but I can't place it."

"Dante's Divine Comedy. It was over the entrance to hell," replied Whitney. She might be the youngest player in the guild but past experiences had taught the guildies that she was very worldly for her age and rarely wrong when it came to literature.

Al Shaytan clapped his hands to gather everyone's attention before beginning his speech. "First off, there will be a few changes in *Lost Lands: Atlantis*. The first being the graphics. Let me just say that they will be very, very intense. Yet they will not in any way slow down your system."

Everyone smiled at that thought. Anytime the game creators can increase the gaming experience without affecting performance, it was a good thing.

"Secondly...death," Al continued. "Since this is a special test phase if you die, you are out of the game. There are no respawn points and third, money. *Lost Lands: Atlantis* has the standard conversion rates but I have strived to make it more of a free-market economy."

Whitney asked, "What does that mean?"

Matthew answered. "The law of supply and demand, the more something is in demand the higher the cost. Simple real world economics."

"Oh," was all she said.

"And lastly, your quest. There's an ancient artifact known as the Dragon Orb and it's missing. The High Mage of Atlantis was the last known possessor of this item. Perhaps he knows what became of it, perhaps not." Al Shaytan looked around at the group for a moment before asking, "Any other questions?"

Mac nodded. "Yes. How long do we have to complete the quest?"

Al Shaytan's smile was fleeting when he answered. "Time is a relative thing. How can one truly measure time?" The red robed wizard shrugged his shoulders. "But suffice to say, you will have plenty of time on the other side of the gateway to complete your quest. Nothing else?" Stepping back, Al Shaytan gestured to the ebony arch. "Then enter brave souls, your destiny awaits."

Mac typed several commands onto his keyboard which activated his normal pre-quest macro, a set of preprogrammed game commands which executed two emotes and a group message. On screen his avatar held up his left hand over his head and gestured in a circular motion before pointing dead ahead. "All right people, let's roll."

Taking his own advice, Mac moved his avatar to the smoke filled archway and stepped through.

If his group mates followed he didn't know or care at this very moment, because the world went black and his ears were filled with the roaring of the wind. Mac felt his gut churning as the world began spinning incredibly fast, almost as if he was caught inside a tornado and then nothing.

* * * * *

When he awoke, he felt the warm glow of the afternoon sun on his face. That's when it registered to him that he was laying on his back. The after effects of the spinning were quickly fading and the roar of the wind was gone. As a matter of fact, the birdsong off in the distance and the cool breeze on his face was very relaxing. Only the slight tap-tap of metal on metal marred the perfection of the moment.

Tap...tap.

Tap...tap.

Suddenly alert, Tao kicked his feet into the air rapidly which in turn catapulted his body upright. Landing lightly, he drew his katana and assumed the stance of the mountain; the posture of ultimate defense.

Blinking away the sunlight, Tao looked around only to find himself standing on a dirt road at the top of a small grassy knoll. There was a slight breeze coming from the fog shrouded lake to his right. Glancing down the road, his eyes followed it as it cut through the rolling hills. It disappeared and reappeared numerous times as it traversed the region until it disappeared into a dark forest several miles away. Turning around, the road ran along the crest of the slope as it wound its way toward an ice covered mountain in the distance.

All around him, there was only one indication of civilization and it was the origin of the tapping sound that had awakened him. Several yards away on the side of the road was a gallows-style gibbet with skeletal remains of its last occupant still inside swinging in the breeze.

Glancing down, Mac noticed that he was dressed in red and black Japanese armor and holding a razor sharp katana with frost visible on the blade.

"Holy Shit!"

Chapter 3

Sheathing his katana, Tao scanned the horizon looking for any sign as to where they were. Of course, if the twin suns in the sky were a clue, he knew where he was. He was inside the game but thought, *'That's impossible. Get a hold of yourself Mac. Mac? Am I Mac or Tao?'*

Shaking his head to clear his thoughts, Tao moved over to the closest of his companions. It was the armored figure of Cozad. At the present time, he seemed to be the only one who was nearly awake. His helmet had fallen off during the transition exposing his face. He was pale, nearly white and completely hairless…literally no hair, no eyebrows, no five-o'clock shadow, totally hairless. Beyond that, Tao guessed him to be human.

Not knowing Cozad's real world name and remembering his own disorientation when he came to, Tao tapped the Dreadknight's metal clad foot and called out. "Cozad! Cozad! Wake up. We're on the other side."

The Dreadknight's eyes flew open and immediately began to glow with a strange reddish light. Snatching up his massive single-bladed battle axe, he rose under some sort of magical power to stand before the samurai. A look of rage contorted Cozad's face as he raised his axe over his shoulder and prepared to strike.

Reflexively, Tao drew his katana and assumed the mountain stance once more.

Pausing, Cozad cocked his head to the side as the features of his face softened slightly. When he spoke, his voice was deep and hollow as if it was coming from the other side of the grave. "Tao?" He lowered his axe and looked around. "Tao? What...what do you mean we are on the other side?"

Relaxing, Tao sheathed his sword and pointed up. "Can you think of any other explanation for that or what you are wearing?"

Cozad glanced first at the twin suns overhead before looking down at his black plate armor. Red flames were engraved on the chest plate and his helmet's faceplate looked like a skull, just how it had been described in the game. He felt the buzzing of his spells in the back of his mind and knew that with a simple thought he could summon a gargoyle to serve his bidding or cast a spell that would wrack the samurai's slender form with disease and corruption. How he knew this, he didn't know or care. Or did he? Speaking softly Cozad finally said, "Edward. My name is Edward."

"Please to meet you Ed." Tao extended his hand. "Back home my friends call me Mac but given our surroundings I think Tao will work just fine."

Shaking hands, the Dreadknight had the intense urge to crush the slender samurai's hand and feed on the pain it would bring forth. Ignoring the urge, the Cozad mind-set fought against the more rational Edward mind-set. It was as if the two personalities were at war with each other with control of the titan's body as the reward. The chaos mindset that was Cozad wanted to crush, maim and conquer all peasants. While the rational mindset that was Edward understood that the urges of chaos and anarchy had a place and time for use and this was not it.

Tao could sense the inner turmoil of the twin sides of Cozad. Instead of resisting or trying to pull back, he took a deep breath and focused on letting his Ki, his inner peace flow, into the struggling Dreadknight.

Whether it helped or not, Cozad finally released his grip and planted his axe deep in the ground. Taking a deep breath, he grinned. "Mac? Tao? You have a thing for three letter names?"

Tao absentmindedly noticed that the smoky glow of his eyes had shifted from red to a deep blue. "Never thought much about it but I guess I do."

"But you're right, given our surroundings I think I would prefer to be called Cozad."

With a nod Tao gestured at the limp forms of their companions. "We need to wake everyone and get this sorted out. We might be safe for the moment but I don't want to tempt fate by lying around. Do you?"

Cozad shook his head. "No. Waiting to be attacked is about as smart as a screen door on a submarine."

Tao clapped him on the shoulder. "I think I like you. This sounds like the beginning of a great friendship."

Cozad grinned and the two moved off to begin reviving the rest of the group.

Whitney turned out to be the easiest to revive and the one who took the least amount of time to adjust to being inside the game. Maybe it's because she was a teenager and her dreams of magic were suddenly real. Or possibly it was that she was now a faerie with the innate ability to fly, change her size and turn invisible. She also insisted that everyone call her Pixi.

Earl and Kaslene were the slowest to fully come around but neither seemed upset at the situation. Earl briefly explained that back home in Alaska, both of them were pushing seventy and Kaslene was completely home-bound due to her medical condition. There was probably a Freudian explanation as to why she chose to play a nature-based healer but Tao had no reason to explore that. They both decided that as long as they were here, they too would go by their avatar names and neither showed any sign of internal struggle with their alter-egos on this side.

Matthew was stressed, plain and simple. In the real world, his fiancé was off at a spa for the weekend getting prepped for their upcoming wedding next Friday. However, as long as he could make it back in time for the rehearsal dinner on Thursday night, he was game. To Matthew, getting a chance to really be Mathias the archer was just the ultimate bachelor's weekend.

Roland seemed to take the whole situation in stride, as if this was just a walk through Central Park. To hear Steve explain it, "I'm a New Yorker and New Yorkers can take anything dished out to us. Hell, if we can survive Nine-Eleven then we can survive anything."

Marvin was another problem. His and Mac's friendship went back over thirty years. They had been friends through many a tough time and Mac could tell that his friend was torn between the excitement of the adventure before them and the guilt of being separated from his family. He was married with two wonderful kids and a third on the way. Of course now he was Gamble, the dwarven skald with skills and abilities he had only dreamed of back in the real world. What that meant exactly, he didn't know…yet.

Arieal and Tariq remained enigmas. Neither would answer questions about their situation in the real world and would only respond to direct questions with short monosyllable answers if at all possible. However, both seemed to be stable for the moment.

By the time everyone was coherent enough for a meeting, the twin suns were beginning to set. Since Pixi could fly and stay invisible, Tao had sent her to search the surrounding countryside but nothing was within easy walking distance. She had found evidence that someone fished this area of the lake. There were several buoys a stone's throw from the waterline but other than the dead prisoner in the gibbet, they were effectively in the middle of nowhere.

Clapping his hands to get everyone's attention, Tao waited until everyone settled down before he began. "We seem to be in a bit of a jam at the moment."

"Ya think!" snapped Tariq.

Tao ignored the snide remark and continued. "I am unsure how or why Al Shaytan sent us through the gateway but it seems we're inside the game."

"Brilliant. Absolutely brilliant," said Tariq.

Everyone ignored the slender rogue except Cozad who turned a harsh eye on him. The glow around his eyes had shifted from blue to purple and seemed to bore into the assassin's flesh. After a moment of squirming, Tariq lowered his head and Cozad turned his attention back to Tao who noted that the gleam had changed colors once more. As the Dreadknight relaxed, the brilliant purple was fading to a pale violet.

Unsure of exactly what had transpired between the two, Tao went back to his discussion. "If we are indeed inside the game, we must assume that the rules of the game govern our actions."

Arieal looked up. "What do you mean by that?"

"Magic, healing, time, money, anything and everything. Don't forget Al Shaytan made a particular point of mentioning death. He said that there are no respawn points in this realm."

Roland asked, "So what happens when we die over here? Do we just get kicked back to our computers? That would be an easy way to get out of here."

Tariq drew his dagger. "We can test that theory easy enough."

Tao shouted. "Tariq! Put your weapon away. Now!"

The assassin hesitated and shifted to face the samurai with the dagger still in his hand. The fading sunlight gleamed off of the green poison which coated the blade. "Why? Who made you boss?"

"I was the designated leader on the other side and you agreed to it by joining the group."

"That was the game. This isn't or even if it is, why do I need you?"

Tao shrugged. "You don't. It's simple. You stay with the group, you follow my orders. I will ask for suggestions and advice but the final decision is mine. If you don't like it, go." Tao pointed off into the distance. "Strike off on your own."

Tariq took a tentative step toward the distant forest before turning back. "Why must it be your decision? Why not Arieal's? I know her. I trust her."

It was the dark elf who came to defend Tao's point. "No. I will not stand for leader. I don't have the skills to get us home." She glanced up at Tao. "That's your intention...right?"

Tao nodded. "Aye. But to do so will take some teamwork and a bit of luck."

Pixi asked, "What do you mean by that?"

"Has anyone else taken an inventory of what you're carrying?"

Cozad raised his mailed hand. "I have. I seem to have everything I can think of that was in my backpack within the game; spare weapons, food, drink and the few other odd and ends that I carry."

Tao raised his left eyebrow. "Recall stone?"

Cozad cocked his head to the side as he mentally reviewed his inventory. Seconds later he shook his head. "No. No recall stone."

Everyone else scrambled to search through their packs but no one had a stone. Tao said out loud what everyone was thinking. "Which means we are not going to be able to teleport back to our guild halls if they even exist in this reality."

Gamble nodded his head as he understood where Tao's logic had already taken him. "But if they do exist, then we could use the magic portal inside to port home which probably means back to the real world."

Tao nodded. "That's what I'm thinking or hoping for at least."

Moira asked, "But if this is a new realm, how do we get back to Camelot?"

"Okay, let me ask everyone another question. Anyone other than Gamble play *Lost Lands* in Beta?"

Only Cozad raised his hand.

Tao continued. "Anyone actually read the history behind the game?"

No one raised their hand.

"Okay, I will try to be brief in my explanation."

Gamble interrupted. "While you do that Tao, I'll get a fire going. It seems like we're camping here tonight after all."

Tao nodded and organized his thoughts before beginning. "From what I understand, the basic theory behind the game was to find a way to let gamers play avatars from different periods of history and have them adventure together. So, the designers came up with something they refer to as the 'Bubble Theory.'"

"The what?" Pixi asked as she cocked her head to the side and absentmindedly fluttered her butterfly wings.

"The Bubble Theory. Every Lost Land is contained in a bubble which floats on the River of Time." Tao pulled out a dagger and began to draw a web-like picture in the dirt to help illustrate his point. "Occasionally, these bubbles touch one another which in turn creates a connection between the two realms. Avalon was the first realm to be developed, based on the legends of the Arthurian Knights. From what I understand it was the only realm in the Alpha test phase but for the Beta phase they added Midgard based on the Viking Age, the Parthenon based on Ancient Greece and Nippon based on Feudal Japan. These became the four original Lost Lands. Over the past three years since the game launched, Infernal has expanded the original realms in size and added two more realms, the Shadowlands based on the legends of Darkness and the Burning Sands based on the Arabian Nights but the one constant through all of this has been Avalon. It seems that every new realm added has a connection to that fabled land."

Cozad picked up the logic. "So, if this is a new realm and they follow their own pattern, somewhere in this realm there's a gateway to Avalon. If we can get back there, we can travel to Camelot and to your guild hall which should enable us to get home."

Tao nodded. "At least that is what I'm hoping."

"And where do you think we can find this gateway?" asked Tariq.

"Al Shaytan is the one who sent us here with the quest to find the Orb of Knowledge and suggested that we seek out the High Mage of Atlantis as a contact."

Mathias said, "You're thinking that was a hint."

Tao shrugged his shoulder. "Occam's Razor."

Mathias asked, "What?"

It was Bjørn who answered. "Occam's Razor states that when all things are equal the simplest answer is usually the correct one."

Arieal absentmindedly toyed with her long snow white hair which stood out in drastic contrast to the ebony skin of her dark elf persona. Finally she said, "But we know nothing of this realm and since we are missing maps, we don't know where we are or where we are going. Correct?"

"True. But I doubt that we were brought here without the means to complete our task. It wouldn't be logical. Al Shaytan stated he wanted us to test his creation which implies to me that there is a method to his madness. We just have to figure it out."

Gamble returned and began stacking the wood he'd gathered into a neat pile. Keeping his voice low he said, "Don't do anything rash but we're being watched."

Chapter 4

To everyone's credit, most of the companions didn't do anything foolish except Pixi. She fluttered her wings once and disappeared from view. Whether it was a conscious action or not, no one knew or cared at the moment.

Gamble continued to stack up the firewood as he continued speaking in low tones. "There are two groups moving in on our position. One along the shoreline and the other coming from the direction of the forest. I couldn't get a good look at them without making it obvious."

Cozad stood up and pretended to stretch. "I can see the ones on the beach. They're trying to hide in the rocks but doing a terrible job. I would guess that they're goblins of some sort."

Roland wasn't so subtle when he hoisted his shield, drew his silver sword, marched to the edge of the knoll and called out, "Creatures of Darkness! Beware!"

Hearing the challenge from the paladin, the goblins yelled and charged.

Moira cursed. "Fool! Of all the hair-brained things you have ever done."

Realizing the need for subtly was passed, Tao began calling out orders. "Everyone form up. Cozad guard the flank to the lake. Bjørn back up Roland on the other side. Everyone else, pick a side and hold."

Mathias began firing indiscriminately. Every arrow felled a goblin but on they came. Pixi popped back into view as she completed her spell and a wall of flame appeared in the path of the charging goblins. She hadn't timed it correctly as the first two ranks of goblins had already passed the wall before it sprang into existence. However, the screams of pain which followed told that many others had felt the spell's deadly effects.

As the goblins closed from both flanks, the numbers were far greater than any had guessed. Not counting those goblins already down or caught in the blaze they were heavily outnumbered.

Standing near the now blazing campfire, Tariq looked nervously over his shoulder and said to no one in particular. "Eight to one…those aren't very good odds."

"Maybe we should let them surrender," said Mathias as he fired his bow out of reflex.

Once the goblins had started their charge, the half-elf just felt the need to retaliate. Continuing his barrage, the archer drew and fired with easy precision, no rush, no fumbling, no conscious thought. Just pull out an arrow, notch it to the string, raise and draw on his longbow in one motion, sight down the shaft and fire between breaths. Then repeat and repeat and repeat. It was the most natural thing in the world for him. One part of his mind, the Matthew part, wondered what his fiancé was doing at this moment; the Mathias part scanned the horizon for more enemies while continuing to rain death on the goblins.

When this was just a game, Earl would just click on a button on the keyboard which would trigger his transformation from Norseman to Were-bear. But on this side, as the goblins approached and the adrenaline began pumping through his system with the impending battle it was completely different. It was at that moment that Earl realized that he was no longer just a retired police officer enjoying a break from reality; he was Bjørn Bluebear, the Norse Berserker. It was a strange sensation as his body began to quiver, as if thousands of ants were running up and down his skin biting him at will. His breathing quickened and his vision narrowed. Gone were his friends. Only the charging goblin horde filled his senses. The urge to feel and taste their blood filled his whole being and the change came over him. His muscles began to swell as his hair lengthened and thickened all across his body, his bones began to pop as they realigned themselves, his nose became a snout and his words were lost as a bestial growl escaped his snout.

Moira also felt strange when she saw the onrushing horde. Somehow, she sensed that these creatures were a blight on nature. Their very footsteps tainted the peace of the land. Feeling the cool earth beneath her feet, she instinctively understood that her powers flowed from the tranquility of nature. Goblins were a bane to her existence and she must destroy them. Reaching out with her mind, she called on the grasses and the roots to aid her. All around the goblins the scrub bushes and tall grasses which they were charging through responded to the druid's call; reaching up and entangling the diminutive humanoids.

Arieal was completely indifferent to the whole situation. Being inside the game was both a wonderful feeling and totally frightening at the same time. Back home, she had begun playing *Lost Lands* to escape the reality of her situation; ex-wife, single mom, business manager, taxi driver, et cetera. Real life always threatened to overwhelm her but when the pressures of her life would get too much, Annie would log into the game and become Arieal. Only in the game did she have peace. She could summon undead minions to do her bidding or suck the life force out of attacking mobs to heal herself. Hell, she could even summon an undead horse to ride. But it was only a game. Suddenly, Arieal knew she could do all those things and even worse, she wanted to do them. It was a chilling and sobering thought.

For Roland, the upcoming battle was different. To him, he had acted in character, doing and saying what he believed the holy side of him would do in this situation. But to be truthful, he was scared shitless. The shield lay heavy on his arm, the helmet was stifling and his sword felt awkward. Nothing felt like it should. He had always imagined the calmness that would flow through him, safe and secure in the righteous knowledge of his faith. Of course, since Steve didn't believe in any higher power than himself, he didn't know how to act as a paladin.

Tariq didn't know what was going on but then, he didn't care either. Somehow Al Shaytan had managed to trick them all into thinking that they were inside the game and this was all real. Brandon knew that it didn't work like that and he was going to prove it to everyone. Looking around at his companions as they formed up to defend themselves against the pitiful goblins, he thought about who he should take out. In the game, he was ranked third on the game server in Player vs Player (PvP) assassinations. He had actually lost count how many 'accidental' assassinations of party members he had completed. The trick was to strike your target in the thick of combat, where the deathblow would actually be assumed from their foes and not a party member.

Tariq's first inclination was the bossy samurai but judging by his fluid movements, a single strike wouldn't be a certain kill and he didn't want to get into a melee contest with Tao. Since he didn't have any grudge against Cozad or Arieal, it wouldn't be them but who? Finally his eyes rested on the back of the goody-two-shoes form of Roland the paladin and a grin crept over his face. Slowly drawing his poisoned dagger, Tariq moved in for the kill.

Tao added the weight of his yumi to rain of arrows pouring from Mathias' bow but the goblins kept advancing. Seeing a charging horde of goblins in game was one thing, actually feeling the ground tremble as their green-skinned bodies scrambled over the fallen to get at you quicker was another thing. The rational portion of his brain that was Mac felt a mixture of revulsion and sympathy at the pitiful creatures. Of course, the logical side that was Tao knew if the goblins could reach them in overwhelming numbers, they would just swarm over them like ants winning the battle by sheer numbers. Once the goblins closed to twenty paces, Tao dropped his bow and drew his swords.

His right hand held his new katana he had received from Al Shaytan last night, part of him regretted having to christen the blade on the blood of goblins but the frost radiating from the blade seemed to increase with their proximity. His left hand held his ever faithful wakizashi which he had created in game after a long drawn out quest to become a Grandmaster Weaponsmith. With a slight grin, he leapt into action. Gone was conscious thought. With the enemy around him, Tao became one with his swords and his every movement became death in motion.

Ed wrestled with the Cozad mindset for all of about ten seconds before giving in. Knowing that the goblins held numerical superiority, the Dreadknight spoke a word of command to summon his pet gargoyle and a hole of darkness opened in front of the foremost goblins as his minion struggled to enter this plane of existence. Unfortunately for the goblins, the gargoyle used their bodies to help pull itself free from the portal in its haste to join its master. Hefting his large axe, Cozad waded into the goblins. Hacking this way and that, anything he hit fell and didn't move again.

They were only minutes into the battle and nearly half of the goblins were dead or dying. A more intelligent creature would retreat after enduring such a slaughter but not the goblins. They kept coming and coming. So, the companions kept killing and killing.

After the initial charge, Arieal had shaken herself free of her immobility and used her magic to animate several of the dead goblins before sending them back into the fray to fight on the side of the companions.

Pixi had reappeared overhead as she launched another attack, this time a lightning bolt spell which claimed the lives of about ten goblins before she disappeared again.

Bjørn was totally and utterly berserk. In his were-bear form, he towered close to eight feet tall and wielded the huge claymore like a scythe cutting through wheat. The few goblins which survived long enough to get close enough to strike the berserker, failed to penetrate his thick blue fur which gave him his surname.

Roland stood back and watched as the goblins were decimated by his companions. Somewhere deep inside himself, he was still convinced that this was nothing more than a dream. Any minute he would wake up and be back in Manhattan. Seeing one of the goblins slip past the werebear and charge at him, Roland raised his sword. His palms were sweaty and his stomach was in a knot but still he paused. As the fear began to overwhelm him, Steve muttered a prayer out of some long forgotten habit.

Suddenly, a calm sense of peace began to flow through his body as he felt strength return to his arms. Not just any strength, the holy strength of the righteous filled him. Raising his sword high with a smile on his face with the knowledge of faith, Roland began to step forward when a sharp pain filled his lower back. He felt his knees begin to give way. He tried to call out a warning but fear swept over him once more as he realized that he was paralyzed and getting weaker by the second. Without control of his body, Roland fell to the ground just as the goblin reached him and began to hack at him with its blunt sword. A loud rushing noise filled his ears and darkness covered his eyes. Steve's last thought was *'what is that light up ahead'* and then he was gone.

Tariq was overwhelmed with elation at his strike. The paladin had been in full plate armor which didn't leave too many openings but there was a single crease in the plates where the upper torso met the waist, just enough room to slide his dagger between and into the paladin's kidneys. Judging from the spasms and twitches after his strike, he knew the poison had done its work and the annoying paladin was dead. Stepping out of the way of the onrushing goblin, he let it hack at the fallen paladin for a few moments before dispatching it with a quick slash across the throat. Looking around, Tariq was pleased with himself. Everyone was so busy with the goblins that no one was watching him, a perfect assassination.

Or so he thought.

Gamble had been overlooked by everyone, goblins and companions alike, which was fine by him. As the twin suns had set and the darkness of night had begun to claim the land, the skald was in his element. As a rogue, dusk was his favorite time of the day. The fading light was at an odd angle in the sky casting strange shadows or creating a glare which could temporarily blind someone, which made it a difficult time to see a sneaking rogue. Gamble quickly realized the advantage of the dwarven darksight.

Darksight was the ability of some races to see in the infra-spectrum or the ability to discern varying degrees of heat. Bodies gave off more heat than the surrounding landscape; their campfire gave off more and Pixi's wall of fire more than that. Gamble could see everyone except Pixi. Somehow her invisibility also masked her body heat.

Since this was a straight up fight, he used his rogue powers which were semi-magical to fade into the shadows. Standing toe-to-toe with superior numbered foes was not within his skill set, not if he could help it. Gamble took up a guard position near Moira the druid, just in case. It was a general rule of thumb when adventuring that the healer must be protected at all cost, everyone knew that. Luckily, none of the goblins had breached the perimeter except one and it was charging the fully armored paladin.

Foolish goblin.

However, the dwarf was stunned when he saw the assassin Tariq take advantage of the distraction and slide his dagger into the back of Roland. From the gleam of the green toxin which coated the blade, he knew that his friend was dead the moment the blade broke his skin.

Gamble glanced back at the others. No one else had seen the act of treachery. They were still busy with the goblin horde. Realizing that it was up to him to capture or contain the assassin, he took stock of his runes.

As a skald, he had access to a specialized type of magic that involved a combination of chanting, praying and the carving of runes into specially prepared stones. Once carved, the runes were stable and able to be used by anyone. Just speak the name of the rune, toss the stone and the spell would go off like the medieval version of a hand grenade. Seconds later Gamble found the rune-stone that he wanted, one imbued with the spell *'Bands of Gyve.'* If it worked just like it did in the game, it would call forth multiple bands of energy that would wrap around any size opponent, totally immobilizing it.

Gamble watched as Tariq easily dispatched the goblin which had been hacking on the corpse of Roland before the assassin moved back toward the fire. The dwarf wanted to puke when he saw the smirk of satisfaction on the Arabian assassin's face. Moving as quietly as possible, Gamble slid up behind the assassin and tossed the rune-stone.

Tariq heard the dwarf's whispered command and turned to block the incoming attack. But he didn't expect it to be a small stone and it slipped past his guard to strike his chest. A mere fraction of a second later, ten black ribbons of energy exploded out to quickly wrap around him. Tariq struggled with all his might for a moment before realizing that he was trapped. He was trussed up like a lamb being carried off to slaughter and completely at the dwarf's mercy.

Chapter 5

As the last of the goblins fled into the night, Tao took a deep breath of the cool night air. Even with the stench of burning flesh, the air tasted sweet. From the past near-death experiences he survived during Desert Storm, he realized of course that it was just the euphoria of being alive. Life is never sweeter than those few minutes after facing certain death.

Turning back to his companions, Tao was confronted with the bittersweet fact of being inside the game. He could see two forms lying prone within the light of their campfire, the still form of Roland and a second one wrapped in black bands of magic which was still struggling against his bonds. The rest of his companions were gathered around them and an argument had already broken out between two party members.

Moira said, "...but he hasn't been convicted."

Cozad folded his arm across his chest. "His actions have condemned him."

Moira turned angrily on Tao as he entered the circle. Thrusting her finger into his chest she glared at him. "What do you have to say about this since you are our fearless leader?"

"What are you talking about?" asked Tao.

Moira pointed at the armored Dreadknight. "He wants to kill Tariq."

"An eye for an eye and a tooth for a tooth," replied Cozad.

Tao waved his hands back and forth. "It would help if someone explained what was going on?"

Gamble stepped forward. "It's simple. While everyone was busy during the battle, I saw Tariq backstab Roland. It wasn't a case of friendly fire or accidental injury, it was a deliberate assassination."

Tao really didn't doubt his friend but he had to ask. "Are you certain?"

In response, the dwarf just knelt down and gently pulled off the dead paladin's helmet. Nobody in the group was a forensic expert but most had seen enough crime drama shows on television to recognize that a swollen and distended tongue that was solid black wasn't normal in death.

Bjørn spoke up, the exhaustion from his berserker rage was evident as his voice was just a whisper. "Only poison could do that to a corpse."

Arieal raised an eyebrow in a silent question but Moira answered for him. "Earl was a detective before he became the police chief. He was on the job for over thirty years before he retired. He's had his share of murders to investigate."

Tao stood over the bound form of Tariq and looked down on him. "You attacked one of our own? During a battle? Are you crazy?"

Cozad took a small step forward. "His actions have condemned him."

Tao held his hand out and the large dreadknight paused. "Wait. Even with my military and law enforcement background, I'm not comfortable being the judge, jury and executioner. It goes against everything that I believe in."

Cozad looked up. His eyes blazed a brilliant red. "Then you suggest letting this piece of scum live?"

"Live? Yes. I can kill an enemy in combat without hesitation but not this, not with him trussed up. It would be an execution and I am not alright with that. Not now, not ever."

Cozad's eyes had changed to a lighter shade of violet as his rage subsided. "What do you propose to do with him?"

Tao turned to the dwarf and asked, "How long will your spell last?"

"Not sure. Back home, the spell would last two hours." Gamble shrugged. "What that converts to on this side, I'm not really sure."

Tao glanced at the dark elf. "How long will your animation of the dead goblins last?"

Arieal cocked her head to one side as she thought. Blowing a stray strand of white hair out of her face she replied, "Up to one full day of game time or until I dismiss them."

Tao nodded. "Okay. Here's the plan. Everyone grab our belongings and prepare to move. We are not spending the night here, we're too exposed." The samurai changed the tone of his voice as he knelt down over top of the assassin. "Tariq, I don't know what possessed you to kill Roland. Steve was flawed but he was a friend. He didn't deserve this but I can't kill you in good conscience. It might be what you truly deserve but I still think it would be wrong. And two wrongs don't make a right."

Tao paused to look around. "But I also can't let you stay with us. So, you're being banished from the group. Whatever happens to you once we leave this campsite is entirely up to you. We are getting back home. How or if you ever make it back, I don't care. However I will give you this one warning; don't try to catch up with us. Don't call, don't write, if you see us on the street, pass us by without a word. If you do ever get close to one of us, I will not try to stop anyone from killing you. Hell, they may have to stop me."

Tao stood up and turned to Arieal. "Have your minions carry him until the spell releases him."

Arieal nodded at Tao's logic and asked, "Which way?"

Knowing that they were going to head toward the mountain by following the coastline, Tao pointed to the distant forest. "That works for me."

Without another word, two of the animated goblins moved forward, lifted the struggling form of Tariq and moved off into the night.

Tao said, "Gather the rest of the dead and mound them high."

"Why?" asked Pixi.

Tao nodded towards the fallen paladin. "His soul deserves the company of the dead on his way to the afterlife."

Understanding what the samurai had planned, the rest of the companions began the tedious work of moving the dead bodies. The magical powers of Arieal and Cozad proved immeasurable during this task. They were both able to animate the dead bodies, although it did eat up a great portion of their energy. Within an hour, the dead were piled high and Roland was laid to rest at their apex.

Everyone was filthy, sore and tired but no one suggested camping for the night.

Hoisting his pack over one shoulder, Tao looked at the still form of Roland then back to his friends. "I'm unsure of why we're here. I don't know if Steve's death on this side sent him back home and he's sitting at his computer sucking down a beer. That's my hope but I fear that isn't the truth. I truly believe that death on this side is permanent."

Tao paused and looked off into the distance where a pale yellow moon was just rising over the water. "I don't know if we will stumble into Atlantis tomorrow or the next day or next year but I know that we'll never stop searching for a way home. And if we stay true to our beliefs and our own personal honor, then we will survive this reality." Turning back to the body of his friend, Tao's eyes were full of tears. "Pixi...burn it."

With a silent nod, she cast her wall of fire spell once more and the mound of bodies roared into flames. Without looking back, Tao turned toward the lake and began walking. One by one the companions fell in behind leaving Roland Darkslayer's pyre to burn deep into the night.

* * * * *

Grigoris grinned when he heard Taote Ching speak these words.

He'd been saddened when Tariq al'Nasir al'Rafiq had succumbed to the temptations of Chaos and had felt his hopes shatter when the companions began to argue about executing him. However, when Moira and Taote stepped forward to defend the assassin, his hopes in humanity were once again restored. He didn't want to get too overconfident or hopeful, the companions still had a long quest ahead of them and his sibling was tenacious.

Chapter 6

Even though the rising of a second red moon was spectacularly beautiful, it was tempered with sadness and tears. The companions had reached the lake and turned toward the distant mountain with slow determination. Each member wrestled with the cold logic that one of their members was dead. After about an hour, Tao called a break. Finding some rocks to use as a windbreak, the companions settled down. The funeral pyre of their friend could still be seen burning in the distance.

Finally, Cozad broke the silence. "Tao...what did Roland do back home?"

"I'm not sure. He never really talked too much about his day-to-day job. I know he'd spent some time in prison for a DUI. When he was just a teenager, he got drunk one night and tried to drive home. He didn't make it. He ran a stop sign, struck a cab and the passenger died. He always said that was his greatest regret."

"He was a struggling artist," Pixi added quietly. Everyone looked up and waited for her to continue. "He was a painter, nothing major. He actually painted houses for a living but was working on his portfolio."

"How do you know that?" Moira asked.

Pixi shrugged and fluttered her wings. "One day I mentioned in guild chat about an art project I had coming up for school. Steve gave me several pointers on how to make better use of shading and blending." She smiled slightly as she added, "I got an A on that project thanks to him."

Bjørn said, "He will be missed."

Cozad stared off to the distance, looking past the burning pyre still visible. "Tariq better not take our mercy as weakness. I'll kill him the next time I see him." The glow of the Dreadknight's eyes changed from the blue of calm to the red of anger as he looked back at the group. "And you will not be able to stop me Tao."

"If he crosses paths with us again, it would be by design not by accident. I won't try to stop you." Tao grinned slightly as he added, "Of course…your blade will have to be quicker than mine on that day."

Feeling uncomfortable with the subject, Moira cleared her throat. "Where are we going?"

Tao pointed down the coastline toward the distant mountain. "If history back home is any sort of a teacher, we should find a village that way."

Everyone looked in the direction he pointed but it was Mathias who finally asked, "Why?"

"Historically speaking, cities and towns were built near waterways, the mouth of a river being the most common since the soil nearest the mouth of a river is typically very fertile. In addition, the city could reap the reward of tariffs for traffic flowing up and down the river and create a port for larger ships which would navigate the lake.."

Pixi asked, "Lake? How can you be sure that's a lake and not a sea or ocean?"

Tao shrugged. "I can't. I don't smell any salt in the breeze but in this realm that might not mean anything. Either way, my best suggestion is to follow the coastline until we find some sort of village. We need information about this land and we aren't going to find it sitting out here in the wilderness."

Mathias asked, "And you think we will find help in the town?"

"Alright listen up." Tao paused until everyone looked at him. "I miss Roland and I will probably always replay the events which lead up to his death to see if I could've done something different to change the outcome. But I can't change it, I can only learn from it. The fact remains that we're here and we're alive. Now we have to figure out how to stay alive and if possible, get back home."

Bjørn stood up. "Tao's right. At this very moment I regret letting Tariq live but that's because I'm still angry. I know it was the right thing to do and if we had let Cozad kill him, then that would've been murder and we wouldn't have been any better than Tariq. Personally, I know I would feel guilty about that for the rest of my life."

Cozad nodded. "No. Tao was right to stop me. As much as I wanted to kill him and still want to kill him, it would've been murder. Plain and simple. Besides, we don't know if it was Brandon or Tariq who killed Roland."

Pixi fluttered her wings and hovered for a second before asking. "What do you mean by that?"

It was Arieal who answered. "He means that there is a second persona lurking in each of our heads that threatens to take over." Seeing the Dreadknight nod, she continued. "Each of us have the powers and abilities our avatars had in the game, right?"

"Correct."

"Well, Brandon, Edward and I chose to play avatars of Chaos to explore the darker side of our nature. Back home, it was just a harmless fantasy, but now…"

Cozad nodded. "Aye. The cold fingers of death are now a part of me. I feel comforted by its embrace."

Arieal glanced back at the burning pyre in the distance. "I too feel that. The stench of death smells as sweet as a rose to me now. It is very unnerving."

"I can imagine. I feel my temper on the edge at all times. Just the simplest things threaten to set me off." Bjørn nodded toward the faerie. "Hell, the flapping of Pixi's wings is nerve wracking."

Pixi settled to the ground and took a small step back from the huge Norseman.

Moira giggled. "Don't worry Pixi. Earl is a gentle giant, here and back home. His bark is worse than his bite." When she smiled, her bright blue eyes seemed to light up the whole gathering. "Besides if he misbehaves, I'll punish him."

Everyone laughed. The thought of Moira, a slender elf weighing less than eighty pounds, punishing the seven foot tall, three-hundred plus pound, bare-chested warrior was ludicrous. Of course, back in the real world they had been married for thirty plus years and Earl had learned the magic phrase long ago and used it now.

"Yes dear."

Tao took the moment of levity to stand up. "Everyone should try to get some sleep. It's been a long day and we can't be sure of what tomorrow holds for us. I'll take the first watch. Cozad, I'll wake you in two hours."

Seeing the logic of Tao's plan, everyone did their best to find a place to lie down out of the wind. The samurai moved off a few steps to be alone with his thoughts and watch over his friends that were still alive. Unfortunately, the death of Steve brought to surface the loss of his wife once more and soon afterwards the tears began to flow.

* * * * *

Callistra reigned in her Nightmare, a demonic horse with fiery eyes and hooves which she had summoned to be her steed. The smell of burning flesh had called to her. Mounting her steed, she had ridden from her cabin to the southeast to investigate the burning pyre. Now that she was here, other aromatic senses called to her soul.

Magic, mighty magic had been cast on this spot.

Climbing down to investigate the area further, Callistra closed her eyes and used her magic to read the remnants of whatever enchantments had been cast on this spot. The vampyre part of her thirsted for the blood that was spilled here. It had been weeks since she last fed and the hunger was becoming unbearable again. Calming herself, she fell into the trance needed to 'see' the battle. In her mind's eye, she watched the ten companions arrive.

It wasn't as clear a picture as those she enjoyed in the past but it was still entertainment. As she watched the battle unfold something in the mannerisms and appearances of some of the companions tugged at her memories but were quickly forgotten when she witnessed the treachery of Tariq. As the companions began arguing, it was times like this when she really missed having sound. Callistra was shocked when the nine companions didn't kill the assassin but let him live.

Weak fools.

However, the trussed up assassin would make for an easy meal. Letting the spell drop, Callistra remounted her steed and turned toward the distant forest. With luck, she would be able to overtake the bound assassin before sunrise, not that she couldn't be out in the sunlight. It was just so damn bright that she preferred the darkness. Either way, she knew she would soon sate her thirst once more.

* * * * *

Chester called out to his older brother. "Sanford, wait up."

As always, Sanford slowed down but chided his younger brother. "Chester, why are you always lagging behind? You know we have to gather the mistletoe before the second moon sets."

"I know. I know. Mother will be very displeased if we don't bring back two full baskets but why do you always rush? We're out of the house and the weather is nice tonight."

Sanford stopped and turned to face his little brother. Closing the hood on the lantern, he plunged the surrounding woods into semi-darkness. "Because we need to be quick or else the Wood Witch will get us."

Chester's face went pale and his eyes widened. "The Wood Witch? She's real?"

"Of course." Sanford struggled to keep the smirk off his face as he added, "However, since this is Wotan's Day, she should be far to the south." Pausing to look around conspiratorially, he added. "But she still could be on the lookout for fresh meat."

When an owl hooted nearby, Chester clutched the sickle he was carrying tighter to his chest and looked around wildly. The fear on his younger brother's face was more than Sanford could stand. Bursting into laughter, he bent over holding his stomach. Realizing that his brother had played a trick on him again, Chester dropped the sickle and leapt on Sanford's back. Momentarily stunned by his brother's wild attack, the two fell to the ground and began wrestling.

Mere seconds into the fight, the cracking and breaking of branches reached their ears.

Forgotten was their argument. Rolling clear, both boys pulled out their daggers and prepared to defend themselves from whatever was plundering through the thick underbrush of the forest. It was only a few minutes before they saw two goblins in the bright moonlight carrying a struggling form wrapped up in some sort of black bands. Neither brother had to ask what to do. Goblins were to be killed on sight. Period. No questions asked and no exceptions. Having lived their whole life under the threat of goblin attacks, the brothers knew how to deal with them and moments later, the two goblin zombies were dead once again.

Sanford moved over to the struggling form of Tariq and poked him with his dagger. "Chester. Get the lantern. I'm not sure what this is but we need more light."

"Gotcha," was all he said and ran off to gather their things.

Sanford knelt down to study the trussed up assassin as best he could in the pale moonlight while he waited. Minutes passed. "Dammit Chester! Where are you?"

A slight rustle of the leaves behind him heralded the soft voice. "He is dead youngling."

Sanford spun around but was dumbfounded at the vision before him.

Dressed in a skin-tight black leather outfit which left very little to the imagination was the most beautiful woman he'd ever seen in his entire life. She had perfect alabaster skin, long silky ebony hair, crystal blue eyes and a body any man would kill to bed. Only the blood dripping from her fangs marred the beauty of the creature.

The dagger fell from Sanford's hand forgotten as he succumbed to her enchantment. He raised his chin and opened his arms to embrace the vision standing before him. He didn't even struggle as he felt his life's blood sucked from his body. His last thoughts were of all the carnal things he wanted to do to the creature which killed him.

Sated, Callistra gazed down at the bound form of Tariq and asked, "And what do we have here?" Leaning down she sniffed the whole of his body. "A creature from the seas of sand by your smell and bound by dwarven magic, interesting."

The vampyress ran her hands over the assassin's body and could feel the different bulges where his weapons were secreted. When her hand grazed over the enchanted dagger he'd received from Al Shaytan there was a spark of magic and she drew her hand back quickly more in surprise than in pain. Carefully, she dug past the magical bands to get at the silver hilt of the dagger. Seeing the ruby pommel and the downward pointing pentagram, she withdrew her hand slowly and studied the bound Arabian once more. Her eyes flashed with anger.

"Assassin, you and I must talk. But first, I must contact Kastle."

Pulling out a crudely fashioned wand, she waved it once over the struggling assassin and he began floating gently into the air. Callistra whistled once and the Nightmare moved closer. Muttering a few words in a language that Tariq didn't understand, the assassin felt himself draped over the saddle and securely fastened.

With another wave of her wand, she transformed into a huge bat and flew off into the night.

As the demon horse began moving south, Tariq stared down at the passing ground and thought, *'What else could go wrong today?'*

Chapter 7

Sunrise found the companions still asleep in the rocks. Tao hadn't awakened a replacement for the night watch once he discovered how calming meditation was in this reality. He had moved away from the rest of the party and had settled down in the lotus position, with ankles folded up onto his inner thighs and entered the trance of the Sensei. It was enlightening. He was aware of everything around him from the ants in the ground to the owls hunting the night sky. With the first hints of the morning sun, Tao had come out of his trance, stood up and felt more refreshed than any other time of his life.

Gazing out at the lake, Tao could just make out the distant shapes of several boats. Probably the fishing fleet from the village he hoped to find nearby. Moving over to Gamble, he tapped the dwarf on his foot.

The skald was instantly awake. "Morning."

Tao looked toward the north where a small plume of smoke signaled the remains of his friend's pyre and said, "Wake everyone. We'll be moving soon."

Gamble watched as his oldest friend wandered off towards the lake. They had been best friends over thirty years and he knew what was bothering the samurai. The Marvin mind-set realized that Mac was still haunted by the men he lost during Desert Storm. Now, Steve's death would have dredged up those memories in addition to the fresh wounds of Cassie's loss only four months ago.

Then, there was the fact that they were heading into unknown territory without any information on the region or culture and it was his friend's responsibility to keep everyone safe. Whether it was the truth or not, didn't matter. It was how Mac viewed the situation. Marvin's problem was how could he best help his friend?

Ever practical, both on the other side and in game, Gamble just shrugged his shoulders and buried his problem for the moment and turned to the task of waking everyone up. Cozad was the easiest to awaken, since his eyes flew open at the dwarf's approach. However, Pixi was the hardest. It seems that fairies have the natural tendency to turn invisible when sleeping, mix that with her ability to shrink down to about six inches tall and you have a very hard companion to find. The dwarf only found her when he tripped over her.

Breakfast for the companions was a mixture of dried fruits and travel biscuits, not the most tasty fare but edible and nourishing. Everyone seemed to want to keep the morning conversation light and about unimportant subjects. Finally Mathias said, "Something has been bothering me."

Arieal was the first to respond. "What?"

"Time."

Moira asked, "Time? What about time?"

"If this is the game and we are governed by the rules of the game, wouldn't time also be affected?"

"How so?" asked Arieal.

"It has probably been eight to twelve hours since we came across, right?"

Bjørn looked up at the twin suns just starting their race across the sky. "Yes. That would be a good estimate."

"So, how much time has passed back home?"

Pixi said, "The same amount, right?"

Gamble shook his head. "No. Game time was much faster than real time. I want to say almost twelve to one." Seeing the blank stares from Pixi and Moira, the dwarf continued. "I'm sure it wasn't a straight twelve to one conversion but I know that every two hours of real time was one full day in game time or twelve game days to one day real time. Does that help?"

Mathias cocked his head to the side while he considered what that meant. "So, only an hour or so has passed back on the other side?"

Gamble shrugged his shoulders. "I'm not sure but if this land follows the rules of the game and that also includes time, then yes."

Tao rejoined the group. "Also remember that Al Shaytan said that time would not be a problem. I can take that remark two ways. Either that time moves much different in this land or more likely, we're stuck here and have all the time in the world."

Mathias grinned. "So, I still have a chance on making it to my wedding on time."

Tao nodded. "It would seem so."

Mathias hopped up. "Outstanding."

Everyone else seemed to be infected by Mathias's sudden good mood and began to pack away their belongings. Within minutes, the companions were ready and followed Tao as he moved down to the shoreline.

* * * * *

A large bat landed on a granite headstone just outside an old stone chapel.

Callistra cancelled the transformation spell and returned to her natural form. One byproduct of the transformation was that the blood was gone from her clothes. She didn't know why or how it happened but she just accepted it and went on with her business. Moving through the graveyard, Callistra thought about the misconception that vampires couldn't walk on holy ground. If that was true, she hadn't run across a holy enough spot to stop her… yet. Hearing singing from inside the chapel, she decided not to use the main door. She didn't relish running into any innocents. Her hunger might be sated at the moment but she didn't trust herself around that much fresh meat. Seeing an open window on the second floor, she leapt the distance and landed gracefully on the small window sill. Sniffing the air, she could smell the humans below but none were close by so she entered the room.

Judging from the furnishings, it was Kastle's room. It had a simple cot for a bed, a wardrobe full of robes and two large tables covered with scrolls and parchments. Covering one wall was a hand-drawn map of Hyperborea and all its known villages. On a second wall was another of Atlantis or at least what was known about the fabled city.

Callistra rummaged through the scrolls while she waited for her old companion. Running across, Kastle's journal she sat back on his bed flipped to the first page and began to read.

'DAY 9: It has been several days since we awakened in the dark forest. Al Shaytan promised us the adventure of a lifetime. I am not sure Wynn would agree with that. He fell in battle to some giants we ran across and we were unable to recover his body since we had to flee or perish. Jagoda didn't take that well and wanted to go back. Only the will of the group overruled him. I will regret voting against him and not going back to the end of my days.'

Tears filled Callistra's eyes as she remembered that day. She could still hear Wynn's screams as the giants ripped off his legs and began eating him while he was still alive. The companions had fled in fear. That was the true feeling of guilt that Jagoda felt. Of course, one thing was still peculiar to her. She fed on the innocent inhabitants of this land to keep herself alive and had no qualms about it but the memory of Wynn's death brought her to tears.

Flipping the pages at random, she read another passage.

'DAY 27: We stumbled into a small walled town today. We thought our luck was improving since we had run out of rations days before but we were unprepared for their fear of outsiders. We had gold but they weren't interested in trading and became an angry mob. We tried to flee. However the mob chased us and when Argos fell to a spear thrown by one of the townsfolk, Jagoda went nuts. We were surrounded and outnumbered. We made them pay but our defeat was inevitable. There were just too many of them. That would've been our last day in this realm if not for the arrival of the Atlantean. Sartael came to our rescue, blasting away at the townsfolk. They fled back inside their walls. Jagoda was still angry and wanted vengeance but since we were all injured, we fled into the night.'

'DAY 33: Sartael has been a wonderful host with a wealth of knowledge. Although he has been very tight-lipped about Atlantis, I have been able to gather that some sort of calamity has befallen the Dragon Kings and the general populace blame them for their lot in life. It is my guess that Sartael is an outcast from Atlantis. I have no proof of my suspicions but there is just something odd about him. On a personal note, Aaliyah and I had a wonderful walk at sunset. Nothing happened but I'm hopeful for the future.'

'DAY 40: Argos is dead. We thought he was recovering from his wounds but he passed away during the night. However, Jagoda discovered bite marks on his neck and accused Callistra of killing him.'

Callistra still remembered that day. Jagoda had actually attacked her but Kastle intervened. Suddenly, their little party was at odds with each other. Sartael, the snake that he was, stepped in and used his magic to subdue her and take her wand. It was not a fond memory. Jagoda had wanted to kill her where she lay but Kastle argued against any such action. She shuddered to think of what might've happened if the Atlantean hadn't chosen that evening to show his true colors.

'DAY 41: The Atlantean attacked us during the night and caught us completely off guard. We lost Bertram and Albiona to Sartael's magic and Kano is missing. The shinobi might've just slipped off into the night but honestly, that doesn't seem like his style. Sartael probably would've gotten all of us if he hadn't underestimated Geirolf and overlooked Callistra. While the traitorous Atlantean fought our werewolf companion, Callistra was able to free herself and then myself. She had wanted to leave Jagoda behind but Aaliyah wouldn't allow it. The four of us slipped away and left our dead friends behind.'

The witch took a deep breath to calm her nerves. One day she would get vengeance on Sartael. She didn't know when or how but it will happen. Callistra flipped further back in the journal and continued to read.

'DAY 97: I think I have lost my chances with Aaliyah. She seems enamored by the rock hard physique of Jagoda and his easy-going smile. She is blinded to his snide remarks. I fear to say anything more as it will just push her further into his arms. On a positive side, it seems that Callistra seems to enjoy my company, although I doubt it will lead anywhere. I know she's married on the other side and completely devoted to her husband.'.

'DAY 166: It finally happened. It was cold and raining last night when Callistra came into my tent. Without a single word, she undressed and climbed into my bed. It was intense, it was magical. I'm sure she just needed the warmth of another body. It wasn't me she truly wanted but I was handy, not that I mind. The sounds of Aaliyah and Jagoda's lovemaking has bothered me for weeks. I guess it got to Calli too. She was gone when I woke up and hasn't been very talkative today. I wonder if it was a one-time thing or will it happen again. I have to admit I am hoping for the latter but only time will tell.'

Turning a few more pages, Callistra felt tears beginning to fill her eyes but she read on.

'DAY 225: We have begun to argue almost constantly. Jagoda has threatened to leave once more. I believe that Aaliyah is leaning toward following him if he does leave. I fear that our days as a group are numbered. On a personal note, Callistra is losing her battle with the forces of Chaos inside her. I fear it was the loss of her wand which truly began her descent into darkness. I fear this will be the end of our union. I cannot abide what she is becoming and fear for her soul.'

Hearing the chapel bells begin to ring, Callistra knew that the service was over and Kastle would be here soon, so she flipped to the last entry of the journal.

'DAY 815: It has been nearly four years since we crossed over and I haven't seen or heard from any of my companions in months. I've heard rumors of a witch living in the Dark Forest to the north, perhaps this is Callistra. It is my hope that she has found some semblance of peace. I've also heard of rumors concerning Jagoda and Aaliyah. Some traveling merchants tell of bandits operating on the coast primarily raiding the Atlantean traders. They say their leader is an Outlander with a sword of fire. This sounds like Jagoda to me. Perhaps I will swallow my pride and journey north to apologize for my harsh words. How I yearn for the days of adventure with my companions or a Domino's pizza and a frosted mug of Budweiser. Better yet, the warmth of Callistra in my bed or the heavenly light of Aaliyah's smile.'

Callistra closed the journal as she heard the approaching footfalls of her former lover as he climbed the stairs. He was right. It had been a long time since she enjoyed the warmth of a body next to her in the night. However, it wasn't Kastle which she longed for. It was her husband back home. Feeling her blood quicken at the thought of sex an old saying came to mind; any port in a storm.

* * * * *

Back in Dallas, Kastle was known as Richard Langford, a mid-level accountant in a large legal firm. Twenty-six, single and overweight, he lived at home and took care of his elderly mother. His greatest release from the stresses of reality had been playing *Lost Lands*. In the game, he was a mighty cleric of Thor the Thunder God, healing the sick and punishing the unrighteous. When he was pulled into the game by Al Shaytan, it was like a dream come true. That was until he saw his friends fall in battle and the reality of their situation had set in. However, losing his chances with Aaliyah to Jagoda and watching Callistra succumb to the Chaos Spirit was almost more than he could bear. Turning aside from the path of the adventurer, Kastle found this old chapel in the small hamlet of Crooner's Gap and began to administer to its residents. It was a good life. If not happy, he was at least content.

When Kastle entered his small room above the rectory, he knew immediately that he was not alone. There was an earthy smell that wasn't normally there. However, seeing the naked form of Callistra on his small bed was not what he was expecting.

"Callistra, what are you…"

"Shh…no words. Come. Warm my body and my blood."

Very few men could or would turn down such an offer, especially from a vision as lovely as Callistra. Kastle was not one of those men. Stripping off his robes, they fell to the floor forgotten as he rushed to accommodate her desires.

*****

"Hold." Tao held up one hand.

According to the position of the twin suns, it was almost noon and the companions could just make out the walls of a village in the distance. Judging from the nets, Tao figured that most of the harbor traffic were fishing boats and they could be seen entering and leaving the port regularly. Most were small, one or two-masted sloops. No large merchant ships or warships could be seen or oar powered slave ships either.

Tao turned back to face his friends. "Okay. Judging from what I can see, this is mostly a small fishing village. In my mind this means simple folk who just want to be left alone. So I'm unsure of our reception. They might have a phobia about elves or dwarves. We just don't know."

Cozad asked, "What's your suggestion?"

"We go in cautiously. Elves keep your faces covered and Pixi stay invisible. Cozad, you and I need to keep our helmets off and hands away from weapons."

"Why?"

It was Bjørn who answered. "If they are indeed an isolated fishing community, they will naturally be suspicious of outsiders. In Alaska, we have many such communities. When I was a State Trooper, they treated me with suspicion and distrust, even when they were the ones who called us in. It is the way of things for small villagers."

Cozad and the others nodded. They were out of their element and realized it.

Walking into an unknown city in the game was easy. The players could tell from a distance if a guard would attack you or not, due to the game mechanics. Anyone that would attack you would be highlighted in red when you selected them as a target. That little trick of the game couldn't be used in this situation. Nor could the companions bypass the village. They needed information and a map of the area if possible.

Tao's first thought was to wait until dark and enter the village unannounced. But that came with its own set of problems. Since it was a walled city, the odds were that they would lock the gates at dusk and not open again until dawn. Not that they couldn't sneak in. As a skald, Gamble would have the necessary skill set to accomplish that feat, the same could be said about Mathias the Archer. Of course, his own training from his days in the Special Forces gave him the skills also but once inside, then what? They couldn't just walk into a tavern and get information or food. This was obviously a small town where everyone knew everyone else's business. There would be no hiding. No, they had to go during the daylight. Of course, he could just send in Pixi since she could stay invisible and just scout out the town. But honestly, he felt that was too dangerous a mission for the teenager. Feeling that he had finally weighed the matter fully, Tao made his decision.

"We go in cautiously. Bjørn will follow up the rear. I don't want his size to be too intimidating to the guards." Tao paused and turned to fully face the dark elf necromancer. "Arieal..."

"I can use my magic to disguise my dark elven heritage. Would you prefer human?"

"Yes. That would help." Tao grinned as he gazed at the beautiful dark elf. Her outfit was very revealing, showing off her shapely legs, a flat tummy and a well-endowed chest. He cleared his throat. "I would suggest a form that wasn't as stunning as this one either. You might draw everyone's attention to yourself but not too homely either, if you get my meaning."

Arieal hadn't received a compliment on her looks in a long time and felt herself blush at Tao's remark but nodded and closed her eyes. Calling on one of the innate abilities of her race, she pictured herself when she was twenty years old; short mousy blonde hair, a button nose and an average figure. Not a head turner but not a dog either. Feeling the spell take shape, Arieal opened her eyes and asked, "How's this?"

"Excellent. Walk up front with me. Everyone else, keep your hands away from your weapons and whatever you do, don't lose your temper."

Everyone nodded and the companions began the short hike to the village.

* * * * *

Callistra climbed out of the bed and wrestled with her conflicting emotions. Back home she was married and honestly, she was unsure if this qualified as adultery. After all, she was inside a game. Callistra wasn't her real name nor was this her real body. Besides, she was stuck in this realm and didn't know if she would ever make it back home again. One part of her was more relaxed than anytime over the past four years. It had been a long time since she had sex and it was very liberating. But as always, the guilty feelings remained.

Kastle watched quietly as Callistra got dressed. It was always the same. Their lovemaking was intense and overwhelming, like nothing he ever imagined back in the real world. Of course, back home he would never have had the chance with a woman as lovely as Callistra and he knew it. He was grateful for the few times they had sex but when it was over, she was always moody and stand-offish. Kastle didn't know why but just accepted it as a normal part of dealing with her. After a moment, he propped himself up on one elbow and asked, "Not that I'm complaining but to what do I owe the pleasure of your visit?"

Callistra sat at the desk and turned to face him. "Al Shaytan has sent another group through the portal."

Kastle nearly jumped out of the bed. "When? Where?"

"Yesterday evening and about ten leagues southwest of Saebroc." Callistra pointed at a small dot on the Hyperborea map. "I was out hunting when I came across a funeral pyre. It seems that ten avatars came through the portal but one was killed during a goblin attack. If I read the battle right, one of their members assassinated another and was banished from the group for his actions."

Kastle moved over to his foot locker and opened the lid. Inside was his armor and adventuring items from the day he crossed over. As he began to get dressed he asked, "How do you know all this?"

Callistra graced him with a crooked smile. "I'm not without skills you know. The banished member is a Hashāshīn. He was bound by very strong dwarven magic. I found him on the northern edge of the Dark Forest."

"How'd he get there?"

"I believe he was carried there by two goblin zombies."

"So they have a skald and a necromancer. That could be good and bad. Any ideas where the rest went?"

Callistra shrugged her shoulders. "I would guess Saebroc. That's what we tried. We went to the nearest village."

Kastle rolled his eyes. "Odin's beard. I hope they find a better reception than we did."

"True."

"Where's this assassin?"

"My cabin."

"Why there?"

Callistra moved to the edge of the window and glanced out at the small hamlet. "I wasn't sure what sort of reception I would get. You and I didn't exactly part as friends you know."

Kastle paused. "True. I know it isn't you, just a condition of your affliction. I have come to terms with that."

"Have you really? What will you say when I need to feed again? I can only resist for so long."

He really didn't know how to answer that question so he just let it go.

She understood his dilemma and didn't press the issue but changed the subject. "Any word from Aaliyah or Jagoda?"

"No, but I didn't expect any either. Remember, we didn't exactly part on good terms either."

Callistra nodded. She remembered the hateful words, the arguments and the sacrifices. She gazed out the window at the small town of Crooner's Gap. The townsfolk were going about their daily lives, content and happy. In a small voice she asked, "Was I right in coming here?"

Kastle moved up behind her and wrapped his arms around her waist. Gently kissing her neck he said, "We might not agree on your lifestyle but you'll always have a friend in me."

As she turned to face him, Kastle could tell that she was feeling guilty about their tryst. Not wanting to complicate things or drive her away, he released her and turned back to his room. "Now, let me gather up a few things and let's go have a chat with this assassin."

Chapter 8

The first thing Tao noticed when they entered the village gates were the guards. They seemed to be either very young or very old. They were probably the ones unable to work the fishing nets. He did notice that they were all dressed in brown leather breastplates and armed with short swords and spears. No bows were visible but that didn't mean they weren't around somewhere.

The companions weren't accosted as they entered but it was obvious that they were being watched constantly. Armed guards walked the wooden ramparts and a few guards followed behind them as they moved through the town. There seemed to be only one road, if that was what the dirt path could be called, which led to the center of town where historically the most important buildings in a village would be found.

With wide eyes, Arieal gazed around at the drab buildings and sarcastically asked to no one in particular. "I wonder if they have a Starbucks?"

Gamble snorted. "I doubt it but it would be nice."

Since no one else laughed at her poor joke, the dark elf in disguise turned her attention back to their surroundings. After a few minutes, she finally realized what was bothering her about the villagers and nudged Tao's shoulder. "They're staring at you."

Dragging his mind away from the martial designs of the town, he focused his attention on the townsfolk. She was right. They were staring. Not at the dwarf or the ladies but at him. Tao looked down at himself. He wasn't very tall, being just over five foot. His skin was the golden hue of the oriental people while his hair was jet black and pulled back into a ponytail. He imagined he looked like Bruce Lee with long hair. He didn't think that he looked intimidating. He had opted not to wear his armor but just a simple black and red silk keiokgi with his swords tucked into his belt. Of course, the silk robe made visible part of his dragon tattoo which ran from the hara, the spot two inches above his navel, up across his chest around his back to the left side of his neck until it ended with the head of the dragon rearing on his left cheek. It was the mark of the Kensai or sword saint in Nippon.

When they reached the town square, the companions were confronted with a large crowd both in front and behind them. Tao made a mental note that every citizen seemed to be armed with some sort of weapon, be it a frying pan or an axe handle. This was not good.

Tao stopped and causally nudged Arieal back to stand with Cozad, Moira and Gamble. Glancing around, he didn't see Mathias or Pixi. The archer had probably blended into the crowd and the faerie was invisible. Good. At least they had a couple aces up their sleeves if things went bad. Tao stepped forward. Out of the corner of his eye, he noticed that Bjørn was standing behind him and slightly to his left.

Keeping his hands away from his weapons, Tao held them up in what he thought would be a non-threatening manner. "We come in peace. We mean you no harm."

Many in the crowd began to mutter amongst themselves and that scared Tao more than anything. A crowd was one thing, an angry mob was another. Seeing the crowd's fear of them growing was like watching the embers of a fire slowly eat at dry twigs. There was heat, there was fuel, now all it needed was a spark and the crowd would turn into a mob.

Tao tried diplomacy again. "I can see that we are not welcome. That's fine. We'll leave. We're just lost travelers and wanted information."

A young guard spoke up first. "Nice try Atlantean. We'll not fall for that line again."

Sensing an opening, Tao focused his attention on the spokesman. "I'm sure I don't know what you're talking about. We're strangers to your land. We're not Atlanteans."

"Liar, you wear the mark!" The young guard looked at the crowd and yelled, "Atlanteans cannot be trusted!"

The crowd roared their approval and many took a slight step forward. The mood of the crowd was shifting and not in the companion's favor.

Bjørn said, "It doesn't look like it is going well."

Tao nodded. "I don't think we're going to get out of here without a fight."

"I agree but they'll be on the losing side."

Before Tao could respond, a high pitched horn blast echoed through the town square. The companions were unsure of what it heralded but the townsfolk obviously recognized it because they surged forward. Emboldened by the arrival of the horn blowers, the brash young guard leveled his spear at Tao's chest and charged.

Back in the real world, Mac had been a student of the martial arts for many years having attained Black Belts in both TaeKwonDo and Judo, not to mention his extensive combat training during his stint as an Army Ranger. One thing he had always read about and only a few times attained was the state of Zanshin.

Zanshin had been called many things over the years; the zone, the empty mind, Zen mind and enlightenment just to name a few. It is the mindset of body and mind working in perfect harmony. Sports celebrities talk about how their game was 'on' and everything was just right, like when the basketball player is shooting from outside the three-point line and sinking every single shot. Marine and Army snipers talk about becoming one with the shot, where they can almost see the wind and visualize the drift the bullet will travel when making a eight hundred meter shot. Zanshin is that moment in time when conscious thought disappears and the body reacts without thought. It is a beautiful thing when it happens. However, to your opponent, it is deadly.

As the guard attacked, Tao reacted. As a by-product of being his avatar, he entered zanshin at the outset of battle. Drawing both blades in one fluid motion, he executed two strikes in the same motion; one strike sliced the spear shaft in half, the other cut a slash across the young man's chest. It was not enough of a wound to kill him but one that would be bloody and painful. Stepping back with both swords at the ready, Tao bellowed loudly.

In the martial arts, the yell was known as a ki-hap or spirit-shout. It was used to startle your opponents and to help focus a practitioner's energy. Tao used it now to startle the crowd and it worked. The surging mob faltered and stopped at the sight of the bloody guard and the fierce warrior with the twin swords, one of which was coated in ice.

They were at an impasse.

The mob was unsure of what to do and the companions feared to move or say anything that might disrupt the delicate stalemate. Time passed and Tao dared to believe that they might make it out of this situation without having to kill anyone. Suddenly, a stray arrow came from the back of the crowd and struck Moira in the shoulder.

As she fell with a scream, pandemonium took over.

The mob surged forward and Bjørn went berserk. Hearing his wife scream in pain caused Bjørn to shape-shift into his were-bear form in a matter of seconds and attack. Anyone and anything in his way became fair game. He was so crazy with rage that his seven foot claymore fell to the ground forgotten. He was just using his massive strength and claws to smash aside anyone foolish enough to enter his range.

Cozad's first instinct was to attack. His Chaos mind-set wanted to crush the foolish peasants but it was his duty to guard the ladies from the onrushing mob. He struggled for a second or two before planting his feet and readying his battle-axe. Anyone who entered his reach was going to pay a bloody toll for their foolishness.

Arieal felt her motherly instincts kick in when Moira went down. Pulling off her scarf, she held it to the wound in hopes of controlling the bleeding. The druid was already pale and seemed to be entering the early stages of shock. Annie tried her best to remember her first aid training. She knew there was something about keeping her warm and elevating her feet. She couldn't remember why but she doubted that she would have time to do it anyway, given their current situation.

Mathias had slipped off to the side at the first sign of the crowd following the companions. He was completely unseen by everyone which was fine by him. Although, his Archer persona was more at home in the wilds, the Matthew mind-set was more comfortable in the crowded cities. Growing up in Denver gave him a familiarity with the abundant shadows and tight alleys of city life. Climbing onto the rooftops had been easy. Moving from rooftop to rooftop unseen by the guards wasn't exactly easy but wasn't too difficult either. Mathias was just about to fire on the crowd when he heard the high-pitched horn. From his vantage-point on the roof, he could tell it was coming from the skies and not the ocean. Scanning the horizon, he caught sight of the five incoming beasts that his half-elf mindset recognized as wyverns.

Wyverns were a distant relative of dragons with large bat-like wings and extremely long tails. Although they didn't have the deadly breath weapon of their larger cousins, wyverns have a stinger on their tails with a poison more lethal than any scorpion venom.

Mathias was as shocked as everyone when the arrow came from the back of the crowd. Dropping all pretense of concealment, the archer began firing indiscriminately at the mob. It was simple. If they were moving toward his friends they were a target. If they were moving away, they were safe from his arrows.

Tao heard the wyvern-riders before he saw them. The flapping of their wings and the shrill cry of the wyverns was unmistakable. He wasn't sure how he knew that but he did. He was extremely busy with the guards to do more than register their arrival. One part of his mind stayed on the problem. Would the newcomers be friends or foes? Only time would tell. When the wyvern-riders swooped down on the crowd, most of the mob fled in panic and it was obvious to Tao that the riders were feared by the townsfolk.

On their second pass, the first two riders fired their crossbows at Bjørn. Neither arrow pierced the were-bear's fur but they did manage to get his attention. As he roared his disapproval of the wyvern-riders, the next pair made their pass. However, they didn't shoot arrows at the lycanthrope. They each fired a net with weights on all four corners. Their aim was perfect. Both nets struck Bjørn and in seconds he was completely immobilized.

The fifth and final rider fired his net at Tao on his pass. However, Tao was more agile than the were-bear and dodged to one side. Before the samurai could recover and move to free his friend, the first two wyvern-riders had swooped back down, grabbed the trussed up lycanthrope and flew off.

Tao took one step to follow before stopping.

This was his worst nightmare. A party member kidnapped, another one injured and the rest surrounded. Out of the corner of his eye, he glimpsed movement and ducked reflexively. A lone guard had used the distraction of the wyvern-riders to get within striking distance of the samurai.

Before Tao could counterattack, a goose-feathered arrow sprouted from the guard's chest. He glanced at the rooftop and saw Mathias's smug grin. Tao thanked him with a nod and pointed at the fleeing wyverns. The Archer nodded once and was gone.

Having a slight break in combat, Tao moved back to his companions and asked, "How bad is she?"

Gamble shrugged. "Unknown. She's unconscious at the moment and has lost a lot of blood."

"Can you carry her?"

Gamble nodded. "Yes. It might not be good for her but I can manage."

"Good. We are leaving. Cozad you have point."

"Understood," replied the Dreadknight. His eyes had already shifted from the blue fire of contentment to the smoldering purple of controlled rage.

Pixi popped into view right overhead. "There's a small gathering of townsfolk trying to block the gate."

Tao replied, "They won't stop us. They'll move or we will move them, one way or the other. Now let's roll."

Gamble lifted the injured druid and followed the armored Dreadknight with Arieal and Pixi in tow. Only a few guards stepped out to meet them and they were quickly dispatched by Cozad. Once they reached the gates, the companions found a gathering of twenty townsfolk. A simple sleep spell from Pixi knocked out half their numbers. Couple that with the sight of the glowing purple eyes of the Dreadknight carrying Bjørn's seven foot long claymore convinced the rest that they had somewhere better to be.

Moments later, they were out of the gates and into the wilds. They hadn't really gained any information for their efforts and one of their companions had been captured but they were alive...which meant they had another chance.

Chapter 9

By the time Kastle and Callistra arrived at her cabin it was an hour past noon. They found the assassin lying on her doorstep still bound by the magical black bands. Kastle lifted the assassin out of the way with ease and followed his beautiful companion inside. This was the first time he'd been invited to visit his lover's home. It was a simple three-room log cabin in a secluded clearing at the northeast edge of the Dark Forest.

Kastle paused as he entered the cabin. Although it was a simple design, it was ingeniously built with the main room, kitchen and bedroom surrounding a large stone fireplace in the center of the cabin where its heat would radiate into all three rooms. Kastle really didn't want to know how she came in possession of the cabin. He gestured with the bound assassin. "Where?"

As Callistra left the main room for her bedroom, she just waved her hand. "Anywhere is fine."

Dumping him in a beautifully hand-carved chair, Kastle pulled out a length of rope from his backpack and began wrapping the arms and chest of the Hashāshīn. Satisfied with his handiwork, he stepped back. "Alright assassin. It's time we had a talk. In a moment we're going to release the magical bands which are holding you but I suggest you don't try to escape until we've had a chance to get to know one another better. Alright?"

Tariq couldn't reply since he was effectively gagged by the sorcerous ribbons but the stare he gave the holy man was full of anger and hatred.

When Callistra reentered the room, both men followed the beautiful vampyress with their eyes as she moved over to a small cage. Lifting the lid, she pulled out a solid black scorpion that was at least eight inches long and placed it on Tariq's chest. Gracing him with a crooked smile she said, "No sudden moves. If my pet feels threatened or jostled, he has a tendency to sting. Of course, the choice is entirely yours."

After a moment she asked, "Do you understand or shall I have my pet demonstrate?"

Tariq nodded, then thought about it and shook his head. He couldn't remember which was the right answer, was it yes or no?

Whichever was the right answer Callistra was satisfied and pulled out her wand. With a simple flick of the wrist, she tapped the tip of the wand to the black bands and they dissolved in to nothing.

Tariq asked, "What right do you have to hold me? I know my rights. You can't hold me."

Kastle chuckled. "First, let's get something straight. You aren't in America or Canada or even East-bumble-fuck Egypt. You are in Hyperborea and here, might makes right. Currently we have power over you which gives us the right to do what we please. We have the right to hold you captive, turn you into a slave or kill you. It is our choice not yours. Is that clear?"

Tariq flexed his shoulders and started to lean forward with the intention of standing up. That was until the scorpion shifted positions and flicked its tail. Tariq hesitated and then slowly shifted his weight back into the chair. He swallowed hard before speaking. "Clear. What is it that you want?"

"Information."

"What kind of information?"

"Let's start simple with introductions. I'm Kastle and the lovely young lady behind me is Callistra. What's your name?"

"Tariq al'Nasir al'Rafiq of the Hashāshīn Order."

"What brought you to Hyperborea?"

"Al Shaytan."

"Where are your companions?"

Tariq spit in the cleric's face. "In Hell for all I care."

Kastle calmly wiped off the spit and looked at his companion. "This isn't getting us anywhere. You want to try?"

Callistra stood up and moved behind the assassin. Leaning down, she whispered in his left ear but loud enough that Kastle would hear what she said. "I can make you talk." She shifted to his other ear. "I know something very important about you, something that you don't even know about yourself."

As she slid her arms around his chest she leaned in and nibbled on his neck, Tariq found it very erotic and enticing. When she shifted her hands lower, he felt his pulse quicken at her touch. However, when she grabbed his dagger and pulled it away, he tensed and started to rise once again. When the scorpion crawled the few remaining inches until it stood over his left carotid artery, Tariq froze.

Callistra moved into view. "This is beautiful. It's a dagger of venom, right? Or should I call it a katar since it's crafted in the Arabic fashion of a punch dagger?"

Seeing the assassin's eyes widen as she handled his blade, she continued talking. "This was the weapon given to you by Al Shaytan. No use trying to deny it, his mark is right here on the tang. Right now you just think this is a magnificent magical item but it is more...much more. Shall I tell you about it?"

Callistra moved over to the sofa about fifteen feet away from the bound assassin and sat down. Tariq had no idea why but there was a tightness in his stomach that wasn't there a few moments ago. He felt feverish and began to sweat. His first thought was that the scorpion had already stung him. When the witch began to twirl his dagger around, he felt his eyes drawn to the magical blade and the longing to hold it in his hands began to grow. It was his blade after all. Why should he let the witch hold it?

Callistra's smile didn't reach her eyes when she asked, "Do you feel it? The need to hold this? Is it gaining strength? Now imagine if I were to drop this in the deepest ocean. How would you feel? I'll tell you how. You would do anything to retrieve it. The compulsion would be so strong it could drive you to try and swim to the bottom of the ocean. And why? Isn't this just a magical dagger? A simple tool?"

The witch stood up and moved closer. As she closed the gap, the pain in his gut lessened and he felt his anxiety lessen. It was strange.

"You see Al Shaytan tricked you. These items are much more than simple magical weapons. They are soul bound to the owner. Should you lose this dagger or it was taken away from you for any length of time, you would feel such anxiety that it would drive you crazy. You would be like a junkie always looking for a fix and nothing, I repeat nothing, can curb the urge." Callistra shifted her gaze to Kastle and some untold message passed between them. Looking back at Tariq she added, "Trust me. I know."

The assassin took a moment to really study the vampyress. Yes, she was gorgeous but now that he was looking, he thought he could see a slight madness in her eyes. Then he actually noticed how crudely fashioned her wand was compared to everything else about her. Her outfit and jewelry was expertly crafted and of superb design, then why the crude wand? Tariq's eyes flicked over to the cleric. He was well muscled and his armor was exquisitely crafted. He was just silently watching him with his hand resting on his warhammer. That's when everything clicked.

"You're both from the other side, the real world?"

Callistra waved her fingers and the scorpion flicked its tail. "Don't think that this place isn't real. If you die here, you die back home...simple as that. But yes, we're from America. Kastle is from Dallas and I'm from Louisville. How about you?"

Tariq tried to remember but it seemed so hazy. "B...Boston."

Kastle leaned forward. "What's your real name?"

Tariq cocked his head to the side as he tried to remember. It should be easy but the harder he thought the more jumbled his memory became. Looking up, his eyes were wide with fear. "I don't know. I can't remember."

Kastle just nodded. "As a minion of Chaos, it is your curse on this side of the portal. The longer you stay, the harder it will be to resist its pull. Eventually the darkness will overwhelm you and you will become your avatar in every way." His eyes flicked over to the witch. "You may even be tempted to try something rash to stop it but in the end, the Chaos will win." Looking back at the assassin he added, "However I may be able to help." Reaching into a pouch, Kastle pulled out a small silver amulet of a hammer and placed it over the assassin's head.

Immediately, Tariq felt calm. Like a cool breeze blowing through his mind clearing away the haze. "Brandon. My name is Brandon."

Kastle grinned. "Good. Now tell me about the people you crossed over with. It's important. Try not to leave out any detail."

Tariq nodded and launched into his tale. He began it on the night of the raid when his guild, the Society of Night had joined forces with the Keepers of the Flame to complete the Tomb of Immortality. Only vaguely did he notice that Callistra tensed up as his story unfolded. The assassin continued his tale all the way through the battle with the goblins, including his decision to backstab the paladin. He didn't leave anything out or try to embellish his actions. He just stuck to the facts. The only detail he really didn't go into were the names of his companions.

Kastle didn't say anything or pass any type of judgment on his actions. He just listened patiently; which actually helped Tariq tell his tale. Once he was done, the assassin sat back and waited.

When Callistra spoke, her voice seemed softer than usual. "This samurai in red and black armor...what was his name?"

"Tao...Taote Ching."

"Oh my God!" yelled Callistra as she collapsed onto the floor.

"Calli!" Kastle rushed to her side only to find her unconscious. Lifting her gently, he carried her into the next room.

Tariq immediately realized that this was the perfect time to slip away. That was until the black scorpion shifted its position once more to remind the assassin that it was still there and just waiting for a reason to sting him.

Chapter 10

The companions were only several hundred yards outside of the gates of Saebroc when Gamble stumbled and nearly fell. Even though the dwarf was amazingly strong considering his short stature carrying the limp form of Moira was quickly sapping his strength and he had to set the injured druid down.

Tao glanced back at the gates of the village and didn't see any sign of pursuit at the moment. Looking east, he could just barely make out the fleeing wyverns. It wouldn't be long before they were out of sight. He knew what needed to be done but hated to divide his group.

"Cozad, you're in charge until I get back. Do your best to keep everyone safe."

The Dreadknight just nodded but Arieal looked up and asked, "Where are you going?"

"After Bjørn. If Mathias catches up to them, he will be vastly outnumbered."

Arieal chewed on a stray strand of hair for a second before saying, "Be careful."

Tao fished through his pouches until he found the crystal vial that he wanted. In the game, it had many names but it was most commonly referred to as a potion of speed. For a brief span of time, everything about him would be sped up, his heart rate, his reactions and more importantly, his foot speed. He knew that too many uses of the tonic would age him or have other dismal side-effects. This was a type of potion he typically saved for dire situations and this seemed like the time.

Popping the cork, Tao downed the red liquid and absentmindedly noted that it had a slight peppermint flavor to it. Seconds later, the world surrounding him seemed to slow down. Gone was the whistling of the wind or the buzzing of the nearby bees. Actually, the bees seemed just to hang in mid-air. It was very strange.

Knowing that the potion wouldn't last long, Tao began running.

Even though he had used this particular potion on numerous occasions in the game, it was completely different this time. When he was sitting behind his computer screen, his avatar would gain several benefits in combat but most common advantage was that he could cover great distances in a short amount of time. So he ran and gained on the fleeing wyvern-riders with each passing minute.

* * * * *

Mathias' first instinct when the wyvern-riders had swooped in was to hide. But when he saw the mob charging his friends, concern banished his fear. Stepping out from behind cover and began firing. That was until the wyvern-riders captured his friend. Concerned that he would strike Bjørn with a badly timed shot, Mathias concentrated his first few shots on the trailing rider. He saw the rider jerk once and slump over in the saddle before the wyvern banked over the walls.

Glancing down at the town square, he saw a guard charging Tao. The normally hyper-alert samurai seemed distracted so Mathias fired off a quick shot and hit his mark center-mass.

He couldn't help but grin when Tao looked up. When his friend signaled for him to follow the wyverns, the half-elf couldn't think of any reason not to, so off he went. Leaping from rooftop to rooftop, then to the ramparts and onto the rocky ground had been child's play. Keeping up with the wyverns was another matter. As a half-elven archer, he was granted certain abilities in tracking, especially over grasslands and through woodlands. Since his prey was flying while he was running, it was only a matter of time before they outdistanced him. Realizing what needed to be done, Mathias angled slightly to his right toward a large group of rocks. Pausing at the peak, Mathias used one of his innate magical abilities to enhance his aim, sighted down the shaft, led his target, timed his release between breaths and let fly his arrow.

Without waiting to see if it struck, Mathias leapt off the rocks and continued pursuit for about seventy feet when he was rewarded with the results of his shot.

One of the two wyverns carrying Bjørn jerked to the side and released its grip on the massive were-bear. The other wyvern was suddenly left 'holding the bag' and couldn't carry the weight solo. It dove under the load for a second before releasing its grip also. Bjørn fell the last fifty feet and landed with a loud thump. The half-elf hoped the Norseman wasn't too injured because he was going to need some help, since it looked like he had angered the proverbial hornet's nest as the five wyverns circled back toward him.

Dropping to one knee, Mathias began firing and muttered to himself, "How in the world do I get myself into these messes?"

* * * * *

When the potion wore off, Tao was close enough to see Mathias' amazing shot. With the five wyvern-riders circling back to attack, he decided it was time to keep the pressure on the raiders. After all, the best defense is a strong offense. With the riders concentrating on Mathias, Tao had a few seconds to study the situation. He was also close enough to get a good look at the riders.

They looked human and seemed to be dressed in leather armor. Their faces were covered with red scarves which instinctively reminded Tao of the bandanas worn by the outlaws in old western movies. Out of the five wyvern-riders, one looked completely incapacitated. He was slumped over in his saddle completely limp while his steed just followed the rest of the herd and another rider seemed to be injured by the way he was holding his leg. The other three seemed fine and completely irritated with Mathias.

On their first low pass, all three fired their crossbows at the half-elf, who just rolled out of the way and loosed a couple shafts of his own. However, his aim was off and the arrows just bounced off the thick hide of the wyverns. Knowing he didn't have the skill of the half-elf with his bow, Tao decided for a more direct approach.

One of the signature kicks in TaeKwonDo was a flying side-kick and it is an extremely powerful technique. As the legends tell it, this particular kick was developed by the Koreans during the Japanese occupation. Supposedly, the peasants used this kick to knock armored samurais off their horses. Tao didn't know if that was true or not but it always sounded good and was possibly practical in this situation.

Shifting several feet to his right, Tao waited about twenty feet behind the same rocks Mathias had used to make his incredible long distance shot from. Keeping low until the wyvern-riders made another pass, the samurai began his run as they came around. Timing was going to be everything on this attack and Tao knew he only had one shot at it. Leaping from the peak of the rocks, Tao knew he had timed it right when the lead wyvern failed to veer away. Both beast and raider were too busy concentrating on the half-elf to defend against Tao's unorthodox attack. His right foot connected with the rider's left ribcage. Even over the noise of the screeching wyverns and hoarse laughter of the riders, Tao heard the bandit's bones crack as the rider was catapulted off his flying steed. Tao reached out and managed to barely snag the wyvern's saddle.

The lead serpent didn't know what was going on with the exception that his master was giving him conflicting signals. By the way he was leaning in the saddle, his rider wanted him to turn hard right. By the way he was pulling on his bit, his rider wanted him to land. Confused, the poor beast of burden did both.

Dropping his right wing, the wyvern executed a diving corkscrew landing. It wasn't pretty…but within seconds, it was on the ground. The other four wyverns were completely confused. Their alpha had just landed and so they followed suit. The one with the dead rider landed first. The other three riders were suddenly too busy trying to convince their flying steeds to stay in the air to defend against Mathias' arrows. Two seconds and two shots later, two more wyverns landed. Only the injured rider remained aloft and although he was still flying, it was obvious that he was fighting his steed to keep it there.

Tao shouted, "Two choices, land or die!"

Mathias nodded and sighted down his shaft once more but held the arrow in the drawn position. Seeing no alternative, the rider signaled to his steed to land. Mathias released the tension on his great yew bow but kept the arrow notched and pointed at the rider.

"Nice timing Tao. I have to admit that I was slightly worried there for a second."

"Glad I could make it in time." With a nod to the injured rider Tao said, "Get him down from there, I want a word with him."

Keeping his hands on the grey wyvern's hide, Tao slowly moved forward toward the head of the great beast rubbing as he went. Not really sure of the flying serpent's mannerisms, he just pretended that it was a really large horse and treated it accordingly. Being from Kentucky, he had grown up with horses. One trick he knew when handling a new horse was to imprint your touch and smell on the beast. It works best on foals but he also knew it to be an old 'horse traders' trick.

After a few minutes, Tao turned his attention to the lone surviving rider. He was definitely human and young, Tao guessed him to be in his late teens or early twenties. Judging from the downward angle of the arrow protruding from his left hip, this must've been the rider Mathias had hit with his long distance shot.

"Incredible shot by the way. I had no idea you could shoot that far. Much less hit anything, I am truly impressed."

Mathias blushed slightly. "Thanks. I guess Lady Luck was smiling on me."

Tao nodded and turned back to the young man who was obviously in great pain. "We could help you if you want. If you don't get that arrow out, you're going to die."

The young man grimaced with pain. "I don't want any help from you Atlantean. I would rather die."

"That is the second time today that I have been accused of being an Atlantean. I guess that isn't a good thing around here. You can believe me or not but I am not an Atlantean, I'm a Kentuckian."

"Liar. Only an Atlantean could've flown up and killed Adok. He was a great hunter."

"Adok?" Tao glanced at the body of the man he knocked from the wyvern. "Oh him? Trust me, it wasn't magic just a skillful kick."

"Trust you? Does a farmer trust the fox that kills his chickens? No."

Tao looked at Mathias. "This isn't going well."

"Maybe if we healed him?" Mathias suggested.

"Possibly." Tao squatted down so that he was eye level with the young man. "We're going to help you. We'll get that arrow out and heal your wound. Then you can go free."

"Liar!" the young man screamed. Pulling out a hidden dagger, he plunged the blade into his own chest, right under the solar plexus and into his heart.

Tao just shook his head. "Be at peace young one."

Mathias just stared at the dead kid. "Why? Why would he do that?"

"Maybe it is part of his culture or perhaps his religion doesn't allow being taken prisoner. I can only guess but for whatever reason, it was his choice."

Mathias turned his attention to his friend with a blank look. "How...how can you be so cold?"

"Don't forget I was in Desert Storm. This wasn't the first young man I've watched take his own life in the pursuit of his beliefs. It was obvious that he thought us helping him was a fate worse than death. He made his choice. We gave him options."

Mathias nodded but looked back at the young man. "But he's just a kid."

"True. But it was his choice, not ours. We cannot change it." Tao placed his hand on his friend's shoulder. "Do me a favor and go check on Bjørn. Hopefully, he just needs help getting out of the net."

Mathias nodded and stumbled away from the dead rider.

Tao went to work searching the bodies for anything useful, all the while being watched by the five wyverns.

Chapter 11

It was late afternoon by the time Callistra finally woke up. From the look on Kastle's face, she knew that she had been out for a while. Gracing him with a weak smile she asked, "How long?"

"About two hours. Are you alright? You gave me quite a scare."

"Yes. I'm sure it was just a combination of feeding overload and a lack of sleep. I went a long time between meals this past month."

Kastle cocked his head to the side. He knew she was lying but realized he couldn't push her to tell him the truth so he changed the subject.

"While you were out, I had a little talk with Tariq. He wants to help and says if we will protect him from the Keepers of the Flame, he'll travel with us." Kastle noticed how she flinched slightly at the guild name but kept silent. "Unfortunately, your scorpion is still holding him hostage and it won't let me get close."

Sitting up, Callistra snapped her fingers and they both heard Tariq yelp in surprise from the other room.

Seconds later Tariq peeked in. "The scorpion, it just disappeared."

Callistra flashed him a crooked grin. "It was never there. It was naught but an illusion."

"But...but I felt it on my skin. I heard the snapping of its pincers."

"Your mind convinced you that it was real but it was naught but a phantasm. However, if you had let it sting you, your mind would've convinced your body that it was poisoned and acted in such a manner."

Tariq wiped the sweat off his brow. "How have you guys survived in this place?"

Kastle looked slightly downcast. "Not all of us have. We lost a party member mere hours after crossing over. And over the next few months, we had to watch as we lost more of our friends to this land, one by one."

Tariq lowered his head. "I think I understand. I will regret my actions to my last breath."

Kastle placed a hand on the assassin's shoulder. "Let's hope that is true. The moment you stop regretting taking a life, then you will know that the Chaos Spirit is taking over your soul once more." Kastle moved back into the main room, pulled out his map and pointed at a small dot on the northern coast. "Calli, from what you said earlier and judging from what Tariq has told us, Saebroc would've been the closest town to where they crossed over."

Tariq and Callistra moved into the other room and studied the map. The assassin pointed at another village further down the coast line. "Unless they went the other direction along the coast."

Kastle nodded. "True."

"No," Callistra added. "They would've gone along the coastline toward the mountains and reached Saebroc."

Both men looked at her but it was Kastle who asked, "How do you know that?"

"I know the Keepers. On the other side, they were my old guild. Tariq, judging from your descriptions, I would guess the party layout was something like this; Tao was the leader with Gamble at his side. Bjørn and Moira are inseparable, so they were there. Pixi was the faerie and you mentioned an archer, which I would guess was Mathias Strongbow. How did I do?"

Tariq had to remind himself to close his mouth since he was so dumbfounded. "Unbelievable." He hesitated for a second before asking, "So...so you knew the paladin?"

Callistra nodded. "Yes, Roland. His real name was Steve but I don't fault you for your actions. I understand the struggle you have with the Chaos Spirit. I fight it every day."

Kastle waited for a moment before asking, "How good are these Keepers?"

"Real good," Callistra replied and Tariq nodded.

Kastle nodded. "Then they should survive the fear and hatred of the townsfolk. So the question remains, where would they go next?"

"Tao will keep working his way toward their goal, no matter what."

"Seriously?"

"He would say that every decision leads to gain or loss and for failure to occur, you only have to do nothing."

Kastle thought about that for a minute. "That is an interesting mantra but what does it mean?"

"It means that as long as Tao is alive he will not stop striving to accomplish his goal."

"Which is to get home."

"Yes. Nothing short of his death will stop him."

"Sounds like you know this guy pretty well."

"Yes...yes I do."

Kastle waited to see if she would elaborate. When she didn't he turned to the assassin. "Are you sure they didn't say anything else?"

Tariq thought about it for a minute before nodding. "Now that you mention it, Tao did say something about a bubble theory and how Avalon was connected to all the other realms in the game. Honestly, I wasn't really listening."

Kastle slapped himself on the forehead. "Holy shit! Why didn't I think of that?"

Callistra grinned slightly. "I told you he was resourceful."

Kastle nodded. "Agreed. We need to find them and hook up. I really want to meet this guy. But where are they now and how do we find them?"

Callistra said, "Aaliyah would know where to find them. After all she is a Sha'ir."

Tariq glanced up. "You came across with a Sha'ir?" Tariq whistled. "Those are rare in game and supposedly one of the hardest classes to play."

Callistra nodded. "She could summon a djinni to find the information we needed." She paused before asking, "Do you know where she is?"

"Probably still with Jagoda."

"Will you be safe?"

Kastle shrugged. "Only the gods know for certain but my apology is long overdue."

"Do you know where to find them?"

Kastle shook his head. "Nope but I know how they can find us."

Callistra raised an eyebrow at that remark but realized that Kastle had a plan and asking him to explain wasn't going to aid in the situation. So, she just began packing her belongings and before long the three companions were off.

* * * * *

By the time Mathias and Bjørn returned to the battlefield, Tao had discovered much about the riders. The other three had been similar in age to the young man who killed himself and their equipment had been of average quality. Their weapons were old and well-used but nothing special. On the other hand, the rider he'd killed with his flying side kick was the only bandit that was old enough to be considered experienced. Only he had anything of worth.

His armor and weapons were of excellent quality, not nearly as good as their own but very serviceable. Along with the standard rations and basic camping items that Tao had found in every saddlebag was a crudely drawn map. This was something they truly needed for it marked several towns. Of course it did not show the reputed location of Atlantis but it was better than nothing. Tao did notice other marks on the map but those would have to wait until later since it was approaching dusk.

Bjørn was limping but seemed no worse for the wear. The large Norseman gestured to the flying serpents. "What are we going to do with them?"

Tao just grinned. "Ride them of course."

Mathias snickered. "Ride them? Are you nuts?"

"Nope. You saw how all four followed the alpha wyvern. They exhibit the herd mentality. They simply follow the leader or alpha just like horses."

Bjørn said, "But they're flying serpents."

"It'll sure beat walking back don't you think?"

Bjørn cocked his head to the side. "There is that but you don't know if you can ride them."

Tao chuckled. "I'm from Kentucky. I've been around horses my entire life. Trust me. It'll be easy."

Too tired and sore to argue, Bjørn relented. "Okay but it's been decades since I've ridden."

Tao talked Mathias through some basic horsemanship skills, grip with your calves not your thighs. Don't jerk on the reins but pull slowly and evenly. Lean into your turns and try to keep your weight in your hips, not your shoulders. Once he felt confident that the archer understood the instructions, Tao had them mounted up.

Bjørn was mounted on the largest wyvern in the herd. It was a reddish brown and seemed the only beast capable of carrying the Norseman. Mathias had opted for one of the two green wyverns which didn't seem too skittish when he mounted.

Tao walked up to the alpha and patted the grey-skinned serpent on the neck. Keeping his voice low as he talked to it, he moved forward to scratch the great beast behind its hooded eyes. "Alright boy, I don't know what your old master called you but you need a name. How about Shadow? It seems like a fitting name?"

Whether or not the wyvern understood him, the serpent leaned into his touch and hissed. Tao wasn't sure what that actually meant but took it as a positive sign and climbed on. Glancing over his shoulder at his friends, he leaned forward and called out. "Lean forward and hang on, cause here we go."

Kicking the wyvern in the flanks like he would a horse Tao called out, "Giddy up."

Even though he was expecting it, the way that the flying serpent shot into the air jerked him back into the saddle and nearly threw him off. Tao peeked over his shoulder at the other wyverns and sure enough, all four serpents leapt into the air to follow Shadow.

Bjørn and Mathias managed to hang on as they circled the battlefield. Tao leaned left slightly and with minimal shifting of the reins, Shadow responded; the same to the right. Through trial and error, Tao figured out the basic commands of controlling the wyvern. It was very similar to a well-trained horse. The gait was a bit different but the view was spectacular. Within moments, they were on their way back to their friends and whoa...did they have a surprise for them.

* * * * *

After Cozad had watched the samurai run off, he began to make an assessment of their situation. Their only healer was wounded, the skald was tired and Arieal seemed shaken to the core. Add in the fact that they were barely out of bow shot from the city and this was a recipe for disaster.

Knowing what he had to do, Cozad moved over to the druid and took a good look at the arrow. It was lodged just below her left clavicle. From the way it was wedged in, he knew the arrowhead had to be barbed. Cozad said to no one in particular, "You know that has to come out."

Gamble nodded. "I was thinking the same thing. But given its location, we won't be able to push it through."

"That leaves two options. Leave it in or cut it out."

That seemed to shake Arieal free of her fear. "But she may bleed to death. She's our only healer."

Pixi popped into view overhead. "The guards are getting organized and the mob is back. I don't think we have long before they come after us."

Cozad's eyes flashed from blue to red in a split second as he glanced at the gates of the city. "Let them come. Many of them won't return to their homes."

"We won't be able to stop them all. Our only hope is to put a bit more distance between us and them before they come." Gamble lifted the injured druid and added. "Lead on. I have enough energy for another run."

Seeing the wisdom in his words, Cozad lead the way. They followed the river south for a short while until he spied a group of rocks. They weren't overly large but they would give them something at their backs when it came time for battle and would make it more difficult for the townsfolk to surround them. Glancing back the way they came, they could see that the mob had actually left the city. They were still milling about the gate. However, Pixi was right, it wouldn't be long before they screwed up their courage enough to follow them.

Cozad pointed at the necromancer. "Arieal, move up to the rocks. It will be your responsibility to make sure no one flanks us."

She chewed on her hair for a moment before nodding. "I'll do my best."

Cozad looked around. "Pixi?" When the faerie popped back into view he said, "Once they get here, I want you to cast your wall of flame again but I want you to let at least five passed by first. I don't care if the rest get caught in the flames or not. Got it?"

Pixi furrowed her brow. "You want me to let a few pass first? Why?"

Cozad pulled off his helm for a moment and scratched his bald scalp. "I have a plan."

Pixi shrugged. "Okay."

Cozad turned to the dwarf. "Skald...you have the hardest task."

"What? Blend in and backstab the leader?"

"Nope. I don't want you to attack at all."

Gamble cocked his head to the side. "I don't understand."

"You were wrong when you said that Moira is our only healer. I too can heal, sort of. When the mob arrives, I want you to cut out that arrow as quickly as possible and staunch the flow of blood. But you cannot act too soon or too late. For when they arrive, I will use my powers to drain the life force from the leading idiots and transfer it into Moira. If you do it too soon, she could die before my spell goes off. Too late and you waste my one spell."

Gamble grinned. "Nothing like a little pressure to calm the nerves."

Replacing his helmet, Cozad took two steps out from the rocks and waited. From the position of the twin suns, he guessed they had less than an hour before dark and he figured the mob would work up their courage long before then. He was right. When the mob came it was almost exactly as he predicted. The guards were sprinkled in throughout the crowd to bolster the mob's courage, while the townsfolk kept chanting, "Death to all Atlanteans!" over and over. A few bows were present but the mob wasn't going to rely on arrows or finesse, this was going to be a mad rush forward meant to completely overwhelm them and Cozad knew it. Using the butt of his axe, the Dreadknight drew a line in the dirt before backing up to the boulders and waiting. The mob got closer and closer, then paused about ten feet short of the line. Keeping his voice low Cozad said, "Get ready."

Hefting his axe into battle position, he yelled. "All right you bastards! Come and get me! You want me? Cross that line and die!"

The mob almost faltered. They weren't expecting someone to stand up to them and didn't know how to act. That was until one of the young guards screamed and charged. A split second later, the rest of the mob followed suit.

Pixi couldn't believe her eyes. Here was a full fledge mob on a rampage like those she had seen on the 'telly' back home, kind of like the riots in Egypt or Libya. She had read about other riots in school but had never expected to see one or worse be the object of one. Feeling her fear grow, Pixi glanced at her friend Moira. She was extremely pale and seemed completely lifeless. Gamble was poised to dig the arrow out of her shoulder and was just waiting for the right time. Pulling herself out of her fear, Pixi began her spell but held off on the last phrase. Once the forerunners crossed the line, she would cast her spell and damn those that were caught in the conflagration.

For Arieal the attack was different. Once danger loomed, her fear fell away. To her it was simple, live or die. She and her friends were going to live, even if the rest had to die. Seeing a few townsfolk break off from the pack and try to flank them, she pulled out some bat dung from one of her pouches. She tossed it at the onrushing mob and waved her wand. Seconds later, a flight of bats spewed forth from her wand to engulf the villagers.

As soon as Gamble saw the villagers begin their charge, he dug his dagger into Moira's skin around the arrow. It was messy but he knew it had to be done. One part of his mind heard the charging mob and wanted to run away. It was the natural 'flight or fight' response built into every human. But he had an injured companion relying on him and he had a job to do. No matter what the cost, he was going to do his best. So, he poked and prodded with his dagger until out came the odious arrow.

Cozad's and Pixi's spells went off almost simultaneously. The young faerie had timed her spell perfectly and allowed seven villagers past the line. The rest were caught in the inferno. The smell of burning flesh and the scream of the dying filled the area.

The wave of heat behind them and the screams of death caused the charging villagers to waver.

However when the leading four villagers just dried up into lifeless husks right before their eyes, they halted. Eyes wide with fear the three remaining looked around for a means to escape. That's about the time they heard the screeches of the returning wyverns and they bolted. The mob wasn't fleeing; it was a full-fledged rout. They dropped whatever they were carrying and ran as fast as they could back to their homes. If a buddy fell, they didn't care, they didn't help…they just ran.

Cozad glimpsed back at Moira. Her color had returned and the arrow was out. His wager had worked. But now, the wyvern-riders were returning and he was unsure how to handle them. They couldn't out run them, which left only one option. Hefting his axe, Cozad strode out to meet them on the field of battle.

Tao, Bjørn and Mathias circled the battlefield once. It was obvious from Cozad's body language that he wasn't expecting them but the raiders. The look of surprise on their faces when they landed was priceless. Bjørn's red wyvern had barely landed when he leapt off and rushed to Moira's side.

Cozad and Tao met each other on the battlefield but it was the dreadknight who spoke first. "I see you have a story to tell."

Tao gestured to the burned bodies. "I see that you have your own story. Both can wait, how's Moira?"

Cozad turned back to the rocks and Tao fell in beside him. "She'll live. The arrow is out and the wound is healing but she's weak and needs rest."

"I think we all do." Seeing Gamble approaching Tao grinned. "Heya mate. How's it going?"

"Not bad. We're alive thanks to Tinman here."

Cozad chuckled. "Tinman?"

Gamble rapped his knuckles on the dreadknight's plate armor. "You know, from the Wizard of Oz? It's a pretty famous movie, perhaps you've heard of it?"

Cozad chuckled. "Yes. I've seen it. I was just finding the humor in your nickname for me. I've been called that before, in real life."

"Really? Why?"

Cozad pulled off his helmet and pointed to his head. "I have a metal plate in my skull from a motorcycle wreck when I was a teenager which left a large scar right here. One of my friends back home started calling me Tinman and the name stuck."

"Works for me," Gamble answered with a sly grin.

Tao knelt down in the dirt and pulled out the maps he had liberated. Cozad and Gamble joined him. Tao pointed to an 'X' on the map that was marked 'Camp Five' and said, "That looks like the closest campground for these raiders."

Gamble asked, "How do we know there aren't more of them waiting there?"

Tao shrugged. "We don't but it looks like our best option. Unless you want to camp here tonight?"

"No thank you." The dwarf nodded his head towards the village. "I've had enough of their hospitality."

"Alright, then lets mount up."

Leading his friends over to the waiting wyverns, Tao went through his spiel concerning riding once more. Bjørn and Mathias added their two cents about liftoff and settled back on their flying steeds. As much as Bjørn wanted Moira to ride with him, they were uncertain if the red could carry both of them, so she rode with Gamble on the other green. Arieal climbed on behind Mathias, which left Cozad on the last wyvern which Tao described as a 'buckskin' since the wyvern's hide was a light grayish-white with black etchings along its wings and eye ridges.

Even though Pixi could fly, Tao knew the wyverns would fly much faster than the faerie so he insisted that she ride with him and had her sit in front of him on the saddle. "Hold on tight, real tight. Takeoff is like the downhill ride on a rollercoaster except we're going up. Understand?"

Pixi gripped the saddle pommel even tighter. "Yeppers. I'm ready."

Unable to resist himself, Tao kicked Shadow in the flanks and called out once more, "Giddy up!"

The great grey serpent leapt into the air with a loud screech. The other four wyverns of his flight followed and the companions were airborne.

Chapter 12

The two guards who had the late watch crowded near the fire pit to warm their hands. It wasn't necessarily cold but the warmth of the fire gave them something to do. Neither guard was happy about being stuck on the graveyard shift and grumbled about their bad luck.

Of course, it's a soldier's lot to complain. To a soldier, there is never enough food or sleep or liquor or women or any number of other complaints. But being stuck with gate duty during the overnight hours on a fortress in the middle of nowhere was the worst or so they thought, until their commander appeared at the gate unannounced.

Jerrick snapped to attention and quickly assessed the condition of his armor and spear. They weren't perfect but far better than his partner's. As his commander strode through the gate, Jerrick surreptitiously scrutinized the dangerous Outlander.

In reality, he wasn't much taller than the two guards but he seemed so much more imposing than his size. His ever present arm and shoulder guard on his left side seemed to accent his broad-shoulders. Of course, he never wore any armor other a wide belt and a leather loincloth. Then, there was the matter of his flaming bronze trident and his quick temper; both had caused his commander to become legendary over the last year. When his commander stopped in front of him, Jerrick swallowed deeply.

"Any word from Adok?"

Surprised at being singled out, the young guard stammered his answer. "No...no sir, there has been no word or at least nothing was passed on to us." His partner nodded in agreement.

Jagoda moved over to the cliff edge and looked down. It was over five-hundred feet to the valley floor and there was no way he could see the lands below but he looked anyway. It had become a habit. Of course, anyone on foot would have to brave the winding mountain trail leading to the fortress and no one could do that safely at night without some form of light. Taking a deep breath, the warrior turned back to the fortress. "Keep a close eye out and have someone alert me the moment Adok returns."

"Yes sir." Jerrick nodded and returned to his duties.

Jagoda moved through his mountain fortress with a restlessness he'd never felt before. He paced the ramparts like a caged lion before a meal. It was nerve wracking. He didn't know why or how but something was wrong or would be soon. Moving to his bedchambers, he found that his lover was still awake and deep in meditation.

Aaliyah was a Sha'ir; which literately meant poet in Arabic. She was a type of wizard from the Burning Sands expansion of *Lost Lands* which could summon and control the ancient djinni. After being with her for nearly three years, he knew that her magic had its limits compared to other spellcasters but the ability to summon a djinn or an elemental to act as a servant outweighed any weaknesses. With their aid, Jagoda had become the master raider of Hyperborea.

Even though he had been able to tame the wyverns which inhabited the Crags, he knew that his winged serpents were no match for their larger cousins which the Atlanteans rode. That thought irritated Jagoda. He had not forgotten his vow of vengeance spoken nearly three years earlier. If anything, his vow spurred him forward and he would not rest until Argos was avenged.

Aaliyah opened her eyes as he entered. "You are troubled."

Jagoda gazed at her perfect body. Even after all this time, she took his breath away. One part of his mind knew that there had to be Freudian explanation to his attraction to her since she looked so similar to Barbara Eden's character from the TV series *'I Dream of Jeanie'* that she could be her twin. Beyond that Jagoda knew she had a gentle soul and that was what had truly captivated him. Crossing the twenty feet between them, he wrapped her in his arms. "It's nothing. I just feel restless; nothing to concern yourself with."

Leaning back, Aaliyah looked up at her lover and frowned. "Anything that concerns you, concerns me. I will have one of my djinni look into it." With a wave of her hand, her air spirit disappeared, off to do her bidding. Aaliyah gave her lover a playful tug and asked, "Now is there anything else I can do to relax my master's body?"

"Now that you mention it, there is something you can do," Jagoda said with a grin and all of his worries disappeared into the night as he pulled the beautiful sorceress into his arms.

* * * * *

Kastle, Callistra and Tariq traveled throughout the evening. Callistra had summoned her customary steed, the Nightmare, while the other two rode conventional horses. Of course, the two normal horses were extremely skittish of the demon steed until the witch cast a simple enchantment on them and they immediately calmed down. Kastle lead them west along the northern edge of the Dark Forest until they reached the remnants of Roland's pyre. It was naught but a smoldering heap but the priest insisted on stopping.

Tariq hated to admit it but he felt a tightness in his gut at the sight but remained silent. Callistra just waited patiently, knowing that she wouldn't be able to sway her friend from his current path. Kastle knelt by the pyre and prayed to the Thunder God for forgiveness for what he was about to do. After a moment, he stood and began rummaging through the ashes.

Tariq slid off his horse and cocked his head to the side. "What are you doing?"

Kastle looked up from his mission. The ashes had already marked up his face. "Simple. I want to see if the sword that the paladin received from Al Shaytan survived the fire. If so, it could be useful in the right hands or extremely dangerous in the wrong hands."

"Why?"

Kastle turned back to his task while he explained. "The magic in the weapons are bound to our souls as Callistra demonstrated. But unbound, the magic could throw off the balance of this realm. These items are imbued with magic far greater than anything else in this land. Trust me on this."

Callistra said, "What he says is true. I just didn't voluntarily give up my wand. It was taken from me and having to deal with its loss has not been a pretty picture."

Tariq looked back towards the dazzling witch and a glimmer of understanding crept into his mind. There was much more to this story than what he knew but one thing for certain, the katar he received from Al Shaytan was more important than he realized. Unconsciously, he placed his hand on its pommel and felt comforted by its touch.

"Found it!" exclaimed Kastle. As the cleric pulled forth the silver blade it glowed with an inner white light which illuminated the area.

Callistra couldn't help but shade her eyes from the holy light. Her demonic steed tossed his head a few times and backed away. Pulling on the reins, the witch struggled for a moment to get her demonic steed under control before saying, "Kastle...would you mind? That hurts."

"Oh, sorry." The priest tucked the holy sword under his cloak to block the divine light. Moving back to his horse, Kastle wrapped the blade with his sleeping blanket and tied it securely to his saddle. "Now let's find Jagoda and Aaliyah."

"Lead on. We have about three hours till sunrise."

Tariq raised an eyebrow. "How do you know?"

Callistra graced him with a little smile. "After living with this condition for the last four years, I know when the sun will set or rise. I can feel it."

Accepting her at her word, the assassin just nodded his head and fell in behind the holy man. He seemed to be the only level-headed one in this bunch and who might know of a way home. Tariq was planning on sticking real close to Kastle whether he wanted him to or not.

Chapter 13

The companions found Camp-Five easily enough given the landmarks on the map. It was located in a grove of trees. No one was exactly sure of the type of trees. They looked similar to birch but they were larger than anything back home, except maybe the famous redwood trees of California. They could tell from the air that there were several huts built in their branches with rope bridges spanning the gap between huts.

Tao had the wyverns circle the camp twice before landing. If anyone was inside, they should've come out to investigate. But to be on the safe side, the samurai sent Mathias, Gamble and Pixi inside to investigate while the rest of the group stood guard. Minutes later the trio returned and declared it empty.

Breathing a sigh of relief, the companions lead the winged serpents into the center of the trees where there was a huge pen woven from the branches like an enormous bird cage. A stream flowed through the center of the cage and several large crates of dried fish were stored under tarps near the entrance, obviously food for the beasts.

Tao's first order of business was taking care of their mounts. Given the lack of specific knowledge on wyverns, he defaulted back to basic horsemanship. After making sure he knew how to strap them back on, Tao pulled off the saddles and placed them on the nearby racks. Using the under-blanket, Tao proceeded to rub the great beast down. After a moment of watching, Cozad, Mathias, Bjørn and Gamble mirrored his actions while the girls disappeared into the huts and several minutes later the aroma of cooking stew filled the small grove.

Once Tao was satisfied that his wyvern wasn't overheated, he led his grey to the small stream that ran through the enclosure and let him drink. After a few moments, Tao pulled his head up and guided him aside. It was obvious that Shadow wasn't done drinking but the samurai knew better than to let the beast drink his fill on the first opportunity. His companions followed his example. It was nearly an hour before all five beasts were watered and fed.

Tired and sore, the men headed to the huts. A small rope ladder had been lowered which allowed access to the lowest platform. Mathias scrambled up the flimsy device easily and Gamble followed not as quickly. Tao looked at the ladder then back at the heavily armored dreadknight. "I seriously doubt that will support your weight."

"No matter."

Calling on one of the innate powers granted to his class, the dreadknight began to float upwards. With a grin, Tao climbed up the rope ladder to join his friends. Once Cozad landed, he pulled off his helmet and smiled.

"Levitation is one of the first spells the crusader class is granted. It is very useful for someone wearing full plate armor. There are tales of knights who died during the Crusades just because they fell off their horses and landed on their backs. Since they couldn't turn over, they baked in the hot sun until they died of dehydration."

Moira stepped out of the small hut which was situated on one side of the platform. Judging from her color and movements it was obvious that she was still weak but she seemed to be in good spirits. She passed out several hand-carved wooden bowls and spoons to her companions. "Whoever designed this campsite did a wonderful job. I found crates full of dried food. Mostly grains, beans and smoked meats. I would guess that there is enough food to keep us fed for several weeks. And to top that off, the grill was already laid out for a fire."

Arieal moved forward with a large pot of stew, set it down between them and began to ladle out portions. "I can't vouch for the taste but it was the best we could manage in such a short time."

Bjørn gently nudged his wife. "I'm sure it's delicious. What is it?"

Moira waited until her husband took his first bite before answering. "Smoked bat meat with kidney beans."

It wasn't two seconds later when Bjørn spewed up the contents. Unfortunately, the disgorged broth coated the entire left side of the armored Dreadknight. There was a moment of silence while everyone waited to see his response. Cozad calmly reached down, ran his finger through the mess and stuck it in his mouth.

"It needs salt."

Everyone burst out laughing.

Cozad calmly threw a chunk of the offending stew onto the Norseman and their laughter became louder and harder. It was infectious. It was healthy. It was cleansing. It was a release of pent up emotions. All their fears, anger and worries about their situation encased in laughter. Several minutes passed before they regained control of their rampant mirth and returned to their dinner.

Mathias asked, "So...what's next?"

Tao stood up. "Sleep. No discussions. No worrying, just rest."

Gamble asked, "Who has first watch?"

Tao shook his head. "No one. The wyverns will alert us if anyone enters the grove."

Cozad cocked his head to the side. "Are you sure that's wise?"

"Yes. Stay awake if you want. I for one am looking forward to a good night's sleep. And by the way, we are going to spend at least a few days here. At least until we get a better lay of the land, so get comfortable." Tao began moving across one of the rope bridges but paused and looked back. "When I say comfortable I don't mean lax, we are still in hostile territory; so be on your toes."

Everyone looked at each other for a moment before realizing the logic of Tao's reasoning. Bjørn and Moira followed first, moving across the rope bridge arm in arm. It was obvious that they were heading off for a long overdue reunion. One by one, the companions moved off to the different platforms to get some much needed rest until only Arieal was left alone. She chewed on her hair for a moment, obviously wrestling with an important decision. Shrugging her shoulders, she made up her mind and went off to find a place to rest.

* * * * *

Hyperborea was technically a large island that was about the same size as Australia which was divided into three major regions; the Westlands, the Eastlands and the Wastelands.

The Westlands was supposedly the oldest settled region outside of Atlantis, the island kingdom. The city of Agharti was originally established as a garrison for the Dragon Kings. It was built in the image of Atlantis with crystal towers and wide avenues. However, centuries ago the inhabitants broke away from the Dragon Kings and built large gates across the only two passes through the Crags, effectively sealing off the Westlands from the rest of Hyperborea.

The area known as the Crags was a mountain range that ran the length of Hyperborea from north to south. It was the home of the dwarves and the nesting areas for the wyverns. The majority of all the precious metals mined in Hyperborea came from this region and the best weapons in the land were forged by the dwarves. It was a rough land and only rugged people settled in this region. There were a few scattered villages but only the dwarves had carved out a major city in this unforgiving region. Valhöll was a marvel of dwarven engineering and spectacular architecture. However, the dwarves had closed the doors of their kingdom to the outside world centuries ago.

On the opposite side of the continent was the Eastlands and it was a widely populated region with the primary inhabitants being humans. Antioch was a human city on the northeastern coast. Actually built as Agharti's sister city, it had been abandoned by the Dragon Kings long ago. Left to its own devices, it became the busiest port city of Hyperborea. There were numerous small hamlets and villages scattered the length of the coast and along the edges of the Dark Forest which covered the southeastern region.

However, deep inside the Dark Forest was Mount Sarai, a long dormant volcano and the supposed location of the lost city of the Elves. The whole region was considered taboo to those not of Sídhe, or faerie-folk, blood.

Between the Crags and the Eastlands was a vast dry, hilly region that was unforgiving to any traveler who was unprepared for its demanding conditions that was known simply as the Wastelands. It was only sporadically inhabited, only prospectors, outcasts and bandits called this arid land home.

Legends tell that once the Wastelands was a land of rolling hills and grassy plains until there was a mighty battle. An alliance of men, dwarves and elves under the leadership of the Atlanteans fought against the Horde, an untold number of goblins and their kind. Thousands upon thousands died during the battle until finally the two leaders; the High Mage of Atlantis and the Goblin King met in a mighty duel. The rules were simple, winner take all. Their battle lasted two full days until in a blinding flash of magic, both leaders were gone. Without the Goblin King, the Horde was defeated and the goblins slunk back to their hovels in shame. However the alliance of men, dwarves and elves was also severed as each race blamed the other for the disaster. Within one lifespan, the green hills and rolling plains had become an unforgiving wasteland and Hyperborea was changed forever.

* * * * *

Kastle, Callistra and Tariq traveled throughout the day and into the early evening before reaching the small hamlet known as Crooked Creek. It was not a very large town, just a handful of buildings; stable, general store and saloon but it was the last town on the East-West road, the only path which wound its way through the Wastelands. Very few caravans stopped here for last minute supplies since it was a lawless town, full of the scum of Hyperborea. There hadn't been a lawman in Crooked Creek for over a year, ever since the last one had been strung up and gutted on the saloon steps. It was the type of a town where thieves, cutpurses and brigands walked openly in broad daylight instead of lurking in the shadows.

The three companions rode into town and stopped in front of the local stable. Callistra's demon steed attracted a lot of attention until she dismissed it with a wave of her wand which caused the townsfolk to shy away from her whenever she turned their direction. Many made the 'Sign of the Horn' over their hearts which was supposedly a blessing that would ward off demons. It didn't work but it gave the townsfolk comfort.

Kastle completely ignored the townspeople and lead the two remaining horses into the stable, paid for a week's care before heading off to the local saloon.

Tariq just followed along, eyes darting from shadow to shadow while trying to come to terms with the knowledge that they were being watched. If the cleric felt it, he gave no indication to the assassin. When they entered the tavern, Tariq felt like he was stepping into an old western movie. The entrance had a swinging door and inside were gambling tables, dancing girls and a piano player. The only major difference was there were no six-guns present and it wasn't as dusty as the movies. Once Tariq leaned on the bar, he reconsidered his thought about the dust. "What are we doing here?"

"Waiting," said Kastle as he downed his first shot of whiskey.

"Waiting for what?"

When the music stopped and the sound of sliding chairs echoed through the room the cleric replied, "That."

The two companions slowly turned around to find five armed men. Two had loaded crossbows pointed at their chests and the rest with swords drawn. Tariq noted that everyone in the saloon had a weapon drawn and was watching the two travelers with suspicion. One of the warriors stepped forward and placed his sword on the holy man's shoulder with the blade touching his throat. "I thought we made it clear the last time you were here that you were not welcome."

Tariq didn't take his eyes off the crossbowman directly in front of him. "Friends of yours Kastle?"

"I came through here about a year ago, shortly after they murdered their lawman who was an acquaintance of mine. I brought Thor's judgment to the guilty parties."

"I might be off base here but I think they're still a little upset with you."

The cleric shrugged. "You could be right."

The swordsmen didn't like that the two men were ignoring him, especially since he had his blade at one of their throats. "Be quiet! You were warned. We didn't kill you in deference to your god but we told you what would happen if you returned."

Several of his men, grunted their agreement with the brigand. Emboldened by their approval, the swordsman grinned and shifted his blade slightly until there was a slight thread of blood on the edge.

Kastle raised one eyebrow. "You ready?"

"I'm gone," was all that the assassin said before he disappeared into a cloud of black smoke.

The saloon erupted into chaos. As the swordsman glanced over to where the assassin had been, the cleric reacted. Using the metal bracer covering his left forearm, Kastle knocked the sword away from his neck, drew his warhammer and attacked. Summoning Thor's wrath with a loud voice, he threw his enchanted weapon at the two crossbowmen. As the mighty warhammer slammed into the brigands knocking them aside with broken ribs, a bolt of white lightning followed in the enchanted weapon's wake. Three of the other warriors began to rush forward now that the cleric was unarmed but stopped quickly when his weapon reappeared in his outstretched hand.

Callistra watched the battle from the safety of the saloon balcony. Upon entering, she had slipped into the shadows and moved up the stairs to wait for the inevitable confrontation. Once the brigands drew their weapons and made their demands, she began casting a simple charm spell. It summoned all the rodents in the general vicinity to her aid. By the time Tariq made his move, she had hundreds of mice and rats at her beck and call. She pointed at the saloon floor. The rodents began climbing and biting on anyone that wasn't her.

It was mayhem. It was chaos. It was glorious.

Tariq had taken a more direct approach. Disappearing into a cloud of smoke wasn't magical, just a simple act of misdirection. Once he threw down the glass bead which contained the liquid smoke concoction, he just ducked down and slid behind the bar which placed him out of sight when the fight actually began. Peeking around the corner, the assassin watched the cleric in action. He was fine. Judging from his movements and gear, there wasn't anyone in the saloon who would be able to stand toe to toe with him. The real bedlam began when the rodents arrived.

However, when the door swung open and two new warriors stepped in, Tariq realized that the real power in Crooked Creek had joined the fray. The first man was huge, nearly as tall as the Norseman Bjørn. He wore a large two-handed axe strapped to his back and wore a cuirass of gleaming bronze. Considering the protective way the fearsome warrior stood in front and slightly to one side of the second figure, Tariq guessed that he must be a bodyguard for the older warrior. He was slightly balding with the grey hair and worry lines of wisdom at his temples. Tariq absentmindedly noted that his chainmail sparkled in the light of the saloon lanterns.

Tariq thought, 'Bodyguard first.'

Pulling out his Katar of Venom, he twisted the gem until it turned blue which indicated a very potent sleep toxin derived from a rare flower only harvested during midsummer in the Crags. He nearly fumbled his dagger when he realized that he shouldn't have known that but he did. Just another example of the twin minds at war within his own psyche. Regaining control of himself, Tariq slipped out from behind the bar. Keeping low, he moved slowly so as not to draw attention to himself until he'd positioned himself behind the two newcomers. Stepping out from the shadows, Tariq sliced the bodyguard once across the back of the neck just above his cuirass but below the helmet. His attack was as swift as a rattlesnake and just as deadly.

The toxin flooded his system in a few seconds. Just long enough for the huge brute to turn toward the assassin draw his axe and fall over asleep. The resounding thud when he landed stunned the rest of the saloon into silence but Tariq had not stopped with his first attack. He had continued past his first victim, grabbed the old man's hair, slid in behind him and placed his dagger on the old man's jugular.

When the saloon fell silent and everyone looked their way, Tariq whispered in the old man's ear. "Tell them to drop their weapons or you will be the next to fall."

The old man swallowed hard but hesitated. When Tariq twisted the blade slightly causing its edge to scrape over his throat, he gave in. "Everyone stand down!"

Callistra waved her wand and cancelled her charm spell. The hundreds of rodents still in the main room of the saloon suddenly knew that they had someplace better to be and scurried off. The saloon patrons hesitated for a moment before lowering their weapons.

The warrior-priest shoved his warhammer into his belt and dusted off his cloak. As he moved closer, Tariq noticed that his grin was huge. Stopping in front of the old man he said, "Hello Ragnar."

"Kastle."

"Tariq, you can let him go. Ragnar isn't going to harm us. Isn't that right?"

Ragnar swallowed hard but nodded. Warily, Tariq removed his blade and stepped back. "Are you sure about this?"

Kastle nodded. "Yes. Ragnar was just testing us. He and I have an understanding, right?"

The elderly brigand rubbed his throat and glanced down at the fallen bodyguard. "Our understanding was that you would leave Crooked Creek and never return. You voided that contract by coming back and compounded it by killing my son."

It was Tariq who answered. "He isn't dead, just asleep. He'll wake up in about twelve hours with a splitting headache but no permanent damage." Stepping over to the sleeping giant, he placed his blade on the back of his neck. "Of course, that can change rather quickly."

Ragnar yelled, "No! Wait!"

Tariq pulled back his katar but kept it near enough to strike if anyone in the saloon decided to be a hero. The assassin just nodded to the cleric and waited.

Kastle picked up his cue. "I'm only here for information. I would've preferred a more diplomatic and civilized meeting but then, your men started all this."

"We did not," came the voice of the first thug who had accosted them.

"Silence!" barked Ragnar before looking back at Kastle. "If indeed my son still lives, then you and I can converse. If not, then no one in this town will let you walk out of here alive."

Kastle cast a quick glance at the assassin and hoped he was telling the truth. Unable to read the his expression, the holy man nodded and stepped away. "Agreed."

Ragnar moved over to his son and checked his pulse. Feeling a strong beat, he sighed heavily and moved over to a nearby table. "Bartender! Bring out a flagon of your best."

Kastle moved to join him and signaled to his friends to do the same. Minutes later, they were all seated around the table and the saloon went back to its normal business. Although the patrons went back to their drinks and card games, they kept a wary eye on the companions.

Ragnar poured four goblets out of the flagon. "A toast."

Kastle held his hands over his and Tariq's goblet and muttered a few words. Their guest gave him a sly look but the cleric just grinned. "Just a precaution in case you tried to poison or drug us." When Ragnar flicked his eyes toward Callistra he added, "Even if your poison got past my magic, it wouldn't affect her anyway. Her chemistry is much different from our own...trust me on this."

Ragnar shrugged his shoulders. "If anyone tried to poison you it was not on my orders."

"Be that as it may, just remember that you'll be the first to die." Kastle paused for a second before adding, "Then your son."

Ragnar glanced at the prone form of his son just a few feet away and downed his goblet. Turning his attention back to his companions the brigand asked, "What can I do for you?"

"Information."

"What kind of information?"

"The kind that could benefit us both."

"I'm listening."

Kastle took a deep swallow of the bitter brew before continuing. "About a year and a half ago, you were deposed from your self-declared throne as the King of Thieves."

Both Callistra and Tariq gave the elderly brigand a sideways glance.

Ragnar gripped his goblet tight. "Yes. It was not a good day for me, thank you for reminding me."

"What was the man's name who took your throne?"

"Jagoda Wartooth. I will never forget it. One day I will have my revenge on him."

Kastle looked over at the witch and smiled. "Perhaps we can help each other."

"How?" asked Ragnar.

"I need to find Jagoda and if things go completely right, take him away from this land."

"You would do that?"

"I cannot force him to do anything. At one time, Jagoda was a friend of mine. Needless to say, we had a falling out but I need to find him."

Ragnar stared hard at the priest for a minute. "I can get you to him. That isn't the hard part. However, he might kill you on sight or totally ignore you. He is too unpredictable to know exactly what will happen."

Kastle nodded. "I understand."

"Are you set on this course of action?"

"I must. I have no other choice."

"If you must, you must." Ragnar stood and signaled to the barkeep. "Rooms have been prepared. You are to be my guest this night and tomorrow you will begin your journey. I will make sure you will be rejoined with Jagoda Wartooth before a fortnight passes."

Kastle stood. "Fair enough. For what it's worth, I'm sorry we had to come to blows before we could talk."

The two gripped forearms before the elderly brigand departed with his comatose son carried by four of his thugs. The three companions followed the chambermaid as she led them to their lodgings. Once she departed Kastle said, "We should be safe tonight. Ragnar has nothing to gain and everything to lose if he kills us."

Callistra asked, "And if he decides to betray us to Jagoda?"

"There is no love lost between them but even if he does, we will still find Jagoda."

"Good point."

"I suggest that we get some rest tonight. The next few days will probably be very tiring."

Tariq nodded and slipped out the door to find his own room. Callistra paused at the door for a moment as if conflicted. She cast a sly glance at the cleric, shook her head and disappeared down the hallway.

Kastle understood her dilemma and didn't press her. He too was thinking about the upcoming reunion and he was also worried. Of course, she was thinking about a different type of reunion.

* * * * *

As the dawn drew near, Tao was at ease for the first time since they had crossed over. Actually, he felt more relaxed than he had at any time over the last three months. Tao glanced at Arieal as she slept and once again admired her naked form. She was asleep facedown with her head on his chest. One part of his mind felt guilty at betraying the memory of his late wife. Another part was completely entranced by Arieal's perfect body.

It had always been obvious that the game designers behind *Lost Lands* were male. The graphics for the female characters were absolutely perfect. Very well-endowed chests, small waists, perfectly round hips and shapely legs...the ideal woman. Of course, seeing it in game and then seeing it in the flesh were two completely different things. Additionally, Arieal was a dark elf which meant coal black skin and ivory white hair. This didn't detract from her beauty in any form or fashion. In fact, it enhanced the exotic nature of her body. No one on Earth could have the skin or hair color of a dark elf and few if any Hollywood movie stars could have a body like hers.

Tao had been shocked when Arieal had entered his hut in the middle of the night. He had actually drawn his katana and assumed a fighting stance when she entered. She hadn't said a word, just slipped out of her robes and stood there silently, letting him drink in the beauty of her body. Once he sheathed his sword and set it aside, she had leapt on him, clawing and tugging at his clothes. Glancing down at his shoulder, Tao spied a bite and several fingernail marks. War wounds from their sexual encounter. There was intensity in their sex that was unexplainable.

Feeling Arieal stir on his chest, Tao felt his lust growing once more. Glancing out the window, he could see the precursor lightening of the sky, a tale-tell sign that sunrise was only about an hour off. Unable to keep his mind off her body, he gently rolled the sleeping dark elf onto her back and began to use his mouth and tongue to explore her perfect figure once more. Hearing her moan and feeling her pulse quicken, he climbed on top and entered her gently. This time, they took their time and enjoyed another romp together. As the morning sun began to climb over the tree tops, the two lovers laid back down on the bedrolls and quickly fell asleep, their lust spent.

When Tao woke up to the smell of frying fish, his room was empty. Donning his black and red keiogki, he went to find breakfast. There were a total of fifteen different huts throughout the grove of trees, all interconnected with rope bridges or ladders. They were ingeniously designed. Tao had chosen the uppermost hut on purpose, wanting the quiet and solitude it offered. But now, he had the most distance to cover to reach the lowermost platform which served as the kitchen. Using a loose rope, the lithe samurai swung down like 'Tarzan' to land next to the armored dreadknight.

"Morning Cozad."

Cozad looked up from his plate of fried eggs and fish. "Morning."

Tao looked around. Only Bjørn and Moira were present. "No one else up?"

Moira immediately began making a plate for him. Bjørn leaned back and pushed his plate aside. "Mathias was here about an hour ago. He ate a light breakfast than went off into the forest to hunt. He said something about wanting venison for dinner. I guess dried fish and powered eggs aren't his favorite fare." The Norseman picked at the remnants of his breakfast. "I think these were powdered eggs. Honestly, I'm not sure what they are but if they weren't eggs, I don't think I want to know what they were."

Moira whacked him on the shoulder with her cooking spoon. "Now don't be crass. You'll eat what's put in front of you and you'll like it."

Bjørn lowered his head and said, "Yes dear."

Moira added with a grin. "Besides, you need to regain your energy after last night."

The Norseman blushed slightly and cleared his throat. "I haven't seen Gamble or the girls yet this morning."

Tao nodded. "Probably just sleeping in. We all needed the rest. I was thinking…"

"Here comes Arieal," interrupted Cozad.

Tao turned in his seat to look back over his shoulder at the rope bridge and sure enough there was the dark elf. Maybe it was the memory of their encounter last night but he caught himself noticing how gracefully she moved. Her ivory hair was pulled back into a ponytail and she was wearing a purple and red lacy outfit that was very flattering to her figure.

It was enough of a distraction, that Moira whacked her husband again because he was staring. Having gotten her husband's attention, she grabbed his plate. "Now shoo, you have chores to do. Don't think you'll be lying around all day. I won't have it."

Bjørn stood up. "You're right. I didn't lie around back home and I'm not going to start now."

Cozad raised an eyebrow. "Where're you off to?"

"Firewood needs to be gathered, fences mended...I'm not sure exactly but I grew up in Alaska. One thing living near the frontier teaches you, there is always something that needs to be done."

Tao nodded. "I can understand that, it's the same living on a farm."

Arieal sat down at the table and mumbled, "Morning."

She didn't make eye contact with Tao but then she didn't make eye contact with anyone. If she was feeling guilty or nervous about their liaison last night, Tao couldn't tell but then he never could read women. His late wife would attest to that. However, he was too much of a gentleman to bring up her discomfort in conversation or question her publicly, so he shifted the conversation to other matters. "I was thinking that we would spend a few days here. I would like to explore the area a bit more and come up with some sort of game plan before we go any further."

Cozad nodded. "I agree. Personally, I would like to know why those peasants attacked us."

Tao pulled out his captured map and unrolled it on the breakfast table. He pointed at the mark for Camp Five. "Well...if we're here, our best bet for information is Antioch."

Chapter 14

The imposing figure of Hákon pulled out his map, unrolled it on the table and pointed at a mark on the coastline. "Given Jagoda's history, our best bet to find him is the area around Antioch. He or his men typically raid the coast."

Neither Kastle nor Callistra could dispute that remark, so they just sat back and waited for the young brigand to explain his plan.

"A convoy is scheduled to come through Crooner's Gap at noon the day after tomorrow bound for Antioch. We have on good authority that it's carrying a very special package for the Head Guildmaster. If we were to intercept it before it reached Crooner's Gap and take the place of the drivers, passengers and escort, then we will be in the perfect position to strike when Jagoda attacks."

Kastle asked, "How do you know that Jagoda even knows about the transport?"

Hákon grinned. "We don't but given his history on similar caravans, it's a safe bet that he does. We don't know exactly where he's planning on striking the caravan but I'm better he will before it reaches the farmlands outside of Antioch."

Kastle leaned forward and studied the map. Since he'd spent the better part of a year preaching in Crooner's Gap, he knew the lands around the town and pointed at a spot a few miles north. "If we ambush the transport before it reaches town, it will alert the Peacekeepers. But if we wait here, this creek always runs fast and high at this time of the year. The stagecoach will have to slow down to a crawl just to get across. Any outriders with them will have to cross before or after them due to the swift current and rocky footings."

Hákon studied Kastle for a moment before a big grin broke out to cover his face. "Are you sure you're a holy man? You sound more like a bandit to me."

"I haven't always been a priest. I was a rogue in another life." He cast a sideways glance at Tariq and Callistra and winked at his companions.

Tariq stifled his own grin. He knew that the priest was referring to playing a different avatar in the game which in turn, caused Brandon to think of some of the other 'toons' he'd played over the last few years. Maybe by remembering those characters and classes, it would grant him more understanding when dealing with the archetypes of this realm. It was something he needed to think about. Realizing that the brigand had asked him a question but since he had no idea what he'd asked Tariq responded, "Huh? I'm sorry. What was that?"

Hákon glared at the little assassin and repeated himself slowly as if he was talking to a child.

"Is…There…Anything…You…Want…To…Add?"

Tariq resisted the urge to draw his enchanted katar but consoled himself by just fingering the hilt and staring at the large brigand. The movement wasn't lost on Hákon. He could tell the brigand was remembering the sting of falling to the assassin's poisoned dagger. Finally Tariq asked, "How many men will Jagoda have with him?"

Hákon shrugged. "I don't know."

"What is the morale of his men? Are they well cared for and highly compensated for their loyalty?"

"I don't know."

"Do they prefer stealthy night attacks or daring daylight raids?"

Hákon took a deep breath. "I don't know."

Tariq shook his head. "It seems to me that there's a lot you don't know."

Hákon placed both fists on the table and leaned forward until he towered over the assassin. "Listen here little man; this is my raid and my plan. You will follow my directions or die."

Tariq just leaned back in his chair, laced his hands behind his head and smiled.

Before the assassin could say anything else that would alienate the brigand anymore, Kastle interrupted. "Hákon, we are not questioning your ability to lead but you must understand that where we come from we were raised with the concept that detailed knowledge of your enemy's movements and disposition to be critical for the mission's success. We understand that you have limited resources but our necks will be on the line just like yours during this raid."

The large brigand looked over at the cleric. It was obvious from the look on his face that he was thinking about what he had just said but was confused as how to reply. "I guess you're right. I'm just not used to being questioned about my attack plans."

Tariq was about to say something when Callistra placed one hand on his arm and leaned forward ever so slightly. The view she offered the huge brigand was vaguely seductive. "If no one ever questions your plans, how do you recognize the weaknesses in them?"

Flustered by his view and her straight question, Hákon didn't have an answer and just shook his head.

Kastle grinned. "When do we need to leave to make it to the ambush location on time?"

"We need to be on the road by noon. Given normal travel times, we should make it about two hours before the target arrives."

"How many men are you taking?"

"Twenty, plus you three."

"Is that enough?"

"It has been in the past. These are all experienced men."

Kastle glanced at his companions but left his doubts unspoken.

Callistra stood up and casually stretched, showing off a fair amount of cleavage in the process. "Very good, we will gather our things and be ready shortly before noon." Turning away, she seemed to add a bit extra sway to her hips as she exited the room.

Kastle and Tariq soon followed. Minutes later, all three were in their room and Callistra leaned in to whisper. "We were being watched."

Tariq looked around. There was nothing in the room except the three of them. He thought back to the earlier meeting. Nothing seemed out of the ordinary except maybe the extreme cockiness of Hákon. "Are you sure? I didn't notice anything. In fact, ever since Ragnar passed the word on us, I've felt welcomed. Well, that is if you don't count Hákon's manners."

Kastle studied his sometimes lover for a moment before asking, "Can you elaborate? Are we in danger from Hákon and his men?"

Callistra shook her head. "It isn't Hákon or his father, it is something else. Something…." Her voice trailed off.

"Are we being watched magically?" Kastle asked.

The witch shrugged her shoulders. "I'm not sure. I can't really explain it. I just know that during our meeting with Hákon we were being watched."

Kastle nodded. "I believe you. We need to be on our toes in the future."

Tariq moved over to the window and gazed out. The townsfolk moved about their daily lives, totally ignoring the thieves and brigands as they went about their business getting ready for the upcoming raid. He nodded outside. "They don't seem alarmed."

Callistra moved up next to him and followed the assassin's gaze. She absentmindedly chewed on her lip. Her actions slightly revealed her enlarged canines which Tariq found unnerving.

After a moment she said, "I don't think anyone else is aware of the spy. I can't explain it but I know we were being watched."

Kastle asked, "Is there anything we can do about it?"

She shook her head. "No."

Tariq shrugged and moved over to the bunk to collect his meager belongings. "Then let's get ready to ride and keep our eyes open. I for one do not trust Hákon."

"Neither do I but our situation dictates our choices." Kastle slapped the assassin on the shoulder. "Didn't Shakespeare write something like necessity makes for strange bedfellows? Our best chance for locating Aaliyah is finding Jagoda and Hákon is our best chance for that."

Chapter 15

Gamble, Mathias and Pixi had left the second morning to scout out Antioch. After the debacle in Saebroc, they were the logical choice. Tao had dropped them off at the edge of the forest within a day's walk of the city. The plan was simple, get in, get information and get out. The companions had pooled their money, so they were well funded. The trio had walked all night and arrived at the city gates an hour after sunrise.

After the simple log palisade of Saebroc, the stone walls of Antioch seemed impressive even to Pixi. Growing up in London, the British teenager was no stranger to castles but Antioch surpassed them all. The walls were of a grey-white marble-like stone that none of them recognized, even the dwarven mindset of Gamble. He judged the walls to be seventy feet tall and smooth to the touch. Even with the stonemasonry skills imparted to him by the transfer, the dwarf couldn't figure out how the builders of Antioch had crafted the impressive barrier.

There were only two gates visible, both chocked full of merchants and farmers bringing their wares to market. Pixi shrunk herself to her smallest size, about six inches tall, and remained invisible as Mathias and Gamble hopped in line to wait their turn to enter the grand city. Mathias kept his hood up to cover his slightly pointed ears and planted a friendly smile on his face.

The guards gave them the once over with a practiced eye before one of them focused his attention on the half-elf. "First time to the big city woodsman?"

Mathias nodded. "Is it that obvious?"

The guard gestured to his partner. "Not to everyone but Mal and I have been working this gate for nigh on eight years now. We can tell the newcomers. You all have the same look."

"I have heard of this city all my life. I finally decided that I needed to see it in all its grandeur."

The second guard with the sour look on his face that the friendly one had identified as Mal asked, "What's your business in Antioch?"

Mathias had been expecting this question and rattled the coins in his belt pouch. "Shopping. My father's birthday is in a fortnight and I wanted to get him something special." By the way both guards nodded, Mathias guessed it was an acceptable reason. "Since we are new here can you direct us to a map vendor? This place seems so huge."

The guards chuckled at his tone and the friendly guard said, "Aye. Pinon's is right around the corner. Best maps in the region."

Mal looked down at the dwarf. "Not the talkative type?"

Gamble jerked a thumb at his firend. "He does enough talking for the both of us."

That brought a grin to Mal's face as he glanced at his fellow guard. "I know the feeling."

As the pair began to walk past, Sal held out his hand to bar his passage. Mathias paused. "Sir?"

"One suggestion, stay away from the docks, that's a rough neighborhood. And hide your purse, you don't want to tempt the street urchins."

Mal spit in the dirt. "That's two suggestions you dummy."

Seeing the guards' attention shift away from them as they began to bicker in what seemed to be a long standing debate, the three Outlanders followed the line of merchants and entered Antioch.

Pixi whispered, "That was easy."

Mathias hid his smile. "Yes it was but I have been through many checkpoints over the years. Crossing back and forth from Canada to the United States on a regular basis you learn a few tricks."

Gamble raised an eyebrow. "Why would you have to distract the guards at the border?"

"Because as much as I hate to admit it, I like my weed and I never leave home without it."

The dwarf just shook his head.

Mathias felt Pixi land on his shoulder as she asked, "Okay. What's next?"

Gamble said, "Just like Mathias asked, first we find a map and then we find something to drink, preferably a nice Guinness."

Mathias shook his head. "I seriously doubt we will find a Guinness here."

Gamble shrugged. "Well, it might take a while to find one similar but I'll enjoy sampling the local brew."

Both Mathias and Pixi laughed as the trio moved through the crowded streets of Antioch in search of a good beer.

* * * * *

Tao enjoyed the solitude of his afternoon ride on Shadow.

They had been in Camp-Five for two days and truth be told, Tao was getting restless, hence this afternoon flight on his wyvern. Even though he was extremely well rested and relaxed, he had no idea where his relationship with Arieal was heading. She seemed to ignore him throughout the day, only answering direct questions and keeping herself busy in a different section of camp. But each night, long after everyone had gone to bed, she appeared in his room, undressed and attacked him with unrivaled passion. Although it was strange, it was in many ways satisfying.

Turning his attention back to his flight, he nudged Shadow slightly downward. He wanted to keep low over the trees as he winged his way east toward the coast. Almost as far as the eye could see were trees; the only remarkable feature was the towering volcano in the distance. He knew from his captured map that Camp Five was actually on the northern side of the Dark Forest with a dormant volcano near its center. It was also the legendary home of the elves before they disappeared from this realm. It was still marked with a rune for 'forbidden' which Tao took as a warning not to travel there.

Shifting in his saddle to his left, Shadow banked slightly to the north. He knew if his map was correct, there would be a village just past the upcoming river and he didn't want to fly over it, so he banked left to follow the river as it wound northeast which would allow him to study the village. This precaution kept him several hundred yards away but close enough that he could study the simple community.

Most of the buildings were simple log built homes but at least two seemed to be constructed from some sort of grey stone, one looked to be a church but he had no idea about the other one, at least not from this distance. If he had to guess, there seemed to be a couple hundred people in the village and no walls present. It actually looked to be very inviting. But he knew that looks could be deceiving. Twice now he'd been accused of being an Atlantean and both times that had heralded hostilities. Why he had been singled out, he didn't know, yet. But it was obvious that the Atlanteans weren't very popular in these parts. Then, there were the original wyvern riders. They had acted like bandits and the townsfolk had obviously been in fear of them. Tao couldn't help but wonder if there was any form of centralized government or ruling body in the region?

Following the curve of the river, the village was temporarily out of sight when the sounds of battle echoed through the trees. From this height, he could tell that this was a robbery gone wrong. It looked as if bandits had attempted to rob a stagecoach only to have it go bad. The bandits had attacked just after the transport had crossed the river. Judging from the fallen outriders, the bandits had taken out the escorts quickly and surrounded the coach. It looked to be an expertly executed robbery. At least until the trap had been sprung.

The stagecoach wasn't full of passengers, it was full of warriors. As soon as the twenty or so bandits concentrated their attacks on the warriors inside the stagecoach, a shrill horn echoed through the trees and suddenly, the bandits found themselves surrounded by more warriors as they emerged from the forests. All the new warriors wore silver chainmail covered by white tabards emblazoned with a red symbol of a crossed key and sword while their heads were covered with some sort of hood.

Tao's first impression was that of a holy order of knights, similar to the Templar Knights of medieval England. They were well trained and supremely disciplined as they attacked, staying in formation and letting their shields cover their partner's flank. It was going to be a massacre but Tao banked his wyvern around for a second pass, curious about the outcome.

* * * * *

Kastle was impressed with the efficiency in which Hákon's men dispatched the outriders. They were clean kills and utterly silent. Of course, the brigands probably had plenty of practice. As the bandits pounced on the stagecoach, something seemed out of place to the priest. Maybe it was the steely eyed driver or the extra doors on the stagecoach? Something seemed wrong. He was about to call out a warning to Hákon when the double doors on the coach flew open and out poured nine Peacekeepers. Kastle knew at that moment that they were toast.

The Peacekeepers were a military order out of the Southland which promised to keep the peace through force of arms and strength of faith. As a priest, Kastle had been treated with courtesy and respect but he had always been leery of the knights. They had arrived in Crooner's Gap six months earlier but knew way too much about the land and its people. He had always suspected that they had some sort of underlying plan for the area. Now it seemed that he had discovered it. They were planning on winning their way into the hearts of the common folk by destroying all bandits. Kastle knew it would work too. The bandits who preyed on the people of the Forestlands were the subject of daily conversations. The simple folk of Crooner's Gap and the other small villages in the area just wanted to be left alone. If the Peacekeepers could do that, then they would find support from the townsfolk.

Of course, Kastle knew that nothing came without a cost. You don't pay a wolf to kill the fox that has been eating your chickens. Sure it will work. Soon you won't have a fox but then, you won't have any chickens either.

* * * * *

Callistra knew something was wrong the moment the two outriders fell to Hákon's archers. She didn't know what or how but everything was wrong. Maybe it was the fact that the escort riders fell soundlessly to the arrows? Maybe it was the impending sense of dread she had felt growing all day? Whatever it was, she held Tariq back slightly as the bandits moved in for the kill.

"Something's wrong," she said in a faraway voice.

The assassin hesitated. He had already realized that there was something special about the witch. The moment the doors flew open and the armored knights attacked, Tariq slipped into the shadows and faded from view.

Callistra was more direct.

Realizing that this was a trap, she turned her attention to the surrounding woods and wasn't surprised to see more of the Peacekeepers charging the brigands. Ever practical, she contemplated fleeing but that meant she would have to leave Kastle behind. He wasn't her husband and she didn't love him but to be honest with herself, she had grown fond of him. Besides she knew that Patrick would never leave a companion behind, no matter the odds and he would never forgive her if he ever found out. So, she pulled out her wand and began casting spells.

* * * * *

As Tao circled the battlefield, he watched in fascination as the bandits fought a valiant but futile battle. Outnumbered, they were quickly surrounded and decimated until there were only two pockets of resistance, one group of five bandits lead by a large warrior with an axe and a smaller group of three with their backs to a large tree. He estimated that there were at least fifty knights in white surrounding the two groups. It was only a matter of time before the knights prevailed.

Tao turned Shadow into a tight circle to keep the battle in sight. He was extremely interested in the trio that was surrounded. The red cloaked warrior with the warhammer was making short work of any of the knights which came inside his reach. A grey robed assassin would pop into view for a split second as he struck a knight before fading away once again. The third member of the trio was a dark haired female who jumped and moved with unearthly grace; sometimes casting a spell, sometimes striking with her feet and hands. There was something about the way she moved which tugged on his memories. The trio had done so much damage to their attackers that the knights were moving men from the other battle to reinforce their position.

As the dark lady completed an attack, she looked upwards and spied him. They made eye contact for just a brief second. Tao didn't recognize her nor did he see any malice in those sapphire eyes. That was until she pointed her wand at him and suddenly, Shadow was falling.

* * * * *

The moment the Peacekeepers shifted more knights over to reinforce their attackers, Callistra knew any chance they had of escaping was gone. Kastle, Tariq and she had proved to be a formidable trio. It was just like in the game. Kastle took on the role of main tank, drawing and keeping their attention while Tariq slipped into the shadows, only to strike from the flanks or the rear wherever the Peacekeepers weren't watching while she used her magic and martial arts skills to add to the damage the small group was putting out. If the Peacekeepers hadn't shifted any of the knights over to reinforce their attackers, they would've been in a position to escape in a matter of seconds. Now, the odds were against them unless something unexpected happened.

That's when she saw the flickering shadow of a circling wyvern. Glancing up, she spied the red armored samurai on the grey serpent and recognized the rider as the avatar of her husband. Not having any other choice, she raised her wand and cast an immobilization spell on the wyvern.

* * * * *

Tao tried his best to keep his wyvern's head up but it was a losing battle. The great serpent was frozen in mid-flap. Luckily, his wings were pretty much parallel to the ground and Tao glided in instead of falling like a rock. Of course, the wyvern had the approximate glide ratio of commercial jet, one to one; which meant that he fell one yard for every yard he moved forward. Unfortunately for the knights in white, that meant he was going to crash right in the middle of them. A few of the knights saw him inbound and opened fire with their crossbows. The arrows did nothing more than bounce off the scaly hide of Shadow.

At the last moment, Tao leapt off and tucked into a roll to bleed off the majority of his forward motion. The stiffened body of his mount gouged out a large groove in the ground and took out five knights in the process. Coming out of his roll, Tao's helmet was left behind as he drew both swords and attacked. The knights in white swarmed him only to die when they entered the range of his blades. Neither their armor nor shields could withstand the enchantment of his frostbrand katana or mastercrafted wakizashi. In a matter of seconds, the tide of battle had turned against the knights.

Callistra felt her heart quicken at the sight of the scarlet samurai. Leaping over two knights, she pressed forward to fight at her husband's side.

Kastle didn't know who the samurai was but given their location and the way Calli acted, he guessed that this was the infamous Taote Ching. Seeing the skill at which he dispatched the Peacekeepers, he was happy that they weren't on opposite sides of the conflict.

Tariq paled when he recognized Tao. The samurai's warning still echoed in his memory but unfortunately, he was too busy with the knights to do more than make a mental note of the situation before he locked blades with another Peacekeeper. Wounded in the shoulder and lower back, Tariq realized that if Tao wanted to kill him, he knew that he was in no position to argue the point; provided that they survived this encounter.

* * * * *

Grand Marshal Jericho watched his Peacekeepers with pride.

They were mostly new recruits to the Order that were untried and un-blooded in battle. However, they had executed his trap with sublime precision. Even though the resistance by the brigands was more vigorous than reports suggested, his men had adapted to the battle well. Only one trio of outlaws was putting up a unified defense but his Peacekeepers had them contained. When this battle was over, he would be able to move on the brigand camp at Crooked Creek without any sort of resistance. Jericho knew it was only a matter of time before he had this region cleansed, ahead of schedule and that would please his master.

With the arrival of the red armored warrior, Jericho saw his plans fall apart. The wyvern riders weren't part of his current plan and he had specific instructions to avoid confrontation with them if at all possible. At first, Jericho didn't believe that one lone wyvern rider would be enough to disrupt his plans. That was until he saw the scarlet warrior slice through his men. He attacked with such controlled ferocity that he didn't seem human. Nothing could stand in his way.

Knowing that his survival was paramount to his master's plan, he prepared to depart. In truth, it wasn't a total loss. He had lost approximately a quarter of his men but the brigands, his target for this mission, were decimated. Signaling the retreat, Jericho turned his horse to the south but paused when the dark haired witch moved away from the security of her companions. Seeing a chance to gain favor with his master, Jericho pulled forth his wand and spoke a word of command. A ball of energy flew unerringly to strike the witch center mass. Within seconds, she was entwined in a cocoon of grey webs and lay helpless before him. Jericho's squires rushed forward to fetch his prisoner and soon followed him as he cantered south. Secure in the knowledge that despite their losses, his mission had been a success.

* * * * *

Tariq was in a sticky situation. He really didn't want to confront the samurai in his current condition. Although, the part of him that was the Brandon mind-set believed Tao would listen to reason. Of course, the Tariq mind-set didn't want to take that chance. When the scarlet samurai crashed into the Peacekeepers and began his attack, the knights completely lost interest in him which gave him ample time to step into the shadows and slip away.

Minutes later, he was further upstream and out of danger when a heavily armored knight rode into view accompanied by three squires. This knight was dressed in full plate armor with a black tabard emblazed with the red crossed key and sword. It was obvious that this was the field commander of the Peacekeepers.

Unsure of what to do, Tariq waited and watched.

His dilemma increased with the field commander's capture of Callistra. He didn't really owe the vampyress anything. From what he had seen, he could just slip away, find a big city and live off the profits gained by his skills. It could be a good life. But leaving Calli to the ministrations of the black knight just didn't sit well with him. Somewhere in the back of his mind, it felt wrong to let her be taken prisoner.

Glancing at Kastle and Tao, he knew that neither was in any position to aid the witch. As the squires moved forward to collect their prize, Tariq knew he had to make a decision. It was now or never. Tariq realized that this was his moment of destiny. His fate balanced on the edge of a knife, depending on the choice he made.

Taking a deep breath, he made his decision and acted.

* * * * *

As the last knight fell to his blades, Tao paused to study his handiwork. His Special Forces training kicked in and he instinctively reduced the dismembered body parts and dying combatants to simple numbers and statistics. He calculated that he had actually locked blades with twenty-four of the knights. Of those, he could account for seventeen kills while the other seven went into the injured or maimed category.

Looking at the battlefield, the hammer-wielding warrior and friends had accounted for at least thirteen dead while the other bandits had killed ten knights before they fell. Glancing at the retreating knights, he quickly counted fifty-seven more warriors before they were lost to the forest. They had survived because the knights retreated, not because they won the battle. That could be an interesting tidbit of knowledge if he ever had to face them again.

Sheathing his weapons, Tao stepped over the dead and dying with little regard to the difference and approached the hammer-wielding warrior who had his head lowered in prayer. Tao took a moment to study the warrior.

He had a square jaw and kind eyes. He was dressed in blue-tinted scale mail with a red cloak and a silver winged helmet. Considering his current actions, Tao changed his mind. He probably wasn't a true warrior, possibly a warrior-priest or a cleric. Stopping several feet away, Tao waited.

Kastle finished his prayer and looked up to find the scarlet samurai watching him. After seeing him in action, the priest had no wish to meet this man in battle and kept his movements slow and deliberate as he stood up. "Many thanks for your timely intervention."

Tao glanced back at the broken body of his wyvern with sadness. "I didn't really have an option."

Kastle nodded. "Be that as it may, your arrival saved my life. You must be Taote Ching."

Tao cocked his head to the side. "Aye, that is the name I currently use. How is it that you have heard of me? I am a newcomer to these lands."

Kastle looked around. "Calli speaks very highly of you and Tariq has shared some stories of your recent adventures. Although, I believe they both understated your skills."

Tao pulled off his right gauntlet and rubbed his chin as he thought about that name. "Tariq? Tariq al'Nasir of the Hashāshīn Order?"

Kastle nodded. "The same. He told me of the dreadful actions he took against your companion and the courageous actions you took in sparing his life. You have my condolences for your loss."

Tao dropped his hand to the hilt of his sword and squinted in concentration as he studied the surrounding forest. If Tariq was hiding, it was beyond his skills to locate. Keeping part of his attention on the adjacent battlefield, he turned back to the cleric. "I'm afraid you have me at a loss. Who are you and where is the assassin?"

"Kastle Rook, a humble priest of Thor at your service."

Tao knew that Thor was the Thunder God from Norse mythology. Nothing that he'd seen in this region indicated a Viking influence especially considering the armor and weapons of the knights he'd just fought so Tao made the next logical conclusion. "You're from the other side?"

Kastle nodded. "Texas, born and raised in Dallas."

Tao felt a few of the puzzle pieces fall into place. "I'm sure there is more to this story but back to my second question, where's the assassin? I don't fully trust him."

For the first time Kastle looked around the battlefield, seeking his companions. "For that matter where is Calli?"

"That's twice you've mentioned that name."

Kastle nodded. "Aye. She should be around here somewhere. Reddish black hair, black leather outfit, stunning body and a beautiful smile. She's kind of hard to miss."

"The witch? I think the knight in black captured her." Tao feared that the cleric was going to pass out considering the way his face paled at his remark.

Wide-eyed, Kastle looked around franticly. "We have to find her."

Tao calmly placed a hand on the priest's shoulder. "If they captured her, they did it for a reason and we have time. Not a lot but I counted almost sixty warriors with the black knight and I do not relish those odds."

Kastle was taken aback at the unruffled mannerism of the samurai. "How can you be so calm?"

"Facts are facts. What we cannot change, we must endure."

Kastle wanted to grab him by the shoulders and shake him but reined in his impulse. "But we're talking about Calli!"

Tao cocked his head to the side. "And?"

"Calli said that she was once a member of your guild."

Tao thought back over all the people who had been in the Keepers over the years and couldn't remember a single person by the name of Calli. Suddenly, the cold grip of fear squeezed his heart. "Calli? As in short for Callistra?"

Kastle nodded.

"Oh my god! Cassie alive?"

Kastle cocked his head to the side. "Cassie? No, Calli."

Tao shook his head. "Cassandra, my wife. She disappeared four months ago in a fire that consumed our house."

"Your wife?"

Tao nodded. "Aye. She had been power leveling a new avatar from the Shadowlands campaign, a vampyress, to aid us in completing the Tomb of Immortality."

Kastle nodded. "That sounds like her."

Tao resisted the urge to chase off after the black knight. However, the facts hadn't changed with the discovery of Cassie's survival, just the urgency. Taking a calming breath he said, "Okay. We need four things to rescue her."

"Which are?"

Tao held up his fingers as he counted down their needs. "Transportation."

Kastle nodded downriver. "We have horses picketed about a mile south of here."

"Information."

"I can tell you what I know about the Peacekeepers."

"Help."

"I might know someone that can aid us. Former companions of ours, also from the other side but finding them and getting their assistance might prove troublesome."

Tao nodded. "The rest of my companions are at a tree fort northwest of here. We'll have their help without question."

Kastle waited a few seconds before prompting, "And the fourth?"

"Luck. Time is not our ally on this endeavor. They might've captured Cassie for a reason but no kidnapper holds onto their prisoners forever."

Kastle nodded. "What do you need me to do?"

Tao moved over to one of the Peacekeeper knights that was still alive. "Gather up the horses and meet me back here as soon as possible."

"What are you going to do?"

Tao looked down at the face of the young man in white. Pain and fear were written all across his face. "Get some answers. It would be best if you weren't around for this."

Kastle hesitated but knew that the samurai was right. He didn't have the stomach for what he guessed Tao was about to do. Nodding, the priest turned south to collect the horses. He was barely out of the clearing when the screams began.

* * * * *

Grigoris winced as he watched the samurai question the injured Peacekeeper.

Although he hated watching the torture, the imprisoned seraph did notice that Tao didn't have any malice or hatred in his heart. It was purely a business transaction. Tao simply had questions that needed to be answered and the young Peacekeeper was the most readily available source.

It didn't make it right but it still gave him hope for the future.

Chapter 16

Cozad spent his days wrestling with the darker side of his personality.

Already a loner in the real world, Ed had always enjoyed the quiet solitude of his job as the night manager of a metal fabrication plant. He only had ten employees to check on and they were all old timers that had been at the job longer than him. He left them alone to do their work and they made him look good to the corporate suits, a perfect pairing. It was his personal life that had always been in shambles. Divorced four times, he was currently not talking with his live-in girlfriend. They more or less tolerated each other and if not for having different schedules, they would've split up long ago. It was probably a combination of all these factors that influenced him to create a Dreadknight in the game.

The game. It was so simple on the other side of the screen. *Lost Lands* was a safe place where he could excise his inner demons without fear of breaking the law and much less expensive than seeing a psychiatrist. He could just pretend to be a minion of Chaos and work out his frustrations in the game. Rape, torture, murder, mayhem, intimidation, fear and pain were all tools of the Dreadknight. It was all harmless fun…until now.

Ed constantly struggled against the Cozad mindset which wanted to do all those dark things. Not just wanted to do them, he longed to do them. He had awakened the last two nights covered in sweat. While his dreams of torture and rape haunted his waking hours. Unsure that he could control his desires, Cozad had awakened on the second day and headed south into the woods to be alone.

* * * * *

Arieal had similar problems. The darker side of her nature called to her but nowhere nearly as strong as Cozad's. Her problem was more of a personal nature. She felt guilty about not being at home with her family but her real anxiety was that she didn't think she felt guilty enough. She was enjoying the freedom of self granted to her by crossing over. Not having to juggle her kids' schedules, dinner plans, paying bills, balancing the budget and every other part of modern daily life was extremely liberating. Currently all she had to worry about was…nothing.

Besides, the late night rendezvous with Tao had been mind-blowing. Annie hadn't been with a man for nearly twenty years. She enjoyed a more alternative lifestyle and was completely satisfied with it even though society still ostracized those in the gay community. Although deep down she knew that she loved her current girlfriend, the spark had been gone from their relationship for many years. Not once had she ever given in to the temptation to have an affair. It wasn't right. Not that it was against her beliefs or anything, she just didn't feel it was right to cheat on her significant other.

But here…here she was someone else and that was a freedom she relished. Her only problem at the current time was wondering when Tao was going to get back so she could jump his bones once more.

* * * * *

Bjørn and Moira spent the days together. It didn't matter what they did, they just spent their time together. They had been married for three decades this past December and both realized that the end of life was close for them. Back in Alaska, they were both in their seventies and Kaslene's health was fading fast. She was on oxygen twenty-four – seven, took lots of meds daily and hadn't been outside their home in over five months. While Earl's health was better, he wasn't a spring chicken either.

This trip inside the game was a wonderful diversion from reality that they both needed. The one difference they had over the rest of their companions was that neither of them were afraid to die. They had lived with the inevitable for so long, death was more of a constant companion than an adversary.

They were spending the morning on the lower platform which the companions had begun to call the 'kitchen' since it was where the cooking area was set up and it seemed that everyone tended to congregate on that platform, just like the kitchen back home. Moira was baking. She had cooked every meal since they arrived. Not being tied to an oxygen tank, she was able to delve into a hobby she missed on the other side. Bjørn was just sitting back, enjoying the quiet morning and watching his wife cook. If this wasn't heaven, it was about as close as he could get.

Unfortunately, the morning quiet was broken by the sound of a shrill horn to the west. Moments later, another sounded to the north.

Bjørn and Moira calmly picked up their weapons and climbed down to the forest floor. They knew the wyvern riders had found them. They had been expecting this. The only question remained was how the encounter would play out. Moving into the clearing just outside the tree camp, they counted twenty wyverns with riders circling the camp. Bjørn calmly planted his seven foot claymore into the soil and waited.

Moira leaned her head on his shoulder and gently caressed his back. "This is the end my love."

Bjørn had seen the look of hatred on the riders' eyes and knew that she was right. "True, but I wouldn't change the last few days for anything. I love you, I always have and I always will."

Seeing the wyvern riders begin their attack, Moira leaned up on her tip-toes and kissed her husband for the last time. "You have always been my rock and I thank you for that. This isn't how I thought I would go out but its better this way. I love you."

Bjørn returned the kiss. "At least we'll be together. The thought of living without you has haunted me these past few years." Taking a two-handed grip on his sword, he pulled it free. "Let's show these bandits how Americans fight."

Moira grinned. "Don't you know it!"

Stepping back to be outside the range of her husband's blade, she began casting her spells. The trees, grasses and insects of the forest answered her call.

* * * * *

When Adak, the commander of the wyvern riders, saw the two strangers exit Camp Five it answered many questions about his brother's missing patrol. Even from this height, he could tell that the large blue-kilted warrior bore the mark of the Atlanteans. They had obviously killed his brother's patrol and taken possession of the camp. Since no dragons were on the way up to confront them, these two were probably just the rear guard charged with the task of holding the camp while the dragon-riders raided nearby.

Adak signaled his flight of five to peel off and to remain on over-watch while the other three flights attacked. He wasn't going to get caught on the ground by the Atlanteans. As his men began their attacks, he had to admire the calm demeanor of the Atlantean and his companion. They did nothing more than talk, kiss and separate. They didn't seem in a hurry or even concerned about the diving wyverns. This actually worried him more than he cared to admit.

Just before his raiders reached them, the tattooed warrior shape-shifted into a huge were-bear. Instead of running away from the diving serpents, it attacked. It was rather frightening. The were-bear's sword glowed with an unnatural light as it cleaved through wyvern and raider flesh alike. His men shot arrow after arrow at him. Some hit, some didn't. Many of the raider's crossbows seem to warp and explode in their hands. While others found that their swords were suddenly so hot that they could no longer hold them. Mere seconds into the attack and Adak counted four of his wyverns down and at least two more injured but flying...barely.

He could tell that both of the Atlanteans were injured as well but neither seemed to be ready to surrender. Knowing he didn't have a choice, he ordered his flight into the attack. Looking over his shoulder at his second in command, he yelled over the wind. "Concentrate our attacks on the female! She's the spellcaster!"

Seeing him nod, Adak turned his attention back to the task at hand.

* * * * *

Moira wiped the blood away from her eyes with an equally bloody hand. She could see that her husband was also injured from the way he moved but she knew that it was nothing serious. Looking down at the arrow protruding from her stomach, she couldn't say the same thing. The only reason she was still standing was the use of a simple spell which dulled the pain. Glancing at the sky, she watched as the wyvern riders began their next run and knew it would be the last. They had injured the raiders but not enough to make them flee. They wouldn't be able to stop them on the next pass and they both knew it.

Bjørn grunted from the pain. Most of his injuries were minor but the one slash on his back from one of the wyverns burned like fire. As the reserve wyverns joined the next pass, he knew they wouldn't survive. Glancing at his wife, he noticed the arrow in her gut and gash on her forehead. He crossed the twenty feet which separated them. "This is it doll."

Moira nodded. "I know. I just hate the fact that we are going to be killed by some low level bandits."

Bjørn let the change back to his human form come over him. "It could be worse. It could've been some goblins."

Moira laughed. "Yes, there is that."

Bjørn glanced back at the wyverns and knew they only had a few seconds left. Picking up his claymore with both hands, one on the tang and the other on the blade, he asked, "Blaze of Glory?"

Realizing what he had planned, she copied his actions with her staff and nodded. "On the count of three?"

Bjørn said, "One…"

They both raised their weapons high above their knees while Moira said, "Two…"

Bjørn looked up. The lead wyvern was only fifty feet away and closing fast.

"Three!"

Husband and wife slammed their weapons over their knees with all the force they could muster.

* * * * *

Adak wasn't reckless. He wasn't the type to lead a charge and it saved his life on this day.

His flight had fallen in behind the survivors of the first run and seeing the two Atlanteans calmly talk in the face of certain death made him hesitate. He didn't know what they were planning but he knew it wouldn't be good for his men. However, the resounding explosion when they broke their weapons was not what he was expecting.

Every wyvern and raider in front of him was engulfed in an enormous fireball.

Adak struggled to keep his serpent in the air as he banked hard to avoid the deadly inferno. The sudden turbulence nearly knocked him from the saddle but he managed to hang on and direct his steed to the ground. It wasn't his best landing but he was alive.

Looking around, he only spied three other wyverns and riders on the ground. The rest were gone. There wasn't a single sign of them or the two Atlanteans, just a charred piece of land.

* * * * *

Arieal hadn't been very deep in the forest when she heard the shrill call of the hunting horn and knew that the wyvern-riders had found them. Running through the trees in reckless abandonment, she arrived at the clearing just in time to witness Bjørn and Moira's last act of defiance.

She had heard of the Blaze of Glory spell before, everyone in game had, but relatively few ever used it.

In game it was a combination spell and action that an avatar could take. It involved sacrificing a mighty magical item and releasing all spells and abilities an avatar had in one monstrous blast. It wasn't used in game very often because that avatar would no longer be available for play. In essence, it was a way of sacrificing your avatar to gain a victory. It would be a costly victory since only master level avatars had the ability. It had taken Annie three years of playing three or four hours a day to get her current avatar to master level.

Unfortunately, she was a bit too close to the blast and it knocked her backwards into a tree. The last thing she remembered before the cool blackness of unconsciousness claimed her was seeing a few of the wyverns land nearby.

* * * * *

Cozad was deep in the forest when he heard the shrill call of the hunting horns. Due to echoes of the tree filled valley that he was in currently, he couldn't tell from where the sound originated.

As the Dreadknight began the process of backtracking to the tree camp, he felt the ground tremble and heard the explosion. He knew at that moment that something extremely bad had happened. Rushing through the trees, he came out of the woods just in time to see four wyverns and riders fly off to the west. The bound form of Arieal could be seen draped across the saddle of the lead serpent.

Of Moira and Bjørn there was no sign, at least not until he studied the ground around the area of the explosion and read the tale of the battle in the dirt. Seeing nothing else to be gained by standing there, Cozad moved in the camp and began packing foodstuffs and other supplies. He knew that Tao would be back soon. They weren't going to let anyone capture one of their companions, at least not without a fight.

With a companion in trouble, the Ed mindset and the Cozad mindset were in total agreement and for a few moments, he was at peace.

* * * * *

Kastle followed Tao as they rode through the trees. He couldn't help but admire the way the samurai sat easily on the horse and how it seemed to respond to his every signal. Even though Kastle was born and raised in Texas, he had never been on a horse before being pulled into the game nor had he taken the skill while leveling up of his character. It always seemed a wasted skill but now, he regretted it.

As they came up to a stream, Tao reined in his horse and patted its neck. "We should dismount and let them drink a little." Putting action to his words, he slid off and led his steed to the stream.

Kastle followed suit and studied his new companion. To all appearances, Tao seemed calm while he felt anxious. Shaking his head he asked, "How can you be so calm?"

Tao looked up. "About what?"

"Calli."

"Four months ago I thought my wife died in a house fire. I had a funeral. I grieved and I drank. I lived for the game. Suddenly, I find myself brought over into the game and I've become my avatar. In some ways it's a dream come true but I've already lost one friend to this adventure. How many more will I lose before it's over? But now I find out that Cassie is still alive? How should I act?"

Kastle cocked his head to the side. "Four months? That's all the time that has passed back home?"

Tao nodded as he pulled his horse's head up from the water. It was bad to let them drink too much too quickly. Kastle followed his example. As Tao climbed back onto his horse he asked, "How long did you think?"

Kastle remounted his horse. "It has been almost four years since we crossed over. We've lost many friends during that time. As far as I know, there are only four of us left, Calli and me and the two who we hope to find, Jagoda and Aaliyah."

Tao didn't speak but began leading his horse across the stream and up the adjoining hill.

Kastle continued. "Jagoda and I had a falling out after we had a run in with an Atlantean."

Tao raised an eyebrow. "What do you know about the Atlanteans?"

"Plenty and nothing."

"That's rather cryptic."

Kastle chuckled. "Well, I've only met one Atlantean since we've been here. Although, he was charming and helpful at first, he turned into a real Mister Hyde in the end. He killed five members of my party before we escaped. On that day, Jagoda swore an oath of vengeance against Sartael and all Atlanteans."

"I'm sure there is more to that story."

"Yes, there is but another time and place perhaps."

Tao nodded. "Gotcha. Maybe you can answer why since our crossing I've been accused twice of being an Atlantean?"

"You bear the mark."

"What mark?"

Kastle pointed at his left cheek. "The dragon tattoo. Only an Atlantean would have such a mark."

"That's why the villagers and the young wyvern rider were afraid of Bjørn and myself. We both have visible tats."

Kastle nudged his horse forward a bit until he was beside Tao. "Which brings up a question of my own, how is it you had a wyvern?"

Tao chuckled. "That is a long story. After we crossed over, we made our way along the coast..."

The rest of his story disappeared into the wind as an explosion shattered the silence of the forest and a huge fireball could be seen in the distance above the trees. Without waiting to see if the priest followed or not, Tao spurred his horse forward. In his heart of hearts, he knew he had just lost a friend.

The distance was greater than Tao thought and it took him nearly a half hour to reach an area within bow shot of the camp. Reining in his horse, he vaulted from the saddle and rushed to the edge of the tree line.

Nothing in sight moved.

Turning back to his horse, Tao noted its heavy breathing and that his coat was covered in sweat. He had not been easy on the beast during the ride. Loosening the straps, he removed the saddle and bridle just as Kastle rode up. Even though it was obvious he wasn't an expert rider, the priest had done his best to keep up and hadn't fallen off in their hasty ride.

Kastle climbed down slowly. His thighs ached like no other time in his life, so much so that it hurt to walk. Hating to waste a spell but unsure what they were about to face, the cleric muttered the words of a simple spell of Endure Pain. It wouldn't take the pain and discomfort away but it did dull it to a manageable level, like taking a super-strength fast-acting pain-killer.

Kastle turned back to find the samurai removing the saddle and bridle of his horse. "What..."

Tao whispered, "Simple. If we don't come back, these magnificent animals would be at a disadvantage and die in the wilderness if we left them with everything on. If we need them again, they will be nearby and we can catch them. If not, I won't feel guilty about leaving them behind."

"I had never thought about it that way but it makes sense." Kastle nodded. Grabbing his and Calli's saddle bags, the priest slung them over his shoulder. "Lead on."

Tao moved slowly from tree to tree, pausing at varied intervals to see if anything moved in the camp. It didn't. Once they got close enough to see the scorched earth, Tao stepped out from concealment.

Kastle lagged behind but didn't approach the samurai. He seemed in deep concentration. The priest could hear the rustling of wings inside the grove of trees. He wasn't exactly sure what that meant yet but he kept one hand on his hammer just in case.

Tao paused at the center of the charred ground and knelt down. There wasn't much left but he lifted up the remnants of a sword and a staff. "I lost two friends this day."

Kastle moved up behind him and gazed down at the shattered remains. Not knowing what else to say, he fell back on the simple phrase, "I'm sorry for your loss."

"C'est la guerre."

"Huh? I have heard of C'est la vie, *'such is life'* but I've never heard that one before."

When Tao stood up, his face was blank of any emotion. "Such is war. It was a phrase the French uttered during the German occupation and has been commonly used among soldiers since World War two."

"Ah," was all Kastle could say. When he looked back into the grove of trees, he saw an armored warrior in battered plate armor carrying a huge single bladed axe step out from the shadows. Pulling out his warhammer, Kastle dropped the two saddle bags on the ground and called, "Ware! Enemies!"

Hearing the warning, Tao reacted out of instinct. Dropping the weapon fragments, he rolled forward to create distance and drew both swords as he assumed the mountain stance. Seconds later, he sheathed both blades and moved forward.

The Dreadknight planted the butt of his axe in the ground, took off his helmet and hung it on his weapon. "About time you showed up."

Tao gripped forearms with the warrior. "I ran into some trouble on the way and had to travel the old fashion way, horseback." He waved the cleric forward. "Cozad, meet my new friend Kastle. He's from Dallas."

The pale skin above his eyes moved and Kastle realized that he didn't have eyebrows or any hair that he could see but it was the soft blue glowing eyes which captivated his attention. Realizing he was staring, Kastle held out his right hand. "Pleased to meet you."

Cozad pulled off his gauntlet and shook hands. However, when they touched hands there was a small jolt which startled them both. "I'm sorry. My affliction doesn't seem to like your god. Whom do you serve?"

"Thor, the Thunder God."

"Ah, that explains it."

Tao asked, "Explains what?"

Cozad replaced his gauntlet. "During character creation Dreadknights have to pick a dark god to serve and I chose Thanatos, the ancient Greek god of death. It seemed a logical choice for my avatar. However, you also have to pick four adversarial gods. I selected Zeus, Mars, Odin and Thor."

Kastle nodded. "You picked the four most common warrior gods. I can understand that."

Tao focused his attention on the priest. "Does that mean you can't heal him?"

Kastle shrugged. "I'm not sure. In the game, only my offensive magic would work on him, not defensive or beneficial spells. But here…" He let his voice trail off indicating that he was unsure.

Cozad stepped back. "One way to find out priest, cast something on me."

Kastle hesitated. "But it might cause you pain instead."

"Pain is life, priest."

Seeing the logic behind the Dreadknight's request, Kastle thought through the spells he had left for the day and selected a simple augmentation spell. If it worked correctly, it would increase his strength and hardiness for three hours. Pulling out his holy symbol, which for a warrior-priest of Thor was his warhammer, Kastle spoke the words of his spell and waited.

Cozad waited patiently for the priest to cast his enchantment and felt the tingle of the magic at work on him. There was a split second where he was certain it would fail but then he felt the extra surge of energy flow through his body. "Strength spell?"

Kastle smiled. "Actually, Aide spell; strength and constitution buff. I take it that it worked?"

"Aye. I feel good."

Tao slapped his friend on the shoulder. "Now that's settled, we have work to do."

Cozad nodded. "They only have about an hour head start on us."

Tao cocked his head to the side. "Who?"

"The wyvern riders. They have Arieal."

Tao felt his heart fall into his stomach. This couldn't be worse if he'd planned it. Two of his friends dead, three on a scouting expedition, one captured by the wyvern raiders and his wife a prisoner of the Peacekeepers. Not seeing any other alternative, Tao just nodded. "Then we have to get her back first."

"First?" asked Cozad.

Tao nodded. "I have a lot to tell you but time is not our ally. We need to leave a note for the others and get after Arieal before the trail gets cold."

Cozad began to walk back into the grove of trees. "Everything is packed and two wyverns are already saddled. I can get a third ready for Kastle. I already left a note. It was troubling at first. It seems that this avatar doesn't know how to write but when I let the Edward mindset come forward, I remembered how to write."

Tao nodded. "That'll work and since it's in English only those from back home would be able to read it. That could prove useful."

Cozad nodded. "That was my thinking also."

Tao offered him a small smile and patted his friend on the shoulder. "Then let's get going."

Chapter 17

Gamble, Mathias and Pixi spent their first day in Antioch exploring the city. By modern standards, it wouldn't really be much of a city. Gamble was from Chattanooga which had a population of about one-hundred seventy-five thousand. Mathias's hometown of Denver boasted over two million residents. Pixi actually spent the school year in London with her mom and the summers in San Francisco with her dad. Both cities had populations of over seven and a half million. Even with those staggering figures in mind, Antioch was still impressive. They had no way of knowing the exact numbers but they estimated the population to be in the low to mid thousands. It was crowded but as long as they had gold, they were left alone by the ever present guards.

Pinon's had been a treasure trove of information. Not only had they been able to purchase a map of Antioch, they got one of Hyperborea with all major towns and trade routes. Pinon the Mapmaker had insisted that it was accurate. However, he balked at the authenticity of the only map of Atlantis. It was supposedly smuggled out by a former slave. Gamble doubted the story but since it was the only map available, they added it to their collection. With a little prodding and a few coins of silver, Pinon also explained the current state of affairs in Antioch.

The city didn't have a King or any type of royalty but was run by the five guilds; the Blades, Shields, Wands, Staves and Coins. These guilds represented the five professions of Rogues, Warriors, Wizards, Priests and Merchants. The Guild Council worked with their counterparts to keep the populace in balance and at peace with the Dragon Kings of Atlantis. Every five years, a new Overseer was chosen from the current Guild Council to watch over the city's affairs. The current chief administrator was on his third term and the guards with the red turbans worked directly for him.

Pinon looked around before leaning in to whisper conspiratorially. "Rumors say that Sanguine Bolt is a refugee from Atlantis, even though he doesn't bear the mark. Of course, he has an awful scar on the right side of his face which could be hiding the mark." The mapmaker shrugged. "Either way, he was young, talented and very charismatic. Joining the Order, he soon rose to prominence in the Wands. I don't know if the rumors concerning his origins are true or not but since he assumed the role of Overseer, we haven't had a single problem with the Dragon Kings." Pinon waved his hands back and forth. "Some think he's been in charge too long. There are some that want him gone so we can go to war against the Atlanteans. Not me. War isn't good for business."

Gamble and Mathias digested the information and bid the merchant farewell.

Their second stop was a local tavern. They found that the ale was in fact very good, not quite a Guinness but extremely refreshing. Gamble and Mathias were careful not to drink too much or ask too many questions at any one location since they didn't want to draw too much attention to themselves.

They failed.

The companions were in their third tavern enjoying a pint when five guards with blood-red turbans walked in and surrounded their table. A quick glance over their shoulders showed that there were at least five other guards blocking the exits. Gamble finished off his ale and dropped one hand to his pouch to draw forth a runestone. He could tell by the feel that it was a flashbang. He would talk but if it came to a fight, he was going to be ready.

Mathias noted the subtle way the dwarf had dropped his hand and started calculating the angles and the odds. Neither were good but they still had an ace in the hole by the name of Pixi. Since Gamble didn't speak, Mathias didn't either and the two companions waited.

The Guard Sergeant stepped forward, placed both knuckles on the table and leaned forward. "Your presence has been requested."

Gamble sat down his empty mug and glared at the guard with an unblinking stare. The four guards behind the sergeant fidgeted nervously. It was obvious that they weren't used to people not jumping to do their bidding. Finally the dwarf spoke. "I don't remember asking you to join us at this table. Nor have we broken any laws, so you can't be here to arrest us." Gamble lifted his empty mug and waved it at the barkeep. "Now if you don't mind, my friend and I were enjoying a pint and we prefer to drink alone."

Turning away from the guard, Gamble shifted his feet ever so slightly as he readied himself to spring into action.

The Guard Sergeant was in a quandary. Never in the past five years had anyone refused the request to accompany them but he couldn't return to his master empty-handed. And what made it worse, the dwarf was correct. They hadn't broken any laws nor could they compel them by force of arms with all the witnesses in the bar.

Uncertain of what to do, the sergeant placed his right hand on the dwarf's shoulders and tried again. "I said that your presence is requested. That was me being polite. You obviously misunderstood this to be an actual request."

Gamble glanced down at the hand then back at the sergeant with a completely blank expression. "Youngster, first off I have boots older than you. Secondly, someone should've taught you proper manners. You don't go around manhandling your elders especially if you aren't arresting them. You're not arresting me correct?"

Gamble casually pulled his hand out from under the table.

The young sergeant grinned. "No sir. You're not under arrest. I just need…"

Mathias could tell that Gamble had something palmed and flexed his fingers ever so slightly to loosen them up. Whatever the dwarf had planned, the half-elf expected him to act soon and he wanted to be ready.

Gamble shrugged his shoulder to throw off the sergeant's hand and slid out of the booth. "If we aren't under arrest, then we choose not to accompany you." Turning his attention to the other patrons in the tavern, the dwarf asked, "Unless it is common practice for guards to take law-abiding citizens away when they hadn't done anything."

From the way the patrons murmured it was obvious that the dwarf had struck a nerve.

"Since when is it against the law to sit quietly in a tavern and enjoy a pint?" Pointing at a well-dressed patron, Gamble changed his tone to mimic the sergeant. "You shouldn't be drinking that, come with me."

The patrons began to give the red turban guards a hard look but Gamble didn't stop there.

Moving over to another table, he leaned his four foot frame on the table in the same manner as the guard sergeant. Staring up at the two warriors sitting at the table, he kept his tone in near perfect mimicry of the sergeant as he said, "Your presence has been requested."

Of course, instead of giving the warriors a hard stare, Gamble proceeded to make a mockery of the guard by his ever changing facial expressions.

The warriors and the patrons laughed.

The red turban guards looked around confused. When they had entered, the patrons were cowed and fearful. Now they were laughing at them. It was a hard pill to swallow. The sergeant's face was flush with anger. He stepped forward and grabbed Gamble's arm roughly.

The dwarf had been expecting this reaction and called out in English, "Flash!"

As soon as the sergeant spun him around, Gamble closed his eyes and threw the stone on the floor. Both Pixi and Mathias heard the skald's warning in time to close their eyes. Since no one else in the tavern understood English, they quickly fell victim to the runestone's magic.

As the stone hit the floor, two mighty spells went off in close secession. A blinding flash of light followed by a loud boom echoed in the tavern room. Even the three companions who had been expecting the spells' effects were slightly disoriented by the spell. It was so loud and forceful, that it rattled their teeth. The guards and patrons who hadn't been prepared for the medieval flashbang were completely blind and disoriented for several minutes at least.

The companions didn't waste a moment and fled the tavern. In her haste, Pixi even dropped her invisibility for several seconds although no one in the tavern was in any sort of condition to notice. Focusing her attention on following the dwarf, she disappeared once again and sped to catch up to her companions.

Gamble led them generally west, left down an alley, then right at the next street and then left again. After several minutes, he slipped in behind some crates that were covered by a large tarp and sat down. Mathias joined him seconds later followed by Pixi.

The faerie landed on the crates and dropped her invisibility. "What was that all about?"

The dwarf shook his head. "I have no idea."

"Then why didn't we just go with them? They asked politely."

"First off, if they had sent two or three guards to ask us, I would've gone without hesitation. That would've been a real invitation. Sending ten guards with all exits blocked, that wasn't a request. It was a summons."

Mathias nodded. "Aye. It didn't feel right to me either. The question remains, why and who wanted us?"

Gamble shook his head. "Well, if Pinon's information was right, they were sent by the city's chief administrator, Sanguine Bolt. But personally, I don't care. We are leaving Antioch tonight."

Pixi said, "But we still have two days until we are supposed to meet up with Tao."

"Doesn't matter. If this Bolt character really wants us, he will try again. The guards couldn't rush us since we were in a public place and they underestimated us. We can't count on that happening again."

Mathias asked, "What's the plan?"

Gamble said, "Simple. We hold up here until nightfall and slip out. Either over the walls, through a gate or by boat. It doesn't matter but come sunrise, we need to be out of Antioch."

* * * * *

The young sergeant and his fellow guards knelt before a heavily cloaked figure with a blood-red cheche; which was a type of turban and veil which concealed everything but the eyes. They had failed to complete their assigned task and they were unsure what punishment the volatile guildmaster would inflict.

Caressing the bone handle of his wand, Sanguine Bolt asked once more. "Are you sure they didn't say anything else?"

The young sergeant racked his brain for anything that might save his head. Suddenly, he recalled something. "The dwarf, he said something right before the explosion."

Sanguine Bolt leaned forward. "What was it?"

The sergeant shook his head. "I don't know. It was in a language I've never heard before. It wasn't dwarvish or elven of that I am sure."

"What did it sound like?"

"Fla....Fla...sssshhh."

"Flash?"

The sergeant dared to look up in his excitement. "Yes master! That was it!"

Sanguine Bolt leaned back in his chair. Flash. An English word. He hadn't heard English uttered in Hyperborea in over a decade. Waving his hand to dismiss his guards, the chief administrator took the time to contemplate the implications. A dwarf that knew English and had access to rune magic could only mean that Al Shaytan had brought another group across. Ringing the brass gong next to his throne, two servants sprinted in to do his bidding.

"Draw up and post a reward for the capture of this dwarf and his half-elf companion; five hundred gold pieces if captured alive...fifteen if dead."

The scribe cleared his throat. "Pardon me master but did you mean fifteen hundred?"

Sanguine Bolt shook his head. "No. On second thought, make it fifteen silver pieces. I want these two ruffians alive and if the reward for dead was higher, it would be easier just to kill them for the bounty. I want the hunters to realize how much gold they'll lose if they disappoint me."

The scribe nodded his head. "Yes m'lord. They shall be posted around town within the hour."

Sanguine Bolt leaned back in his throne, deep in thought about home and not for the first time.

* * * * *

Tariq al'Nasir al'Rafiq wondered, and not for the first time, what possessed him to leap onto the underside of the black knight's squire's horse? Internally he knew it was a desperate act of penance for his assassination of Roland. He was truly committed to trying to rescue Calli. He just didn't know why in the world he was still hanging onto the front breast collar of a galloping horse. Of course, if he let go now, he would be trampled underfoot and that would tend to ruin his day. His wounds throbbed and ached but he forced those thoughts aside. At this current time, it took all of his concentration to do two things; keep up the spell that kept him invisible and hold on for dear life.

Just when he thought that he wouldn't be able to hold on for any longer, the horses slowed down to a walk.

Tariq opened his eyes to find that they had entered what looked to be a large military camp with white tents and plenty of soldiers.

The horses came to a stop near the center of the camp and the black knight dismounted. Moving up to the squire's other horse, he casually lifted off the bound form of Calli and entered a large tent without a word to anyone. The well-armed and armored guards on both sides of the entrance had come to attention and saluted with their pikes. Once the knight commander was inside, the guards shifted back into their more relaxed but still very attentive position.

The rider of Tariq's horse hopped down and grabbed the reins of his master's horse and led the three weary steeds off. Unsure of where to go exactly, the assassin waited until they passed behind a large tent with several wagons parked behind it before dropping off. Rolling underneath one of the wagons, he crawled the few feet until he was next to the tent wall and out of sight before collapsing.

Tariq wasn't sure how long he lay there but it was dark when he opened his eyes. Struggling into a sitting position, he studied the camp. Torches and lanterns were lit all around the camp. This really wouldn't complicate his mission, both light sources created flickering shadows which to an assassin was as good as darkness. However, Tariq was weak. Weaker than any other time in his life that he could remember. He felt worse than the time he had run, well actually jogged and walked, the Boston marathon.

Tariq checked the wound on his shoulder. He could hardly move his left arm but the good news was that the gash was only oozing blood instead of running free. Reaching behind with his good hand, he found the wound in his lower back and his hand came away coated in bright red blood. This wasn't good. Now he knew why he was so weak. He'd lost more blood than he realized.

Pulling out some gauze from one of his pouches, he shoved it into his tunic over the wound as best as he could. Sticking his wounded arm inside his tunic, he wiped the blood from his hand on his already filthy robes. Pulling out his enchanted katar, he dialed up one of his most deadly poisons. Taking a deep breath, he summoned up a hidden reserve of strength and slipped into the shadows.

Tariq al'Nasir al'Rafiq of the Hashāshīn Order was going hunting and beware to anyone who crossed his path.

* * * * *

Cassie cursed herself over and over at her foolish behavior. She'd known better than to rush into the open like some lovesick schoolgirl. But she had. Seeing her husband after nearly four years had overwhelmed any sort of rational thought. Thinking back to their brief encounter, she was sure he hadn't recognized her. Of course, she wasn't his Cassie anymore. She was different. She was Callistra, the vampyress, killer of innocents.

She wasn't even sure how Patrick's sense of honor would handle the fact that for her to survive in this land, she needed to drink blood. Only time would tell, but she forced herself to think of herself as Calli. It was a subtle reminder of the changes in her.

Turning her attention back to her dire situation, she studied her surroundings. The knight commander had dropped her just inside his tent and went about his business without a single word to her. Of course, she was still bound by the magical webs and without her wand, she couldn't dispel them. She took a deep breath as she considered her lost wand…again. If she ever got out of this, her powers would be severely limited. At least, she knew how to construct one now, that is if she lived through this.

She was unsure how long she lay there. It was late afternoon when she was carried inside but now it was dark. Servants had arrived to light the lanterns inside the black knight's tent. With the new lighting she took some time to study her adversary.

He was tall and handsome in a rough sort of way but his face and eyes seemed incapable of showing any emotion. When some of his subordinates had been inside the tent, one of them had cracked a crude joke. Everyone laughed, including the Grand Marshal but his smile and laughter seemed forced. His eyes were cold, like those of a shark. The evening meal came and went and still he ignored her. There was a constant flow of soldiers in and out of the tent. It was obvious that the Peacekeepers were up to something. If Calli had to guess, it would be that they were staging an invasion or a major military campaign.

Near midnight, he focused his attention on her. Grabbing a chair, he reversed it and sat down where he could stare at her. Rubbing his chin, "Now my dear, what am I to do with you?"

Since she was still gagged, Calli took that as a rhetorical question and did nothing but return his stare.

After a minute or two, he clapped his hands loudly and two knights dressed in the white tabards of novice Peacekeepers walked in. One had his left arm in a sling and the other seemed to be favoring his left side. The Grand Marshal fixed his eyes on them and gave them the once over before commanding, "Your names?"

The limping guard responded, "Yeltzer, m'lord."

The guard with the sling bowed his head. "Benedict, m'lord."

The Grand Marshal nodded his head. "I see you were both wounded in battle. Crooner's Gap?"

Yeltzer nodded. "Aye m'lord."

Benedict nodded but remained silent.

The Grand Marshal turned his attention back to the bound witch. "You men did well there and you'll be rewarded. I admire your dedication to your duties to assume new roles while injured. I won't forget that."

"Thank you m'lord." Benedict answered. After a brief pause he added, "How may we be of service to you m'lord?"

The Grand Marshal pointed at the witch. "Take her to the prison wagon. I want her placed in cell three and a guard on her at all times. It is now your responsibility. If something goes wrong, you two are to blame. You have no other duties from this moment forward, if your brigade commander has any questions send him to me."

Yeltzer snapped to attention and saluted with his right fist to his heart. "It shall be done m'lord."

Benedict mimicked the salute but just a tad slower.

The two guards lifted the witch and disappeared into the darkness of the camp. The Grand Marshal watched them for a minute before returning to his maps and charts.

* * * * *

Arieal knew the moment she woke up that she was in trouble.

She was bound, feet and hands, with a gag in her mouth and a bag over her head. She could also tell by the motion that she was airborne. Aside from that, she had no idea where she was or where she was going. For that matter, she didn't really know who or why they had captured her. She struggled against the ropes which held her until she felt a sharp whack across her back.

"None of that you demon. We will be back at Akrôtiri shortly and then you can explain your actions to the King."

Unable to talk due to the gag, Arieal realized that she couldn't do anything except wait and wonder. This hadn't been a good day and it didn't promise to get any better.

* * * * *

Tao, Cozad and Kastle moved to the aerie and quickly saddled one of the green wyverns for the priest. Cozad had already saddled Bjørn's red which Tao claimed as his new mount. The Dreadknight was mounted on his buckskin and had the last green loaded down with supplies. Tao nodded. It seemed that Cozad had already thought this through and knew that if they rescued Arieal, she would need a ride. If not, they would need the extra supplies to survive the Wastelands.

Tao unrolled his map. "Judging from the direction you said they were flying, there are only two locations marked on the map along that course, one is marked as Camp One, the other as Akrôtiri."

Kastle asked, "Akrôtiri?"

Tao turned his attention to the priest. "Yes. Why? Is that name important?"

"Well, in the time I've been in Hyperborea, I've done some research into these lands. It seems that Akrôtiri was a city that was destroyed during the Cataclysm, which is what the locals called the magical battle between the High Mage of Atlantis and the Goblin King."

"If it was destroyed, then why is it marked on their map?" asked Cozad. He scratched his chin for a second before adding, "Unless they've converted ruins into their base of operations?"

Tao nodded. "That would be my guess. Anything else you can tell us about Akrôtiri or these bandits?"

Kastle took a deep breath. "Akrôtiri was built on top of a lone butte, kind of like the Devil's Tower back in Nevada. There is only one path up or down so it is nearly impregnable to siege."

"But with wyverns, it would be a perfect base of operations," added Cozad.

Kastle continued. "The wyvern bandits are led by a former companion of mine who crossed over with me. He's a gladiator by the name of Jagoda Wartooth. Alongside him will be Aaliyah, a Sha'ir of great power. Jagoda is angry at Sartael, the Atlantean who is responsible for the murder of his best friend Argos. On that day, he made a vow to have his revenge on Sartael and all Atlanteans. The wyverns and the bandits are just a means to that end."

Tao seemed lost in thought for a minute. "So our true threat is this Jagoda."

Kastle nodded. "Don't forget about the djinns that Aaliyah can summon."

"Or the bandits that he commands," added Cozad.

Tao shook his head. "No. The body cannot live without the head. We must strike at the commander and I have a plan at how we can do it."

Chapter 18

Jerrick was again on gate duty when Adak's hunting party returned with the ebony demoness. He hadn't gotten a great look at the witch but the camp was abuzz with her description. She was supposedly black as ash with snow white hair, on top and below. To hear the other warriors describe her she had the perfect body, a small waist, a plump behind and huge tits. There had been a debate in the chow line earlier if she was a succubus or not. The argument raged back and forth. The most common comments were since she didn't have horns, wings and a tail, she was not in fact a true demon but maybe the spawn of a demon.

Jerrick couldn't wait until his shift was over and could see for himself. He was hoping that Jagoda would open her for use of the soldiers, especially if she was as good looking as the rumors said. He rubbed his eyes and looked out over the wastelands. Aušrinė, the morning sun, was about an hour away from setting and she bathed the desolate landscape with her reddish light. All seemed quiet on the desert floor, as if it wouldn't be. Akrôtiri was located in the middle of nowhere, several days ride from any semblance of civilization.

Glancing to the north, which was also part of his responsibility along with the eastern approach, Jerrick did a double-take. There was a wyvern and rider approaching. Jerrick scratched his head. There weren't any patrols out. Squinting against the morning light, he could tell that the serpent was a large red. He knew that there was only one red currently flying and that had been one of the guys in Adok's patrol. He couldn't remember the brute's name but he was a big son-of-a-bitch.

When the wyvern came to rest next to him, Jerrick was shocked to see that the rider wasn't the big bastard he was expecting but a warrior in the oddest looking crimson armor that he'd ever seen. The stranger's face was covered with a mask of black.

Calmly the scarlet warrior dismounted and said, "I'm here to see Jagoda Wartooth."

Jerrick's partner reacted out of fear and tried to stab the newcomer with his spear. He was dumbfounded at the speed and ease that the warrior drew both swords, one sliced the spear in half, the other disemboweled his partner.

Calmly, the scarlet warrior sheathed both weapons and spoke again. "I am here to see Jagoda Wartooth. Would you be kind enough to take me to him?"

Nowhere in his deepest nightmare had Jerrick ever imagined a crimson demon arriving on the heels of the ebony witch. Not knowing what else to do and having no desire to offend the warrior, he nodded. "Right this way, sir."

Jerrick lead him through the main entrance and through many winding turns. A large procession of bandits fell in behind them. Tao couldn't help but grin. His gamble was paying off.

It wasn't long before they entered a large open air courtyard and Tao's smile fled when he saw Arieal. She was gagged and stripped completely naked. He felt his anger quicken at her treatment. She didn't look like she had been violated, yet. Her eyes pleaded for help once she saw him.

Ignoring his escort and the following bandits, Tao crossed the courtyard and studied her restraints. She was suspended by her limbs by some sort of earthen creature with eight arm-like appendages. It stood absolutely still as Tao approached but he could see that it watched him with its two eyes of coal.

The bandits had stopped at the far side of the courtyard and watched.

Tao realized that the creature must be an earth elemental; a being summoned from a different plane of existence. He racked his brain to try and remember everything he could about elementals, which wasn't really much. Mac had always hated playing spellcasters. He remembered that elementals could only be summoned by an extremely powerful mage and they weren't very intelligent. Their existence on this plane was to serve its master in whatever function it was ordered, without questions or hesitation.

When Tao got within striking range of Arieal, he drew both weapons. The elemental shifted slightly and moved the dark elf to the samurai's right and out of his striking range. The elemental was obviously ordered to hold her securely and to keep her safe from harm.

Tao grinned. If that was true, then he had an advantage. To test his theory, Tao swung his frostbrand katana at the dark elf's midsection. Nowhere near full speed but one that if she didn't move would disembowel her. He could see Arieal's eyes widen in surprise and fear. The elemental twisted the dark elf out of reach and took the blow on its back. A huge chuck of rock flew off.

Tao grinned underneath his helmet and exploded into action. His katana pulsed with hoarfrost as he rained blows on the elemental. Every strike chipped off a piece of the creature. Whenever the creature began to turn back to confront him, Tao would swing one of his swords at Arieal and the elemental instinctively turned away. Within minutes the summoned creature was shrinking as Tao whittled away the soil that made up its body.

The earth elemental made one last attempt to move away from the scarlet samurai.

Tao ki-happed loudly. Leaping high into the air, he landed on its back with his katana gripped in both hands and his body weight driving his enchanted blade down through its head and deep into its body. The elemental shuddered once and fell apart as the magic which held it together was torn asunder by the samurai's attacks.

Arieal fell on top of the pile of rubble that was once her captor and Tao rushed to her side. Tossing aside his helmet, he ripped off her gag. Her violet eyes were filled with tears and Tao found that he couldn't resist the temptation to kiss her. Arieal responded.

Before the two lovers could say anything to each other, the sound of a single person clapping echoed loudly in the courtyard.

* * * * *

Cozad and Kastle flew in from the east. They were careful to keep Saulè, the second sun of Hyperborea, at their backs. This had been Tao's idea. He would land earlier and completely distract the guards. Kastle doubted that he could do it but didn't have a better plan. Cozad had just nodded when the samurai outlined his idea. The only modification he suggested was the mission once they landed. Tao had wanted them as high guard in case things went wrong. The dreadknight had suggested an alternate objective. The two spiritual warriors were to infiltrate the cliff fortress and capture Aaliyah, the bandit's lover and only exploitable weakness.

Kastle had mixed feelings about his part in the plan. By all accounts, Aaliyah was still his friend. It was her words of reason which calmed the volatile warrior on that fateful day three years ago. They had parted as friends even though Jagoda had threatened to kill him the next time they crossed paths. Not having any other options, Kastle agreed to the reckless plan.

They had come in low over the horizon with the twin suns at their backs but it was all in vain. When they had arrived, there wasn't a single guard in sight. Whatever the samurai had done, it had captured the attention of everyone. They landed near the largest and most ornate structure that was still intact. Both warrior and priest had to admire the stonework involved in the construction. It seemed to their untrained eyes that it was a mixture of southwest adobe style buildings and those seen in Egypt.

Leaving their mounts behind, Kastle used one of his spells to locate Aaliyah. It wasn't perfectly accurate but it did point them in the right direction. Mounting the stairs, they heard the sounds of fighting and had to resist the urge to rush to the samurai's aid. They had to trust that Tao knew what he was doing and continue with their plan.

Cozad used his magic to levitate the pair over the thirty foot wall to reach the upper apartment. They landed lightly and could see the Sha'ir on the far side of the balcony watching whatever was transpiring in the courtyard below. The Dreadknight signaled that he would go to the right and moved off more quietly than the priest thought possible.

Kastle paused for a moment to drink in the beauty of Aaliyah. Yes, he had always found Callistra gorgeous in a dark, mysterious way. Nevertheless Aaliyah was just stunningly beautiful with her long legs, blonde hair, small waist, large perky breasts and dazzling smile. It was like trying to decide between a Ferrari and a Lamborghini. Kastle shook his head and took a few steps forward before clearing his throat.

Aaliyah whirled around to face him with her wand raised in preparation of casting a spell before she froze and their eyes met. First, there was confusion. Then recognition and finally, her eyes sparkled.

Kastle knew in that moment that he was still in love with her and that was the real subject of contention between himself and the gladiator. "Aaliyah."

"Kastle? How…"

Whatever else she was going to say was lost to the wind as Cozad came up behind her and entrapped her in an invisible fist of air pinning her arms down.

Kastle hated to do it but he rushed forward and gagged his friend. "I'm sorry."

Her eyes showed a mixture of betrayal and anger. The priest couldn't tell which one hurt more.

Cozad nodded. "That was easier than I feared. Now, let's get below before this spins out of control."

The priest noticed that the dreadknight's eyes were smoldering a pale blue, he didn't know what that foretold but he nodded and lead the way. Kastle was very conscious of the accusing eyes on his back as they made their way down the step and into the courtyard below.

* * * * *

At the sound of the mocking applause, Tao disengaged himself from Aerial and turned to face the bandit leader. The Mac persona immediately compared the warrior in front of him to the actor who played King Leonidas in the blockbuster movie *300*. He couldn't remember the actor's name right off the top of his head but he noted that Jagoda was about the same size and build. Which meant, totally ripped with probably less than five percent body fat.

Jagoda was dressed in the traditional Gladiatorial armor. He was bare-chested while his left arm was covered with a bronze embossed leather bracer, arm and shoulder guard. A weighted net was tucked into his belt and he pointing his flaming bronze trident directly at the scarlet samurai.

"You! How dare you come into my kingdom, kill my subjects and attempt to free my prisoner!"

Tao slowly walked forward to stand in the center of the courtyard. "First, I only killed those who attacked me or my companions. Secondly, you had no right to capture my friend. Thirdly, you are not a king. You are Jagoda Wartooth, a simple bandit leader and an Outlander to this realm."

Tao had questioned Kastle extensively on everything he could remember about Jagoda and Aaliyah before they were pulled into the game. He realized that it might be the difference between getting through to the modern mindset of his opponent or not. However, the first facet of unlocking the past was speaking in English. "I know your secret Leon. That is your real name is it not? The one you left behind when Al Shaytan pulled you into the game."

Jagoda's trident wavered a bit as he tried to recall those memories. It was strange. Jagoda hadn't heard English in almost four years, yet it sounded comfortably familiar. However, everything beyond that seemed more like a dream that he could only vaguely recall. Mere fragments of another life.

Tao kept his hands away from his weapons and turned to keep facing the warrior as the gladiator began circling the samurai. He also kept his voice low and even as Tao continued speaking.

"I know it has been a long time for you. I can empathize with that but I can tell you that it has only been four months in real time. I cannot imagine everything you have been through in this realm but the real world waits." Tao gestured at the dark elf laying at the edge of the courtyard. "Arieal has a family back home. Kids, a job, things she would like to return to. What about you? What did you do for a living back home, before Al Shaytan pulled you into this realm?"

Jagoda hesitated and lowered his trident slightly. "Do?"

Tao could see that the warrior was forcing himself to recall his past, so he kept it up. "Your job. I was a Deputy Sheriff for a small town in Kentucky. Nothing glamorous but it paid the bills."

Whatever Jagoda was trying to recall was lost when he spied Cozad and Kastle enter the courtyard with the magically bound form of Aaliyah in tow. Tao knew at that precise moment that he'd lost him by the expression on his face. One moment it was thoughtful and kind, the next it was full of rage. Jagoda's trident snapped up level with the samurai's chest and he pulled free his net.

"Betrayer!"

Jagoda's first strike was lightning fast but Tao was ready for it. He had hoped to avoid armed confrontation with the gladiator but it looked like that option was past. Tao had assumed the Stance of the Water Spirit, a very defensive and deceptive fighting posture, one that ebbed and flowed like the tide. As Jagoda's strike came in, Tao moved out of its path and back to his original position in a matter of seconds. Instinctively, he knew he could counter-attack but held back. As the gladiator's next strike came in, he rolled away and again assumed his defensive posture.

Wanting to try one more form of diplomacy, Tao called out to his companions. "Kastle! This is her only chance!"

* * * * *

The priest nodded and turned to face the Sha'ir. Without removing her gag, he began to talk.

"I know you care for Leon. You always have. I know that now. I guess I always did but I didn't want to admit it, not to you or to myself. But this isn't about you or me, or what could have been. This is about the future." He paused and thumbed her attention to the crimson samurai. "As you can guess, Al Shaytan has brought another group across. Tao is Callistra's real life husband and she's in trouble. She's been captured by the Peacekeepers. Which is one of the reasons we are here, we need your help to find her. Secondly, the dark elf is one of Tao's companions and Jagoda made a big mistake in capturing her."

Aaliyah's eyes flicked from the priest to her lover and back again. There was fear and concern in her eyes but also a questioning look.

"You have one chance to talk Jagoda down. I convinced Tao to let you give it a try." Kastle's tone changed, becoming softer. "I know he's no longer Leon. I can see it in his every move. I know you can too. Let me guess, his temper has gotten shorter and shorter. He's become more condescending to everyone he views that is lower in stature than himself, including you."

Aaliyah eyes widened but she nodded.

"It's the Chaos Spirit at work on him. A person can only resist for so long but we can discuss that later, if he is still alive." Kastle glanced at the deadly dance happening behind him before adding, "Tao has yet to counter-attack. He will only wait for so long before he must. Once he attacks, Jagoda will not be able to withstand his assault. Trust me on this."

Seeing her nod, Kastle removed her gag and signaled to the dreadknight to release his spell.

With a simple thought, the crushing grip was gone and she could breathe again. She cast a dismissive glance at Cozad before pointing a finger at the priest. "You and I are not through. When this is over, one way or the other, we are going to finish this discussion."

"I wouldn't have it any other way."

Aaliyah turned her attention back to her lover and the crimson samurai. Although she was angry with Kastle she had never known him to lie, at least not about anything important, other than his feelings. She also had no reason to doubt him. In the past four years they had never seen or heard of a dark elf or a samurai in this realm. They had to be Outlanders. Additionally, how else would the samurai know English? As she watched the two combatants, she knew that Kastle was right. Every move that the samurai made was completely defensive and she could tell that he was passing up numerous opportunities to counterattack.

Concentrating her attention on Jagoda's face, she tried to read his emotions. If she had to name it, she would call it rage. She'd seen him like this a few times over the last three years and it was never pretty. The last time was when one of the new recruits had flown his wyvern into Jagoda's prize serpent and injured it, enough so that the Gladiator had to put it down. Jagoda had gone in such a rage that it didn't end until he had killed the young recruit and seven civilians of the town they were raiding at the time. Unsure if she would be able to reach him through his rage, Aaliyah resolved to try her very best. She owed it to him even if he was buried beneath the rage of the Chaos Spirit.

Taking a deep breath, the beautiful Sha'ir stepped into the courtyard.

* * * * *

Tao once again rolled out of the path of the flaming trident. This time it was close enough that he felt the heat from the red-hot fuscina. Tao swung his katana at the gladiator, not with the intent on striking him but with enough force to make him pause for a second.

Tao chanced a glance at his position. They were in the center of the courtyard with about fifty bandits a stone's throw to his left, Arieal was slightly behind him and to his right. Coming down the steps was one of the most stunningly beautiful women he'd ever seen in his life. Tao knew that this must be Aaliyah.

Rolling out of the way of another attack, Tao held his breathe as the bandit-king noticed her and paused in his attacks. Tao was too far away to hear their conversation but watched in amazement as the rage seemed to fall away from the gladiator's face. Aaliyah moved closer until she was in between the two combatants and still she spoke. For a brief moment, Tao thought that they would get through this without any more bloodshed.

That was until, she said something wrong.

Tao noticed it immediately. It was like a switch flipped inside of Jagoda and the rage overwhelmed him once again. Using the back of his fist, Jagoda smashed Aaliyah aside and screamed, "Harlot!"

There is an old saying about *'seeing red'* when letting your anger take over. Mac had only thought it to be a cliché but when the gladiator smacked the beautiful Sha'ir, Tao literally saw red.

Hitting your opponent in battle is one thing, a preemptive strike on a foe is another thing, striking a woman in combat or training is also acceptable but this was none of those. To Tao's personal code of honor, Jagoda's strike on a defenseless female was the act of a bully and he was forced to act.

Shifting to the Stance of the Fire Spirit, a purely offensive stance, Tao went on the attack.

Jagoda did his best to block or avoid the Samurai's attacks and failed. Numerous blows slipped through and scored wounds to his body, none were serious but it was only a matter of time.

Tao continued his assault and worked Jagoda's defenses up high. When the gladiator raised his trident high to block, Tao shifted tactics and executed a jump spinning side kick.

This was another one of TaeKwonDo's signature kicks. Not as flashy as the flying side kick but more useful in combat. The martial artist would leap straight up into the air, chamber his kick by pulling his back leg up to his chest while turning one-hundred and eighty degrees in a split second. As soon as he completed the spin, the martial artist would lash out with his leg, striking with the heel of the foot. The extra force of spinning and the large muscles of the leg combined to make a devastatingly powerful kick. If the martial artist was extremely skilled, and Tao was, the kick would land in a very vulnerable spot on the human body; solar plexus, groin, ribs, etc. which would multiply the effectiveness of the kick.

Jagoda felt all the air leave his lungs as he was catapulted backward several feet. Landing on his back, he couldn't think of anything except the need to breath. At this exact moment, he didn't know where his shield or spear was nor did he care. He just wanted his lungs to work.

Tao followed up his devastating attack by immediately moving to the downed gladiator and placing his swords in an X over his throat but paused before making the final blow when he heard Aaliyah screaming at him to spare him.

Placing his knee on the larger warrior's chest, Tao stared down at his defenseless opponent. "Do you yield?"

Jagoda answered between breaths. "Why would you spare my life? I wouldn't hesitate to end yours."

"I'll give you two reasons. First, Aaliyah asked me to and only the gods know why after what you did to her. Secondly, I'm betting you weren't always this way. This isn't the real you. As Kastle would explain, it is the Chaos Spirit at work inside of you, struggling to take control." Gesturing with his head to the compound around them, Tao continued. "I bet that none of this was in your plan. I don't think you set out to be bandits, it just happened. From what I've been told, an Atlantean killed your best friend and you vowed vengeance. Completely understandable. Nevertheless you had the mentality that the end justifies the means." Tao nodded his head toward Arieal. "Nothing justifies what you did or intended to do to her."

Jagoda looked from the dark elf to Aaliyah. Kastle was tending to her wounds. Judging from the bruising around her tear filled eyes, she had a broken nose. The gladiator focused his attention back on the samurai. "If I yield you will just let me up?"

"Is not the word of a King the same as the law? Or am I mistaken?"

Jagoda tentatively shook his head. Careful not to cut himself on the razor sharp blades at his throat. "You are not wrong."

Tao searched his face for any of the tale-tell signs of Jagoda's earlier rage. Not seeing anything he asked, "Then I can let you up?"

"You can let me up."

Tao slowly removed his blades and stepped back. Surprisingly, the Gladiator didn't immediately get up but laid there checking his wounds. Once Tao had put about twenty feet between him and the defeated warrior, he sheathed his blades and turned his attention to Arieal.

* * * * *

Jagoda watched the crimson samurai move away with barely disguised hate. It had taken every ounce of control to keep it off his face. There was no way that he was going to forgive the humiliation he received from this peasant, especially since it happened in front of his men. The samurai must die.

Shifting his gaze to Aaliyah, he watched as she let her injuries be tended to by the false priest. Kastle wasn't there because she was injured. He was there because he wanted the Sha'ir. Seeing how tenderly he touched her made his blood boil. Aaliyah was his woman. No one was allowed to touch her without his permission.

Glancing around, Jagoda spied his trident a mere foot away. Rolling over, he grabbed it, whispered a word of command and it burst into flames. Hurling it with all his might, it flew straight and true right toward the priest's back.

* * * * *

Once again, Tao moved with such lightning speed that it was amazing. The samurai had suspected that the gladiator had given in too easily and remained on high alert. One skill that both mindsets, Mac and Tao, practiced religiously was Iaijutsu which is often translated roughly as the *'art of mental presence and immediate response.'* It is the Japanese martial art of drawing the sword. It was designed for the samurai to be ready at any moment for combat. To draw and cut with the same motion greatly enhanced readiness.

Tao used this skill to cut the flaming head of the trident off in mid-flight, just a few feet short of its target.

Cozad had also reacted, though not as quickly nor as flashy as the samurai. The dreadknight knocked the two friends aside and brought his weapon up to a ready position. The flaming spines of the broken trident harmlessly bounced off the huge blade of the dreadknight's axe.

Both Kastle and Aaliyah were shocked and realized in that instant if it hadn't been for the quick actions of Tao and Cozad that they would've both been skewered.

"That's twice you have vexed me! Not again!" Jagoda roared. Drawing his bronze sword, the Gladiator charged the samurai.

Part of Tao regretted his next action for a long time to come. He instinctively knew it was necessary and even unavoidable but that didn't make it any easier to live with. Jagoda's rash charge was basically the same as *'suicide by cop'* back in the real world. Tao didn't have any choice but to act. That didn't lessen the fact of taking a life. Killing in combat is one thing. He'd done it dozens of times in Desert Storm. He'd even done it several times since being pulled into the Game but this was completely different. Jagoda had dropped all pretense of defense and ran at him.

The bandit-king made one downward swing which Tao blocked with his mastercrafted wakizashi which shattered the weaker blade. The samurai reacted out of pure instinct and immediately counterattacked. His frost-kissed katana slid straight through the Gladiator's unprotected chest and ruptured his heart.

Jagoda Wartooth was dead before his body hit the dirt.

Chapter 19

Tariq moved through the Peacekeeper camp with ease. That first night, wounded, tired and in pain, he had gone in search of death. His intention had been to kill anyone and everyone in his path in a vain attempt at rescuing Calli.

Tariq shook his head. He still didn't understand why he was here trying to rescue the witch. She wasn't his lady. Hell, he hardly knew her. So why was he risking his neck for her?

The memory of his assassination of Roland the paladin flooded his mind and he knew why he was wandering around the enemy's camp in disguise. Atonement.

Forcing his mind back to the matter at hand, Tariq or Benedict as he was now called moved through the chow line. His wounds were healing nicely thanks to the medical care of the Peacekeepers. A grim smile flickered over his face as he recalled how he had gained his robes.

On that first night in camp, Tariq had stumbled across the medical tent and found some poor sap sitting with his back to the door and no one else in sight. It was a simple matter to slice his throat and pull him into the darkness. He noticed that the victim had similar enough wounds to himself. But more importantly, that he was wearing a chadri, type of burqa that covered the entire face except a small region around the eyes. Tariq recalled that all of the attackers back at Crooner's Gap had been wearing similar head coverings but hadn't given it much thought. Now with this dead body at his feet, a crazy plan began to form. Stripping the body, he checked for any tell-tale marks or tattoos, there weren't any. He disposed of the body in the nearby pig pens, knowing that the omnivores would make short work of the corpse.

Donning the soldier's garb, he returned to the medical tent and was bandaged by the Peacekeeper healer. He attached himself to the platoon of injured soldiers and spent the next few days following orders. It was rather simple to blend in. So, he followed orders and scoped out the camp. It was obvious that the Peacekeepers were preparing for something big but what that was, neither he nor his bunkmates knew. Even though Tariq had gotten himself assigned to the guard detail on the prisoner wagons, he hadn't found a chance to talk to the witch alone.

One thing for certain, Calli was in bad shape. None of the Peacekeepers had touched her but it was obvious that she was getting weaker by the day. They brought her three meals a day which she politely refused. Tariq knew why she wasn't eating but couldn't say anything for fear of discovery. He knew that as a vampyre, Calli couldn't gain any nourishment from eating normal food. She needed blood to survive.

Seeing the cook preparing to head out to the pens gave Tariq an idea. Putting on his best smile, he flagged down the cook. "Gavin!"

The large cook paused and turned back. "Yes?"

"I just wanted to thank you for your wonderful food."

Taken back by the compliment, Gavin grinned. "Thanks"

Tariq flexed his injured hand. "Between your fare and the doctor's care, I'm getting my strength back." When Gavin didn't respond, Tariq continued without pause. "It just so happens I have a few hours before my next shift and I was always taught to return kindness with kindness."

Gavin looked around doubtful and wiped his hands on his already filthy apron.

Tariq gestured with his chin. "I see you are heading out to the pens. Need any help in the slaughtering?"

Gavin's face brightened. "Help? Hell yes. I can always use another set of hands around here." Grabbing a second cleaver, he gestured for the assassin to follow him. As Tariq moved to follow, the cook pointed to his mask. "Don't forget your chadris. You don't want Jericho to see you without it until after your vows."

Tariq nodded and pulled the mask up. "Thanks. Even after all this time, I have a tendency to forget."

Gavin grinned and showed off his missing teeth. "No worries. All you recruits forget from time to time." Turning, he headed back out to the pens. "Now, have you ever slaughtered a pig before?"

Tariq shook his head. "No. But I'm a fast study."

"No worries. It isn't unlike killing a deer. We'll start by stunning them with a mallet, then slice their throats and drain their blood before removing the hair. All this before the butchering begins."

Tariq took a deep breath as the large cook continued to ramble on about the art of slaughtering a pig.

* * * * *

Calli was in a bad situation.

She had heard of the Peacekeepers, everyone in Hyperborea had but she had never considered the possibility of being captured by them. She knew that the Peacekeepers were from the Westlands and only recently had made their way into the Forestlands. She had even attended one of their revivals last season and was shocked at what she had heard. It was the rhetoric of hatred. Sure it was subtle but it was there.

The orator was talented. During the sermon he began to talk about the good old days and how they were a time of prosperity. Once he had the crowd agreeing with him, he switched to the problems across the land, such as the bad weather or poor crops. Then, he picked on someone to blame for all the problems. First, he blamed the Dragon Kings. Never mind that according to Hyperborea legends, all humans were descendants of the Atlanteans. Once the crowd was agreeing with him, he switched to blaming the elves for the bad weather and the dwarves for the poor crops. Soon, it was everyone who wasn't aligned with the Peacekeepers.

The scariest thing for Calli was watching the simple and peaceful farmers become a mob at the behest of his words. If a lone elf had walked into the tent that night, they would've torn him apart with their bare hands. Having seen that, Calli knew that she had to keep the fact that she was a vampyress a secret. If the Peacekeepers discovered her affliction, she was dead. However, if she didn't feed soon, she was dead anyway. She was in a quandary and didn't know what to do or how to get out of it.

Hearing movement outside of her cell, she placed her back to the wall and waited. The food slot popped open and in fell two pink objects that landed with a squish. The slot closed quickly and she heard the soft sounds of footfalls fading away. But still she hesitated, that was until the overwhelming scent of blood filled her nostrils. Moving closer, she studied the pink objects in the steady light of the four glow stones hanging in her cell.

Glow stones were a magical lighting source that gave off light but no heat. No chance of accidentally burning down a house. They were popular with peasants since they were cheap to purchase and tended to last a full year before needing a refreshing spell.

The pink objects turned out to be pig bladders full of blood. It was either a trap or she had a friend nearby. As she picked one up, she noted that on the outside of the bladder a symbol had been traced in blood. It was a colon, a dash and a parenthesis :-) the smiley symbol used all across the internet. The image of the injured guard with the dark eyes who had escorted her to the cell came to mind. She racked her memory for a name.

Benedict. As is Benedict Arnold? The turncoat? Holy shit! Tariq was the guard!

Lifting the first bladder to her mouth, she bit into it and felt the still warm fluid run down her throat. Almost immediately, she felt strength returning to her limbs as the blood did its work. But it was hope for tomorrow which truly fueled her soul. She had a friend nearby and she knew that Tao was outside the camp somewhere. She just had to bide her time until one or the other freed her.

Chapter 20

Tao ignored everyone as he lifted the limp form of Arieal and carried her inside the dilapidated fortress. Subconsciously, Tao could hear the mixed cries of disbelief and outrage from the bandits over the death of their leader. However, it was nothing but white noise to him. A friend was injured and her safety was all that mattered at the moment. Wandering through the winding passageways of the ruined palace, he stumbled across the renovated chambers of the harem with a large bathing area.

Fully armored, Tao stepped down into the steaming water and gently lowered the dark elf into the water. She was either unconscious or fainted, he didn't know which and at this moment, he didn't care.

Seeing that she wasn't going to slip underwater, he climbed out and quickly stripped down to his loin cloth. Gathering up a sponge and soap from a nearby shelf, he reentered the pool and began the process of cleaning the dark elf. All of her wounds were superficial, minor cuts and bruises but it was the injuries to her soul which mostly worried him. She had been helpless and humiliated, two things that weren't particularly good for a person's soul.

As he sponged down her perfect ebony body, Tao felt himself getting aroused and the guilty feelings that came along with that. She was his friend and she was injured. Not to mention that he had just learned that his wife was still alive. He had no reason to be lusting after another woman. Of course, one part of his mind knew that psychologists had always argued that there was a correlation between combat and sex. Something to do with how the brain was affected. That didn't excuse his condition or his guilt. But here he was, fully aroused and yearning for the dark elf's body.

* * * * *

Arieal had passed out sometime during the battle between the Gladiator and the Samurai only to awaken at the gentle touch of Tao and the warm water caressing her skin. Cautiously looking around, she noted that she was in a sandstone room with tapestries and drapes covering the walls. A large pool lay in the center of the room which is where she was floating and Tao was sponging her down.

It was a strange feeling.

Annie hadn't been with a man for nearly twenty years and had never even considered having an affair on her current girlfriend. Her little romps with Tao over the last few days had been strangely satisfying but this…this was more erotic than anything she had ever imagined. She just closed her eyes again and enjoyed the feeling. Letting her mind drift back over the events of the last few days, she thought about everything that had transpired. Now that she had time to think about it, even her kidnapping and being put on display stripped naked was slightly stimulating.

Giving in to her lust, Arieal reached out with one of her hands and grabbed Tao's manhood. As he started to object, she grabbed him with the other and pulled him down into a kiss.

He resisted for all of about five seconds before giving into his own carnal desires.

* * * * *

Kastle watched as Aaliyah moved over to Jagoda's body. He tried to sympathize with her as she mourned his death. Even before they had crossed over, he and Leon weren't friends. They were cordial to each other but that was about it. Richard had always thought that Leon was overbearing and rude but the others had liked him.

His relationship with Aaliyah was different. They had always been friends. He had always hoped for more and had been working up the courage to ask Ashley out when they had been brought across by Al Shaytan. However once Leon, in his Jagoda persona, got a good look at Ashley in her Aaliyah persona, he began to flirt with her. Richard found that even as Kastle he was shy around her. In the end, she became Jagoda's lover and he found solace in Calli's arms. Now here they were standing together over his body and Kastle really didn't feel any remorse over her loss. He had sympathy for what Aaliyah was going through but that was about it.

Feeling uncomfortable with the silence, Kastle looked around and spied the large group of bandits standing around. Pointing at the closest bandits, he commanded. "You two! Find a shield and come here! The rest of you, gather some wood for a funeral pyre." Seeing them hesitate Kastle added, "Now!"

As the bandits scurried off to do the priest's bidding, Cozad placed a gauntleted hand on his shoulder. As he turned to face the dreadknight, Kastle absentmindedly noted that his eyes were glowing a soothing yellow although his voice still sounded as if it was coming from beyond the grave.

"Take her away from here. She should remember him at his best, not like this." The priest started to object but Cozad interrupted him. "Go. I will handle the funeral preparations. It will be at sundown."

Seeing the wisdom in his words, Kastle led the sobbing Sha'ir back into the palace. She walked stiffly, content to be escorted. Once they reached her bedchambers, she sat on the bed and finally looked up. Her eyes and cheeks were red from her crying and the faint blackness around her eyes from her broken nose could still be seen.

Personally, Kastle never thought she looked more beautiful.

Finally, she choked out a question. "Why....why did you come here?"

Kastle had been expecting this question and answered quickly. "We need your help."

"Why? Why me?"

Kastle shook his head. "Not us...you. Only you have the power to save Calli." Seeing her start to object, the priest waved her silent. "Let me fill you in on my new companions."

Aaliyah listened patiently without interrupting. When Kastle was done and leaned back, she asked. "Let me get this straight. You originally needed my help to find Tao and his companions but during your journey you ran across the Peacekeepers and they captured Calli, which is in fact Tao's real life wife?"

Kastle nodded.

"Does he know that you two are lovers?"

Kastle paused for a split second before shaking his head. "That was over a long time ago. Besides, it was never more than a physical thing between the two of us. Neither of us were looking for a commitment..."

"Looking or incapable?"

"Looking. Calli was, and is, still in love with her husband. And I...well, let's just say I wasn't looking either and leave it at that."

Aaliyah thought about pressing him more on the matter but the fact that he wouldn't meet her gaze once more gave her the answer. Ashley was still puzzled about why he hadn't pursued her once they crossed over. She knew that Richard was extremely shy; especially around women. It had taken nearly six months of gaming together before he would even talk to her about anything that wasn't game related, even when they found themselves adventuring as a duo. She leaned back and studied her old companion as he made himself busy in the small room.

Once they crossed over, she thought he would change and become more aggressive and confident. He was, in every area except her. He still seemed unsure of himself when talking to her. That's when Jagoda entered the picture. He was charming, witty and a smooth talker, both on this side and back home. He had tried his charms on Calli. She was cordial but cold to him. However, Ashley was unused to all the attention and fell prey to his charms. She knew that now. She had known it for months. But she found herself stuck in an unwinnable situation in a foreign land and had strived to make the best of the situation.

The reality of the situation suddenly hit her. She was free. Free to do what she wanted. Free to talk to whomever. Jagoda had been intensely jealous and once killed a man because he had whistled at her as she strolled through the town. That had been six months ago and since that time, she had sequestered herself in the palace and only came out at Jagoda's bidding. Now she could go anywhere and do anything.

She looked back at Kastle and felt a longing for him. She didn't realize how much she missed his friendship until this very moment. Maybe it was his shyness, maybe it was the euphoria of freedom but suddenly she knew what she wanted and she wasn't going to wait on him any longer.

Standing slowly, she noted that the priest stopped in mid-motion and looked up at her. He had kept himself busy and gave her the personal space she needed by making tea. The water was steaming and he had set out two cups. But she had no desire for tea. Stepping up, she wrapped her arms around his neck and pulled herself up and pressed her lips to his.

Kastle hesitated for a split second in surprise but when he responded she was overwhelmed at the passion in their first kiss. A second followed and third. After that Aaliyah lost count as she let her passion loose and they didn't know anything else for hours.

Chapter 21

Mathias glanced over his shoulder once again. His half-elven nature granted him excellent vision. As long as there was some sort of ambient light he could see relatively well, even the reddish glow from the twin suns setting in the distant east. "We're still being followed."

Gamble cursed again. Since it was in dwarvish neither of his two companions understood exactly what he said but his tone spoke volumes.

Pixi popped back into view. "The forest is probably less than twelve kilometers miles away. Unfortunately it's mostly uphill."

Gamble held his sides as he struggled to catch his breath. "Have they gotten any closer?"

Mathias peered at the trackers through the fading light. Unable to make out fine details, he could tell that a group of ten, maybe twelve, soldiers were following them but they were still a good distance off.

The twin moons of Hyperborea had already climbed into the sky about an hour ago but when the night truly fell, the companions would be forced to slow down. Granted, Mathias's night vision and Gamble's darksight would allow the trio to keep moving but the companions had been on the run constantly for almost a full day with very little rest or nourishment and they were tired, especially Gamble. His short legs and stout frame were not designed for long distance running.

Mathias turned back to his friends. "They're still a bit off but making steady progress. They have us outnumbered by at least three to one."

He gestured at the flat plains around them and added, "We cannot make a stand out here in the open."

Gamble nodded. "I know…I know. We have to make it to the safety of the trees." Taking another deep breath, he nodded as he began to move forward once again. "It would just be easier if I knew why we are being followed."

Mathias nodded but didn't say anything else as the three friends once more began their run toward the imagined safety of the forest.

Chapter 22

When the twin suns sank below the Hyperborea horizon, they lit the sky afire. Maybe it was the elevated position of Akrôtiri or the remnants of the magical battle which had turned this region into the Wastelands but whatever it was the sunset was spectacular. None of the Outlanders had ever seen a sky with such dramatic colors. Even the bandits who were used to the strange sights of the Wastelands were moved at the sight. No one could ever remember seeing a more red sky. Normally, there were mixtures of purples and yellows but not tonight. It was red on red and highlighted by more red.

Everyone was gathered in the courtyard around a large pile of logs which were neatly stacked about waist high and as long as a man. Just as the first sun completely disappeared behind the horizon, the doors to the palace flew open and out came Jagoda's corpse. He had been cleaned up and dressed in his finest battle array before being laid to rest on his shield which was carried by Kastle and Cozad.

About ten paces behind came Aaliyah. She was dressed in a black silk skirt with a long slit up one side for ease of movement. Her matching halter top of black silk accented her bare stomach and shapely figure. She was carrying Jagoda's bronze helmet which had been polished until it gleamed and reflected the burning sky. Even though the faint traces of her broken nose and tear filled eyes could still be seen, none could deny Aaliyah's beauty, including Arieal.

The dark elf had even tried to hate the Sha'ir. She was just so beautiful, almost painfully so, but Aaliyah had such a wholesome quality about herself that disarmed everyone she met. Arieal had been forced to talk with her about borrowing some clothes since those she arrived in were ruined. Within ten minutes of meeting the Sha'ir, Arieal felt as if they had been friends her entire life.

The last to enter the courtyard was Tao. He was bearing the broken parts of the gladiator's enchanted trident. Kastle and Cozad placed the corpse on the unlit pyre and stepped back to stand next to Arieal.

Aaliyah paused and looked down at the body of her dead lover. Feeling slightly guilty at the tryst she had enjoyed with Kastle, she contented herself knowing that she hadn't betrayed him while he was alive. Leaning down, she kissed him one last time and slid the bronze helmet in place before stepping back to stand beside Kastle.

Tao had stopped several feet short of the pyre and watched the Sha'ir say good-bye. When she was done, he moved forward and placed the broken trident on the chest of the corpse and turned to face the gathering. Scanning the crowd, he noted that there were only one or two who would even meet his gaze and they only did that for several seconds. Tao felt that this was less a sign of guilt and more a habit learned for self-preservation. Everything he had heard about the dead gladiator spoke of someone who would interpret eye to eye contact as a challenge. Tao let the silence linger and the bandits get nervous. He knew from conversations earlier that day with Kastle and Aaliyah that prolonged periods of silence with Jagoda heralded fits of uncontrolled rage which usually only ended with someone's death. Taking a deep breath, he began. "My friends, it might seem strange for me to be the one to deliver Jagoda's..."

He wanted to say eulogy but found that there wasn't a similar word in the native tongue of Hyperborea. When they crossed over each Outlander had gained certain skills that they could access without conscious thought, speaking the common tongue of the land was one of them. They didn't even realize they were speaking another language until something like this would pop up. Realizing that he had paused longer than intended, he tried again and gestured to the four outlanders and Jagoda's corpse.

"Many of you know that we are Outlanders to Hyperborea. Where we come from it is customary to have someone speak in behalf of the deceased. Usually it is a family member or close friend who would stand up and tell a story from the past. Only Kastle and Aaliyah knew Jagoda before they crossed over but neither wish to speak tonight."

Tao paused and gestured to beautiful blonde. "However, Aaliyah asked if I would speak in behalf of the fallen warrior. Jagoda 'Leon' Wartooth didn't start out to be a bandit. This I know. I've talked with his friends. Even though I never met Jagoda before this morning, I know the type of man he wanted to be. He was a man of strong convictions and strong emotions. These were both his boon and his bane."

Glancing down at the corpse, Tao paused for a moment as he searched for the right words.

"When Jagoda's best friend was killed by an Atlantean, he made a vow of vengeance. There was nothing wrong in doing so and it was completely understandable. Nevertheless Jagoda let hatred into his heart and it corrupted his mission. It corrupted him. Jagoda was a gladiator, a man of iron principles. He didn't set out to become the man you knew, a common bandit. I'm sure it was a gradual process, committing some small infraction or sin in favor of the mission, under the guise that the end justifies the means."

Tao gestured at all those gathered. "That was wrong. What right do you have to raid simple farmers and traders? Does might make right? Where is the justice in that?"

Tao studied the bandits again. Many were looking around at each other with guilty looks over their faces; however some looked angry at his words. Tao made a mental note about those who looked upset.

"Preying on the weak stops now. I will not let Jagoda's legacy be that he was a bandit. By the gods, he was a man of honor. I will return that honor to him."

Tao gestured to Kastle and the cleric lit the pyre. The flames greedily ate the dry timber. Those gathered stayed and watched for a few minutes as the fire consumed the corpse. One by one, the crowd broke apart. Many of the bandits headed to their quarters needing the time to think on what the future would hold for them now that Jagoda was gone. Some headed to the saloon, one of the only renovated buildings in Akrôtiri. Both Tao and Cozad noted that the ones which seemed the most upset by the Samurai's words were in this second group.

Tao nodded to his companions and the Outlanders spilt into three groups to attend to their assigned tasks.

Aaliyah and Arieal headed to the stables. It was their job to make sure that none of the bandits stole any of the horses or wyverns. Tao believed that this would be the night of the most desertions and he planned on making sure that no one made off with any of the flying serpents. Also, Tao wanted to see if the two spellcasters could look in on their missing companions. He knew that Mathias, Gamble and Pixi should be on their way back to Camp Five by now.

Cozad and Kastle had the hardest part. They were to contain those bandits which went to the saloon and use their best judgment on how to deal with them. Cozad just nodded at his orders, truly understanding what the deadly samurai meant while Kastle was confused.

The priest believed that there would be trouble. Those bandits which went to the saloon were probably the ones that enjoyed the pillaging the most, the thugs and cutthroats. Kastle briefly wondered what they were supposed to do, that was until he saw the grim look on the dreadknight's face and the smoldering purple glow of his eyes. That's when Kastle realized that if push came to shove, they were to use deadly force to gain compliance.

By sending the two of them, Tao had taken himself out of the equation. He could become the focus of their hatred and rage but by not being there, he wouldn't be the spark the bandits needed to ignite their anger. It was devious. It was smart. It was a masterstroke of strategy and Kastle was impressed.

* * * * *

Tao watched as Cozad and Kastle departed. The two spiritual warriors made an interesting duo. They were like two sides of the same coin. Both were powerful servants of their gods and he knew that if the bandits stepped out of line, they would be able to take care of any problem.

Which brought Tao's attention back to his own problem.

The majority of the bandits had gone back to the barracks. It was his job to figure out what to do with them. He didn't particularly want his own army but he just couldn't leave these brigands leaderless. Without a strong, honorable leader they would be back raiding the peasants of the region within a week.

Entering the barracks was a mixed feeling of stepping back into time and walking into his own memories from his time in the Rangers. It seems that barracks in ancient days and modern times were nearly identical. There were rows of bunk beds down each side of the building and two footlockers could be seen under the lower bunks. Of the twenty or so men that were housed there, twelve were gathered in the back of the building around a table; four were playing cards while the rest sat around drinking and talking. Tao had made sure not to wear his armor since it seemed to intimidate the men and that wasn't his intention. He quietly moved through the barracks but paused just shy of the bright light around the table. It seemed that the bandits were discussing his speech as they played cards.

A young bandit with dark hair and a beard played a card and drew two from a nearby deck. "I think the red warrior is a devil. How else could he defeat Jagoda?"

A burly warrior with a bald head and a ragged scar down the left side of his face said, "I don't know nor do I care. All I know is that he isn't one of us, therefore he has no right to lead."

The young guard that was on duty earlier that morning when Tao arrived slammed his fist on the table upsetting the cards and coins. "Dammit, Jagoda was an Outlander and you followed him. What's the difference?"

The burly warrior glared at him. "Jagoda promised to make us rich."

Seeing his cue, Tao stepped into the light. "And how's that working out for you?"

All the bandits jumped at his voice and many drew their weapons. Tao ignored them, picked up a fallen chair, reversed it and sat down at the table. Leaning forward on the back of the chair, Tao looked around. To all appearances the samurai seemed completely at ease and comfortable at the table.

One by one, the bandits sheathed their weapons and returned to their seats. However, it was Jerrick who spoke first. "What was that m'lord?"

Tao shook his head. "First off, there isn't m'lord this or m'lord that, its Tao or Captain if you must. But let's get back to your comment. Jagoda promised to make you rich, correct?"

Tao saw several heads nods. "How's that working out?"

Most looked around, obviously uncomfortable with the conversation but it was Jerrick who finally broke the silence. "Umm...well, it hasn't actually happened. I mean, we've done plenty of raids but we haven't seen any of the profits."

Tao nodded. Reaching into his belt pouch, he pulled out a small leather bag and dropped it on the table. The clink of gold was unmistakable to the bandits. "That doesn't surprise me. I haven't completely searched the fortress but I did find several chests of gold in what used to be Jagoda's quarters. It seems that he'd been keeping the lion's share of the profits."

Tao saw a few of the bandits get slightly upset at his statement. Was it the thought of Jagoda short changing them or the fact he just insulted their former commander? Not that Tao really cared. It was the truth. He'd found out long ago that the truth wasn't always popular but that wasn't his problem. Hell, Cassie used to get onto him constantly about how abrasive, or blunt, he was in conversations. A wave of mixed emotions rolled over him at that thought. Guilt concerning his resent tryst with Arieal, concern over Cassie's whereabouts and even the joy he found with the knowledge that she was still alive.

Bringing his attention back to the matter at hand, Tao gestured at the pouch of gold. "There is a bag like this for each of you, considering we come to an agreement. Consider it payment for past services rendered."

The burly bandit placed both fists on the table and leaned slightly forward. "Listen here little man, this gold is ours. Won through our blood and sweat, not yours. It isn't yours to give away."

Tao locked eyes with the bandit. He'd been expecting a challenge of some sort. This was it. He let a small smile creep over his face but he was positive that it didn't reach his eyes. "The way I see it, you have three choices. You can take this money and depart Akrôtiri." Tao held up his fingers as he counted down their options. "You can work for me for the betterment of Hyperborea and receive triple this amount, or you can bitch and moan some more and leave Akrôtiri flat broke in the morning."

The burly man with the scar grinned. "You left out one option. I could throttle you right now and take all the gold. Then we could live like kings in Antioch."

Tao calmly looked around and saw that the braggart did have the support of at least three of the bandits judging from the ice cold glares that they gave him. Five looked to be on the fence as to support him or not, while the remaining looked to be against the burly braggart.

Tao nodded. "You're right in the fact that I did leave out an option but you're wrong in your description. The final option is that I kill you where you stand and anyone else that raises a hand against me. Then, I go back to my first three options to those left alive."

The burly warrior grinned. "I'd like to see that. We have…"

Whatever else he was going to say was lost as the samurai executed a perfect draw and slice. Technically, the attack was called tameshigiri and Tao had used the tsuihei, horizontal cut. His frost-kissed katana streaked out of his scabbard in a perfect arc and severed the braggart's neck. Blood sprayed all across the table and barracks as the headless corpse fell backwards. The severed head flipped through the air for several seconds before landing with a loud thud.

After the initial shock from Tao's preemptive strike, the three bandits who were the braggart's buddies drew their weapons and hesitated. Yet, none were eager to attack after what they had just witnessed.

"Damn fool." Without so much as a sideways glance at the headless corpse or those bandits with weapons drawn, Tao calmly sheathed his katana and turned his attention to Jerrick. "Did you understand my warning?"

"Yes m'lord…I mean, Captain."

"As I was saying before I was rudely interrupted, I have need of brave souls but I will not lead bandits into battle. I need soldiers. Those who stay with me need to know that I expect them to walk bravely into the dragon's lair but they should also know that they will be well paid."

Tao picked up the small bag of gold and stood slowly. Making eye contact with each man in the room he added, "Those that want to depart should see me in the courtyard for their severance pay. But be advised, you will not be leaving here with a wyvern or horse. I will make sure you have transportation to a local port but that is it." Tao focused his attention on the guard Jerrick. "Those that stay on will receive back pay and further instructions concerning our mission." He started to walk out but paused and looked back. "You have until dawn to make your decision."

Jerrick jumped up and rushed forward. "I don't need until dawn. I pledge my sword to your cause."

"What is your name son?"

"Jerrick."

Tao handed him the bag of gold. "Consider yourself promoted. Meet me in the courtyard an hour before dawn." Without saying another word, the deadly samurai departed the barracks.

* * * * *

The tavern fell silent when the two spiritual warriors stepped into the room.

There was nothing special about this building. It was built of sandstone like every other building in Akrôtiri. But long rows of tables filled the room and along one wall were three huge kegs of rum. The tavern was nearly half full, probably thirty bandits, all armed and already drinking.

Without discussing his plans with the priest, Cozad moved into the center of the tavern and planted his axe. Raising his voice, his eyes smoldered a bright purple. "Listen here scum. You have two options before you. One, follow Tao's leadership and get paid or leave Akrôtiri. Those that choose to leave, have two options… walking or feet first. This is not negotiable."

Kastle walked up to him and shook his head. "That was real diplomatic."

Cozad shrugged. "It was the truth…plain and simple."

"But you didn't take time to explain it. They deserve to know what the risks are and the rewards."

"Why? They are nothing more than random elements of the Game."

Kastle shook his head. "No, they are living breathing beings with feelings and dreams of their own."

"So you say."

"I have lived amongst them for nearly four years. They are as real as you and I."

Cozad looked back at the bandits. His eyes glowed red. "No, they aren't."

The gathered bandits were confused and nervous watching the two armored warriors argue. Finally, one of the bandits had enough and made a break for the door.

Cozad saw the peasant running and stopped him cold with a single spell. Using a *'Word of Power'* curse, the dreadknight channeled his magical energy into the curse which caused the young bandit's heart to explode.

The rest of the patrons quaked in fear. It was one thing to fight an opponent. It was another to watch a buddy fall dead with a single word.

Even as they pulled out their weapons and contemplated their options, Cozad lifted up his axe. Kastle stepped between the dreadknight and the bandits with his hammer at the ready. "No. They have the right to choose."

"They are nothing but peasants. They live and die by our whims."

"No, that isn't true. They have a right to live. Anything less and you are as bad as any tyrant from back home. Do you see yourself as another Saddam Hussein? How about Hitler? Do you want to start carting them off to the gas chambers just because they have the wrong eye or hair color?"

The Dreadknight paused at the names of the infamous dictators. Even if the Cozad mindset didn't know who they were, the Ed mindset did and the simple accusation of being compared to the architects of modern genocide was sobering. Whatever it was, it forced the Edward mindset to the forefront and Cozad's eyes stopped glowing. "Maybe you are right, priest."

Kastle took a deep breath and stuffed his hammer back into his belt. "The Chaos Spirit is strong. You must constantly be on guard against its influence."

Cozad hesitantly nodded. "I shall try priest, I shall try. Now deliver Tao's offer and let us be gone from this place."

Kastle pulled out a sack of coins and tossed it onto the closest table. Once he explained the samurai's offer, the two spiritual warriors departed and the bandits were left to discuss the offer among themselves.

* * * * *

Arieal and Aaliyah both summoned a servant to guard the entrances to the stables. Aaliyah kept it simple and summoned another Earth Elemental. Since Arieal didn't have a body handy, the dark elf summoned a Shadow to do her bidding. A Shadow is an incorporeal creature made entirely of sentient darkness. Its touch saps the strength of living creatures and appears as a patch of mobile gloom with a more or less humanoid shape.

They set their servants to guard the door and moved inside talking. Arieal filled in some of the highlights of the last four months back home. Nothing political or sports related but more about the latest fashions and celebrity gossip…typical girl talk. Once they were situated, the two spellcasters joined hands and calmed their minds.

The plan was simple.

Aaliyah would summon a Jann to search for Arieal's missing companions. The advantage of a using a Jann was that it was a purely magical creature formed from the four basic elements of the world. It would be more powerful and intelligent than a typical elemental but not as strong as a true Djinn, nor as fickle. True Djinni are formidable servants but resist servitude and tend to twist their instructions ever so slightly. Janns were different. Since they were only called into being by the power of the spellcaster, they relish the chance to serve.

However, what made this summoning different was that Aaliyah didn't know anything about the people she was sending the Jann to locate other than what she'd been told. Which wasn't really enough to safely send a true Djinni. On the other hand by using their magic to meld or align their minds, Arieal's memories of her missing companions would influence Aaliyah's summoning and enhance the odds that the Jann would find them quickly.

At least that was the plan. It was still a long shot but it was all they could do at the moment.

* * * * *

Arieal did her best to relax. It was scary to think of someone else entering her mind and having access to her memories. She forced herself to think of this as a medieval version of the Vulcan Mind-meld from the classic television show *Star Trek*. Concentrating on her breathing, just as she had been instructed, Arieal felt the onset of the merge and it was nothing like she expected. Arieal had expected it to be intrusive but it wasn't. It was like warm water flowing through her mind and filling up her senses.

Suddenly, she wasn't alone and for that matter, she wasn't Arieal any longer. She was Annie and Ashley was with her, hand in hand, as they walked through her memories. At first, it was Arieal's most recent memories. Primarily her latest liaison with Tao. As the two of them watched, Annie found that she wasn't embarrassed at all. If anything, she was slightly aroused.

Ashley gave her hand a squeeze and pointed to one side. Annie glanced over to see Aaliyah's romp with Kastle. Evidently, the merge went both ways and even as they delved into her memories, they would see some bleed over from Ashley's mind.

Memory by memory, the two spellcasters worked their way back until Ashley felt that she knew Gamble, Mathias and Pixi. In the process, Ashley got to know Annie intimately. Her wants and desires. Her fears and doubts. Everything that was Annie and Arieal. The more Ashley got to know her, the more she liked her. Annie felt the same way. The merge not only helped Ashley learn about her missing companions but helped Annie discover the truth about how Ashley had survived in Hyperborea.

Having the information she needed, Aaliyah broke the connection and leaned back. Coming out of the trance was sobering and slightly lonely. Having another person's thoughts, feelings and memories in your mind was strange but at the same time comforting. With a flick of her wand, Aaliyah's Jann was off to do her bidding.

Now all they had to do was wait. The Sha'ir lowered her gaze and offered the dark elf a mischievous grin.

Arieal wrapped her arms around the gorgeous blonde and leaned in. Aaliyah lifted her face and their lips touched. Moments later, their clothes were thrown aside as they began exploring each other's bodies just as they had their minds earlier.

Chapter 23

With the lightening of the sky, the fleeing trio knew that dawn was approaching and they were just plain tired. They hadn't made the safety of the forest nor had they lost their pursuers. In fact, more hunters had joined the chase and a second, much larger, force had moved across their intended path. Destroying their plans to escape into the solace of the trees. Only the darkness had truly hidden them from their pursuers but now with sunrise quickly approaching, the Outlanders were getting desperate.

Pixi popped into view overhead. "They're getting closer."

Between heavy breaths Gamble asked, "Which group?"

"Those behind us."

"How far to the ruins?"

"Less than a kilometer."

The dwarf nodded. "We can make it."

Mathias looked to the southeast. "We better. The other group has changed directions and is moving toward us."

Gamble looked in the direction the half-elf was pointing but couldn't see anything, not that he doubted the Archer. He just looked out of habit. Taking one last deep breath he grumbled, "Let's get this last sprint over with."

Without another word, the companions started running again. They knew that their only chance of survival was to reach the ruins ahead of their pursuers. Outnumbered as they were, solid defenses would be the only thing between a short battle and a quick slaughter. Even then, their odds were abysmal but surrender wasn't an option.

Even as they traveled the last hundred feet or so to the ruins, Gamble scoped out the defenses with the expert eye of a stonemason, courtesy of his dwarven mindset. It was once a tower of some sort and the remnants of a stone spiral staircase could be seen protruding above the walls by twenty feet or so, which would probably be a good perch for Mathias' archery. There was only one true entrance to the ruins but the attackers could climb over the walls easily enough since they ranged in height from eight to fifteen feet. It wasn't a perfect location for a defensive stance but it was the best they could hope for under their current situation.

The truly frustrating part was they didn't even know why they were being chased. They hadn't robbed or killed anyone nor broken any laws that warranted this much attention. Which left Gamble to deduce that it was because they were Outlanders but that thought carried its own set of worries.

Pixi interrupted his thoughts. "Okay, we're here. Now what?"

Gamble reached into his pouch and pulled out his last five runestones. He looked them over with an experienced eye. The first two were primarily utility spells, light and darkness, but they could still be useful. The next two were offensive spells and could prove extremely helpful, web and stun. However, both were limited to one attacker. His last runestone was a powerful but fickle buff spell. Gamble hated to rely on something so unpredictable but he didn't see any other choices. His mind made up, he gestured to the ruined stairs.

"Mathias, climb up there and make it costly anytime they get too close."

The half-elf skipped up the stairs, looked around and judged the range. After a few seconds he returned to his friend's side. "No problem. There's enough elevation to give me a clear field of fire for their entire approach except the last twenty feet or so. The real problem is that I only have eighteen arrows left."

Gamble grinned. "They don't know that. Just make sure not to waste any of them and the bloodier or more gruesome your hits are, the better. We need to make them fear us."

"I can do that but it's only a temporary reprieve and you know it."

"Aye, that I do." The dwarf lifted up one of his runes. "This is a Serendipity runestone. Once the attack starts, I'm going to cast it and hope for the best."

Pixi had enlarged herself to near normal size and was currently visible when she asked, "What does it do?"

Gamble shrugged. "I have no idea."

The teenage faerie cocked her head to the left and chewed on the inside of her lip for several seconds before asking, "What do you mean by that?"

"Back home in the game, everyone nearby would gain bonuses to all stats, rolls, attacks, defenses, saves, et cetera. Additionally, some sort of random beneficial effect would happen." Gamble paused for a second and flipped the small stone in the air. "Traditionally speaking serendipity means a 'happy accident' or 'pleasant surprise' specifically the accident of finding something good or useful while not specifically searching for it. Oddly enough I know that serendipity was once voted to be one of the hardest words to translate or accurately describe."

Mathias grinned. "So, you're gonna cast it and hope for the best."

"Yep, unless of course you have a better plan?"

The Archer shook his head. "Nope. Sounds like fun."

"That it will be," replied the dwarf. "As to the rest of the plan, it's simple, don't get dead."

Pixi giggled. "Great plan. Let's do it." Flapping her wings, she shrank down to her smallest size and disappeared from view.

Mathias just nodded to his friend and climbed back up the ruined stairs.

They didn't have to wait long. Within ten minutes both groups began to converge on the ruins. Gamble did a quick head count, there had to be at least thirty hunters between the two groups. Luckily for them, they seemed to be arguing. Just when he thought that they could just slip out over the back wall, he spied several soldiers being sent out to guard for just that sort of action. They were trapped.

Now that they were closing in on the ruins, Gamble got his first real look at the pursuers. With the exception of the two leaders and one old man, they looked like out of work soldiers; men who had fallen on hard times and turned their military skills to mercenary work. The only good news was that he only spied three crossbows in the whole lot and no long bows. That meant they would have to get up close and personal, which was a slight advantage.

Even as Gamble was trying to figure out the best way to handle their attack, Mathias' bow rang out and one of the lead mercenaries fell to the ground with an arrow protruding from his throat. His screams echoed through the gathering and stopped them in their tracks. He was a long time dying and it was bloody and noisy; just what Gamble had asked for. Of course, it's one thing to desire something and another thing to see it in effect. The poor man was suffering but it was buying them some much needed time. That was until the two leaders stepped forward. One ended the injured man's suffering with a quick slash of his sword while the other one began cussing out the hesitant soldiers. Then, one by one, the mercenaries commenced their attack and Mathias' bow began to sing.

Out of some old habit, Gamble whispered a portion of Psalm Twenty-three. "Ye though I walk through the valley of the shadow of death, I shall fear no evil, for you are with me..."

He kissed the magical rock, spoke the command word and tossed the Serendipity Runestone on the ground.

"I hope you work." Drawing his twin daggers, he called on one of his Skald special abilities and faded into the shadows. He wasn't completely invisible like Pixi but it would hide him from view from the first soldiers through the opening. Even though he could no longer see them from his new vantage point, he knew when the mercenaries began their charge by their blood curling screams and the sound of heavy boots on the ground.

Within seconds, they breeched the open doorway and the battle was joined in earnest.

* * * * *

Grigoris had watched in silent resignation as the gamers wrestled with the hazards of being inside the game. He was both saddened and proud of the twin sacrifice made by Bjørn and Moira in the face of such insurmountable odds. Yes, they had killed themselves but in doing so, they had gained a moral victory. They had died like they had lived, together.

Now he watched as a trio of gamers, or Outlanders as they were now called, defiantly face overwhelming odds. None of the three had even considered the possibility of surrender. They were determined to face their assailants head on. That was a quality he had to admire.

Nonetheless, Grigoris was most proud of Tariq. After committing such a heinous act as to murdering another gamer, he had acted unselfishly in trying to rescue the witch, Callistra. But now, Grigoris knew that his brother's greatest pawn was moving against the witch and the assassin. He didn't want to lose them, not when they were both fighting valiantly to regain their humanity.

Grigoris sat down with his legs crossed in front of the silver mirror. Folding his wings around himself, he focused all his attention and limited power on sending a warning to Tariq. The seraph knew that if his spell worked and slipped past the magical barriers that kept him bound to this tower, the assassin would be warned about the impending danger. If not, his spell's energy would just add more power to al'Shaytăn.

Not to mention that Grigoris would lose two very powerful pawns of his own and his game pieces in this realm were very limited.

Chapter 24

Tariq al'Nasir al'Rafiq watched the rising of the twin suns of Hyperborea with mixed emotions.

He was glad in the fact that his current shift was over and he could get some much needed rest. But saddened by the fact another day had passed without an opportunity to break Callistra out of jail. Which meant another day inside the Peacekeeper camp. The only bright side had been that he believed that he'd found a weakness in their perimeter. He hadn't worked out all the particulars of the jail break but a plan was forming in the back of his mind.

Tariq was heading to the mess hall to grab some breakfast when a horse and rider came galloping into camp and nearly ran him over. Without so much as a sorry, the rider leapt from the horse and rushed inside the Grand Marshal's tent. There was nothing unusual about riders coming and going but this one was different. In the first place, the horse looked about to die from exhaustion. The messenger had obviously ridden it hard, long and unforgiving. Secondly, the clothes of this messenger were completely different. He wore the colors and tabard of the Peacekeepers but these were of the finest silk and not rough spun cotton.

Oddly enough, Tariq felt a weird pricking sensation in his fingers.

A long forgotten quote he last heard in Mrs. Rector's English class in South Boston High School came to mind, *'By the pricking of my thumbs, something wicked this way comes,'* MacBeth, Act Four, Scene One.

How or why he suddenly remembered that, he had no idea. He also had no notion what the sensation meant but for some reason he suspected it to be a bad omen. Especially since the pricking occurred with the arrival of the Peacekeeper messenger.

Not one to ignore a gut feeling, Tariq stepped behind the nearest tent and checked his surroundings to make sure the coast was clear. Seeing no one nearby, he called on one of the innate abilities of the assassin class and faded from sight. Moving silently, he crept up to the back of the Grand Marshall's tent and knelt down. Pulling out his dagger, he cut a small hole in the fabric and peered inside.

* * * * *

Grand Marshal Jericho had been studying maps and planning troop movements when the royal page burst in. He hadn't been expecting a summons from his master but then, the Overlord could do as he pleased.

The royal page walked in and handed him a glass orb. Without a single word, the messenger pulled out his dagger and plunged it deep into his heart. The page died without a word.

Jericho dropped what he was doing and moved to the center of his tent. Kneeling down onto one knee in what he hoped was a submissive pose, he crushed the orb in his right hand and dropped its contents on the dirt floor. Smoke and broken glass swirled throughout the room like a mini tornado, knocking things over and blowing loose paper all around. Jericho didn't dare raise his face or try to shield it from the flying glass. Either action would be seen as disrespectful to the Overlord.

After several minutes the wind and smoke died down and coalesced into the image of a heavily hooded figure. When the Overlord finally spoke, his words seemed hollow and devoid of any emotion. "Report."

"Master. The trap set against the bandits of Crooked Creek was a great success. Casualties among the new recruits were approximately twenty-five percent. The rest of your troops will be in place to eliminate the remainder of the bandits in two days."

The image of the Overlord cocked his head to one side. "I sense that you're holding something back."

Jericho swallowed hard. "Although the trap was a success, we encountered stiff resistance from a strange trio; a holy man in blue armor, an assassin and a dark haired witch."

"And?"

"A wyvern rider in red armor."

The Overlord shook his head back and forth slowly. He gave the Grand Marshal the same disappointing look a parent would give its child when it's done something it knows to be wrong. "I warned you about the wyvern riders."

Jericho glanced up. "It was unavoidable. The red warrior crashed his serpent into my men and proceeded to cut through them like a scythe through wheat."

The smoky figure made a slight gesture with his left hand, a kind of choking motion and the Grand Marshal couldn't breathe. "That sounded like an excuse to me. You know I don't believe in excuses. Give me one good reason why I should let you live?"

Jericho clawed at the unseen hand that was choking the life of him. He knew he didn't have long before he was dead. He only had one chance. Between gasps for air, he croaked out. "I captured the witch. I captured the witch."

The Overlord relaxed his crushing grip ever so slightly, not enough for his subordinate to move but enough where he could breathe. After all, Jericho had always been loyal and useful.

"And why is some witch worth sparing your life?"

Jericho sucked in the precious air and struggled to get enough breath so he could explain. "There is something special about her. I can't explain it but I sensed it. The same could be said about the red warrior who decimated my men."

The Overlord had his *'Hand of Force'* squeeze hard again and Jericho found himself lifted several inches off the ground and unable to breathe once more. "First off, they are my men...not yours. You live and die at my whim. Your only purpose is to serve me...understood?"

Jericho couldn't answer but managed a weak nod.

"Secondly, you better be right about this witch or I will be very angry. You wouldn't like me when I'm angry. Trust me on this." The Overlord released Jericho and the warrior fell to the tent floor in a heap. "At dawn tomorrow, my courier will arrive. Have her ready for pickup."

Jericho shifted position enough to nod and whisper, "As you command Master."

* * * * *

Even as the Overlord ended his spell, Tariq shifted the small segment of the tent back into place and quickly added a few whip stitches from his handy sewing kit to keep the fabric in place. Sliding away from the Grand Marshal's tent, Tariq ducked behind a nearby wagon and dropped his invisibility spell.

Entering the mess hall, the assassin ate his morning meal automatically as he digested everything he heard and saw. If he had any hope of freeing Callistra, it had to be before the courier arrived. The logical side of him also realized that he needed a least a few hours of sleep before attempting the jail break.

For good or ill, he was going to try his crazy plan. He didn't have time to come up with anything else.

Chapter 25

Even as the twin suns of Hyperborea began to creep higher in the morning sky, Tao and his friends waited in the courtyard for the rest of the bandits to make their decision known.

A small group of ten bandits lead by Jerrick had joined the Outlanders before dawn. They were mostly the young idealists that had been recruited by Jagoda with the promise of throwing off the yoke of slavery; not that any of them had actually been slaves. They had always been told that they were serfs to the Atlantean Empire and they believed it. After some intense questioning, Tao had discovered that none of them had ever seen an Atlantean nor had they ever paid tribute to the Dragon Kings. It was just something they were raised to believe and so they did.

That left thirty-one bandits unaccounted for...Tao shook his head. Actually the count would be twenty-nine. He'd forgotten to subtract the two idiots both he and Cozad had killed.

Tao frowned when he realized that he'd so easily dismissed the killing of the young braggart. That was a slippery slope and he didn't want to fall into apathy over killing someone. Even though part of his mind kept telling him that this was nothing more than a game and everyone was just part of the intense computer graphics. Of course, the rational side of him argued against that thought. Their blood looked and smelled real enough, as did the sounds of their death screams.

Hearing movement from the tavern, he buried his doubts. He was a soldier. It was his job to fight and die for his country. He didn't have to like it but he did have to do it. That was one of the mantras he'd told himself over and over during his time in the 'Sandbox'. It might be harsh but then survival in a time of war was harsh. And like it or not, Tao knew that they were basically at war while they were stuck inside the game.

Even before the bandits stepped into the light, he knew what to expect. Greed had taken hold of their hearts and they had found courage in the bottom of a bottle of strong spirits. So when they stepped into the courtyard with bared blades he wasn't surprised.

Nevertheless, Kastle was. The priest leaned his head toward him and asked, "Tao?"

The scarlet samurai ignored him and turned completely around to face Jerrick and the new recruits. "No matter what happens or is said, you are not to draw your weapons. Period. I don't care if they call you by name or insult your mother, do not draw your weapon. Even if they rush forward and attack one of us, do not draw your weapon. Only if they get past me or my friends and are threatening your life are you authorized to draw your weapons. Understood?"

Jerrick nodded. "Aye Captain."

Tao cocked his head to one side. "I'm serious about this. If any of you cannot follow this simple command, then you will be dismissed from my service. No questions and no excuses."

"Understood Captain." Jerrick answered more forcefully and glared over his shoulders at his squad. "It will be as you command."

"See to it."

Tao turned his attention back to the waiting mob and stepped out to meet them.

Kastle matched his stride.

Tao began making a mental list of the little nervous nuances each bandit displayed. From the beads of sweat on their forehead or upper lip, to which ones nervously shifted their weight from side to side or fidgeted with their armor or constantly fiddled with their weapons. All these 'tells' foreshadowed what each bandit was planning on doing if it came down to battle. Tao didn't do this consciously but unconsciously as part of the blending of the Samurai warrior spirit with his own military training. When they were about ten feet away, the two Outlanders stopped and stared hard at the waiting bandits but neither of them drew their weapons.

The mob stopped moving and slightly bowed itself around them in a slight semi-circle. No one talked or moved for several minutes. It seemed as if they were waiting for something. Tao knew what it was even if they didn't. The mob was waiting for a spark, a reason to attack and by not being threatening; neither Tao nor Kastle had given it to them...at least not yet.

After several long agonizing minutes, Tao finally spoke. "You have two choices before you, live or die. It's as simple as that. I gave everyone here a chance at greatness but no...you wanted to be greedy. So that offer is gone. I also gave you a chance at a life away from here with a small fortune but no, you wanted more. So that offer is gone also. You now have two options left, turn away and live or stay and die."

Finally one of the bandits took one step forward. "Do you really think that you'll be able to stop us? All of us?"

"Probably but it's not me you need to worry about. It's him." Tao grinned and pointed to one side.

Even though the bandits were suspecting a trick, they couldn't help but look.

On cue, Cozad stepped out of the shadows. However, the darkness seemed to cling to his frame and slowly drip off his armor like black raindrops off a hot tin roof. It was chilling to witness, even for those who had crossed over with him.

The bandits looked back at the samurai and then back at the dreadknight. Fear was clearly written on their faces.

"Still can't decide?"

Tao signaled again and the ladies stepped into view, one on each side of the bandits. Each spell caster was flanked by their minions. Aaliyah by two Earth Elementals, the easiest to summon considering their location, and Arieal by the animated corpses of the bandits Tao and Cozad had killed last night. It was a frightening sight especially since the bandit that Tao had decapitated was carrying its severed head in one hand while the other held a sword.

It was also at this point when the bandits realized that they were surrounded.

"Still like your odds?" Tao asked. When they didn't answer the deadly samurai continued as if they had. "You still have a chance to leave here alive but the door of opportunity is closing fast. Those that wish to live should drop your weapons and move over to the Elementals." When no one moved, he added more forcefully. "Now!"

Seven bandits hesitantly did as they were told and moved out of the mob. The rest gripped their weapons with sweaty palms and looked around with wide-eyed expressions.

Tao shook his head. "Maybe I didn't explain myself well enough." Turning his back to the mob, he faced his new recruits and singled out Jerrick. "Did you understand my proposal?"

Jerrick nodded. "Yes Captain."

Tao turned back to face the hold outs and rested his hands on the pommels of his swords. "Well they understood and your comrades understood. Therefore, I can only guess it is one of two things; either you want to die or you're too stupid to know how close to death you really are."

Tao nodded subtly to Cozad and he took his cue.

Calling upon the dark powers at his command the dreadknight summoned his pet gargoyle. The sight of the winged demon crawling its way out of the flaming pit of darkness was enough for the rest of the bandits. Dropping their weapons, every single one of them rushed to the safety of the Earth Elementals.

Kastle moved up beside the samurai and whispered, "Nice bluff."

"It wasn't a bluff. That was their last chance."

After setting his pet to watch over the cowed bandits, Cozad joined them. "You should've just let me kill them. It would've been easier. After all, they're nothing but NPCs."

Tao knew the acronym stood for 'non player characters' – a generalized term that referred to any character in a game that wasn't an actual player. It was a holdover from the old pen and paper role playing games like *Dungeons and Dragons*. He also realized that Cozad was struggling with the same problem he was, accepting that everything around him was real. After all, they were inside a game. Why should they care what they did to non-players?

Kastle shook his head. "I can tell you after living among these people for the last four years, they are not just computer generated images. They have lives, dreams, worries and problems just like any person back home."

Tao nodded and said, "If you prick us, do we not bleed? If you tickle us, do we not laugh?"

Cozad cocked his head to the side. "Huh?"

"Shakespeare, the Merchant of Venice."

Kastle grinned. "I vaguely remember that play. Wasn't the character Sherlock?"

"Shylock, a Jewish moneylender but that isn't the point. I don't remember the whole play but that line always stuck with me, especially while I was in Iraq. It was hard not to hate all Iraqis or Kurds or Sunnis or whoever was shooting at us on any given day. But whenever I felt my hatred threatening to overwhelm me and I wanted just to group everyone in the same pot and kill them all, that simple line came back to me time and time again."

Cozad asked, "Why?"

"Everyone is an individual. Each person is responsible for his or her own actions. Those that took arms up against me or my brothers were the enemy. Everyone else was just trying to live with the cards that had been dealt to them. They just wanted to survive, day by day…just like us."

The dreadknight slowly nodded. "You're trying to convince me that these peons are really people and not just sheep that need to be slaughtered."

The deadly samurai just shrugged his shoulders but remained silent.

Kastle rubbed his chin with his right hand as he thought about how to best explain his position. "Look, try to accept the fact that your natural viewpoint on this side will be colored by the Chaos Spirit. It may not seem that way but it's a fact. It is part of your burden for choosing an avatar of Chaos during character creation." The priest shifted his attention to Tao. "But don't discount the Chaos Spirit just because we didn't start our avatars that way. You saw what happened to Jagoda. There's an old saying; power tends to corrupt and absolute power corrupts absolutely."

Tao nodded. "Lord Acton."

Kastle cocked his head to the side. "Who?"

"Lord Brandon Dalberg-Acton, an English politician from the turn of the century."

The priest shrugged. "Wow. I didn't know that. I was quoting from the Superman-Batman comic book."

Cozad chuckled. "I thought that you were quoting from the Marvel X-Men comic books from the Phoenix storyline in the late Eighties."

"Either way, the concept is the same. If you stay long enough on this side, you will learn that we are far more powerful than any of the general populace and even most of the rulers." Kastle gestured at his soul bound hammer. "And these weapons are like WMDs when compared to anything else in the land. Trust me on this."

Tao chewed on his lower lip for a second. "Sounds like there's a story behind that remark…"

"There is."

"Later. Right now we need to get these guys sorted out before one of them decides to act stupid."

The two spiritual warriors nodded and moved off to implement the next part of the samurai's plan.

With Jerrick's help, Kastle began sorting out the subdued bandits into smaller groups. Cozad and five of the new recruits headed to the aerie to saddle up some wyverns. The plan was to disarm, blindfold and shuttle them to different locations, far away from Akrôtiri. No one group would have too many of the troublemakers in it nor would they be left in the middle of the desert to die. Each group would be dropped off safely, with their weapons, water, food and two pieces of gold per individual.

Tao knew that it was actually going to be a logistical pain in the ass to complete but it was the only way he could come up with to safeguard the civilians of the region. Even with the difficulties of the plan, Tao wished that finding and rescuing his wife would be so easy. He also wished, and not for the first time, that Marvin was back. He needed his oldest friend's advice. He wondered if Aaliyah's servant had been able to locate his missing friends but before he could ask, Jerrick signaled for him and he began the process of putting out fires. A leader's job is never done.

* * * * *

Gamble took advantage of a brief lull in the assault to assess their situation and bandage his wounds. None of his injuries seemed critical but the gash on his forehead hurt like the dickens. However, it was still better than the alternative of decapitation.

The three of them had proved to be a formidable trio and had repelled the hunters' assaults twice. He wasn't sure if they could or would be able to stop their next charge. Mathias was completely out of arrows, he was out of runestones and throwing knives and Pixi was low on power. To top that off, all three were wounded and tired.

The only two positives in the whole situation had been that they had killed or severely wounded over half of the attackers. Unfortunately, that hadn't been enough to convince them to retreat. If anything, it had infuriated them even more. In the first assault, not a single attacker had carried a bladed weapon. They'd all been using clubs, which had actually helped the trio in their defense. For some reason, the hunters were going for crippling attacks.

They didn't know why but the Outlanders had taken full advantage of that fact and repelled them.

The second attack the hunters had tried to flank them with a small group attacking the opening while two larger groups had tried to climb over the walls. It was obvious when Pixi appeared out of thin air and burned them, that they hadn't been expecting the faerie. Two of the surviving hunters had lost their clubs in the conflagration but pulled out swords and attacked. They both died but not before wounding the half-elf and the dwarf.

Gamble looked out at the remaining hunters and recognized what they were planning. Turning back to his friends, he steeled himself for the upcoming argument but knew they didn't have a choice. "We won't be able to stop the next charge."

Mathias finished tying off the makeshift bandage on his thigh and nodded. The dressing was already blood-soaked but he ignored that fact. "You figure they'll do a mass charge?"

"I would. We've stopped the last two and that's the only thing they haven't tried."

Pixi was currently visible and near normal size. "So? We'll stop them." She pointed at the surrounding corpses. "Look what we've already accomplished."

Mathias shook his head. "No. We won't be able to stop them this time. It's simple numbers. When they rush forward en mass, they will completely swarm over the defenses and us. And there's nothing we can do to stop it."

Gamble nodded. "Except one thing."

Pixi raised one eyebrow. "What's that?"

"Mathias and I can keep their attention on us during the fight, which should allow you to slip away and find Tao. You have to tell him what's happened."

"No! I won't leave you!"

Mathias frowned but nodded. He had realized the truth of their situation just as the dwarf had. "It's the only way. What we cannot change we must endure."

Pixi stopped protesting and thought about what he'd said. "That's a good philosophy."

Mathias snickered. "I wished I had come up with it. My fiancé is an avid reader. It's a line in some romance novel she was reading. I can't remember the author or even if it's an exact quote but it stuck with me."

Gamble couldn't pass up the opportunity to jab on his friend. "A romance novel that SHE was reading…right." The dwarf nodded and grinned. "I believe that."

The half-elf's eyes went wide and the slight flush of embarrassment rolled over his fair skin. "Seriously."

"Hog wash!"

Whatever either of the friends were going to say next was forgotten as they spied movement in the hunter camp. Their attackers had fanned out and were moving towards them. They knew that they only had seconds until they charged. Gamble turned back to the faerie.

"It really is our only hope. If you don't tell Tao about the hunters he'll never know what happened and he might even send more of our friends into Antioch. However, if we do survive their attack and are captured, it'll be up to you to make sure we're rescued."

"But…but…"

Mathias pulled his twin matching daggers and moved to one side of the open door. "Good-bye Pixi...Whitney. I hope to see you again real soon."

Gamble moved to the opposite side. "Take care of yourself ya little Limey."

Pixi hated the thought of leaving her friends behind but she knew that they were correct. Someone had to escape and warn the others. She was the logical choice but that didn't mean she had to like it. Calling on the innate abilities of her faerie avatar, she shrank back down to her smallest size, about six inches or so, and turned invisible. Flying straight up to a height of about fifty feet, she hovered and watched. She might not be able to help them but she wasn't going to abandon them, at least not without knowing the whole story.

Mathias and Gamble looked out at the rushing mob of hunters. There was no give in their eyes, only rage. They had been humiliated with their futile assaults and meant to redeem themselves this time and their payment would be blood. As the first two hunters rushed through the open doorway, the Outlanders struck.

Even as the hunters fell, two more took their place. Gamble and Mathias tried their best to remain near each other for a better defense but as more bodies poured through the doorway or over the walls, they were forced apart. They blocked and parried, stabbed and slashed, dodged and jumped to the best of their abilities but they both knew the end was near.

Suddenly the very ground beneath their feet began rumbling, violently. So much so that everyone, attackers and defenders alike, were knocked down.

Someone yelled, "Earthquake!"

When the stone doorway came apart and reformed into a vaguely humanoid shape, Gamble seriously doubted that was what it was. The stone creature surveyed the area but didn't move. That was until two stupid hunters attacked it. Anyone with any sense would have realized that attacking a thirty foot tall creature made of stone with a two foot piece of sharpened steel as a futile gesture. Maybe that was their last thought as the stone creature shifted its form and slammed twin pillars of spinning rock down on top of them...squishing them like a bug.

That was enough for the rest of the bounty hunters as they broke formation and fled into the wilderness. The rock creature seemed to watch them flee for several minutes before it shuddered once and broke apart.

Gamble looked over at Mathias. The half-elf simply shook his head and shrugged his shoulders. He had no idea what had happened. Of course, the old saying about 'not looking a gift horse in the mouth' came to mind. No matter why it had happened, they were alive and that meant they had something to be positive about.

* * * * *

Sanguine Bolt shook his head as he listened to the reports from his hunters.

It was obvious that earlier reports about the Outlanders had left out one important fact. That they had a spellcaster with them, a wizard by all accounts and one that was very skilled in elemental magic. This was both good and bad. Good in the fact that the wizard might be strong enough to help him but bad because Sanguine Bolt had missed an important opportunity due to bad intel, or should he say incomplete intelligence.

He had tried his best to organize and train his own brand of intelligence network. They were nowhere near as sophisticated as MI-6 or the CIA but they were getting better. They were the ones who had discovered the Outlanders in his city in the first place. He made a mental note to chastise them about not realizing that they had a spellcaster with them but then it was his own fault for not taking that possibility into consideration himself. The only glimmer of good information had been from the old tracker that had been leading the chase.

When everyone else had fled, the old tracker had hunkered down and watched. Sometime around midday, a flight of wyverns had arrived and picked up the Outlanders. The old tracker had watched them fly off to the west before returning to Antioch.

The involvement of the wyvern riders was peculiar. By all reports the bandits preyed on anyone weaker than themselves and particularly focusing on anyone aligned with Atlantis. However the really odd part was that he'd never heard of them returning to pick up stranded warriors. Just one more thing that was strange about the whole situation. Plus, he had to take in consideration the latest reports about a large force of Peacekeepers camped near the small hamlet of Crooked Creek. He knew that the religious order was becoming more and more militant and sooner or later would take a stab at Antioch. It was the only logical reason for them to be operating in this region.

Wayne, or Sanguine Bolt as he was known in these lands, leaned back and contemplated the strange circumstances he found himself in. One day he was Alpha testing a new game and the next he was trapped inside that same game. However, it was in this realm where he really seemed to flourish and he found that the organizational skills he gained from his years of working in the Human Resources department of an up and coming software company began to pay off. He'd been able to pair his management skills with his new found magical abilities and work his way through the Wizard's Guild. Originally in Atlantis but after Sartael stole one half of the Dragon Orb and the calamity that followed, Sanguine relocated to Antioch and proceeded to take over the Wands.

It would really help if he could figure out what Al Shaytan's endgame was or at least what his next move would be. After all, he was the true enemy. The Outlanders and even the Peacekeepers were just pawns in his little game, just like the Goblin King and the High Mage of Atlantis had been a century before. Sanguine Bolt's real challenge would be figuring out how the new Outlanders fit into Al Shaytan's grand plan or if Sartael was directly involved somehow.

Not one to shy away from dangers, Sanguine Bolt rang the gong next to his desk and in rushed his servants. He didn't even look up as he began giving orders. "Prepare my gryphon. I will also need supplies for a full week, although I don't expect to be gone for more than a few days. Alert Vladimir over at the Guild of Blades that he's covering for me for the foreseeable future. When he asks, be vague about my whereabouts."

Jareal had been his manservant for the past ten years and knew the drill. "I'll give him the usual spiel that you're off communing with the spirits. He won't ask any more questions after that."

"Good…there are a few things I need to take care of and I think it's past time that I visited my wife again."

Jareal kept his gaze averted. He didn't want to see the pain in his master's eyes at that confession but at least he knew what to expect when his master eventually returned. He'd been through this before and would be prepared.

Chapter 26

The twin suns of this strange land had already set when Tariq al'Nasir al'Rafiq set his plan in motion.

When Yeltzer and he, as Benedict the injured Peacekeeper initiate, had been assigned the task of watching over the prisoner, they had divided the detail into two equal shifts, day and night. Tariq had let Yeltzer think he was getting his way when the Peacekeeper had chosen the day shift. Tariq had wanted the night shift. As an assassin, or a Hashashin as he was properly called, he felt more at home in the darkness than in the bright sunlight.

Arriving late to relieve Yeltzer had been part of his plan. The Peacekeeper would be hungry and race off to the mess tent instead of hanging around to chat. At least that was the plan. As Tariq limped up, he made sure the new bandages were visible to his counterpart.

"Sorry about being late, the Sawbones took his time in changing these out."

"Dammit Benedict, I'm hungry."

Tariq shook his head and hunched his shoulders in what he hoped would be a sympathetic gesture. "I know, I know. Tell you what, sleep in an extra hour." He lifted up his bag of rations. "I packed plenty of food since I knew I would miss chow with my visit to that quack of a doctor."

Yeltzer brightened up at his suggestion. "Seriously? Thanks. I'm sorry about all the mean things I said about you over the last quarter hour."

Tariq laughed. "No worries. I'm sure I deserved it."

Yeltzer smiled and disappeared into camp.

Tariq opened the food slot and pushed in another pig's bladder full of blood. He waited for at least a half hour before opening the door for two reasons. First off, he really didn't want to see her feed and it took him that long to pick the lock. Back in the game, as an assassin he had the skills of a typical thief but he didn't really waste his limited skill points in pickpocketing or lockpicking. Those weren't typically useful skills for an assassin, at least not back in the real world when he sat in front of his computer screen playing the game.

Opening the door, he got his first good look at Calli. She was pale, more so than normal, but seemed no worse for the wear. "M 'lady, your carriage awaits."

Calli rushed forward, surprising the assassin with a hug. "You're a sight for sore eyes."

Tariq returned the hug and moved aside so she could exit the cell. "We need to get moving just in case someone swings by." He handed her his bag. "There's an extra robe inside with another chadris to hide you from prying eyes as we make our escape."

Callistra simply nodded and slipped on the baggy clothes but paused when she went to put on the hood due to the horrendous smell. "Ugh...where did you get these?"

"The medical tent. Its original owner won't have any more need of it." He made the cutting of the throat gesture with one hand and turned back to the cell. He pulled free all four glow stones, wrapped them in a blanket before stuffing them in his bag. Tariq relocked the door and turned back to her. "These might come in handy and if someone just glances in, they won't be able to see if you are inside or not. It might buy us a few more minutes."

Calli just nodded and fell in behind the assassin as he moved through the camp. He walked quickly, like someone on an important errand and no one stopped to question them. He wound his way through the camp and even seemed to backtrack on himself before ducking behind a wagon that was parked near the picket lines.

Hidden in the lee of the wagon, he pulled off his Peacekeeper robe and hood. Throwing them into the back of the wagon he grinned at her. "Although they were useful, I'm happy to be rid of those garments." Reaching into the wagon he produced two backpacks and an assortment of weapons; daggers, swords and bows. "I couldn't find you a wand but hopefully you can use some of these."

Calli pulled off her disguise and grinned. "I'm from the hills of Kentucky. I know my way around a bow. Personally, I prefer a compound but this recurve will do nicely."

She tested the pull. It was stiffer than what she was used to but she felt that she could still fire it. Slinging it over her shoulder, she strapped on both quivers of arrows and four daggers. She knew that she wasn't really familiar with a sword but she grabbed one anyway. Without her wand, her magic was severely limited so she would have to rely on weapons and her martial arts skills.

"Okay, what's next?"

"Here's the situation, whoever Grand Marshal Jericho answers to is sending some sort of messenger to take you back to his base of operations. It's supposed to arrive at dawn. So we need to be as far away from here as possible. On top of that, the Peacekeepers are about to attack Crooked Creek."

"We have to warn them."

"That's the plan. I wasn't able to get my hands on a map but I did get a glimpse of one. Crooked Creek is due west of us but I'm unsure of the exact distance. Logically, Jericho would've tried to place this staging area close enough to get to the village with an easy ride but not too close to be stumbled on." Tariq shrugged his shoulders. "I would guess that it's at least ten, if not fifteen miles away but that's only a guess."

Callistra nodded. "That's a lot of distance to cover on foot. So, we best get moving."

Without another word, Tariq turned toward the west and headed off into the darkness with the vampyress right beside him.

* * * * *

It was in early morning hours by the time Gamble, Mathias and Pixi arrived back in Akrôtiri.

The wyvern riders had been forced to fly along the coast due to reports of increased Peacekeeper patrols in the Forestlands. Jerrick explained that he was under strict orders to avoid the Peacekeepers at all cost. This meant that they took frequent breaks and changed their flight path often. It was during one of these breaks when he also related to the rescued trio as much of the story that he knew. It was obvious that Jerrick was in complete awe of the crimson samurai as he talked.

Gamble just shook his head in disbelief as the raider told the tale and muttered, "Patrick always did have the gift of gab."

"Excuse me sir, what was that?"

"Nothing...nothing."

Jerrick didn't push the subject as they remounted their flying serpents and resumed their journey. Landing in Akrôtiri the raider led the Outlanders to the tavern which Tao had converted to a war room. Charts, maps and books were laid all about the room, covering nearly every table.

The deadly samurai looked up when they entered the tavern. "Heya mate! About time you showed up."

Gamble laughed. "You know, it's so hard to get a taxi in these regions."

Tao crossed the short distance between them and gave his oldest friend a hug, patted the half-elf on the shoulder and winked at the faerie. "Damn, it's good to see you."

Mathias laughed. "It's good to be seen. It was touch and go there for a while."

"I have so much to tell you guys."

Gamble gestured to their surroundings. "It sounds like a hell of a story."

Tao waved his hand in a dismal manner. "Not all this. This is nothing...Cassie is alive."

Gamble's jaw literally dropped. It was the furthest thing from his mind. Even though they were in a world full of magic, he would've never guessed that. "What? How?"

Tao launched into his tale concerning the Peacekeepers, the other Outlanders and even how he managed to become the leader of the wyvern raiders. The trio listened quietly until it was their turn to tell their story. By this time, all of the Outlanders had joined them in the war room and Tao made introductions all the way around.

After a moment, he stepped back and gestured at the map of the region that he had spread out on the table. "Now that we are all back together our next order of business is finding Cassie. The only thing we know for certain is that she has been taken hostage by the Peacekeepers. From what I can see, the order has at least four base camps spread out around this region."

Aaliyah stood up and pointed at a dot on the map. "As of an hour ago, Callistra was just outside of Crooked Creek and heading that way." Tao raised an eyebrow in an unspoken question and the Sha'ir explained. "One of my servants located her. She and one other are on foot running toward the hamlet."

"Running? From what?"

"Peacekeepers," she responded. "Evidently she escaped and is on the run."

Tao looked at the map and tried to judge the distance between their current location and the town but couldn't. There was no proper scale to the map nor did he know how long it would take the wyverns to traverse that distance. But he knew someone who would.

"Jerrick!" Tao's loud voice echoed slightly in the converted tavern.

Seconds later his newly promoted sergeant-at-arms came running in and slapped a fist to his chest in an odd salute. "Captain?"

"How long would it take for our entire force to reach Crooked Creek?"

Jerrick cocked his head to the side and chewed on the inside of his cheek as he quickly did the calculations. "We could have the entire flight of wyverns ready in less than an hour and once we're airborne, we could be onsite in another hour. Ground forces would take most of the day to reach the town."

"How many wyverns do we have?"

"Fifty-seven. The rest are too old or too young to carry anyone."

"Do we have enough riders?"

Jerrick nodded. "More than enough, Captain."

Tao nodded. "Alright, spread the word. We fly in one hour. Every man that wants to go, goes. If we have to fly two per serpent, we do. We are going to need all the swords we can get for this."

Jerrick was obviously confused. "Captain? We're raiding the village?"

Tao shook his head. "No. We are planning on rescuing them. The Peacekeepers are about to lay siege to that town and we're going to stop them."

Jerrick's grin was nearly as large as his face. "Aye Captain, that'll help morale. Many of us have been itching to strike back at the Peacekeepers."

"Pass the word."

Jerrick sprinted off to get the former bandits organized. He was barely out the door when the Outlanders heard him yelling orders.

Cozad stepped forward. "Do you think they're ready for something like this?"

"No but they've been parasites on society for too long, preying on the weak and the unprepared. This will either galvanize them or break them. Either way, we will need them if we have any hope of fighting the Peacekeepers." Tao pulled out a blank sheet of parchment. "Without proper intel, I really don't have any way of planning our assault."

Kastle cleared his throat. "I can give you a general layout of the town."

Tao brightened at that suggestion and it wasn't long before the Outlanders had a plan of action.

* * * * *

When dawn broke over the Peacekeeper camp, Grand Marshal Jericho was already mobilizing his troops. Only an hour earlier, he had discovered that the witch was missing and had ordered a systematic search of the camp. That is when they had discovered the bodies of several other Peacekeepers.

Yeltzer had been brought to him in chains and questioned about the location of Benedict. He hadn't been very helpful. Not because he didn't want to help but because he didn't know anything. That hadn't helped Jericho's mood but then, Yeltzer's beheading hadn't either.

Jericho ordered an immediate attack on Crooked Creek. It was the closest and only location the missing initiate and the witch could reach. The Grand Marshal searched the skies for any signs of his master's messenger. Not seeing any, he spurred his horse forward. His only chance to forestall his master's displeasure was to recapture the witch before it arrived.

* * * * *

Callistra and Tariq stumbled into Crooked Creek just as the first rays of the first sun broke over the horizon. In their heart of hearts, they knew that the Peacekeepers weren't far behind them. Much to their surprise, the whole town seemed to be asleep, totally unaware and completely unprepared for the coming raid.

Tariq didn't owe this town or their leader Ragnar anything but the thought of the Peacekeepers riding in unmolested upset him. "We have to warn them, somehow."

Calli nodded toward the stables. "The stable-boy sleeps in the loft. He would know how to rouse the town in case of a raid."

Even as they crossed the threshold of the stable, they heard shrill cries of multiple war horns in the nearby forests. The Peacekeepers had arrived.

Lights flared on all over town as the villagers responded to the imminent danger. Some stumbled into the streets in their bed clothes, these were the shopkeepers and regular townsfolk, but the majority poured out armed and armored. These were the ex-bandits and Ragnar was among them. Spying the two fugitives, he pointed at them and shouted. "You! Where's my son?"

Calli pointed to the distant forest. "Peacekeepers. They set a trap and your son died. Now they are coming for you."

"You led them to us?"

"Nay...we came to warn you."

It was obvious that Ragnar wanted to discuss the death of his son in further detail but the impending danger of the Peacekeepers overrode everything else and he began shouting orders. From the actions of the bandits, Callistra could tell they had trained for the possibility of such a raid before. Nevertheless seeing their numbers and defenses, she knew they wouldn't survive.

"They won't be able to stop the first wave of attackers."

Tariq nodded. "I know. This town is in a poor location." He pointed to the tall hills behind the stable. "Since it's basically a cul-de-sac there is no easy way out. The Peacekeepers only need to place a small group of archers in those hills to keep anyone from fleeing that way."

They witnessed all the non-combatants move away from the only entrance to the town and congregate in the stables. The bandits hastily constructed a barricade with wagons and barrels across the street. The sound of charging horses reached their ears and soon the twang of bows as the bandits responded. Even to the untrained eyes of Tariq and Calli, they knew it was a hopeless cause. The Peacekeepers were just too well trained and organized to be stopped by such a weak defense.

Tariq glanced at the woods behind the stable and momentarily considered fleeing into them. With his skills he knew he could avoid the scouts scouring the woods but that meant leaving behind the vampyress. One look at her face and he knew she wouldn't leave. That's when he took a good look at the faces of the villagers. They were scared. They knew that death was coming for them. The Peacekeepers had labeled them as undesirables and that meant their destruction was assured.

Tariq looked back at the line of defenders.

The first wave of Peacekeepers had reached them and the barricade was already about to collapse. When the second wave of more seasoned warriors reached them, it would collapse and there was nothing that the bandits could do to prevent it. A baby began to wail as one of the villagers watched her husband fall to the blades of the attackers. Tears rolled down the mother's cheek as she turned away and moved deeper into the stables.

Even without a conversation, both Tariq and Calli knew where they would make their final stand. They followed the villagers into the stable and barred the door. Death might be coming for them but not without a fight.

Chapter 27

By the time Tao and his crew arrived at Crooked Creek the town was ablaze.

As they made their first pass, Tao changed his initial assessment. There was one building not on fire but judging from the surrounding Peacekeepers it wasn't too far from destruction. The soldiers were being kept at bay by whoever had barricaded themselves inside the stable. Tao could see pitch forks, shovels and even sticks poke through the open places in the wooden walls to push back the attackers. However, it was only a matter of time before the Peacekeepers just set fire to the building and stepped back to watch the devastation.

Tao looked over his shoulder and yelled over the rushing wind at his passenger. "Hang on mate, we're going in."

Without waiting for a response, Tao nosed his wyvern down. Even without looking back he knew that the rest of the flight followed.

Gamble gazed down on the attacking army and did a quick head count. There had to be over two-hundred Peacekeepers below which meant that they would be outnumbered almost three to one. Not that the odds really mattered to Patrick. They both knew that if Cassie was still alive she would be inside the besieged stables. Woe to anyone that stood in his friend's path.

Tao guided his winged serpent past the largest group of Peacekeepers but pointed at them for those that followed behind him. He didn't need to look to know that Cozad and Kastle were leading the rest of the reformed bandits to a landing right in front of the soldiers. Even as the Peacekeepers tried to form up in defensive lines, the two heavily armored warriors vaulted from their steeds and attacked.

The Outlanders had to give the Peacekeepers credit, they tried to hold their formation but they had never faced a deadly duo like Cozad and Kastle. They were like two peas in a pod, yin and yang, positive and negative.

Cozad was a blend of raw power and dark magic. He would attack with a vicious slash with his huge axe, beheading two or three soldiers with one swipe, before summoning an unseen fist that would knock an entire group aside. Summoning his pet gargoyle, Cozad grinned as it clawed its way to the surface of the fiery pit and pulled any unfortunate souls to thier doom.

Kastle was both similar and different at the same time. He was more like the chained fury of a thunderstorm mixed with compassion for his fellow man. His strikes were direct and effective but nowhere near as deadly, by design not lack of ability. He would bash right and left, knocking aside nearby warriors before throwing his enchanted warhammer at onrushing Peacekeepers. Every once in a while, he would raise his hammer high and summon a huge bolt of lightning that would leave him unharmed but fry his enemies.

To top it off, behind them came the fifty-seven reformed bandits. None were as deadly as the spiritual duo but they were fighting for something they believed in for the first time in years. That gave them passion and a belief in what they were fighting for, something that had been lacking in their lives for a long time. Couple that with the deadly rain of arrows coming from Mathias and a small group of archers that remained aloft on their wyverns.

Tao had no idea where the ladies ended up but as he guided his beast toward a small opening just shy of the stables, he soon had other distractions. His new steed had been Jagoda's prime mount. It was a dark, dusky grey and larger than any other wyvern in the herd. But beyond that, Tao discovered that it was superbly trained and took only the simplest of nudging to get it to do his bidding. He only had to guide it with his legs while he fired indiscriminately with his bow as they came in for a landing.

Touching down, Tao dropped his bow, leapt off and went on the attack. He crossed blades with two young Peacekeepers as soon as his feet touched the dirt. The first one he disemboweled with a wicked slash while the second only received a gash across the cheek. Then, Tao was past them and they were forgotten. He knew that Gamble had his back. Marvin had always had his back ever since High School. The dwarven skald might not have any runestones but that only meant that he would have to rely on his deadly daggers.

As Tao locked blades with the next group of Peacekeepers, he discovered that the dwarf wasn't the only assistant he had in this battle. The winged serpent that he had ridden wasn't content at being left behind and lashed out at targets of opportunity with its extremely long tail. The scorpion-like stinger blasted through armor and defenses to inflict its deadly poison on anyone that got near its new master. Then, there was the matter of its long neck and deadly jaws or its huge wings that it used to buffer nearby soldiers away, the wyvern was not going to be ignored.

To put it bluntly, the Peacekeepers were in complete disarray. They had expected minimal resistance for their assault on the town and had planned accordingly. They also figured that there would be some stragglers that would barricade themselves somewhere or flee into the woods. These were situations that they had planned for...not the unexpected assault of the wyvern riders.

As Jericho witnessed the deadly efficiency of the Outlanders, he knew that all of his plans and dreams were about to disintegrate. He had one chance to turn the tide of the battle back on itself. He had to take out some of the Outlanders. The closest and seemingly most disheartening pair to his men's morale was the huge armored knight with the battle axe and the red-cloaked priest with the warhammer. Seeing no other option, the Grand Marshal of the Peacekeepers drew his sword and waded into battle.

* * * * *

Sanguine Bolt rarely thought of his life before being pulled into the game.

Those memories were almost like the dream that had happened to someone else and not real life. Of course, he'd discovered that the one real truth of the game long ago, one person's dream is in effect another person's reality. The truth of the matter was that he was trapped here in Hyperborea. That was a fact. It was originally designed as a game world, another fact. But even though logically he knew it was naught but a game, it could kill you as outright as a psychopath with a gun. A long forgotten quote ran through his mind. *'If you prick us do we not bleed? If you tickle us do we not laugh? If you poison us do we not die? If you wrong us shall we not revenge?'*

Shakespeare. Sanguine knew it was Shakespeare but he couldn't recall which play or movie it was from. The Wayne mindset remembered the famous actor Sir Laurence Olivier speaking that line in some old nearly forgotten movie but that was about it.

Taking a deep breath, Sanguine shook his head to clear it of the times before he was pulled into the game and turned his attention to the amazing scenery.

His gryphon was flying along the northern edge of the forest that dominated the majority of this region of Hyperborea. It was shorter to fly over the water in a straight line to Atlantis but it was nowhere as beautiful. A person can only stare down at the unbroken waters of the oceans for so long before it gets boring. Or at least that's how it affected him.

Suddenly, his gryphon tucked in his wings and dove with a loud screech.

Grabbing on the reins, Sanguine pulled back with all his strength but the hybrid eagle-lion wasn't responding to his commands. He'd been flying on gryphons ever since he'd left Atlantis and its dragons behind years ago. This had never happened before. Leveling out mere feet from the tree tops, the gryphon flapped his mighty wings and picked up speed. He screeched again but this time he was answered from below. Not just one shriek but several echoed through the trees.

Since the flying beast wasn't listening to him and all he could do was hold on, Sanguine hazarded a look over his shoulder and noticed nine large figures break from the canopy of trees behind him. They were similar in size to his steed but these looked different in some aspects. As they quickly drew abreast of him, he noticed that they were a hybrid of a gryphon and a horse, more commonly referred to as a hippogriff.

Several questions ran through Sanguine's mind. Why would his gryphon suddenly not respond to his commands? And why would it call to hippogriffs? And for that matter, why would they answer him? But more than that, where were they going in such a hurry? Not that he had any answers or any other choice but to hang on and find out.

* * * * *

At this precise moment, Cozad was as close to Nirvana as he could get in life. He was surrounded by numerous enemies and he could kill with impunity. He was truly and fully a servant of Thanatos, the god of death. The only thing that bothered him was the fact that none of his current opponents even offered him a challenge. They died easily and messily by spell or blade. Granted, that would make his god happy but it did nothing to quench his need to conquer an enemy of true worth.

When his eyes fell upon the Grand Marshal of the Peacekeepers, Cozad smiled.

* * * * *

Tariq couldn't hold back a grin as he watched the scarlet samurai cut into the Peacekeepers. It was weird to think of Tao as the cavalry especially since he'd threatened to kill him but at this point, the assassin would take his chances with him. He knew what the Peacekeepers would do to them if captured and it wasn't pretty. At least with the samurai, he had a chance and with Callistra in his corner, he liked his odds.

He stepped back from his vantage point in the hay loft and looked down into the stable proper. The witch had done wonders with the villagers that had sought refuge in the old stable. She had organized the ladies and elderly into a formidable defense that had actually repelled the invaders twice. The older children had been put to work keeping the horses calm and out of the way, while the youngest kids had been given scouting jobs all throughout the barn. It was make-work but the kids believed they were helping and that kept them out from under the adults' feet and possibly out of harm's way.

Tariq could tell from Callistra's mannerisms that she hadn't seen the arrival of her real world husband, probably due to the fact that there was still a mass of Peacekeeper bodies trying to burst through the stable door. He was unsure of how she would react when she saw him but he knew that he couldn't, no shouldn't, keep that information from her. "Calli," he called out, "the cavalry has arrived."

The beautiful ginger haired vampyress paused and looked up. "What? Who?"

The assassin pointed to the opposite wall. "Tao has arrived and it looks as if he brought a bunch of friends."

Calli dropped the pitch fork she was using and rushed to the ladder that led to the loft. "Patrick is here?"

Tariq moved back to his vantage point and nodded. "Looks that way, I don't suppose that there are too many crimson samurais in the neighborhood."

She smiled at his sarcastic remark.

Tariq pointed to the left. "And it looks like Kastle is with him."

Calli shifted her attention to the area he'd indicated and sure enough, she spied the warrior-priest of Thor as he locked weapons with Grand Marshal Jericho. It was sword and shield versus lightning-kissed war-hammer. A servant of the thunder god versus the right arm of the Peacekeepers. It promised to be an epic battle until a cloud of darkness engulfed the warrior-priest, hiding him from sight.

"What the..." Callistra asked before she spied the imposing armored figure of Cozad step forward.

Tariq swallowed hard and mumbled under his breath. "That doesn't bode well for Jericho."

* * * * *

Cozad had felt the rage of jealousy flow through him when the priest engaged the enemy commander. Somewhere deep inside him, he heard a small voice ask, *'How dare that upstart steal your kill?'*

Cozad shook his head even as he killed a young warrior with a backhanded slash. "Kastle should know better."

'He doesn't believe you have it in you to do what's necessary,' came the voice, only this time it was stronger.

Cozad continued to cut his way across the battlefield in a straight line toward the two warriors. "He knows that I will do whatever is necessary to accomplish my goal."

'If that is true, then he wants the glory for himself and his god.'

"Not on my watch." Calling forth the dark powers at his command, Cozad dropped a globe of darkness on the priest and stepped forward. Raising his huge axe, the dreadknight entered the fray.

* * * * *

Tao and Gamble made a formidable duo.

They had cut straight through the invaders until they'd reached the besieged stables and turned to one side. Mathias and his archers were decimating the enemies to his left, so Tao had turned to his right and began cutting deep into their ranks. Unknowingly, or better yet unconsciously, the samurai had caught the majority of the Peacekeeper force between them and the two holy warriors.

Tao sliced and stabbed with deadly precision as he constantly moved forward. He had switched to the same tactic he had used the last time he had run afoul of the Peacekeepers, his attacks became less about killing and more about wounding. Gamble was like his shadow on a cloudy day, always one step behind him but never seen for long. One moment he was on the samurai's left, the next on his right. Always present but never prominent. The skald would silently slide forward and slice an Achilles tendon here or whack a downed warrior on the temple there, whatever was needed to aid his friend.

* * * * *

Even though the Peacekeepers still outnumbered the Outlanders, the invaders were now on the defensive and felt as if they were caught between Scylla and Charybdis or more commonly known as a rock and a hard place.

Grand Marshal Jericho sensed all this and knew that he was outmatched by the dark knight with the axe. Jericho still had the slimmest glimmer of hope that he could turn it around right up to the moment his sword broke. Falling onto his backside, the Grand Marshal raised his battered shield in a feeble defense and called, "Parley!"

* * * * *

All around the battlefield, the Peacekeepers stopped fighting, dropped to one knee, lowered their weapons and looked to their leader. The Outlanders paused in their attack and followed their gaze.

Unseen by all, there was still a battle raging but it was inside of Cozad's psyche. The Ed mindset was fighting a losing battle against the Chaos Spirit. The more Cozad had waded into battle, killing indiscriminately, the stronger the Chaos Spirit became. With each passing second, Ed felt the chains of hatred bind him deeper and deeper within his own self. So much so, that he could no longer speak. However, a new voice had taken his place. A sweeter voice that continually whispered words of lust, malice and greed. Cozad looked down on the battered form before him. The enemy commander was bleeding from numerous wounds but instead of bearing them stoically like a true warrior, he was calling for a parley.

"Only a coward would ask for mercy."

Raising his axe high, Cozad brought his weapon down with as much force as he could muster. The soulbound axe seemed to scream in delight as it cleaved through the Grand Marshal's shield, armor and body.

Chapter 28

Grigoris shook his head in a mixture of disgust and despair as he watched the Dreadknight split the Peacekeeper commander in two. Not for the fact that one of game's constructs had died. Death was only the logical conclusion of life. Without the threat of death, one cannot truly know the value of life. That was a universal truth.

No, it was more than that. Cozad had killed an enemy that was beaten and had in effect surrendered. He did this willingly which showed that his brother's influence had won out. He was now an instrument of the Chaos Spirit.

Grigoris turned his attention back to the other Outlanders. One of them must be the key. As always, he could do nothing but watch and pray.

Chapter 29

Tao couldn't believe what he had just witnessed. Yes, he'd seen and done some horrible things during his time in Iraq but this was different. What Cozad had just done topped them all, including the stuff the damned CIA Spooks did to Iraqi insurgents. Tao ignored those around him as he rushed across the battlefield. When he saw the Dreadknight move toward the nearest Peacekeeper and raise his axe once more, he screamed, "No!"

However, it wasn't his command that halted the Dreadknight nor the fact that he had a change of heart. It was the arrival of a new combatant on the field. A large dragon-like creature with rust colored scales, a long tail and the head that was reminiscent of a rooster landed next to the corpse of Jericho. Sitting on its back was a man that had the look of a typical wizard; black robes, brass spectacles and pointed but floppy wide-brimmed hat. However, he seemed very spry and alert despite the long grey beard.

"By the Maker, that's a cockatrice," came a voice in Tao's ear. The scarlet samurai glanced quickly to his left to find that Jerrick had joined him and Gamble on the battlefield. The reformed raider kept speaking. "I didn't think anyone, not even the Atlanteans could tame them, at least not enough to ride on."

Tao nodded toward the wizard. "You know him?"

Jerrick shook his head. "Nope and I don't think I want to."

The black-robed wizard stood tall in his saddle and looked over the battlefield. "And what do we have here?"

Tao assumed that was a rhetorical question and kept silent. The wizard's voice had a slight nasal quality to it but more than that his tone was full of confidence. Nonetheless, Tao started moving to one side toward the dreadknight and one that might give him a better angle on the cockatrice if it came down to a fight.

The wizard hopped off and gazed down at the body of the grand marshal. "He was a good commander, once. Lately he's been making too many mistakes." He patted the huge Dreadknight on the shoulder like one would a pet. "You saved me the trouble of killing him. Thanks."

Cozad planted the butt of his axe in the ground and looked down on the newcomer. "And just who do you think you are?"

The wizard cocked his head to one side and was about to speak when another voice echoed across the battlefield.

"Sartael!"

The wizard turned and smiled, although Tao noticed that it didn't reach his eyes. "Ah, Kastle. How good of you to come. Did you finally get tired of preaching to the little people in Crooner's Gap?"

Kastle moved forward slowly with his warhammer still in hand. "But...but you are an Atlantean. Why would you be leading the Peacekeepers?"

The wizard waved off the priest's concerns with one hand while the other one caressed a strange looking device that was stuffed in his belt. "Oh Kastle, you are so naïve. I am no more an Atlantean than you are a Norseman."

The priest stopped moving and cocked his head to one side. "What? But you bear the mark and you said you were from Atlantis."

"I lied. Actually, I'm from Seattle."

"You're an Outlander?"

Sartael glanced over at the Dreadknight. "Is he always this dense?"

Cozad nodded. "Yes."

Sartael shook his head. "I used you and your companions because you had something I needed."

Kastle's eyes flicked down to the wizard's waist and recognition flooded his face. "You needed our weapons. But...but why?"

"It's simple. In this land there are only two types of people, those with power and those too weak to seize it for themselves. The rest of you are in the latter category. I knew this from the moment I met you. I thought about asking you to join me but all you and your companions wanted to do was complete some lame quest and return home." Sartael's eyes flashed with excitement as he spoke. "This is truly the land of opportunity. If we want something, we take it. No rules, no cops, no jails. We can be gods here."

"But that is so wrong. Might does not make you right."

Sartael shook his head and sighed. "I had hoped that a few years living with the little people would've changed your mind but I see you are beyond hope."

Cozad moved up to his side. "I bet you have a plan."

Sartael smiled again but this time it was more like the one a cat gives the mouse that it was about to eat. "Yes, yes I do. Kill them and bring me their weapons."

Cozad lifted his axe. "Why?"

Sartael pulled out a strange device and held it aloft. It looked like some kind of staff with a crossbar about a foot from the top where one half of a black globe on top of it. As the black robed wizard lifted it higher, Tao could tell that the cross-bar was actually two wands.

"This is only one-half of the Dragon Orb. I've been experimenting with it for the last few years and I've discovered that the weapons Al Shaytan gave us when we crossed over have enough energy to power this device." Sartael waved it around proudly. "I can already control the lesser dragon-kind. Hopefully with the addition of their weapons, I can control the dragons. Let me demonstrate."

Sartael lifted the device high overhead and it began to glow with a black light. Every wyvern screamed as if in pain. Those that were still flying immediately turned on their riders, while those on the ground attacked whoever was closest, friend or foe.

It was pure anarchy.

The worst part to Tao was hearing Cozad's laughter. Taking two steps forward, the samurai pointed his frost covered katana at the wizard. "Stop it."

Sartael lowered his caduceus and raised one eyebrow. "Hmmm...a samurai. You must be an Outlander, Al Shaytan told me he was sending me some new recruits."

Cozad hefted up his axe. "His name is Taote Ching and he is quite formidable."

Sartael began to pace as he looked the samurai up and down. "Can you take him?"

"Yes," Cozad answered quickly. Almost too quickly.

"You know, I believe you. But then, if he's as dangerous as you say, you may get injured and that will delay my plans. So…" The black robed wizard grinned like the Cheshire Cat when he waved his caduceus.

Two terrible things happened. A horde of goblins rushed out of the nearby forest to attack anything that moved. But worse than that, the cockatrice attacked. The rooster-headed serpent must've realized that the samurai was the greatest threat because that was its first target. Tao would've died in the initial attack if it hadn't been for Jerrick.

A cockatrice was not only a fierce fighter able to rend flesh with its mighty beak and sword-length claws, it possessed a most terrifying breath weapon…petrification.

As the beast exhaled its deadly cloud of poison, Jerrick dove forward and knocked his new commander out of the way. Unfortunately, that also meant he took the full brunt of the toxin. One moment Jerrick was full of life…a living, breathing person. The next, he was a statue of solid rock.

Not wanting to waste his friend's sacrifice, Tao became a blur of motion as the cockatrice leapt forward and shattered the newly formed statue. Tao rolled and slashed, dove and stabbed but he could've been pissing on a forest fire for all the good it was doing. His blades cut into the serpent's hide but not deep enough to do any major damage. Tao's only advantage was the fact that he was extremely agile and by staying underneath or near its legs, the cockatrice couldn't bring his breath weapon to bear on him. Or at least that was the plan and it was working, right up to the moment that the ground exploded underneath him.

Tao felt himself flying through the air. It was a strange sensation. The world seemed to slow down and a loud ringing filled his ears that drowned out all other sounds but he was aware of everything else.

The goblins had broken through the perimeter and were threatening to overwhelm the humans. Kastle and Gamble were battling Cozad. Mathias, Arieal, Aaliyah and Pixi were all fighting the berserk wyverns and through all of this confusion, the power-hungry wizard was calmly walking his way. Tao even noticed that Sartael had an evil grin plastered on his face with his pet serpent at his side. Tao felt all the air leave his body when he slammed against the stable wall and the world went fuzzy. He knew at that moment that he was at the mercy of his enemies and there was nothing he could do about it.

He had failed.

* * * * *

Arieal couldn't believe her eyes. The wyverns that she had come to think of just as big, ugly, winged horses had turned on them. Luckily for Mathias, he and a few of the archers had dismounted only moments before. The rest of the reformed bandits were already lunch for the wyverns. But then, the beasts were only following the commands of the black robed wizard.

Even from this distance, the dark elf could feel the power which radiated from him, or more importantly from the strange device he was wielding. It was intoxicating. It called to the necromancer part of her soul. It promised pain and suffering to all living things and the power to have the dead permanently walk the land.

She, Aaliyah and Pixi had taken position off to one side of the battle. From here, the three mages had been able to aid each other while directing their spells and servants all across the battlefield. However with the attacking horde of goblins on one side and the wyverns on a rampage on the other, it was only a matter of time before one faction or the other reached them. Arieal had been secretly hoping for the goblins. But no, the huge beast Tao had ridden into battle turned towards them and with a couple flaps of its mighty wings it was on them. Thankfully one of Aaliyah's stone constructs was standing in front of them acting as a guardian and intercepted it.

Arieal was about to cast a spell against the beast when she spied Tao flying through the air towards the sole remaining building. To complicate matters, a band of ten hobgoblins broke through the line of defenders and were heading toward the archers. Mathias had his back to the onrushing enemies and didn't realize the danger he was in. Arieal knew at that moment that she would have to make a choice, aid the samurai or the archer. She didn't have time to do both. Biting her lip as she made her choice, cast her spell and hoped for the best.

* * * * *

Callistra and Tariq watched the raging battle from the vantage point of the hay loft.

The assassin's first instinct had been to rush out and help his former companions. Actually that wasn't true. His first instinct was to slip in the shadows and out the back. With his skills, he could make a decent living anywhere in this world but he had made his choice several days ago by choosing to aid Calli and he still felt he owed some penance. Therefore, he would stand by her side. What he was most shocked about was that it was the vampyress' idea to quietly wait. He thought she would leap out of the loft when the rooster-headed dragon creature attacked her husband but other than chew on her fingernails and a few whimpers, she remained silent.

Finally, Tariq nudged her. "What are we waiting for?"

"Our one chance," she replied without looking away from the expanding battle. "I was captured by Jericho because I acted rash. I didn't think. I reacted out of emotion, not logic. Fool me once, shame on you. Fool me twice, shame on me." She pointed at the wizard. "That's Sartael. He is a very powerful wizard. He aided my original party when Al Shaytan brought us across. But he killed my friends and would've killed us if we hadn't escaped."

"Why? Why would he do that?"

"Because he wants power, absolute power and domination over all living things in this realm."

Tariq cocked his head to the side. "How do you know all this?"

Callistra pointed at Sartael's jerry-rigged wand device. "Because he has my wand."

Tariq squinted at the device, not that he could make much out of it from this distance. "Are you sure?"

"It still calls to me although not as strongly as before. It is slowly becoming his. I can tell you this, he's using it to power that black orb on top of his staff and that's what giving him dominion over the dragon-kin. We need to separate it from him if we are to have any sort of chance."

Tariq looked incredulously at the witch. "Are you serious?"

"Yes, but Sartael isn't your concern. He's mine."

"And what did you have in mind for me?"

Even as she pointed toward the rooster-headed cockatrice, she flinched as Sartael's bolt knocked her husband for a loop. "You must take out its eyes. That is our only hope."

Tariq swallowed hard. "Surely you can't be serious."

Callistra flashed him a crooked grin. "I am serious...and don't call me Shirley."

Before the assassin could say anything else, the witch drew her two daggers and jumped out the window.

* * * * *

Sartael was pleased with himself as he gazed around the battlefield. His day had started bad when he'd received reports that the witch had escaped but now he saw that as a blessing. If she hadn't run, then the other Outlanders wouldn't have arrived on site to rescue her.

Sartael did a stuttered step as that thought rolled through his head. The witch. She was unaccounted for. From all descriptions that had reached his desk, he could only guess who it was. That's when he felt a slight twitch in his caduceus. She was close.

Seconds later, he found out how close she was when she landed five feet in front of him and directly in his path to the fallen samurai. He did notice that she was wearing a form fitting black leather body suit that was extremely flattering and holding a pair of knives. Considering the fighting stance she was in, he guessed that she knew how to use them. Not that it really mattered to him. He could tell that they weren't enchanted which means they had no hope of penetrating the magical shield radiating from his caduceus.

Plastering a smile on his face, he summoned his most persuasive voice. "Callistra my dear, it is a pleasure to see you again."

"Liar! You might've stolen my wand from me but you will not take my husband from me."

That revelation shocked him enough to make Sartael jerk backwards slightly. "Your husband? Wow, Al Shaytan wasn't kidding when he said that he had a present for me. I can only imagine the power his blade will add to my caduceus once it's joined with your wand."

"You won't have a chance since you're not leaving here alive."

Sartael couldn't hold back his laughter. "You are outnumbered and powerless against my army. You have lost already, you just don't know it."

"As John Paul Jones once said, I have not yet begun to fight." And the vampyress attacked.

Back in the real world, Cassie had been training in TaeKwonDo for over a dozen years. She was no where near as skilled a martial artist as Tao was in this realm or even Patrick back on the other side but then, her real self wasn't nearly as fast or as strong as this body. Since Calli had lost her wand, she had relied on her marital arts skills many times to get her out of sticky situations and had become downright deadly.

However she hadn't counted on his magical defenses. She started her assault with a jump spin side kick that landed square on his scepter. She had hoped it would be knocked out of his hand but it was only knocked aside. It did allow her the opportunity to stab with her daggers. Both scored direct hits in the center of his chest but the blades seemed to pass through Sartael's body and robes without injury.

The sickening grin plastered on his face only angered her.

Channeling her fury into her attacks, Callistra let loose with a dazzling series of kicks followed by more knife attacks. Sartael seemed to be moved backwards from the force of her attacks although he didn't seem to be hurt by them at all and once again, the non-magical daggers just passed through his body without injury. Regrettably for Calli, her last series of attacks actually put her out of position and almost directly under the raised head of the cockatrice.

"My turn," said Sartael as his caduceus began to glow with a reddish light.

Calli hazarded a quick glance upwards and saw that the deadly serpent was sucking in air, not a good sign. Her eyes flicked to the body of her husband and she saw him move, not much but at least he was alive. Refocusing her attention onto the wizard, she tensed in expectation of his spell. She would only have one chance to dodge whatever spell he was about to cast and she needed it to count. One wrong move and she was toast or a statue.

Neither sounded like a good option to her at this particular time.

* * * * *

Mathias reached over to his shoulder to grab another arrow only to find empty air. Not that it should surprise him. He'd been firing arrows non-stop since they had begun this assault. He'd already gone through the two quivers of fifty he'd strapped onto his hips before the raid. And now his back quiver of one hundred arrows was also empty.

This was not good.

The half-elf began scanning the nearby corpses for arrows. None that were close seemed to have any usable arrows protruding from their bodies. Not that they didn't have arrows stuck in them, they did, but most seemed to have been bent or broken in the enemy's death spasms.

Damn it! Here he was an archer without arrows but plenty of targets.

Expanding his gaze, he saw the ivory skinned witch backing away from the black robed wizard. Even though Matthew hadn't officially met Cassie's current avatar, he knew it was her. And now she was caught between the wizard and the cockatrice. She couldn't dive to her left since that would put her back to the wall of the stables and nowhere else to dodge. If she dove to the other side, it would be easy for the cockatrice to breathe on her. If she stayed still, the wizard had her.

The Matthew part of him couldn't help but think, 'Lord, if only I still had some arrows I could help.'

Mathias felt the enchanted bow vibrate in his hand and right before his eyes, an arrow of pure magic formed across the riser. It was solid white and seemed to pulse with its own heartbeat. Sighting down the shaft at the rooster-headed serpent, Mathias Strongbow held his shot as he witnessed a dark shadow leap from the barn loft onto the cockatrice's head.

* * * * *

Brandon couldn't believe what he was doing. But then, he wasn't Brandon at least not entirely. At this precise moment he was Tariq al'Nasir al'Rafiq of the Hashashin Order. He was the Silent Blade of the Burning Sands. He had been given the challenge of killing the cockatrice. And a Hashashin never backs down from a challenge.

Biding his time, Tariq had waited until the serpent's attention was fixed on the witch before he struck. He had dialed up the poison in his katar to its most deadly venom. He doubted it would do anything more than slow the beast down. His only hope lie in his first strike and then his agility.

The knowledge of anatomy imparted to him by his assassin avatar did not cover the vulnerable parts of a dragon. He had to trust in the witch's suggestion of attacking the eyes. It was only logical. Even if it didn't kill it, at least it would put the great beast at a disadvantage. And that might make all the difference.

As soon as he leapt, he knew that he'd timed it perfectly. Tariq landed and stabbed his magical blade deep into the serpent's left eye. What he didn't take into consideration was the speed at which the beast would react. The cockatrice jerked back so violently that he was flung off its neck. Tariq flipped over in mid-air and bounced off of the nearby barn. Meanwhile, his katar was still lodged in the ruined eye socket of the cockatrice and it was now pissed off and after him. This didn't bode well for his immediate future.

Chapter 30

Callistra would've smiled at this situation if she was still back home sitting at the keyboard.

Actually, that was incorrect. Cassie would've smiled. There was a distinct difference in the two and she forced herself to remember that. Back home the worst thing she'd ever done was a speeding ticket or smoked a little pot. But over here, she was a killer. She'd had to drink the blood of innocents to survive. She was still unsure of how Patrick's sense of honor would react to that fact. Although, she hoped to have the chance to find out and that all depended on the next few minutes.

Tariq's attack on the cockatrice had caused Sartael to pause but not enough for her to escape. Now, he was about to cast a killing hex. She knew this through her faint connection with her former wand. It still answered to her but only slightly. It was slowly being drained of power and soon wouldn't even recognize her. Even as Sartael cast the spell, she leapt high in the air to avoid its deadly effects but it still struck her.

As she was knocked back through the air, she knew the only reason she was alive was her wand. It had resisted the killing aspect of the spell but in the process she could sense that it was done. It was no longer attuned to her and now only responded to the black robed wizard.

Callistra came to rest against the corpse of a wyvern that still had its saddle and bags strapped to its back. Something about the saddle rig tugged on her memory but she couldn't concentrate. The world was fuzzy.

Sartael calmly walked toward her. His brow was furrowed as he chewed on the inside of his lip. "You're supposed to be dead. Why aren't you dead?"

Callistra grimaced when she tried to move. At least one rib was broken, that much she could tell. Not that she was worried about it. If she lived through the next few moments she would heal and heal quickly, one of the few benefits of her vampirism affliction. If Sartael had immediately cast a second spell, there would not have been anything she could have done to defend against it but the wizard wanted to talk, so she would talk.

Grinding her teeth together at the pain, she shifted to a more upright position and looked the wizard in the eyes. "It's simple, I wasn't supposed to die."

That brought Sartael up short. "What do you mean by that?"

"There are more forces at work in this realm than your precious Al Shaytan."

Sartael rubbed his chin as he considered her implications. "You're bluffing."

She licked her dry lips and knew that there was blood on her tongue, typically not a good sign. "Think so? Then why didn't your spell kill me? I know that was your intention."

"True."

She nodded toward his makeshift caduceus. "Why do you only have half of the Dragon Orb? Because that is how the powers that be want it."

Callistra could tell that her words were causing him doubt. She could almost see the uncertainty flooding his face. But more than that, she saw that her husband had pushed himself up to his knees. He needed more time to clear away the cobwebs but she didn't know if her current bluff would give it to him. Out of the corner of her eyes, she saw the half-blind cockatrice as it chased the nimble assassin through the onrushing horde of goblins, who quickly discovered that they were just as susceptible to the serpent's devastating breath weapon as Jerrick had been.

The witch nodded toward the wounded cockatrice. "Your pet isn't faring well."

Sartael glanced in that direction and shrugged. "No matter. He is only one of many. The same could be said about the goblins. They are naught but pawns to be used and discarded when they've outlived their usefulness."

Calli shifted to her left and felt a jolt when her hand brushed up against a familiar object wrapped in a blanket which had been shoved into a saddlebag. Sartael didn't seem to notice her actions since he was still talking.

"This world is nothing but an elaborate chessboard. Anyone and everyone are just pieces in the game. Nevertheless I'm playing to win. I'm happy to trade pawns for nearly any gain but more importantly, I've traded a simple knight for a powerful bishop. Hell, I don't even mind trading my cockatrice for the death of your friends." Sartael nodded toward the rooster-headed serpent. "Behold. Bear witness to their destruction."

Calli couldn't help but look and the sight crushed her hopes.

The cockatrice had Tariq pinned underneath one claw with scores of broken and shattered statues of goblins and men surrounding them. Not far from that spectacle, Kastle was down with blood flowing from a head wound. Gamble the dwarven skald was standing over top of him, injured and putting up a brave but futile defense against the massive dreadknight.

"Now it's time to end this. However, don't take this personal. It's just business." Sartael raised his caduceus and spoke the command phrase of his strongest and most painful curse.

Calli gripped the hilt of Roland's sword and pulled it free. Thrusting it in front of her in a desperate measure of defense she couldn't help but mutter, "Oh Lord, let this work."

* * * * *

Tariq looked up from the flat of his back at the massive cockatrice as it raised its head high and took in a deep breath. This was it. He was trapped and didn't have a single trick left to play.

"By God, I didn't think this was how it would end."

* * * * *

Something had told Mathias to hold his shot. He wasn't sure why but he'd held the arrow of energy and waited for the right moment. Seeing the cockatrice rearing up overtop the prone form of the assassin, he knew it was time. Exhaling slowly, the half-elf sighted down the shaft and trusted his archer instincts on the wind and release his shot.

The mystical bolt flew straight and true.

* * * * *

As the fog cleared from Patrick's mind, he took in the battlefield in a single glance.

It was bad.

About fifty feet to his right, the wizard was standing overtop of Cassie and looked to be about to cast a spell. While off to his left and much closer was Cozad, who was about to strike a killing blow on Gamble. Tao knew he could intervene only on one, not both. His head told him to help Marvin, his oldest friend, yet his heart ached for him to aid Cassie.

"Jesus, how do I choose?"

Chapter 31

Grigoris grinned as he felt the infusion of power from the Outlander's prayers.

Technically, they hadn't prayed to him but to his Father. However, he still felt the energy flow into him. It wasn't enough for him to break free of his prison but it was enough for him to influence world events. Of course, one of the major differences between him and his brother was the fact that al'Shaytăn tended to interfere directly in the lives of the mortals while he liked to work in the background, guiding and influencing events from afar.

Just like now.

Grigoris released the pent up energy in a series of spells that might not change the present day situation but would facilitate a positive outcome in the future. He realized long ago, when you're playing for the souls of innocents, the long run is the most important aspect.

Chapter 32

It was the hardest decision of his entire life but in the end, the Tao mindset won out. It was more tactically sound to save two friends over one unknown entity, even if that individual happened to be the avatar of his wife. The Patrick mindset had wanted to rush to Cassie's aid but somehow the Tao psyche suspected that she would be fine and he turned his attention to the deadly Dreadknight.

As a samurai, Tao had access to numerous skills and weapons. As a real world martial artist, a similar but different set of skills but as an ex-Army Ranger, he had an even broader array of skills that he could use in any given situation. It was these latter abilities he drew on at this time. Considering the distance between him and the Dreadknight and the position of Cozad's heavily enchanted axe, Tao knew that he couldn't close the distance in time to save his friend...but a knife could.

Tao drew his tanto, a Japanese style knife crafted in the same manner as a katana and with the same legendary armor piercing point. Flipping it once so that he was holding it by the blade, Tao cocked his arm back and threw the knife. It tumbled end over end and struck point first with amazing accuracy. The offending blade landed right under Cozad's upraised arms and directly in his right armpit where his plate armor was weakest. The strike caused the deadly Dreadknight to flinch which disrupted both his aim and the power of his downward strike.

Given the circumstances, Gamble was able to deflect the glowing axe aside with his own magical dagger. As Cozad turned to face his new attacker, the skald slipped into the nearby shadows and faded from sight.

The Outlanders had actually gotten used to the hollow tone of Cozad's voice but this time it was different. It held no trace of emotions and absolutely no warmth when he spoke.

"Tao, I should've guessed that you would side against me."

Cozad turned his back on the fallen priest and shadow-cloaked skald. Hefting his axe, he began moving towards the samurai. Tao picked up his fallen blades and also moved forward.

"It doesn't have to be this way."

"Yes it does. Since the day we crossed over, I've been wondering which of us is better. It's like an itch that I just had to scratch."

Tao shrugged. "That's strange, I've never even considered this possibility."

Cozad laughed. It wasn't a wholesome sound. "You lie. Every warrior sizes up the competition. It's only natural."

Tao knew what he was referring to and the Dreadknight was essentially correct. When two warriors meet, they immediately compare their strengths and weaknesses against the other. Sometimes this is done intentionally but most of the time, it is an unconscious act that instinctively happens. However, Tao saw a flaw in Cozad's wording and seized on the opening.

"Oh? So we have been competitors since we've crossed over? That's strange, I considered you a friend and ally."

Cozad paused in his forward motion and cocked his head to the side. "Okay, rivals."

"Rivals? What, like Pepsi versus Coke? Or Ali versus Frazier? Those are rivals. Hell, even when Muhammad Ali was stripped of his heavyweight title in 1968 and banned from pro boxing, Smokin' Joe Frazier was a huge supporter and an advocate of getting Ali's ban lifted. There ain't too many rivalries worse than them."

"That's….that's not what I meant and you know it."

"Really? Up until a few minutes ago I thought we were friends."

"Only the dead are my friends."

Tao shook his head. "That is a lonely path you have chosen."

"The path to power is littered with fools and weaklings. I am neither. Sartael and I will rule over this land with an iron fist. All shall know fear."

"To quote Master Yoda, fear is the path to the dark side. Fear leads to anger. Anger leads to hate. Hate leads to suffering." Tao shook his head and brought his twin swords up to the ready position. "And that I cannot allow."

Cozad seemed to paused as he tried to remember who this Master Yoda was that the samurai was quoting but couldn't. Somewhere buried deep inside his psyche, Edward pounded on the chains which kept him bound. The more the Cozad mindset contemplated the identity of Master Yoda, the more slack the chains gained. Not enough for him to break free, the chains still held him firm but at least he could move. Ed considered screaming out the answer but decided to keep that knowledge to himself. Maybe, just maybe, this was a weakness his friend could exploit. Cozad was so frustrated that he couldn't remember, that he just screamed and attacked.

Tao dodged to one side and countered with his own attacks. Just like that, their conversation was over and the two warriors began their deadly dance.

* * * * *

When the gryphon riding Sanguine Bolt crested the edge of the forest, he saw the battle raging below. He now knew why his mount had vectored to this location and why his gryphon called on the hippogriffs for aid. An army of goblins were attacking the village of Crooked Creek. Every building save one was ablaze. But more than that, the goblins had the support of a dozen wyverns and one cockatrice.

It was common knowledge throughout Hyperborea that gryphons and their kin were the mortal enemies of dragons and their kin. Each species constantly sought each other out in an effort to annihilate the other. According to the local lore, gryphons and hippogriffs were the favored steeds of the lost elves of Hyperborea. After the disastrous duel between the High Mage of Atlantis and the Goblin King, a great rift opened between to three kingdoms. There are even stories of open conflict between the Dragon Kings and the Elves. But that all changed when the elves disappeared from Hyperborea. Where they went or why they left had become the stuff of legends. And ever since that time, the two species had been at odds with each other.

As the gryphon and hippogriffs swooped in on the town, Sanguine Bolt noticed that the rooster-headed serpent had someone pinned down with one of its massive claws but he was still too far away to be any help. Suddenly, the cockatrice's head was knocked backwards when a bolt of pure energy exploded on the inside of its open mouth. Roaring in both pain and surprise, the massive dragon-kin turned towards its newest attacker.

An explosion near the back of the hamlet caught Sanguine's attention and he immediately recognized his former friend. Leaning forward in his saddle, he drew his wand and nudged his gryphon steed toward the black robed wizard. The question remained, would he arrive in time to save whomever Sartael had targeted?

* * * * *

Calli was alive. That was her first thought following the explosion. She didn't know why or how, just that she was alive. When she felt the sword throb in her hands, she realized what had saved her. But more than that, the shining silver sword wanted to retaliate against the black robed mage.

Callistra had never trained with a sword but Cassie had played softball since she was a little girl. Taking a solid baseball grip on the hilt, she swung it as she would a bat. Given her sitting position, it wasn't a very strong swing but it was enough to make the wizard pause in his attacks.

Sartael stammered as he stepped backwards. "What? How? How is it possible that you can wield a Holy Avenger?"

Callistra forced herself to stand up. The pain in her ribs was nearly enough to make her pass out but she ground her teeth together and brought the holy blade up. "Simple. I believe."

Sartael's head jerked back. "Believe? Believe it what?"

"The Holy Trinity." Every second Calli held the blade more strength flooded into her system. "I told you there were more powers at work here than you could ever imagine."

Sartael furrowed his brow. "That doesn't make sense."

"That's because you don't believe. Come on, let's test your magic against the might of the Holy Trinity."

Callistra took a step forward and swung the paladin's blade again. It was sloppy and slow by the standards of a veteran swordsman but it seemed to do the job. But more than that, a white light which had begun in the pommel of the sword ran up the length of the blade and with every swipe radiated outward and seemed to eat at the black illumination given off by the wizard's caduceus.

Sartael cast another killing spell. Once more it was knocked aside by the holy blade.

As the witch continued to move closer, she kept swinging the sword back and forth. Somewhere in the recesses of her mind, Cassie recalled one of the nuns at Saint Gabriel School citing Psalms Ninety-one. Sister Mary had repeatedly called it the *Qui Habitat*, the Psalm of Protection. Giving the dark wizard a crooked grin, she couldn't help but recite part of it out loud.

"I will say of the Lord, he is my refuge and my fortress. In him I will trust."

Sartael was vexed. Somehow, the witch had been able to draw on the powers of the Holy Avenger blade lost by the fallen paladin. It shouldn't be possible. She was a vampyress and a witch; one of the minions of Chaos. However the wizard believed his eyes. Nevertheless there was more than one way to skin a cat.

"Okay Callistra, I will test your theory."

Pointing his caduceus at the ground, Sartael used its powers to influence his own wizardly spells and opened a portal to the Abyss. A huge pit of fire appeared between them with a howl of rage.

Summoning a demon was always a bit tricky and potentially dangerous to the summoning mage but with the witch wielding the Holy Avenger, whatever fiend answered his summons would automatically focus its rage on her since the blade was a bane to its very existence.

* * * * *

Whitney couldn't believe her eyes. The cold reality of being stuck inside the game was becoming more and more harsh. At first, the pure excitement of being 'Pixi' was overwhelming. She could fly, change her size at will, turn invisible and even cast spells. It seemed like a dream come true.

Then, Roland had died.

Somewhere in the back of her mind she felt that Steve was gone also. She knew if she ever made it back home, it would be strange not to hear his New Yorker accent on the guild chat channel. Even when they had been chased out of town and she had to use her magic on the townsfolk, it still felt like a game or better yet, a dream. Well, not so much a dream as possibly watching some super intense 3D fantasy movie directed by Quentin Tarantino or Peter Jackson.

Whitney had to admit that it was sad to think of the loss of Kaslene and Earl and the sacrifice they had made but the reality of their situation hadn't sunk in, at least not until this battle. When the cockatrice had attacked Tao and all their pet wyverns had suddenly turned on them, she had been scared. Almost too scared to do anything but watch. All around her, men and women fought and died by spell, blade or beast. The screams of pain had been horrifying. Even though she kept telling herself that this was nothing more than a game, their blood looked the same. It even smelled the same if not magnified.

Honestly, she probably would have stayed frozen in fear if a stray arrow had not clipped her wings. The pain had shocked her into action. Turning invisible, she began casting her spells but now she was careful about selecting her targets. The goblins looked and acted like monsters, so it was easy to use her magic on them. The Peacekeepers not so much. Not saying that she didn't cast her spells on them, she just refrained from using her more powerful and deadly spells on them.

That was until one of the Peacekeepers had broken through the defensive barrier and rushed the small band of archers nearby. Mathias had recruited about ten bandits and they were using an overturned wagon as a perch. The archers peppered wyverns, goblins and Peacekeepers with their deadly arrows.

However, Mathias and the other archers had their backs to the rogue Peacekeeper and Whitney suddenly realized that she could lose another friend. And not just lose them. She would have to witness their death, all the while knowing she could've prevented it.

Even as she pointed her wand at the charging Peacekeeper and summoned forth five flaming balls of fire that streaked across the sky to blast the warrior in the back, she had an epiphany. Even if it seemed unreal to be inside the game, this was real. They could die.

It was a lot for a teenager to grasp. Hell, she didn't even have her driver's license yet. But at that very moment, she made choice. Actually, she made two choices. One, she was not going sit idly by and let anyone hurt her friends. And two, she was going to remain true to herself. That meant from this moment forward, she was going to be Whitney, not Pixi. Pixi was her avatar. It was a character inside a game and that was where it would stay.

* * * * *

The moment his arrow of energy exploded in the cockatrice's mouth, Mathias regretted it. Not because he's saved Tariq's life but because the damn rooster-headed serpent was now angry at him. The huge dragon-kin covered the intervening gap with one flap of its mighty wings and crushed the wagon he had been using as a perch. Fortunately for Mathias, he was nimble and had already abandoned his former position. The deadly serpent roared with anger and swung its head back and forth, trying to get a bead on the offending half-elf.

The half-elven archer contemplated calling forth another arrow of energy but when he spied several creatures flying in from the east, he held back and waited. There was no telling if they were friends of foes and since the cockatrice didn't know where he was at the moment, there was no reason to betray his position.

* * * * *

Tariq was alive. It hurt to breathe but he was alive. Rolling over onto his stomach, the assassin pushed himself to his knees. All around him, the battle raged but for the moment, no one was targeting him which gave him a chance to take stock of the situation.

The remaining wyvern riders had joined up with the remnants of the townsfolk and were fighting side by side against the goblins, the Peacekeepers and the rampaging wyverns. The goblins still numbered in the hundreds, although there was only about twenty of the Peacekeepers left. The villagers had gathered around the Outlanders and were holding their own but they were clumsy and outnumbered. Sooner or later, the goblins would break through their defenses. Then, there were the wyverns. They had taken to the skies and were constantly swooping down on the defenders, swiping them with their dangerous beaks or worse, striking out with their scorpion-like stingers.

Hearing a scream of pure hatred, Tariq glanced over his shoulder and did a double-take at what he saw. A flaming pit that radiated pure evil had opened up between the dark robed wizard and the beautiful witch. A huge clawed hand could be seen clutching at the lip of the hole in an attempt to gain enough purchase to pull itself up.

"Holy shit!" was all that Tariq could think to say. The wizard had summoned a demon and it wouldn't be long before it entered this plane of existence.

The assassin frantically looked around. The cockatrice was off to his right with his enchanted katar still lodged into its eye. Tariq knew that if it came down to a fight against the demon, he would need his weapon. It was the only enchanted blade he had and nothing short of a magic weapon would even scratch the fiend's hide.

Then, his eyes landed on the epic battle between the samurai and the dreadknight. To the assassin's surprise, they actually seemed evenly matched. Both were wounded but neither would back down.

Tariq instinctively knew what he had to do. Grabbing up a fallen dagger, he faded from sight.

* * * * *

As soon as Tao had engaged the dreadknight, Gamble had slipped into the shadows and off of Cozad's radar. There was an old idiom, out of sight out of mind but that didn't mean the skald had left the area.

Gamble waited until the two warriors were fully entwined in their battle before he uncloaked and rushed to the side of the fallen priest. Kastle had valiantly fought the dreadknight but had been no match for him. The priest was bleeding from numerous wounds including a large gash that had split open his abdominal cavity and the skald could see that his intestines had spilled out.

The Marvin mind-set knew from first aid classes back home that you weren't supposed to move an injured patient but he was sure that the Red Cross hadn't considered the fact that he might be in the path of two titans battling each other with medieval style weapons.

Grabbing the priest's arm, Gamble dragged him several yards away. Ripping apart the priest's cloak, he applied pressure to his wounds in a vain attempt to stem the bleeding. It wasn't much but hopefully, it would be enough to save his life. Hearing a screech coming from the skies, Gamble looked up and spied the incoming gryphon and hippogriffs. Not knowing if they were friend or foe, the skald decided that discretion was the better part of valor and pulled the priest a few more feet back to hide behind the corpse of a fallen wyvern.

* * * * *

Tao had to admit it, Cozad was good. Real good. Granted, the samurai was still holding back since he really didn't want to kill his friend but the huge dreadknight was more agile than Tao would've guessed for his size. Tao had staying in the stance of the water spirit since it was both defensive and offensive but if something didn't change soon, he would have to step up his attacks and take this battle to the next level. When the samurai heard the screeches of the incoming gryphon and hippogriffs, he wanted to look but couldn't chance taking his eyes off the deadly dreadknight.

However, the scream of pure evil as the fiery demon pulled itself out of the flaming pit caused both of them to pause.

Cozad gestured with his axe. "Ah, I see my ally has summoned another pawn to the game."

Tao hazarded a glance and immediately regretted it. Cassie was standing with her back to the barn holding a shiny silver sword that glowed with an inner white light. A massive fiend with wings of fire was moving slowly towards her. In one hand, the demon was dragging a multi-headed whip of fire through the dirt, the other held a flaming sword that was the size of a typical canoe. Anyone who had read or seen Tolkien's *Lord of the Rings* would've recognized the demon. It was a Balrog, one of the most powerful demons from the Abyss.

Cozad shifted his position until he was between the advancing demon and the samurai. Hefting his axe back into a battle position, the dreadknight grinned. "To reach your wife, you will have to go through me."

Tao readied his weapons and shifted into the stance of the Fire Spirit. "If that is how you want it. I lost her once and I'll be damned if I lose her again."

"Yes, you will be damned," replied the hollow voice of Cozad. Raising his axe, he stepped forward to start his attack but suddenly jerked back in pain and screamed.

Tariq appeared behind the heavily armored dreadknight and flashed Tao a little grin. "Go! Help Calli! I've got this."

Tao had mixed feelings about leaving the Hashashin to face the dark knight. He was unsure if the assassin was truly up to the task but then Tariq had made his choice and had bought him an opening. Racing across the body strewn ground, Tao prayed that he would reach his wife's side in time.

Chapter 33

Sartael threw his head back and laughed when the demon emerged. The dark wizard had been hoping for a powerful minion but since he hadn't taken the proper preparations and arranged for a suitable sacrifice, this was beyond his wildest dreams.

Sartael was a demonologist, a specialized subclass of Conjurors. He had summoned many demons during his time in Hyperborea but never a Balrog. According to published literature on *Lost Lands* there were only seven demon-lords in existence. He knew that this limitation was loosely based on notes by the literary genius J.R.R. Tolkien. Personally, he didn't know their names but he was certain he would learn this fiend's name soon enough. Since once he knew its name, he could summon the fiend at will.

Sartael felt his caduceus quiver and turned to see his old friend and nemesis Sanguine Bolt riding to the rescue. Casting a lightning bolt at the diving gryphon, he yelled. "Once again you are late to the party. Do you ever arrive on time?"

Sanguine flicked his wand and deflected the spell. Unseen to his adversary, the spell landed amongst a group of goblins and blasted them to smithereens. Leaping off his steed, the wizard executed a flip and landed gracefully several feet away from the dark wizard. "There is an immeasurable distance between late and too late. I'm here now, therefore I am right on time."

"Ha! I wonder what Amerisky would say about that? Oh wait, she can't, can she? She's dead."

Sanguine brought his wand up in a pose that was reminiscent of a fencer's stance. "She is not dead. One day I will find a way to reverse the spell."

Sartael waved his caduceus and two swords of solid darkness sprang into existence between the two rivals. "Once a fool, always a fool. We had a chance at greatness once but you stood against me and look what happened. You lost your wife and became a nobody. But it's not too late, you can still join me. Together we can lift the curse over Atlantis and rule this land like gods."

Sanguine wiggled his wand and two swords that had fallen on the ground during the battle answered his call and interposed themselves between himself and the shadowy blades of his opponent. "We are not gods, not now not ever. We are nothing more than gamers trapped inside this reality."

Sartael made a gesture and his swords leapt to the attack.

However, Sanguine's floating swords blocked and parried every assault. When the dark wizard called forth three more swords and sent them after his old friend, Sanguine Bolt took a step backwards and summoned more help. Two daggers and a discarded shield sprang to life to aid the wizard.

Once again Sartael laughed. "I can keep this up all day. What about you Wayne? Were you expecting a wizard's duel this morning when you memorized your spells? I bet not. Sooner or later, you will run out of spells or energy. It's only a matter of time."

Sanguine Bolt knew that his former friend spoke the truth.

Even as powerful a class as wizards were, they had three limiting factors; the number of spells they can memorize, which spells they chose and how much power they have available. Characteristically speaking, a wizard's energy is limited by their level. Basically the higher level, the more power a wizard had to use. Kind of like a battery of magical power. When it was depleted, the wizard had to stop casting. Only time and rest would allow them to regain their power. Back when Wayne and Alex were just playing the game, their power was just a number on the screen. But here, in this realm of existence it was more than a number. It was in effect, their life force. Wands and staves were used to focus the wizard's magic and acted as a storage device for energy. Casting through a wand or staff made the spells more efficient and therefore, more powerful.

Sartael's caduceus which was basically a wizard's staff but somehow he had rigged it to draw power from the captured weapons of the fallen Outlanders. As much as he hated to admit it, his opponent was correct. Sanguine hadn't anticipated a wizard's duel this morning and only had a limited number of spells that would be useful against his former friend. Overall, this promised to be one interesting fight.

* * * * *

Tao had no idea who the newcomer was but if he was fighting the black robed wizard than he was a friend. Even as he raced across the ground, both Tao and Mac mindsets searched their collective memories about anything and everything they knew about demons. Which wasn't much. He knew that they were powerful extra-planer creatures that thrived on death and destruction. And the fact that only very powerful magic items could harm them.

With that in mind, he sheathed his mastercrafted wakizashi and took a two-handed grip on his frost-kissed katana. Accelerating his last few steps, Tao leapt into the air with his sword high above his head.

* * * * *

Callistra dodged to her left as the Balrog swung its flaming scourge at her. The many thronged whip blasted the wall of the barn asunder and boards went flying everywhere. Out of the corner of her eye, she spied her husband racing across the battlefield to help her. She knew at that moment, it was her responsibility to keep the fiend's attention on her and give him a clear shot.

Besides, now that there was a demon nearby the sword seemed to have a mind of its own. When the Balrog brought its flaming weapon down to smite her, Calli's first instinct was to dodge aside but that wasn't what the Holy Avenger wanted. It leapt forward and dragged her along with it. The blade slid into a perfect guard position over her head with the point of the blade toward the demon and her hands to the rear. Somehow, Calli knew this was known as the Ox Guard position and she calmly placed her left foot forward but kept the majority of her weight on her back foot.

The Balrog's blade crashed against the Holy Avenger and bounced off. Calli felt nothing more than a light tap on the blade. She sensed the blade wanted to counterattack immediately and let herself be led by the magical sword. Thrusting forward, she shifted her weight forward and watched as the silver blade bit deep into the Balrog's left hip.

As the demon reared up in pain and rage it screamed. It was a deep, cavernous sound that once heard would be hard to describe and impossible to forget.

* * * * *

Whatever Cassie had done to the demon, it worked.

Tao's greatest fear had been that the fiend would see him and turn to intercept. Because once he leapt into the air, he was committed. There wasn't much he could do to change his trajectory or defend himself against an attack. This was an all or nothing attack.

Tao landed right between the wings of fire and thrust his katana deep into the Balrog's back. His strike was fueled by his momentum, the strength in his arms and the fear of losing his wife. The enchanted blade buried itself all the way to the tsuba, the hand guard on a katana.

The Balrog roared again and spun in place as it tried to reach the offending samurai.

Tao held on for dear life as the flames ate at the circle of cold which radiated from his blade. Tao instinctively knew to let go meant death but to hang on promised pain and suffering. Between the two, he chose the latter and prayed that he would survive.

* * * * *

Mathias was glad that he'd held his shot when he saw that the hippogriffs immediately attacked the dragon-kin. They dove and slashed the wyverns and the cockatrice. Once the dragon-kin realized that their mortal enemies were amongst them, they forgot about anyone else.

Suddenly, the defenders only had to worry about the goblins and the Peacekeepers. The half-elf glanced at the knot of defenders. He could see the three girls toward the back, protected by the last of the bandits and numerous elementals. Mathias did a double-take as he watched one of the bandits get skewered by a goblin spear but didn't fall. The bandit calmly ripped out the offending weapon and use it to kill the goblin. Mathias grinned when he realized that Arieal must have animated the dead bandits and was using them to defend her and the rest of the survivors.

Mathias looked around the battlefield. The dead and dying were everywhere. This was nothing like he imagined but then, everything was different here. Back home, the game was just a simple way to escape reality. No harm, no foul. Just log in, play a few hours and leave the problems of the real world behind. But now, this was his reality and the other world seemed like the dream.

Hearing a frightening scream from the far side of the battlefield, Mathias began sprinting toward the sound but skidded to a halt when he turned the corner of a burning house. There were three battles raging in this area. Two mages were having a wizard's duel, a demon was thrashing about with what looked to be Tao on its back and Cozad was fighting Tariq. If the stakes weren't life and death for his friends, he would just sit back and watch. It promised to be memorable.

Once again, Mathias was faced with the decision of who to help. Honestly, he wanted to help Tao but that meant he'd have to leave the assassin to the ministrations of the dreadknight. Although Tariq had killed Roland in cold blood, he seemed to have a change of heart and once more was with the Outlanders. Mathias willed an energy arrow into existence, drew back on the bowstring and fired.

The bolt of pure energy crashed into the dreadknight's back and knocked him aside.

Tariq took complete advantage of the distraction and thrust another dagger between the plates in Cozad's armor. That made four blades sticking out of him. None of them were poisoned or magical but he was certain they were painful. Rolling out of the way from one of his opponent's strikes, Tariq couldn't help but taunt the dark knight.

"How's that feel Ed? Does it hurt?"

"Ed? There is no Ed here. I am Cozad the Conqueror and I will destroy you." Another bolt of energy crashed against his helmet and the dreadknight glanced at the archer. "Ah, another peasant has decided to take up arms against the nobility. You too shall perish."

Summoning a globe of darkness, Cozad centered it on top of the archer and lashed out with a kick at the assassin.

Tariq hadn't been expecting such an unorthodox attack by the knight and was taken completely by surprise. He felt one of his ribs break as he was launched backward.

* * * * *

Sartael gazed at the battlefield and sensed that the tide had turned against him. His goblins and Peacekeepers were nearly decimated. The wyverns were dead and his cockatrice was mortally wounded. It was only a matter of time before the gryphon and its cousins killed his pet. On top of that, the samurai and the witch seemed to have critically injured the Balrog. Then there was his newest recruit, Cozad. He was wounded but still in the fight. Nonetheless, a wise leader knows when it was time to retreat.

Sartael made sure that his shadow swords were keeping his nemesis occupied before he contacted his ally. *'Cozad, it is time to depart. The field is theirs.'*

Cozad recognized the voice from earlier and so did the Edward mind-set but since he was still chained deep inside the dreadknight's psyche and could do nothing but listen. *'I do not like to flee. There is no honor in retreat.'*

'True, but then the dead have no honor. I did not anticipate Sanguine Bolt's interference nor the possibility of a Holy Avenger sword being in play. However, I have many more pawns to use in this game. They just need a general capable of wielding them correctly.'

'You have an army for me to lead?'

Sartael grinned despite himself. The dreadknight had been so easy to read and in turn, manipulate. 'Yes but we must depart before our enemies join forces against us. Come, join me and I will whisk us away to my kingdom.'

'On my way.'

Sartael watched as the dreadknight cloaked the archer in a globe of darkness and couldn't help but wince as he kicked the annoying assassin. Yes, Cozad was the right person for the role he had in mind. When the dark knight reached his side, the demonologist drew the outline of a door with his caduceus and a shadowy portal opened up. Gesturing at the opening, the dark knight stepped through and disappeared.

Sartael couldn't help but gloat at his escape. Tipping his head and his hat to his former friend he quipped, "Farewell Sanguine Bolt, we will meet again."

As soon as he stepped through, the shadow portal slammed shut and Sartael's ethereal blades dissipated into wisps of smoke.

Sanguine just shook his head and spoke to the empty air. "You are right about that, we will meet again and next time the outcome will be different."

Hearing the screams of pain from the samurai, Sanguine Bolt took in the situation with a single glance. The Balrog was critically injured but as long as the portal to the Abyss was open, the manifestation of its mortal form couldn't die. Therefore, the portal had to be closed.

Mentally reviewing all the spells he had left for the day, he only had one that might do the trick. As a specialist mage, Sanguine gained bonuses to certain types of spells but had penalties in other areas. Wayne had chosen to be an Elementalist which was a wizard that specialized in the four elements; earth, air, water and fire. As such, he had a useful utility spell called *'Move Earth'* which was basically a magical version of a giant invisible backhoe.

Sanguine knew that the pit was extremely deep and it would take a lot of dirt. Not that he could really fill the pit since it was in fact a portal to another dimension but the introduction of enough soil could break the Balrog's connection to its home plane. The real danger lie in the fact that once he cast this spell, he would be defenseless.

Glancing at battle between the Balrog and the Outlanders, Sanguine knew he had no other choice. Not if he wanted to aid them. Summoning all the power he could muster, both from inside himself and his wand, Sanguine pointed his wand at the hillside behind Crooked Creek and cast the spell. Nearly one third of the hillside lifted up into the air. It was as if a giant unseen hand, reached down and scooped up a large portion of the hill.

Beads of sweat broke out all across Sanguine's forehead as he concentrated on moving the dirt to the correct location. Inch by inch, foot by foot, yard by yard, the mound of dirt floated toward the gaping pit. Just when he didn't think he couldn't hold it any longer, he was there. Cancelling the spell, the hillside came crashing down on the flaming portal.

Sanguine dropped to his knees with exhaustion but couldn't tell if his gamble had worked since there was a huge mound of dirt in between him and the Balrog.

* * * * *

Tao had been injured an untold number of times, both as a martial artist and soldier. But at this very moment, none of the pain he felt in the past was anything like was he was experiencing at this very moment. The oddest part was the fact that the flames were both hot and cold at the same time. The flames burned the skin but sent a chill to his very soul. He was afraid to open his eyes since he imagined that his hands and arms were nothing more than charred flesh by now. A logical person would let go but then, a rational person wouldn't have jumped on the back of a giant fire-winged demon either.

Suddenly, the burning was gone. He was still being thrashed around but it was getting less and less violent.

Daring to see what was going on, Tao opened one eye. The first thing he did was look at his hands and much to his surprise, they seemed normal. No burn marks were visible. Opening up his other eye, Tao chanced a look around and noticed that the beast's fiery wings were gone. Then came the realization that the fiend was shrinking. But more importantly, he ached all over. It was as if every muscle in his body was having a charley horse at the same time.

Tao tried to force his body to respond to his commands but nothing would move. He couldn't even relax his hands enough to let go. He had no choice but to hang on and ride this out.

* * * * *

When Cassie heard her husband scream, she went crazy. She had no reason to believe that he would survive his kamikaze styled attack but she prayed that he did. Her fear and rage fueled the bond between her and the Holy Avenger sword. What had started out as the sword dragging her to a proper position, became something else. Calli became the living embodiment of righteous vengeance. She stabbed and thrust with impunity. She blocked, parried and moved as gracefully as a professional dancer.

The Balrog was in pain but it was far from being defeated until something odd happened. A large chunk of the surrounding countryside lifted up into the air, floated into town and crashed down behind the demon. However, that wasn't the bizarre part. The Balrog's wings of fire disappeared and it began to shrink with every swipe of Calli's sword. She didn't know what was happening but she kept up her attacks.

The Balrog decided to make one last suicidal attack, dropped its scourge, took a two-handed grip on its sword and chopped down with all its might. Unfortunately for the demon, Callistra was ready for it.

The Holy Avenger had anticipated such an attack and guided the witch to the perfect spot for a counterattack. Stepping underneath the massive body, Callistra leapt straight up and swung her own mighty weapon. The shining silver blade slid right through the demon's neck like a knife through butter and the Balrog fell to the ground, decapitated and very dead.

Chapter 34

Grigoris exhaled deeply when the demon fell. Actually, he hadn't even realized he had been holding his breath as the battle raged but evidently, he had been. When Sartael the Snake had arrived and seduced Cozad to the side of Chaos, he had begun to doubt the outcome. When the wyverns turned on their riders and the cockatrice had attacked the samurai, he knew that their demise was imminent. Additionally, the summoning of the demon had all but sealed their fate. Once again, he felt that his brother was going to win.

To see them prevail in the face of such long odds was more than the imprisoned seraph could hope for. But it was more than that and Grigoris realized it. He had begun to cheer for them and felt invested in their struggles. He knew it was dangerous for him to get attached to the Outlanders. For him to win this contest against his brother, he may have to sacrifice one of them to assure ultimate victory.

Grigoris shook his head and chastised himself for his thoughts. It was not his place to sacrifice one or all of the Outlanders. That was the real truth here. His involvement was limited to ensure that the Outlanders maintained free will. They deserved the opportunity to decide their own fate. That was the will of his father, freedom of choice in all things. That was the true secret of life.

Chapter 35

Calli held her pose for a few seconds and took in the battlefield with a single glance.

The whole town was ablaze and bodies filled the streets. Nevertheless, it was the disintegrating corpse of the Balrog which captivated her attention. Primarily because the severed head of the demon was still looking at her with hate-filled eyes. Its mouth opened and closed several times while its forked tongue flicked in and out. Even as the light in its ebony eyes faded, it croaked.

"We shall meet again you traitorous witch."

Before Callistra could respond, the severed head of the demon hissed once and crumbled into dust. It seems she had made another enemy this day.

Unbidden, an old nearly forgotten quote ran through her mind, *'A man cannot be too careful in the choice of his enemies.'* She had no idea who said it but it seemed fitting somehow.

When the last of the demon had dissolved into nothingness, the Holy Avenger sword relaxed its grip on her body and she could move of her own accord. Rushing forward, she stabbed the sacred blade into the dirt next to her husband's body. He was lying face down with his hands still wrapped around the hilt of his katana.

"Patrick!"

When he didn't respond, Callistra felt the cold hands of fear grip her heart.

* * * * *

The moment the dark wizard and Cozad had stepped through the magical portal and disappeared from the battlefield, the remaining goblins and Peacekeepers lost their desire for battle. The goblins tried to flee back into the surrounding countryside but the villagers wouldn't allow it. They ran after them and killed every last one. The Peacekeepers were another matter. They called for parley and threw down their weapons. A few of the villagers had wanted to continue attacking the invaders, that was until the remaining wyvern bandits stepped forward and stopped them. They had already seen what would happen if one of them countermanded an order given by their new Captain.

Aaliyah and Arieal sat down right where they were and took in a deep breath of air. It might have been full of the stench of battle but it was also life affirming. The two conjurers had worked together, sending their minions wherever they were needed. It had been touch and go a few times. Once, a crazed band of five hobgoblins had broken through the wall of defenders and threatened them directly. It was at that moment when they both realized that a well-placed whack with a staff or a slash with a dagger was worth its weight in gold. The hobgoblins had thought they would be easy pickings but the two casters were more in sync with each other than they imagined. Possibly a side effect of the merger but they had been able to fight as one effective unit and they had dispatched their attackers quickly.

Now they just wanted to sit and relax for a moment. But it was not to be. Mathias came running up and both casters could tell that he carried bad news.

"Aaliyah...come quickly."

The blonde beauty stood up. "What is it?"

Mathias licked his lips. "Kastle is asking for you."

The next few moments would be forever seared into Ashley's memory. Rushing across the battlefield, she didn't even notice the scattered bodies and pools of blood. Her sole attention was fixed on the prone form of her lover.

Kastle was lying on his back with his feet propped up on the carcass of a dead wyvern. Gamble had made a pillow for him out of the remnants of his cloak. The rest he had used as a makeshift bandage, first on the priest's forehead and then on the large gash across his abdomen. The first thing Ashley really noticed was the fact that the priest was pale, too pale.

She glanced up at the dwarf, who just gave her a subtle shake of his head. Reaching out, she grabbed his hand. "Kastle....Richard. I'm here. I'm here darling."

Kastle's eyes fluttered open. "Ash? Ashley, is that you?"

His voice was weak. Weaker than any time she had heard it.

"Yes my love, I am here."

Kastle turned his head slowly as his eyes focused in on her. "You are so beautiful."

Aaliyah's tears were flowing but still she blushed. "You're just trying to sweet talk your way back into my pants."

Kastle tried to lick his lips but his mouth was too dry. "No, not your avatar. You. I've always loved you Ash. I'm sorry I was too afraid to say it before now."

Aaliyah leaned forward and kissed him gently. "Shhh....my love. Save your strength. You will have plenty of time to tell me this."

Kastle started to say something but began coughing violently and he quickly covered his mouth with a rag.

Aaliyah frantically looked around for help but when she saw the look in the eyes of Arieal and Mathias, she could tell that they knew the truth also. He didn't have much time left. They knew it and so did Kastle.

* * * * *

Tariq edged his way over to where Callistra and Tao lay.

He really didn't want to intrude on their reunion but he felt that the witch would want to be there before the priest died. Besides, it was time to confront his past. He had failed the group when he had assassinated Roland. Although he had strived to atone for his crime, he realized now that Tao was the judge he had to face. For better or worse, it was time to pay the piper.

Softly clearing his throat Tariq said, "Calli?"

* * * * *

Cassie felt the tears running down her face as she rolled the avatar of her husband over. It was strange seeing him like this. Logically, she knew this was Patrick but it wasn't him. From the slant of his eyes to the shade of his skin, everything was different. But in her heart, she knew this was her husband.

Leaning forward, she kissed him gently on the lips. They felt warm to her but they were lifeless. Suddenly, one arm shot up, wrapped around her waist and pulled her close. But it was the passion and warmth in his kiss that truly got her attention.

Minutes passed before she leaned back and looked into his eyes. Even though the shape of them were different, Cassie could swear they were the same as Patrick's back home.

Tao spoke first. "Hey doll."

The wall holding back Cassie's emotions broke down at those words. Those were the same two words he said to her when they first met all those years ago. She had been out with some girlfriends in a bar and they had guys hitting on them all night with cheesy pickup lines after pickup lines. Patrick had walked up and said those two simple words. What had made it so different was the fact that he only made eye contact with her, totally ignoring her girlfriends, and that he only stared into her eyes.

Cassie laughed and more tears fell as she responded the same way she had back then. "Hi there."

Neither one of them said another word for several minutes as they squeezed each other tightly. They only broke their embrace when they heard someone clear their throat behind them.

"Calli?"

The scarlet haired witch glanced over her shoulder and smiled. "Brandon…" Whatever else she was going to say fled as did her smile. "What's wrong?"

"It's Kastle." Tariq lowered his head. He didn't have to say anything else, the couple knew it was bad.

Tao tried to push himself up but every muscle in his body ached and refused. Tariq moved forward and helped Calli lift him. Tao simply nodded and said, "Thanks."

Tariq grinned in spite of himself. Just like that, Brandon felt that he was once more a part of the group. It seems that his past actions might not be completely forgotten but at least they were forgiven. It was a good feeling.

As they walked up, Tao took in the priest's condition with a single glance. He was a goner. Actually, it was a testament to his willpower and constitution that he was still alive. Arieal and Aaliyah were already there and so was Gamble. Calli rushed forward to the priest's side, knelt down and grabbed his hand.

Judging from her body language, they had been more than friends. One part of Tao's mind, the Mac persona felt a slight twinge of jealousy. It wasn't logical. He had been unfaithful with Arieal several times since he crossed over. Of course, he knew from conversations with Kastle that they had been trapped inside this reality for nearly four years. Tao forced his jealousy down and knelt beside the fallen priest.

Kastle shifted his head to the side and made eye contact with the samurai. "Tao, don't judge Calli. We have all done things we aren't proud of to survive."

Tao flashed him a reassuring grin. "No worries, Kastle. I am not in a position to judge. Rest easy my friend. You have done your part."

Kastle gestured feebly with his left hand. "Gamble...keep my hammer. I suspect you will need it before this is all over."

"I will priest, I will." Gamble reached over and picked up the mighty weapon. "Don't worry, I'll keep it safe. "

Aaliyah leaned forward and kissed him once more. "Rest now Richard. Know that I will love you to the end of my days."

Kastle smiled. Reaching out, he caressed her cheek one last time.

"I'll be waiting for you." And with those final words, he died.

Chapter 36

Mathias had not been idle while the priest was saying his goodbyes. He had seen the look on the dwarf's face and knew that Kastle wasn't going to make it. And personally, the half-elf didn't want to watch him die. So, he had moved away to supervise and organize the survivors. A small group of the wyvern bandits had already begun moving through the fallen, dispatching wounded goblins and moving wounded defenders over to a makeshift triage area. However, they were giving one area a wide berth. The region surrounding the cockatrice.

Perhaps it was the corpse of the rooster-headed dragon-kin that scared them but Mathias figured it had more to do with the fact that the gryphon and hippogriffs were feeding on its carcass. The archer couldn't help himself as he paused to watch. It was as if he was watching a super high-definition version of the Discovery Channel.

Pixi popped into view right above his left shoulder.

"It's equally cool and gross at the same time. Don't you think?"

"Pixi…I was wondering where you were at."

"Whitney." She nodded to the carnage all around them. "I decided that if we're stuck here and this is my destiny, than I'm going to be who I am. Nothing more, nothing less."

Mathias grinned. "Whitney. I'm glad you're okay. I admit, I was a bit worried about you."

The faerie flipped her long blonde hair back over her left shoulder in a very teenager like fashion. "I'll admit, I was scared but..." She stopped in mid-sentence and stared at the gryphons.

Mathias glanced back and hesitantly took a step backward. "What the?"

All nine creatures had stopped their feasting and had moved toward them. Stopping about five yards away, they had all taken a position that seemed unnatural to the majestic beasts. Their heads were lowered and their front legs were bent, as if they were bowing.

Whitney couldn't explain it but she felt drawn to them. Somehow, she knew they wouldn't hurt her. Letting herself grow to where she was almost normal size, she took a hesitant step forward.

"They haven't seen a Sidhe in decades," came an unfamiliar voice from behind them.

Mathias whirled and drew back an arrow of energy in one fluid motion but held his shot when he recognized the speaker. It was the wizard with the red turban that had rode in on the majestic creatures. Lowering his bow he said, "I don't know you but given your actions earlier, I'm willing to listen."

The newcomer limped his way closer and gestured to the 'griffs. "They were bred to be servants of the Sidhe."

Whitney shifted to near normal size and turned to face the wizard with a few flaps of her dragonfly wings. "Not to be rude, but who in the Hell are you?"

The red cowled wizard bowed low. "Sanguine Bolt, Overseer of Antioch, formerly of Atlantis and before that, Portland."

That remark caught their attention but it was Whitney who asked, "You're an Outlander like us?"

Sanguine nodded. "It's a long story but yes. I came across with Sartael back in the Alpha Test Phase of the game." It was obvious to the wizard that they had plenty of questions but Sanguine wasn't ready to delve into everything at this very moment so he gestured to the griffs. "You might want to let them relax."

Whitney jerked back. "Me? What do mean?"

"They are paying you homage but I'm certain that isn't the most comfortable position for such a magnificent creature."

Whitney cocked her head to the side as she gazed on the griffs. They hadn't moved a muscle since they assumed the awkward position. "How?"

Sanguine grinned. "Just say éirigh. It is Sidhe for arise."

Whitney chewed on a strand of hair for a moment before saying, "Éirigh." The griffs stood up. "That's amazing."

"Not as amazing as finding you in Hyperborea," replied Sanguine.

"Why?"

"As I said earlier, it has been decades since a Sidhe has been seen in these parts."

Mathias asked, "Sidhe?"

"The faerie folk; faeries, centaurs and elves. After the debacle with the Goblin King and the High Mage of Atlantis, they left Hyperborea for Avalon."

Mathias felt his heart skip a beat. "So it is possible to get to Avalon from here?"

"Well yes and no..."

Whatever else the wizard was going to say had to wait when all nine hippogriffs and the gryphon raised their heads and screeched in unison. It was both terrifying and beautiful.

Whitney looked over at the wizard. "What? Why are they doing that?"

Sanguine pointed at the gathering of Outlanders. "A Champion of Law has crossed over the veil of death. Personally, I haven't seen them honor anyone like this since the death of the High Mage."

Whitney looked over at the half-elf. "Who died?"

Mathias lowered his gaze. "Kastle, the warrior-priest. He fell in battle with Cozad."

Whitney slapped her hand to her mouth and her eyes grew wide. "But he and Aaliyah just got back together! It's not fair."

From the look on Sanguine's face, Mathias could tell that the wizard was starting to realize how young Whitney really was. The archer began walking back to the group. "Come, let's say our goodbyes."

As they joined their companions, Tao stood up slowly and faced the red-cowled wizard. Holding out his hand, the samurai nodded. "Taote Ching at your service."

"Sanguine Bolt, at yours." The wizard nodded toward the fallen priest. "I would like to honor his service."

"How?"

"He deserves a proper burial. I would suggest him being interred in the Hall of Heroes in Atlantis."

Tao raised an eyebrow. "And how do you propose we accomplish that?"

Sanguine gestured to the griffs. "We take him there. We can be in the crystal city within two hours."

Tao glanced at his companions. Everyone was injured, tired and saddened by Kastle's loss but Aaliyah seemed to be overcome with her grief. It was obvious that she was in no condition to make any sort of decision. Tao glanced over at the avatar of his wife and once more his heart leapt at the thought of her being alive. It didn't matter that she was different. Hell, he was different. But she was still his Cassie, no matter what she had done in this reality to survive.

"Your offer is generous, extremely generous, but honestly we need some downtime. Since we have arrived, we have gone from the frying pan to the fire."

Sanguine nodded. "I bet but you have questions and Atlantis holds many of those answers. I can also guarantee that you will be safe from all outside forces in the crystal city. Although, you may also be saddened by what you find in Atlantis."

Tao nodded. "It's a deal. Come on, let's get busy."

* * * * *

Once the decision was made, the Outlanders got to work.

A litter was quickly constructed with timber from some of the fallen buildings. Kastle was laid out respectfully before being tied down. The Outlanders retrieved their weapons and bound their wounds as best they could.

Tariq couldn't help but take one of the cockatrice's feathers as a keepsake. Tao talked with the remaining bandits while Calli handled the villagers. The idea was simple, they needed to join forces and either rebuild the town or relocate to a more defensible position. At first the villagers were hesitant but then reality sank in and the two groups of survivors joined forces.

Within an hour, the Outlanders were airborne.

Whitney had discovered that when she placed her hands on the griffs, she could almost feel their thoughts. Sanguine Bolt explained it as an empathic bond between them and the Sidhe. Whatever it was, it was wondrous. She spent time communing with each hippogriff but in the end it was obvious that the gryphon was the alpha and as such, positioned himself to be the faerie's steed. With a simple thought, she directed it to carry Kastle's corpse while everyone else rode on the hippogriffs. The Outlanders found that riding on the hippogriffs was much more enjoyable that riding on the wyverns. Their gait was almost exactly like a normal horse.

Callistra sat behind Tao with her arms wrapped around his waist and her head resting on his back as they headed north. It wasn't long before they were over the water. In the distance the Outlanders could make out a large object on the horizon. It was hidden by the clouds but it was obviously their destination. As they got closer, the city itself became visible. There were numerous towers of crystal which sparkled in the sunlight and several dragons could be seen flying about. Tao couldn't help but notice that this was the same viewpoint of the picture that dominated the DVD jewel case that the *Lost Lands: Atlantis* disk came in and almost exactly how he imagined it to look. He did notice one major variance. The dragons were not moving. Even as they came within a stone's throw of one of the massive beasts, it hung motionless in midair. It was as if it was frozen in place.

A dozen of questions poured through Tao's mind but he shunted them aside as the lead gryphon dove through the low flying clouds.

They were about to enter Atlantis.

Chapter 37

Sartael stepped out of the portal split seconds behind his newest recruit. Cozad had stopped moving the moment he arrived in the dark wizard's spell chamber and looked around. The wizard knew the dark knight was well outside his comfort zone, no matter which mindset was in control at the moment. Sartael ignored the dreadknight's discomfort and moved passed him. Throwing open the balcony doors, he gestured to the land below.

"Behold Cozad, your army."

The dreadknight moved up beside him and gazed out. From their vantage point, he could see a multitude of soldiers training in three distinct areas. From this height, Cozad couldn't tell what race the soldiers were but then, he really didn't care. If they could fight and follow orders, he could lead them into battle. The mere sight of the vastness of the troops melted away any apprehension he might have felt moments before. Hoping to hide his excitement Cozad asked, "Is this the entire army?"

Sartael shook his head. "No, this is about one-third of them. You will meet your sub-commanders tomorrow."

Cozad removed his helmet and tucked it under one arm. "I do not like to wait."

Sartael turned and moved deeper into the tower.

The dreadknight followed. "What about Taote? He is a formidable opponent."

"Let me ask you this, what is the anathema of a samurai?"

Cozad shook his head. "I have no idea."

Sartael flashed him a Cheshire Cat grin but remained silent. As they approached the doorway at the end of the hallway, the double doors opened to reveal a large chamber. Dozens of warriors, male and female, tumbled and climbed their way through the deadly maze which filled the entire room. One misstep and the nearly naked warriors would fall to their death or be skewered by the many blades which populated the maze.

However, it was the warrior dressed in all black which captivated the dreadknight's attention. He was calmly sitting in the lotus position in the middle of the room surrounded by all the bedlam. Realizing that he had company, the black garbed warrior stood up and clapped his hands twice loudly.

All around the chamber, the scantily clad warriors leapt off the platforms, no matter the height, to land gracefully all around the room. As soon as they landed, they dropped to their hands and knees, prostrating themselves before the black robed wizard.

The shinobi warrior moved forward to stand before his guests. Placing both hands by his side, he bowed. "You win battles by knowing the enemy's timing…"

Sartael nodded his head in greeting. "Kano, I would like you to meet Cozad. He is my new general and will lead our armies to victory."

Kano continued speaking as if he hadn't been interrupted. "…and using a timing which the enemy does not expect."

Sartael shook his head and turned to face Cozad. "Never mind him, he always talks like some sort of Chinese fortune cookie."

Kano removed his mask and grinned. "The ninja are Japanese, not Chinese."

Suddenly, an image of black clad assassins surrounding and attacking the samurai flashed through Cozad's mind, even though he had no idea where they came from but with their influx came knowledge and he immediately understood what the wizard had in mind.

Deep inside Cozad's psyche, Ed recognized the images as a mixture of several movies, ranging from the *American Ninja* in the early '80s to the *Last Samurai*. None of this helped him break free from the chains which bound him but now Ed had an idea what Sartael had planned.

Now, Ed just had to figure out a way to warn his friends.

Epilogue

Amanda came home early from work and expected to find Marvin sitting at the keyboard playing *Lost Lands* but he was nowhere to be found. The car was still in the driveway and the computer was still on.

She thought, "Maybe he went out for a run?"

Dismissing her concerns, Amanda quickly changed her clothes and began her nightly chores even though it was a Saturday and it was supposed to be 'date night' since the kids were at her mother's house. It was unusual for her husband to run at this hour but then, she had been bugging him to get back in shape and she was home early. Closing the lid on the washing machine, she stared at the dirty dishes in the sink. She really didn't want to wash them, at least not right now. Casting a glance into the next room, she could see her husband's computer monitor. The image of their guild hall filled the screen and beckoned to her.

Pulling her hair back into a ponytail, Amanda sat down at his computer. It had been days since she had enough time to play *Lost Lands*. She normally played on her own laptop but didn't want to take the time to boot it up. Logging off her husband's account, she logged in her own avatar, Andraste. She was an Elven Warden; a hybrid class of healer and warrior from the Avalon Campaign. They could cast spells, wear armor, carry shields and wield nearly any type of one-handed weapon.

As the screen refocused, Amanda slipped on the headset and microphone but more than that, she couldn't believe the graphics. They seemed so much more vibrant than any other time she had ever played. It was amazing. As she maneuvered her avatar around the guild hall, something was out of place. A huge glowing portal which seemed to beckon for her to enter.

"What in the name of the king is that?" came a familiar voice.

Amanda turned her avatar around to discover Marrok. The knight was resplendent in his silver armor. "I'm not sure. It was here when I logged in. What happened last night?"

Marrok shrugged. "We beat the dungeon and met some crazy wizard named Al Shaytan but I'm sure Marvin told you all about that."

Amanda's avatar automatically shook her head as she typed the emote command for no. "No. I had to work early and was asleep when you guys finished the raid. And I was gone before he woke up. We haven't spoken since yesterday."

John quickly filled her in on the particulars of the raid in the Tomb of Immortality and the offer of the red robed wizard. Amanda listened but continued to stare at the portal.

"Do you suppose that this has something to do with the wizard's offer?"

Marrok shrugged. "I guess so. It wasn't here when I logged out last night."

"Where's Pixi?"

Again he shrugged. "Don't know. She was supposed to meet me here several hours ago. I've been downstairs crafting while I wait."

"Marvin isn't here. I'm guessing he went out for a run or something." A mischievous thought filled Amanda's mind. "Want to step through and find out what's on the other side?"

Marrok grinned. "I have been tossing around that idea myself. Sure, let's do it. What's the worst that could happen? Besides if Whitney or Marvin log in, we can just use our Recall Stones to get back to the guild hall and group up."

"Good point." Amanda moved her avatar to the portal and stepped through.

John followed suit and the two friends found themselves standing before another portal. However, this one seemed different. It was a huge ebony archway that was filled with swirling smoke. Ivory letters marked the face of the arch which read: *'Abandon All Hope Ye Who Enter Here.'*

No one else was around. Marrok immediately moved forward but Amanda held Andraste back. She absentmindedly chewed on a strand of hair before remarking, "I don't know about this."

Marrok paused and glanced back at her. "We can't stop now."

"But we don't know where it leads."

"Nothing ventured, nothing gained."

Amanda offered him a small smile. John was right. After all, it was only a game. What is the worst that could happen? Stepping up to the archway, she stepped into the swirling smoke.

If Marrok followed she didn't know or care, because the world went black and her ears were filled with the roaring of the wind. Amanda felt her gut churning as the world began spinning incredibly fast, almost as if she was caught inside a tornado and then nothing.

To Be Continued...

Author's Notes:

Sometimes the idea of a story hits me at the weirdest times.

One day at work, a buddy of mine and I were chatting about online gaming. He's a WoW addict -- ie World of Warcraft -- while at the time, I was playing EverQuest 2. We were comparing some of our adventures and the spark of a story emerged. Grabbing a pen and a notepad, I began writing and scribbled down about ten pages.

Unfortunately, without more thought and planning the story went flat. But the spark was still there and several months later, it began to burn again. I happened to share the idea of this story to some online friends of mine. They were excited and intrigued by the storyline. That was nearly three years ago. I would work on it for a bit before moving it to the 'back burner' for more pressing stories.

If by chance you enjoyed this novel, please do a couple of things for me. One, take a moment and post a review on Amazon. It doesn't have to be much, just your opinion on the novel. Believe it or not, reviews (good, bad or indifferent) help. Two, pass the word about my novels. As a self-published author, I rely on the oldest form of advertising....word of mouth.

DrewMcCullough
February 2014

Author's Bio

Drew and Felicia McCullough – circa 1996

Andrew was born in Munich, Germany while his father was stationed overseas with the US Army. Growing up a military brat, Drew became an avid reader with Fantasy, Science Fiction and Detective Thrillers being his favorite genres.

Drew served in the U.S. Coast Guard from 1982-88 and began training in TaeKwonDo in 1985. In 1994 he moved to Louisville, Kentucky to open his own TKD studio and taught for 11 wonderful years where he met and married his wife, Felicia, and gained a great step-son, John Michael. In 2005, he closed his studio and switched careers.

He currently works as a Corrections Officer with Louisville Metro Corrections and writes in his spare time. Unable to live on the beach, he resides on a farm with his wife and animals: 5 cats, 3 dogs and 2 horses.

Novels by A.E. McCullough

Available on Amazon in print or eBook format

Tales of the Wolf Saga
The Coming of the Wolf
Enter the Wolf
Darkness Falls
Coming Soon
Grimstalker

The Last Spartan Series
The Last Spartan: Different Paths
The Last Spartan: DJ's Mission
Coming Soon
The Last Spartan: The Great Hunt

The Lost Gamers Series
Lost Lands: the Game
Atlantis (Book 1)
Coming Soon
Lost Lands: the Game
Avalon (Book 2)

Made in the USA
Middletown, DE
31 July 2017